<u>WHAT READERS ARE SAYING</u>

"A smart, gripping sci-fi thriller that explores the dangers of blind patriotism and the challenges of self-knowledge." – *Kim Wozencraft, NY Times Bestselling Author of RUSH*

EDITOR'S PICK "Seupel presents this prescient story in a well-earned gritty style. Harsh details, subtle emotion, and political machinations permeate this sweeping saga, which takes seriously the traumatizing impact of violence—even revolutionary violence. This emotional story of revelation and resilience will keep readers of all ages turning the pages. Future books in the series will be eagerly awaited." – *BookLife, from Publishers Weekly*

"A compelling page-turner that satisfies both adrenaline junkies and readers seeking deeper thematic exploration of autonomy, identity, and moral responsibility." – *Troy Bond, Author of SLICER*

"With such strong forward momentum, the material will not require psychic pushes to compel readers to barrel through in one sitting. A bracing headlong rush of SF action and angst."
– *Kirkus Reviews*

"Libraries seeking either a coming-of-age or dystopian YA story that operates a cut above others with its moral and ethical underpinnings will welcome Girl with the Silver Hair into their collections. With its survey of extraordinary abilities and the choices that accompany them, Girl with the Silver Hair creates a masterfully compelling saga that proves hard to either predict or put down." – *Diane Donovan, Midwest Book Review*

"Celia Seupel is a writer totally in control of her story world, and this precise and confident prose makes for a gripping blend of dystopian thriller-action and emotional depth that has you constantly reading with your heartbeat in your ears." – *K.C. Finn, Readers Favorite*

THE SAMSON PROJECT - 1

GIRL WITH THE SILVER HAIR

CELIA SEUPEL

Girl with the Silver Hair
Copyright © 2025 by Celia Seupel
Cover illustration by Victo Ngai
Cover design by Youness Elh
Interior and map design by Ashton M. Smith Designs
SFF Publishing, Inc. PO Box 235, High Falls, NY 12440
http://www.sffpublishing.com
sffpublishing@gmail.com

Library of Congress Control Number: 2025905890

979-8-9928504-0-6

What will give the meaning to your life—love or power?
And what if choosing one excludes the other?

—Anonymous poem

My actions are my only true belongings.
—Thich Nhat Hanh
The Heart of the Buddha's Teaching

Climate Change USA 2088

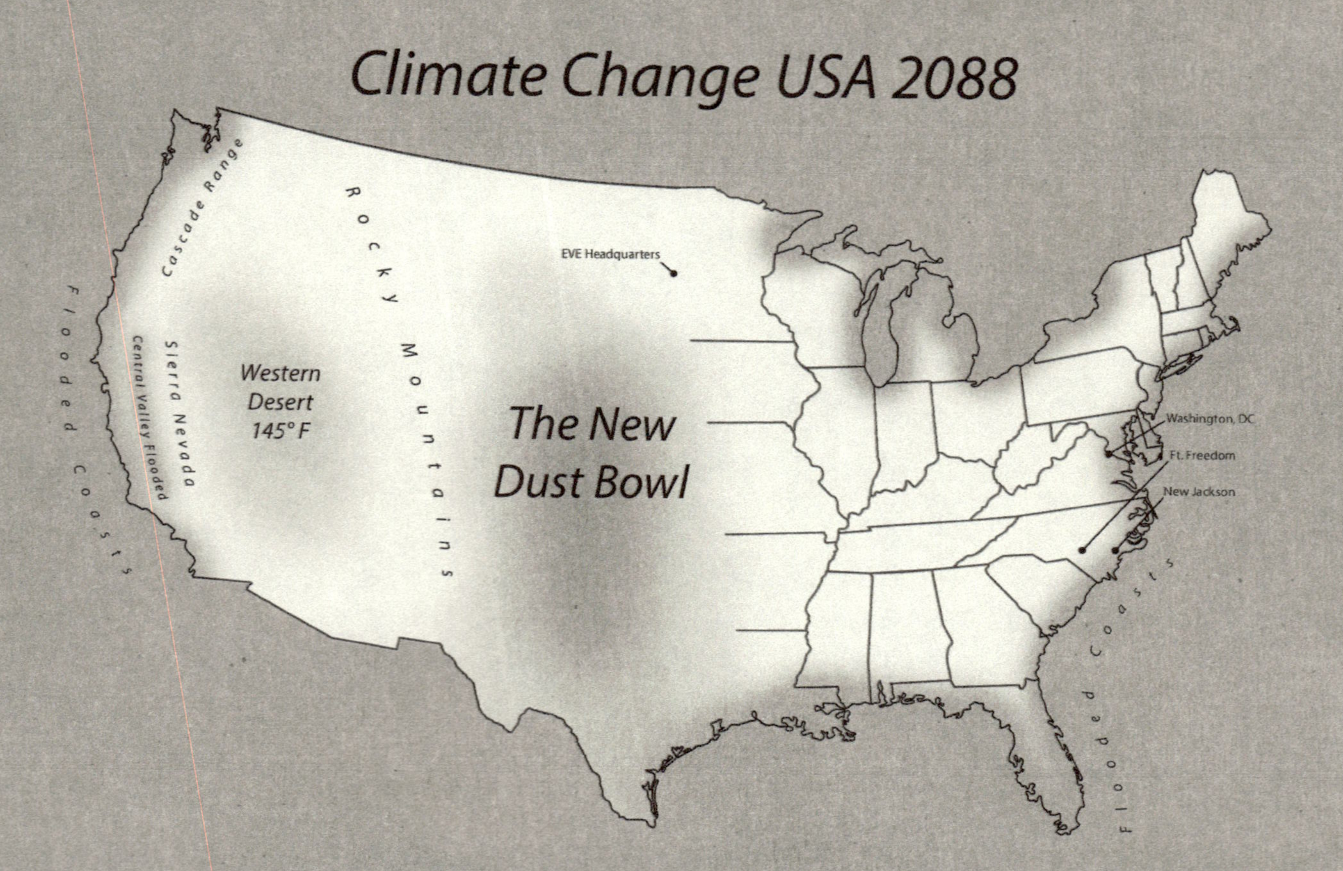

PART I: WAR

Why war? Why would human beings invent such an awful practice, and, having experienced its horrors, repeat it over and over again for thousands of years?

Toward a Theory of Peace
by Dr. Randall Forsberg

Chapter 1

My little sister and I crawl on our bellies toward the ruined house. A guard sits in front, still as death. One sound, and it will be all over. The test has begun.

It's chilly. Illumination is late evening. Somewhere out of sight, down a rubble-strewn alley packed with more bombed-out buildings, a streetlamp flickers. Light glints off the guard's helmet. The rest of him is shrouded in black: coat, scarf, MK15 slung over the back of his chair.

Teetu has stopped breathing. Or moving. Her eyes are huge; her mouth hangs open. Her terror makes me feel sick. She's too young for this, or at least too small. I was so much bigger for my first test.

I touch her arm. "Breathe," I whisper. Her nostrils flare as she takes a deep breath. "Jump the gun away, then keep going. Hurry, but quiet." We have to get close enough for her to terminate the guard before the EyeSpy shows up.

She nods and stares hard at the guard's rifle. It vanishes. I hope she's Jumped the gun back into the weapons closet where it belongs and not under her bed. The silver strands in her black curls undulate like sea grass in the dark. She's like a pearl, nestled in a dark shell, so fragile my heart aches. I don't think Mom will punish her if she fails, but the possibility makes me angry, and I must bend my thoughts away. Self-control, at all times, is paramount.

Before Teetu can move again, a familiar sound freezes us. Now it's me holding my breath. *Tk-tk-tk-tk-tk.* The ticking whines upward like a question, stops, then starts again.

A small device, the size of a grapefruit, glints blue in the faint streetlight. It hovers in the air, then moves bare centimeters to the left and hovers again. Like a bright hummingbird from times before. It's the EyeSpy, searching for us. If it sees or hears movement, it will fire.

I cringe against the floor as the device swoops closer, hovering beside the guard. If only we'd had another minute!

From behind her safety goggles, Teetu's frightened eyes tilt toward me. "Now." I mouth the word without sound. We can't crawl any closer, not with the EyeSpy watching. I hope we're close enough.

Teetu's face draws together in concentration, her brows fierce. The silver strands threading her hair ripple. Her breath comes short and quick; her mouth screws up tight and her nose wrinkles as she tries to explode the guard's "head" with her mind.

But we're not close enough. The guard's helmet just jiggles a little, but that's enough to make the EyeSpy erupt with gunfire. It strafes over our heads with shattering, rapid bursts, rising higher, hunting us. They're only rubber bullets, but they can break bones.

I throw a shield around us, tumbling molecules of air so fast and tight the bullets are deflected. Shielding is pure reflex for me now, but it's something Teetu can't do yet. We launch ourselves forward, scrambling under a haze of fire. Teetu rolls over once, twice, three times, out from under my shield.

"Dammit," I mutter, lunging for her, thinking she's disoriented, but suddenly she stops, rises to her knees, and, with her fingers interlaced overhead, hammers her fists forward into the air, her baby teeth bared.

The EyeSpy flies backward, smashes into the wall of a building, and drops to the floor, destroyed.

I can't believe she just did that. She's never *thrown* anything like that before. It's a complex skill. You have to manipulate the air, bunch and snarl it into a mass of power that bludgeons an object. The EyeSpy flew as if hurled from an ancient catapult.

The sudden silence is enormous. Her focus swivels, and she lashes out, sweeping a hand in the guard's direction. He's still about four meters away, but his "head," which is actually a pumpkin on the body of a mannequin, explodes with a pop.

Orange pulp and slimy seeds spatter against the wall. I look away in disgust, unable to suppress the suggestion of real brains, real flesh. Real assassination. It makes me nauseous.

Immediately, shame flushes my cheeks. I used to be a great soldier. Dad once said, "The greatest assassin of all time." But it's getting harder. This secret illness, this growing repugnance, it's a curse. I fear I don't love my country enough to do my job anymore. I don't care about the earth enough to sacrifice for its salvation.

"I did it," Teetu signs triumphantly, then claps her hands.

"Yay!" I say, trying to hide my lack of enthusiasm as she throws her arms around my neck.

Illumination flashes full daylight with a hum. Pain lances through my temple as lights ten stories up crisscross the enormous gym. We stand up in the fake "ruins" at the center of the gym, with sports equipment spread out to the sides and the running track circling the wall.

"Okay, Teetu," Dad announces. His voice, deep and resonant, sounds very close. But he's not close. He's three flights up in the control room. Shading my eyes, I glance up at the window, but all I see is reflection. "You passed the test."

"Congrats, sis," I say, relieved. At least, there will be no punishment. A real smile touches my lips. "You did great. I can't believe you smashed that EyeSpy."

"Good work." Dad's voice booms through the speaker. "You are now officially Private Teetu."

With a big grin, Teetu turns toward one of the vidcams, leans back against me, and salutes. "Thank you, sir," she says in American Sign Language. Teetu can hear like everybody else, but she was born with no vocal cords. She speaks ASL.

I hold my sister's shoulders. The solid, warm weight of her grounds me. I take a deep breath and try to relax.

Our twin brothers and sister Jaysx burst into the gym and race the whole distance toward the central ruins, hollering with celebration. The boys dash up and rumple Teetu's hair, which she hates, and Jaysx squeezes and hugs her, hopping up and down.

Teetu manages to move her sneaker in time to prevent Jaysx from crushing her toes.

"Pretty good, kiddo." High praise from Mom. She strides toward us across the gym floor. Her face sports the ghost of a smile, her blonde hair pulled into a bun, skin stretched tight around her pale blue eyes. She's dressed in her usual, trim military uniform—khaki trousers, white shirt, tie. The silver oak leaf pinned to her collar glints.

"But I'm wondering." Mom stops at the edge of the ruins, arms folded. She taps a foot on the glossy wooden floor. She showed me once, years ago, removable steel shanks in the soles of those soft, black leather boots, each sharpened to a point.

My brother Gethre and I exchange glances. Her mind is so shielded, we can't Sense what she's feeling. Usually, we can Sense the feelings flickering through other peoples' minds. We don't hear thoughts, but we can see images and feel other people's emotions. With Mom, though, it's hard. Is she unhappy with Teetu's performance? Is she going to override Dad's *Pass* and give Teetu a *Fail?*

"Why did you try to explode the soldier's head *before* you were close enough? All you accomplished was rattling his helmet and alerting the EyeSpy."

Teetu looks up at Mom, then at me, biting her lower lip. Everybody falls quiet. My fingers curl into fists. Why can't she just praise Teetu instead of correcting her? I hope she isn't going to fail her now. I glance toward the control room again. Is Dad still up there, listening to this?

"You weren't close enough," Mom continues. "On a real mission, if there'd been a squad of soldiers inside that building, you would've been toast."

Teetu takes a deep breath and squares her shoulders. "Yes, ma'am," she signs. "I…" She steps uncomfortably from foot to foot. I'm rocking back and forth in unison with her. "We couldn't get closer because of the EyeSpy." She glances at me again, then back to Mom. "I had to take the risk."

Teetu looks every inch a soldier, shoulders back, chin up, her deep violet eyes clear. I'm so proud of her. Even under Mom's scrutiny, she's brave.

"And yet, you deactivated the EyeSpy," says Mom, tilting her head with a quirk of her thin eyebrows and a quizzical little smile.

I break in, unable to contain myself. "Deactivated? Mom! Did you even see? She *threw* the EyeSpy. She crushed it!"

"You're kidding," says Gefor. "She *threw* it?"

"She threw it up against that wall and smashed it!" I point to the wall and the boys hurry over to look at the damage, echoing "awesome" to each other.

"She's amazing," I say. "I couldn't throw anything till I was six years old!"

"I'm already eight, and I still can't do it," our sister Jaysx mutters despondently, too low for Mom to hear.

Mom nods at me, her smile slightly bigger. Can a smile look like a knife? "Exactly my point," she says. "Teetu, how could you have accomplished the job without triggering gunfire?"

I try to keep my mouth shut, dig my nails into my palms. Self-control is getting harder and harder these days.

Teetu frowns, her eyes unfocused for less than a second before she snaps to attention and signs, "I throw the EyeSpy as soon as it shows up, and while the guard is distracted, I rush in and blow up his head!"

Mom holds her hands out like she's presenting something to Teetu. "Right. You see? Next time, you can do it perfectly."

What bull! Teetu didn't even know she could throw things—she got mad and the skill manifested for the first time. We often develop new skills like that.

Teetu grins like Mom just gave her a prize. Not likely!

"All right," says Mom, clapping her hands. "Lunch."

I try to shake off this whole test thing. Today is Friday, pancakes-for-lunch day. After that, the others will have free time, but as the eldest, I study *Religions of the World*, a dangerous but exciting subject. Mom says religion is brainwashing, but Dad says it's important since wars are fought over religions. I'm learning about Zarathustra, the ancient Iranian prophet who said God made the world as a battleground for good and evil.

What I want to know is: Do the good guys ever win? Do they get to stop fighting?

CHAPTER 2

*P*ancakes-for-lunch Friday is normally the best day of the week, not only because of the pancakes, but also because my favorite guard, SamJay, eats with us. I should say "our" favorite guard—my brothers and sisters love him, too—but SamJay saved my life when I was very young, when my older brother disappeared. He's had my back ever since.

Today, though, I can't shake my bad feelings. A grim darkness has been stalking me for months. I fight it, but sometimes it invades like a tide in an underwater cave. I feel drowned in it. Mom and Dad say kids like us are the latest evolution of *homo sapiens*, forged in the aftermath of nuclear war. I wonder if this darkness comes with it.

If so, it's not the case for my brothers. On the bench opposite me and Teetu, the boys are wilder than usual. They're thumb-wrestling and somehow their whole bodies got involved. Their legs flail around under the table and a fork clatters to the kitchen floor. You'd think they were ten, not practically teenagers.

"Stop it," I snap, grabbing a couple of glasses of orange juice rattling on the wooden table. "Cut it out, will you? You're acting like babies."

Nana pulls out a huge griddle from the lower cabinet and clucks her tongue. "Boys, settle down," she says. As if they ever listen to her. "Pay attention to your sister." As if they listen to me, either.

"I win," says Gethre.

"Not fair," says Gefor.

Gethre sits up, pushes his long, golden curls off his sweaty forehead, and pulls the front of his T-shirt up to wipe his face. "Congratulations, Teetu. How'd you figure out how to throw the EyeSpy? That was amazing."

Our sister is grinning madly, her round, little cheeks flushed dusky gold, big violet eyes bright. I resist the urge to smooth back her fluffy cloud of hair, shot through with the silver strands that glint under the bright kitchen lights. "I was so mad, I just did it," she signs. "I'm going on a mission soon and I'll throw the bad guys till they die. I'll throw them and smash them."

"Oh, no," I say, my gut twisting inside of me. She doesn't know what she's saying, *smashing* people. "No missions, Teetu, you're still too young."

"I was five on my first mission," says Jaysx from the end of the table.

"Yeah, us too," say the twins simultaneously. "So were you, Eten," adds Gethre.

I can feel the heat rising in my throat, my ears, the anger rippling under my skin. I try to push it back. "She's too *little*, can't you see that?" My voice comes out louder and sharper than I intended, but the others pay no attention.

Teetu raps on the table so we'll look at her and says, "I'm not too little. Mom said. My first mission is soon. A week maybe." The pale scars on the sides of her neck, three on each side—Mom calls them her "anomalies"—flush reddish-brown. She's angry.

The familiar, helpless frustration balloons in my head, making my skull feel like a million puzzle pieces ready to burst apart. "It's not right."

"Nana, chocolate chips today?" asks Gefor, as bright and oblivious as a light bulb. The boys don't get it. Teetu is too little to start *killing* people. Even if they are terrorists.

"Blueberries," says Nana, ignoring Gefor's grumble. Her wide body blocks the well-lit counter as she mixes up the batter. She holds the big bowl under one arm as she gently stirs it with a whisk—one, two, three—not too much, she says, keep it lumpy. It's a good maxim. Sometimes, when I get really anxious, afraid I'll make a mistake, I whisper to myself, "*Keep it lumpy.*"

On the wall in front of her, there's a painting of an open window showing grass and sky and blue flowers, with a red bird on the sill—a cardinal. Nana can actually whistle its song. Years ago, Nana asked Mom if the window could be painted there. She likes to look at it while she cooks. She says it reminds her of outside in the old days. Nana is so old, she can *remember* the old days. Before everybody had to live underground.

Today, she's wearing her long green dress with the yellow flowers and the big ruffly yellow apron that ties in a bow behind her back. It's faded, but it's still pretty. She's the only one in our pod who doesn't wear a khaki uniform or boring T-shirts and sweats.

She plugs in the griddle and turns on the overhead fan that sucks up cooking smells and smoke. When I was little, I thought the fan vented all the way up to the earth's surface. I pictured giant bugs on the burnt wasteland, or mutant rats, sniffing at pancakes through a pipe poking out of the ground, clamoring to crawl down. It gave me nightmares until SamJay explained that venting didn't work that way.

The griddle sizzles and the smell of butter and bacon and crisping pancakes fills the kitchen. At the far end of the table, our sister Jaysx groans. "I'm so hungry. When is SamJay coming?"

"Just a few minutes," says Nana.

SamJay is never late. I glance up at the clock. It's 11-56. Lunch starts at 1200 hours, but Jaysx is always ravenous. She's growing so fast, she's almost as big as the boys. Broad shoulders, square chin, blunt nose, determined, dark eyebrows. The same golden skin as the rest of us, but maybe a shade darker, more like Teetu. Even Jaysx's hair looks powerful—bold, thick, glossy dark brown, the silver strands flashing. She likes to keep it short, though you can't cut our hair shorter than just above the shoulders, where the silver ends. Unlike regular hair, silver hair bleeds. My brothers and sisters and I are the only ones in our pod with silver hair—Mom says that's because our pod has so few people. She says there are lots of others in bigger pods with hair like ours.

Jaysx scrunches her face up and holds her stomach as if she were in agony. Despite her appearance, Jaysx is kind of a wuss.

Teetu pokes my shoulder. As soon as I turn, she signs, "I'm ready for missions. I'm strong." She holds up her arms, fists tight, and flexes her muscles.

She is so adorable, I can't help but smile. I poke her arm. "I don't know—is there a muscle in there?" I poke her other arm and tickle her. She's trying to wiggle away, her bubbly, hissing laugh making me grin when the door to the forbidden corridor unlocks and SamJay limps into the kitchen. His leg was damaged in the Rebellion, the conflict that came after the nuclear holocaust, but SamJay is still a big and powerful man. His bald head gleams, his warm brown eyes sparkle and his smile lights up the room. As the door slams shut behind him, he slaps our hands in high fives. He's wearing his usual sergeant's uniform: khaki pants and a white shirt. He always leaves his hazmat suit by the elevator.

My spirits lift as soon as I see him. "How's everybody in your home pod, SamJay?" I ask.

"Good, good, just fine," he says.

He always says fine. He never tells me anything. Every Wednesday night, SamJay dons his hazmat suit and goes to the surface to return to his large home pod—which, he once let slip, is called "Bulee Creek." That's when I found out our pod is called "Fort Freedom," and we live in what used to be North Carolina. I'm burning with curiosity about the people who live at the Bulee Creek pod, especially if there are other teenagers like me, but I can't get SamJay to talk about it. All I know is he used to live with a wonderful man who was the love of his life, but he died and now SamJay lives there alone.

"Any new people? Any teenagers?"

"Naw, everything's the same."

I'd give anything to meet another girl my age.

He holds out his arms, and Teetu slips off the bench and runs to him. "Hey there, little bit." He grabs her and throws her up into the air. When he catches her, she signs at him rapidly. "You're a…You're a…" he says, frowning. "What?" He looks over at me. SamJay is a bit slow with ASL.

"She's a private now," I tell him, feeling bad again. I don't want to think about Teetu and missions. "She passed her first test this morning."

"Congratulations," he grins. Teetu struggles out of his arms and claps her hands, skipping around the wide kitchen.

"All right," says Nana. She turns, holding her big, blue platter with one hand and the old silver tongs in the other. "Everybody sit down." Steam rises from the plate. She serves each of us two big pancakes and two pieces of bacon, except for SamJay, who gets three.

We compete—as we always do—to give Nana the most creative, extravagant compliments ever. Today, I win with, "Your pancakes are so magical, they make me feel like stardust!" Pretty good for somebody who's never seen the stars. Then, it's quiet as we dig in. Nana sits on her high stool near the counter—with, I suspect, *more* than three pancakes on her plate. Just when I'm thinking I might enjoy this Friday after all, Mom walks in. I didn't even Sense her approach.

"Eten," she says, "come with me."

I go rigid. Her anger is so palpable, we all can Sense it. Even Nana, who can't Sense anything, clasps her hands together and looks down. Teetu gets scared; I squeeze her shoulder and whisper that everything is okay.

SamJay is on his feet and salutes. "Lieutenant Colonel Nowak."

Mom salutes back. "Sergeant." She doesn't look angry. She looks anxious, which is unusual for Mom. But still; she shouldn't make everybody so uncomfortable.

Just to be contrary, I take another bite of pancake. "What's going on?"

She turns her eyes on me like twin beams of ice-blue energy. "We need to review your next mission. Something ..." She hesitates. "Something new has come up."

Suddenly, the pancakes taste like dust. I *so* don't want to talk about a new mission right now. "Mom," I say, "can I just finish…?" I motion to my pancakes, though I doubt I could eat the rest.

Surprise overtakes Mom's face. "Aren't you finished yet? Well, Nana will keep it warm till you get back."

Nana reaches for my plate and I mutter to her, "It's okay, I don't want any more," and slide off the bench.

Mom seems to become aware that everyone has stopped eating. "Please, enjoy." She rolls her hand, which is supposed to indicate that people should recommence their activities. "We won't be long." She turns and walks away without another word, assuming I will follow. Which I do.

EYES ONLY   EYES ONLY

US DEPARTMENT OF DEFENSE
SPECIAL OPERATIONS
WASHINGTON, D.C. 20223

CLASSIFIED

ULTRA
TOP SECRET

NO DISSEMINATION OR DECLASSIFICATION

THIS DOCUMENT CONTAINS INFORMATION AFFECTING THE NATIONAL DEFENSE AND SECURITY OF THE UNITED STATES OF AMERICA. TRANSMISSION OR REVELATION OF ITS CONTENTS TO UNAUTHORIZED PERSONS IS PROHIBITED BY LAW. REPRODUCTION OF ITS CONTENTS IN ANY FORM IS STRICTLY FORBIDDEN BY LAW.

DEPARTMENT OF DEFENSE
Office of the Under Secretary (R&E)
VIA COURIER
EYES ONLY   ULTRA TOP SECRET

```
FROM: Dr. Joseph Duroc, MD, PhD, US Under Secretary
TO:   Major James Hamilton, Director of Operations
CC:   Lt. Colonel Monica Nowak, Project Director
RE:   PROJECT SAMSON: MISSION DIRECTIVE
DATE: 30 March 2088
```

```
Place:    City Center Plaza, Xapalt, South Kongolia
Target:   Sayan Hann
Action:   Termination
Date:     17 April 2088
Time:     1100 Hours Local Time
Priority: Priority One
```

Your orders are to terminate "President" Syan Hann at his outdoor rally, 17 April, 1100 hours local time. Use a Project Samson operative. Maintain clandestine presence. Close-ups, satellite photos, and maps are enclosed.

As usual, President McCarthy lends his full authority to these orders.

Do not file.
Project Samson forbids use of text or instamail.
Deliquesce this memorandum after reading.

DEPARTMENT OF DEFENSE

Special Forces

VIA COURIER

EYES ONLY   ULTRA TOP SECRET

From: Lt. Colonel Monica Nowak, MD, Project Director
      Major James Hamilton, Director of Operations
TO: Dr. Joseph Duroc, US Under Secretary
RE: PROJECT SAMSON: MISSION DIRECTIVE
DATE: 31 March 2088

<u>Obstacle:</u> Project Samson operatives can approach Syan Hann in Xapalt only by going outside.

As you yourself have frequently pointed out, Project Samson operatives must grow to maturity before they are permitted outside. To allow them to experience the battlefield first-hand is to risk rebellion, especially during adolescence. To allow them to go outside at all is to risk their escape, as we know from bitter experience in 2075.

We are aware of the urgent need to recapture Xapalt and restart New American oil production in South Kongolia. However, it is not possible to transport a Project Samson operative into Xapalt inside a travel pod at this time. No vehicles will be permitted within one kilometer of President Hann's rally. Even our eldest operative can't work from that far away. We strongly recommend against allowing operatives outside to complete missions.

<u>Solution:</u> Wait until we can approach President
Hann in another part of South Kongolia.

Do not file.
Project Samson forbids use of text or instamail.
Deliquesce this memorandum after reading.

DEPARTMENT OF DEFENSE

Office of the Under Secretary (R&E)

VIA COURIER

EYES ONLY   ULTRA TOP SECRET

```
FROM: Dr. Joseph Duroc, MD, PhD, US Under Secretary
TO:   Major James Hamilton, Director of Operations
CC:   Lt Colonel Monica Nowak, Project Director
RE:   PROJECT SAMSON: MISSION DIRECTIVE
DATE: 1 April 2088
```

You don't need to remind me of your failure to contain a juvenile operative in 2075. With the rising rebellion throughout the former republic of Mongolia, it is not practicable to wait. Another New American oil field has just been attacked. 17 April will be Hann's first known appearance in six months.

Proceed with original orders.

As usual, President McCarthy lends his full authority to these orders.

Do not file.
Project Samson forbids use of text or instamail.
Deliquesce this memorandum after reading.

CHAPTER 3

Under the bright corridor lights, I follow Mom past Dad's office. The blind in his window is pulled shut, but we can hear Dad talking on his com. Through dark wood and glass, his voice rises vehemently. "Dr. Duroc, please reconsider. I know it's Priority One. Yes, sir. Sir, please, read our memo again. It's too soon to send her outside."

To send her outside? Who is he talking about?

Mom lengthens her stride. Dull red flushes the back of her neck.

Dad says, "Sir, it's been thirteen years ..." His voice stops abruptly.

Thirteen years? A flash of memory pierces me: My big brother Beeta, standing on a chair by my crib, saying goodbye. Thirteen years ago. My head suddenly feels wobbly, too big for my body. Something weird is going on.

Mom marches to the living room corridor. She's so worked up, her mental guard slips a little. I glimpse the image of someone I've seen before in Dad's mind: A man with wire-rimmed glasses, talking fast, a man who avoids your eyes when he's speaking to you. He has gray hair, closed-cropped, and chiseled cheekbones. His front teeth overlap slightly. I'm pretty sure this is the guy Mom's really angry at.

She mounts the two steps and throws open the door.

The "living room" isn't actually a place for living. It's a room for lectures. Sometimes, punishment. It's big, stiff, and formal. There's a hard, white couch and a matching chair with curved wooden arms, a tall cabinet faced with glass that holds lots of old porcelain cups and plates, and a big, gold-framed mirror on the side wall. More chairs—all uncomfortable—line the walls, plus there's a side table with little figures of girls and boys on it. When I was little, I used to play with the porcelain girls and boys. Until I broke one.

Mom stops short in front of the sofa. "Damn it!"

The boys left their War Seeker board game in here, cards and tokens scattered all over the place. *So* not good.

"I'll get it, Mom." We're not supposed to play in here, but sometimes the boys sneak in when they should be studying—the room has no surveillance. Before Mom can get more pissed, I Jump the game pieces into our bedroom. They vanish.

Jumping something from one place to another is easy; we're born doing it. But Jumping many things at once is a skill we learn. I Sense the *thisness* of the game pieces, call up the place I want them to be—Gethre's bed—then I fold it all together. Mom says it's folding time/space, which is why the transfer happens simultaneously, but it just feels like holding the essence of many things inside of me at once and kind of *fusing* it.

Mom heaves a sigh and drops to the couch. "I'm sorry I got angry," she says.

"Oh, it's okay." I'm surprised by her apology; I don't know what else to say. We're not allowed to get angry in our home; anger can lead to dangerous behaviors. But Mom would never do anything dangerous. I'd believe her self-control ranks in the range of *ultra*. Sometimes, though, she does do something unexpected. Like apologize.

I lower myself to the edge of one of the hard chairs. It's a particularly bad chair because I can see myself in the mirror on the wall across the room. I'm too skinny. I have muscle but almost no bulk. Jaysx has muscle *and* bulk. I'm twice her age, and I look like a child, with my small nose and quiet eyes, my golden skin, and long black hair with the silver streaking it. My hair cascades over my face as I twist in my seat to focus on Mom.

"You have a new mission," she says. "You'll have to go outside."

I shrug and shake my head. "We always go out for missions."

"No," says Mom. "I mean completely *outside*. Without a travel pod."

Without a travel pod? Shock like cold water in my face rocks me back on my chair.

I always fight from my travel pod. It's a shielded, windowless, four-meter square cube equipped with special air filters, a bed, travel chair, and tiny bathroom—plus a minifridge with snacks (snacks are crucial). It gets transported—with me inside of it—from our underground pod, up the huge freight elevator from the gym to the surface, and on to the mission site by truck or by plane. Sometimes, once we're on-site, I transfer from my travel pod into a minipod that can fit onto a smaller truck. So I'm always protected. Never actually *outside*.

Something catches in my throat. For a moment, I can't breathe at all. My face goes hot and my head feels wobbly again. I should be excited. Gethre and Gefor always talk about sneaking outside before they're old enough.

Am I old enough? I thought I had to be 21.

"Mom," I finally say in a long exhale.

"It's going to be fine," she says.

It's not going to be fine. She and Dad are both upset. My heart begins to thump.

"The radiation?" My voice trails off.

Since the nuclear holocaust, outside has become hazardous, especially to growing children. Survivors in the U.S.A. live underground now. Adults go out only in hazmat suits. Ozone depletion has made the sun's rays lethal, and nuclear radiation causes disease, mutation, and death.

She frowns and waves a dismissive hand. "No, no. Radiation won't be a problem." I Sense her mental shield snap tighter. "You're going to New America in what was pre-war Mongolia. A rebel-controlled region called South Kongolia. Nuclear radiation isn't a problem there."

I nod. I'm not sure why worldwide, lethal radiation and the frayed ozone layer aren't a problem in East Asia, but she'll just get annoyed if I ask.

"The target is a terrorist leader named Sayan Hann. He's been attacking New American oil fields, killing our people."

Abruptly, Mom stops speaking as Dad opens the door. He closes it gently behind himself and crosses the room. His usually cheerful face looks dour. He's as pale as Mom, his short, brown hair sticking straight up in front where he pushes it back when he's worried. He sits heavily on the couch. She raises her eyebrows at him. He shakes his head and says, "He wouldn't budge."

Dad can't shield his emotions as well as Mom, and for a moment, a crack splinters the length and breadth of his mind. His true feelings bubble out. He's scared, and he's angry he's scared. And the image of that stern man with the wire-rimmed glasses haunts his feelings.

He looks over at me and smiles. "You'll be fine, kiddo," he says. "We've still got two weeks to prepare. We leave the 16th."

Okay, the day after my birthday. Which Dad's probably forgotten—he always forgets birthdays, even his own.

"You've trained for this all your life," Mom says like she's trying to reassure herself. "Hand-to-hand. Shielding. Disarm-at-will. We knew this day was coming. Just obey orders. Do your job. You'll be fine."

Yeah, I knew this day was coming, but not *now*. When I'm 21, not when I'm about to turn 16. My heart skitters in my chest. My throat throbs and my mouth goes dry, tasting of metal. I stare at the floor and try to keep my voice steady. "So why do I have to go without my travel pod?" The mission sounds like the usual. Wherever we go—Malaysia, Nigeria, Venezuela, even in the U.S.A.—it's always the same story. Terrorists. Oil fields. Rebels. People who won't let the war go. People I have to kill.

"We can't get our vehicles close enough," says Dad.

"Will I have a hazmat suit?"

Mom brushes the air, dismissing my fears. "Listen, I don't want you to worry about radiation. Just focus on the mission. The earth is recovering in South Kongolia. It's a good thing." She smiles. "Isn't that what we're all fighting so hard for? The recovery of the earth?" She reaches out a hand toward me, then drops it.

"I thought we were fighting for world peace." I know I'm being a brat, but I can't help it. Mom and Dad always preach that scientists are working day and night to save the earth, and the rest of us are in the military, fighting for world peace.

"That too," says Mom.

"I don't get why I can't even go in the minipod." I can hear myself whining. Not very soldiery. But at the moment, I'm more scared of outside than I care about military discipline.

Normally on missions, I fight through Dad. Dad finds the target while I'm close by in my travel pod. All I have to do is Sense Dad's mind. I can merge with his mind perfectly. I see the target through Dad's consciousness, and I know who to terminate. Through Dad, I can Sense the target, slip into their body—the warm skin, the heavy bones, the zing of nerves in muscle, the blood shushing steadily. I follow the blood back to the heart itself.

Which I then crush.

Mom's eyes harden as she looks away. "I wish you could stay in the minipod, believe me, but it's just not possible. Security is so tight, they're not allowing any vehicles in. Everyone is walking. This is a very important target, Eten. Sayan Hann is a big deal all through Asia. He's blowing up our oil fields."

"Wait," I say, increasingly worried by what Mom said. "*Everyone* is walking? Who's everyone?"

Mom and Dad look at each other. "Well, that's what we wanted to discuss with you," says Dad. "There will be some crowds. Strangers. Hann's followers, people who gather to see this man speak. We'll be walking among them to get to the site."

My mouth goes dry. I've seen crowds in vids. But that's a fantasy thing, not real. I can't imagine being inside a crowd. "Like, how many people, do you think?"

Mom shrugs. "A hundred, maybe?" Her eyes are full of pity as she gazes at me. That look scares me more than anything else. "To be honest," she says, "it will be more. Hundreds more. It's a big rally."

"But I'll be with you every step of the way," says Dad.

"Oh," I put my hands over my face. "Hundreds." I try to picture it. Being surrounded by unknown faces and strange bodies. A river of people jamming the street. I shiver.

"I know it will be hard for you," says Dad. "We thought you'd have more time. I'm sorry, but it's got to be done. This mission is really, really important. And only you can do it."

Wow, I'd feel really, really special, except for the fact that *every* mission is really, really important and only I can do it. I'm so tired of the military *hoo-rah*. I know we're working for world peace, but why does there have to be so much killing? I long to be something other than a soldier. Like a healer. I met a doctor once when my finger broke after a particularly bad punishment. All he did was x-ray my hand and tape my fingers together. I was the one who healed it, Sensing the bone and helping the cells to build back strong. I could be a *good* healer.

"Our safety is going to depend on you, Eten," says Dad. Raw uncertainty edges his voice. "There will be new sounds, new sights. You'll have to focus. Okay? Can you do that for me?"

I take a deep breath, pushing back the anxiety. He's depending on me. "Of course I can, Dad," I say. A good soldier may feel fear, but fear does not control her. I take another breath and begin my mantra. *I am a part of all things, and all things lift me toward the center.*

"You've seen crowds on your vids," says Dad.

"Yes," says Mom, "it will be similar." She turns to Dad. "Should she watch vids to prepare?"

Oh, my God, my vids are a hundred years old. Another deep breath. *I rest in light. My spirit flows forth unencumbered.*

Dad shakes his head. "We'll practice in the gym."

SamJay thinks my mantra is an ancient poem. I learned about mantras in my *Religions of the World* course. That's when I began to use this one to calm myself.

"You know, going outside might even be fun," says Mom. "You'll be wearing foreign clothes." I just nod as she pushes this bit of nonsense. She's really reaching. I take another deep breath. *I am embraced by the stillness, and the stillness fills me with power.*

"Okay," I say as the power of stillness seeps into my body. I'm connected. With what, exactly, I don't know, but that's what the mantra does for me—it makes me feel connected to something infinite, calm, and good. "I'll be okay," I tell them.

They finally let me go and I return to the kitchen. Lunch is over; SamJay is gone. The promise of the day has vanished, and I struggle to maintain that connected feeling.

"You want your leftovers?" asks Nana, who's washing dishes. "I think the others are playing that game in the bedroom, that War Hunter thing."

"No, thanks Nana." All we do is missions; why do my brothers and sisters want to play at war, too? I head for the study lab, the mantra lifting my breath:

I am a part of all things, and all things lift me toward the center.

I rest in light. My spirit flows forth unencumbered.

I am embraced by the stillness, and the stillness fills me with power.

CHAPTER 4

Tonight, we get free play. That means I get to talk to SamJay. I need to ask him something, but I'm not sure how to say it. *Why do I hate being a soldier these days?* Or, *Lately, terminating evil terrorists makes me feel sick. Why is that?* SamJay was once a great soldier—he'll be ashamed of me turning into a coward.

Only the basketball court is lit—you can't even see the ruins at the center of the gym. SamJay sits down on the bench to rest his bad leg, and I take a time-out with him. We're both sweating. SamJay pulls off the red bandana tied around his head and wipes his face with it.

The boys and Jaysx play another round of 21-Skip while Teetu sits on the floor and watches something on her vidscreen—probably one of those ancient *Father Knows Best* shows. She loves those.

"SamJay, why were families from the time before so different from now?" I ask him, even though that's not really what I'm worrying about. "I mean, I know there was the war and all. But everybody seems so happy in those old vids."

SamJay shrugs. He watches vids with us, and he loves *Father Knows Best* almost as much as Teetu. "Those shows were made before I was born," he says. "I don't know why all your vids are so old."

"What?" I sit up straighter. "Mom said all the newer vids were destroyed in the war."

"Oh, that's right," says SamJay, not very convincingly.

"Come on, is she lying?"

"No! Of course not." SamJay looks around nervously for surveillance cams.

I shake my head, disgusted. I can't believe SamJay can't Sense them. "There are no close vidcams here and no soundbugs at all," I murmur.

"Well, I don't know," he says, rewrapping his headband snugly. "Doesn't your mom say the 1950s and '60s were the 'golden age' of America?" He makes little air quotes with his fingers. "That must be why the families all seem so happy. Maybe your mom wants you guys to watch happy vids."

"Yeah, but the moms and dads in those vids are nothing like Mom and Dad. And the kids are nothing like us. They don't even know how to fight. Do you think those vids are realistic?"

SamJay frowns and puckers his lips.

"Come on. Truth."

Ever since I was little, SamJay and I have had a special truth bond. When one of us says "truth," we have to be honest. SamJay started it. He taught me you have to tell the truth to the people you love. Lies, SamJay says, are like bricks that create a wall between friends. You tell too many lies and there is no more closeness.

Mom tells lies all the time and that's why we're not close. Dad tries to tell the truth, but sometimes he struggles. SamJay's the only one who's always honest. Sometimes, SamJay has to say something is "classified," which means it's a secret that belongs to someone else, so he can't reveal it. But at least that's honest.

I wish SamJay could be my dad instead of Dad. There's a closeness between us that began when Beeta disappeared from our old pod. SamJay was a new guard, and I remember I just couldn't eat or drink anything after my brother vanished. I was just shy of three years old. I remember being so empty and tired. I didn't want to be awake. Beeta was always in my mind before. After he left, I was alone, drifting into darkness. Nana fussed, trying to force me to drink from a bottle, and Mom kept trying to spoon applesauce into my mouth. I remember people shouting. Mom yelled I was dying. I didn't care; I just wanted to sleep.

Then someone new picked me up. He didn't try to get me to eat. He just held me next to his chest, inside his shirt, rocking back and forth. And he sang to me. *"Bright angels around, my darling, shall guard. They will guide thee from harm. Thou art safe in my arms."*

Later, he told me that was a very old song his mother used to sing to him called Brahm's Lullaby. I could feel the song rumbling in his chest. He rocked me for what seemed like hours, and every so often, he would kiss my head and push his fingers gently through my hair. I could feel the little silver strands of my hair curling around his fingers, and he just let them slide between his knuckles, across his hands, connecting. My cheek and ear pressed into his bare skin. For the first time since Beeta left, my Senses found a warm place where they could rest. SamJay was like a warm blanket in a cool, dark room filled with song. I began to fall asleep when I felt something warm and soft on my lips. Milk. I drank.

After that, I began to live again. Always with my protector nearby.

SamJay turns and looks at me. Then he grins. "Truth? I don't think those families are realistic."

I laugh. "Neither do I. So, are most families like our family?"

SamJay lets out a low sound, almost a grumble. I look up. He shrugs and smiles. "Classified," he says.

That makes no sense, but I don't pursue it. Something closer to what I'm really worried about tumbles out. "I don't want to go on missions anymore."

"Mmm," SamJay grunts, staring at the floor as if my confession isn't that surprising. "It was a long time ago you started."

"When I was five."

"Mmmm," he grunts again.

"At first, I was excited. But I didn't understand what I was doing. I mean, I know we have to fight for our country and restore world peace and everything, but, SamJay, I just don't want to kill people anymore. Even if they are bad."

SamJay is looking at me now with a strange expression on his face, his mouth pulled together in a tight knot and his brow furrowed in a mighty frown. I realize I'm twisting my fingers and I shake out my hands. "It's okay, never mind," I say, embarrassed. "I'll be fine. I can do my job."

"Are you scared about the new mission, you know, outside?"

I shrug and blow out a breath. "Yeah, I guess so." But that isn't what's bothering me, and the frustration brims over. "It's just, you know, isn't it wrong to kill people? To murder people?"

SamJay draws a sharp breath in through his teeth as if stung. "You can't think of it like that, Eten," he says. "It's not murder. It's totally not the same. This is war."

"I don't see the difference," I say. "The whole thing makes me sick. I mean, physically sick to my stomach. I don't want to go on any more missions."

SamJay turns his attention back to the floor, his hands on his knees, shaking his head. "War is tough," he says. Which isn't very helpful. "But we have to defend ourselves."

"That's another thing. Why do these terrorists keep attacking us? Wasn't the nuclear holocaust enough? What do they want? It must be important, or they'd stop after all these years. Mom and Dad say we're fighting for world peace, but when will it happen?"

"World peace is tough," says SamJay. Equally unhelpful.

"I want to be a healer, SamJay. I think I could be a good healer."

SamJay nods with that same intent, unhappy frown. "Yes, you would." He's still not looking at me.

"Do you think—" I hesitate to ask, then plunge on. "Am I turning into a coward?"

SamJay throws his head back and laughs out loud. He throws an arm across my shoulders. "No, no, no, no, no," he says, shaking his head and still laughing. "Girl, you are no coward."

I don't see what's so funny about it. "Well," I say, "I am terrified of going outside."

SamJay's broad face goes serious. "Listen, you take care of yourself. Just be careful, okay?" He sits back down and speaks quietly. "You Jump yourself away if anything dangerous happens, okay?"

His words surprise me. "I've got to do the mission," I say.

He looks at me seriously. "I know, but your safety is more important than the mission. Remember that." He shakes his finger at me. "If anything compromises your safety, you Jump yourself back to your travel pod."

My mouth hangs open a little—I can't believe what I'm hearing. Jump myself back to the travel pod if it's dangerous? Isn't *that* being a coward? He's never said anything like this before. But then, I've never gone outside on a mission before. Dad's priority is to complete the mission successfully. He wouldn't tell me to abort a mission unless we were about to be killed. And even then, he might not.

"Uh—okay," I say, wondering if it will come to that.

It's funny. SamJay's not a dad, but he's a lot more like the dads in *Little House on the Prairie* and *Father Knows Best* than Dad is. I guess SamJay's just old-fashioned that way. Or is he unrealistic? Telling me to abort the mission if I'm in danger is kind of unrealistic.

Gefor and Jaysx are calling us back onto the court. SamJay and I run out there, and I pull Teetu up from her vid. I'm going to help her score this time. The boys don't want her to play with us because she's so little, but I insist. When you're a family, you include each other. You take care of each other. I guess I'm a little old-fashioned that way, too. Hopefully, not unrealistic.

CHAPTER 5

I hate live target practice. I loved it when I was little and gung-ho. Now, it's unnerving. Things happen too fast and people can get seriously injured.

I push on the gym door. "Don't forget," I say to the others. I can't see their eyes behind goggles and helmets. "Don't hurt anybody." We're in full body armor; it's the prisoners I'm worried about. My heart ratchets up a notch.

"Are you kidding?" says Gefor, his voice muffled. "How do we not hurt them? We're supposed to shoot them."

"They're terrorists," adds Gethre.

"They're prisoners now, okay?" I say. "Just don't kill anybody." I know our training is important, but using prisoners like lab rats—it's repulsive.

As today's leader, I enter the gym first, throw my back against the wall, and grip the rifle to my chest. In quick succession, my brothers do the same. Jaysx is last; Teetu, thank goodness, is still too little for this.

Dad told the others that today's practice is for me, to get me ready for my new mission. But it's not for me. He's testing Jaysx. He says she has to toughen up. Sometimes, on missions, she freezes, which of course screws everything up. We're not in any real danger inside our travel pods. What makes her freeze is fear of making a mistake. Exchanging bullets with prisoners isn't going to help my sister with that.

The automatiks echo in the distance.

Jaysx coughs. She tends to cough when she's scared. This is her first live target practice ever. I lean over, take one look at her face, and my heart sinks. Her expression is rigid, her dark, full lips pressed into a grim line.

The practice won't last long, but rubber bullets hurt—a lot. "You'll be fine, Jaysx." I try to project warmth and reassurance the way Teetu does. I'm not very good at it.

"The automatiks don't hit anybody," says Gefor. "They're just for distraction."

"I know!" My sister's emotions swirl like water down a drain. She isn't ready, even though she's heavy and strong and eight years old. I did my first live target practice with Dad when I was six, just a skinny brat, but I loved it. Big and strong doesn't mean ready.

I told Dad this wasn't going to help, but he said it would. There are too many missions, he said. Jaysx is running out of time, he said.

Running out of time? What does that even mean? A dark thought flickers in and out of existence in my mind. *They wouldn't dare,* I think, my skin going cold.

Jaysx squares her shoulders, the dim "afternoon" light reflecting off the sweat on her high cheekbones and chin.

I lean across the boys. "Focus on your shield, Jaysx."

Gethre puts his arm around our sister's shoulder and squeezes. "Come on." He jiggles her. "You're gonna ace this."

"You'll be great," echoes Gefor. "You're a natural-born warrior."

Jaysx nods.

"Okay," I say. "Ready?" I point my finger and we advance.

The only sound is the chattering automatic gunfire. The air tastes acrid and dry.

I Sense eight terrorists hiding in the fake ruins. All male. They're mostly confused and scared by this assignment, though one is angry. It's like he's seen all this before—he must be a long-term prisoner. They don't even try to shield their minds. Two are on a roof together. Three more in another house, two moving from one house to another. One, a new prisoner, is hiding by himself.

"Hold it," I say. The boys look at me, annoyed. I keep my voice low. "Can you Sense them, Jaysx?"

She nods eagerly.

I know how much my sister wants to do well, to show Mom and Dad she can pull her own weight.

"Don't forget," I whisper. "No blowing up heads, no matter what." Again, I give the go-ahead. Gethre crouches and slinks off to the left. Gefor surges right, headed for the guy who's by himself.

"Damn it!" I mutter. I wanted Jaysx to fight the single guy. Already, my sister has allowed her shield to slip. Her pulse is racing; she still hasn't moved.

I touch her shoulder and make a circling motion with my hand. Jaysx focuses on continuously Jumping a sphere of molecules all around her body. A shield is difficult at first; it requires constant attention when you're new to it.

I help strengthen her shield. She gives me a thumbs up, jogging from foot to foot, blowing a couple of breaths out hard. Gunfire bursts from the roof of a building, and Jaysx flinches as bullets ricochet off her shield. She knows they're rubber, but still. The assault is alarming.

Suddenly, everybody begins to fire. The noise is deafening. Atop the building, a man cries out in pain.

I nudge Jaysx toward two terrorists who are lying on their bellies, training their guns on us through a hole in the wall. I give her a go-ahead signal.

Jaysx sprints toward them, yelling.

I split left through a new hail of bullets. Three terrorists are hiding on the second floor of another house. I duck past the cement casing of the doorless building.

Inside, it smells of dust and debris. Sudden quiet falls like a drape. The men upstairs are waiting for me. I place my boots carefully on the cement steps, avoiding anything that might crunch, and make my way up. First step, second, third. Then I pause.

The stairs in this house have a blind spot. The vidcam on the ground floor can't see me now, and the cam in the stairwell is focused too high. This is because I tilted it up years ago, during another target practice.

As I reach the blind spot, I Jump myself into the room behind the terrorists and underneath the vidcam, where it can't see me. I suspect

Mom and Dad know we can Jump ourselves, but I'm never sure, and I don't want it on camera.

Overhead, dust swirls upward through the catwalks and the dim lights. I press my back to the fragmented wall. The terrorists don't hear me. Three men stand at the edge of the stairwell, pointing their weapons down. They're coiled, tense, waiting for me to come up the steps so they can shoot me, as instructed.

If this were a real battle, they'd be dead already. For a single moment, I try to Sense them, but all I get is a rush of fear. I wish I knew what motivated them. Why are they terrorists? Why do they choose to destroy things when the world needs so much healing?

I greet them with a sigh. "Hi there, soldiers!"

All three cry out and spin, convulsively firing their weapons.

But I'm still shielded. The bullets fall harmlessly to the floor. I Jump the rifles from their hands to the weapons closet. Two of the men shout fearfully, shaking their empty hands, but one—a big, white man who looks familiar—stares at me, stolid, resigned, his hands in the air. He crouches down, making himself small, and covers his head with his arms. As he does this, one of the others scurries backward and tumbles with a yelp into the stairwell. I Jump him back up so he doesn't break his neck, but now he's a terrified blob, jabbering broken phrases in Hamgyŏng, a Korean dialect, holding his head and hopping around as if he stood on a hot stove.

It's awful, frightening grown men this way. Even if they are terrorists. It's not right.

"It's all right. Go ahead," I tell them, motioning with my rifle. I learned to speak Hamgyŏng a couple of years ago, when the U.S. pacified

Korea. I'm up to ten languages now, not including Mongolian—five more than Dad. Languages are easy for us kids, like math. "We're done," I continue. "All done now. Go back to the elevator." Terrorist prisoners come and go via the cargo elevator at the back of the gym— the same one we use for our travel pods.

The two Korean men hurry away, but the hulking, white man stops at the top of the stairs and looks back at me. He's the one I Sensed had been here before, the long-term prisoner. I can tell he's about to say something. I should threaten him with the gun. I'm not allowed to talk to terrorists.

"Who the hell are you?" he says in English. "*What* are you? And where the holy fuck am I?"

Surprise ripples through me. How can this terrorist not know where he is?

If a soundbug hears us, we'll both be punished. "You shouldn't talk to me," I tell him in a low voice. "I'm not allowed to talk to you."

The man ignores my words, peers down the stone steps into gloom, then up over the roofless wall. Sporadic gunfire echoes. "What is this place?"

"It's just a pod." I shrug. *Your prison*, I was going to say, but I don't want to call my home a prison.

"Do you know why I'm here?"

I frown and gape, amazed. Seriously, does he not know why he's here after all this time? I Sense his mind spin, his confusion. My helmet suddenly feels uncomfortably hot and tight, and I pull it off. "Because you're a terrorist!"

"Oh my God, you're a kid! Americans are recruiting children now?"

I bristle. "I'm not a child."

"I'm not a terrorist," says the man. "I'm a climatologist."

I know what that is. He must be lying, but I don't Sense a lie. Images of a broad room full of vidscreens flicker in his mind, vids of black clouds swirling in a huge circle, of cities flooding, pictures of desert soil cracking under the sun. I don't know what to say.

"Don't you realize they're manipulating you?" His voice is too loud.

"Shhhh!" I hiss at him. "Be quiet."

The man lowers his voice. "Whoever you are, whatever you are, you should know you're fighting for the *wrong side*."

CHAPTER 6

Suddenly, I'm really scared. I motion with my gun. "Go back to the elevator."

But he doesn't. He crouches down and talks in a low rush. "Military officials arrested me. Your military."

My heart pounds again and my lips feel numb. "You're a terrorist," I say. But suddenly I'm not sure.

"I'm a climatologist," he insists again. Now that I can see his face, I realize he's older than I first thought. Under his dark hair, worry creases his forehead, and the pale skin around his eyes is marred with shadows. I Sense his dismay, his urgency. "Climate change is destroying the earth. Don't you know? People are starving, burning up. Drowning. I was testifying before U.S. state representatives when military police arrested me. Don't you get it? I don't belong in this prison."

"That's enough," I growl, terror blooming through my body. I can't listen to this treason. Instinctively, my mind lashes out, squeezing the muscles in his neck as I Sense their moist, gentle throb. His face goes grey; he chokes and gasps for air, his hands flying to his throat.

I step back with a gasp of my own, releasing my mental grip. I don't want to hurt this man. He wheels, his breath ragged as he coughs and runs down the stairs.

How could he say such things? My brain is throbbing. Around me, the shooting has stopped except for the chatter of the automatiks. I look up at the vast space above, at least 30 meters to the ceiling. This isn't a prison; it's my home, one pod among many. But I can't help wondering: Can a home be a prison?

There's another burst of gunfire and pain slams me. I stagger. Jaysx has been hurt. Nearby, Gethre screams as I sink to my knees. With an effort, I withdraw from my sister's consciousness.

There's more gunfire and I hear my brother shouting, "Motherfucker." I can't believe he even knows that word.

"No," I call out, and Jump myself into the familiar building where Jaysx lies on the floor. Gethre crouches next to her, his gun pointed at a hideous sight.

Two men, their faces and hands just visible, are *embedded* in the concrete wall. It's like the wall has been poured around them, leaving only their hands and faces sticking out of rough cement.

"Gethre!" I whisper, shocked to my core. "What did you do?" I throw my rifle on the floor, run over, and tug a flashlight out of my vest.

The men are still alive. Their fingers twitch and their eyes roll. Their mouths hang open, tongues purple and swollen. Their lips writhe as they try to force air into their trapped lungs. Their faces are turning blue.

"They shot Jaysx," says Gethre.

"They're *supposed* to shoot at us! It's live target practice." I Jump the men out of the wall and onto the floor. A trail of rubble follows them. Two chest-sized holes gape in the already crumbling wall. "You're not allowed to kill them. I told you."

The men gasp, oblivious to everything but pain. One utters broken phrases in Hamgyŏng. I think he's praying.

"They didn't shoot *at* her," says Gethre. "They shot her."

I crouch over Jaysx. She's lying on her back, trying to hold her side, her violet eyes wide and frightened. Her body armor is barely attached with Velcro on the sides, and it gapes open. It's too small. The bullet hit under her left arm. She groans as I try to pull the Velcro off from underneath her.

Gefor comes running in.

"What happened?"

"They shot her," says Gethre.

"She let her shield down," I say.

Gefor falls to his knees next to her. He grabs his side, moaning. He's become embedded in Jaysx's mind, and he's losing consciousness.

"Come on, Gefor," I snap. "Withdraw your Senses."

"Okay, okay," whispers Gefor, slowly recovering. Tears flood his face and his nose runs. "It's hard when it's your sister."

"Come on, guys, help me with her before Mom and Dad see this." We all look up to the corner of the room. The vidcam is gone. We got lucky.

"I moved that one," murmurs Gethre.

"Good. Come on, we have only a minute." I'm still trying to get Jaysx's vest off. "Next time, just tilt the vidcam up instead of moving it, okay? They're going to get suspicious." I motion with my chin to the wall where the men were embedded. "How'd you do that?"

Gethre shrugs.

"Don't tell Mom and Dad," I say.

Mom and Dad go nuts when one of us manifests a new skill. They get so wound up, it's pathetic. After Teetu threw the EyeSpy during her test, they spent a day examining her. They make us try all kinds of weird things to figure out what we can and can't do. Like, "Can you attach the rat's tail to its head?" (The answer to that one was, "No," and a dead rat.)

"Are you kidding? I'm not an idiot," says Gethre.

"They could have killed her," mutters Gefor, still choked up.

He's not wrong; rubber bullets can kill if you're close enough. But we're supposed to be able to shield ourselves. That's the whole point.

Jaysx lies on her back, moaning, breathing in a shallow pant, holding her side. The boys each put a hand on Jaysx's leg and radiate calm, trying to absorb her pain in small doses.

One of the terrorists makes a noise. I'd forgotten them. They're still lying on the floor, pretending to be dead.

"It's all right," I tell them in Hamgyŏng. "I'm sorry you were hurt. You can leave."

The two men crawl to their feet and limp out of the low doorway. "Devil hell," one mutters in English.

"I don't know why you're so nice to them," says Gefor. "They're terrorists."

"They're bad," says his twin.

"Yeah, well, now they're just prisoners, aren't they?" I stroke Jaysx's forehead. She looks up at me. "Can you heal it?" she asks. She knows I wish I could be a healer.

My insides flutter. I'm not sure.

The loudspeaker blares to life. "Let's go, crew," booms Dad's voice. "Where are you?"

"Hurry up. Mom and Dad are going to get mad," says Gefor. "They're already pissed Jaysx screwed up those missions."

"Oh, no," moans Jaysx.

"She didn't screw them up," snaps Gethre. "She was too far from the targets."

"Please…don't let Mom know I got hurt," Jaysx says faintly. "I dropped my shield."

"Just relax, you're probably just bruised." In fact, I'm not sure what happened, but I've got to get her on her feet. "It's not your fault, okay? Your body armor is too small."

"Come on, boys and girls," booms Dad. "No horsing around. The enemy is already on the elevator."

"Coming, Dad," shouts Gethre.

Grabbing Jaysx's hand, I let my Senses flow into her body.

Her rib isn't just bruised—it's cracked. It hurts each time she breathes. Blood seeps, and there's a splinter of bone…But now I've lost it.

"A splinter," mutter Gefor and Gethre simultaneously.

I find it again. A tiny, sharp splinter of bone, *moving through viscous, injured cells toward the lung…*

I jump the fragment out of Jaysx's body onto the floor. *Out now.* My brothers grunt in satisfaction.

The brokenness of her bone echoes in me like a thin, dark whisper. I slide up to the narrow crack, wrap myself around and into it, as if I were a fog seeping into her body.

Dad's voice says something from a distance. A flicker on the edge of consciousness.

"Hurry," says Gethre.

But I'm falling away from him. I'm seeping through warm blood, marrow. Cells form about me in a matrix. I am a dark red glow. Infinitesimally tiny fibers fill the dark space, spongy and new. A hard, flexible layer surrounds us, holding us together. The lungs expand; the rib holds.

Gethre pulls on my shoulder and I tumble backward. I'm looking at the ceiling. Gefor reaches to catch me, then turns in slow motion. It's like waking up from a deep sleep.

"We gotta go," Gethre hisses.

Overhead, all the lights flare. Daytime lighting.

"Oh, crap," says Gefor.

"Where's the vidcam feed?" Dad's voice booms over the intercom again.

Gefor and Gethre run out into the gym and I help Jaysx to her feet. She stretches and her eyes go wide. "Better," she says.

A buzzer sounds. "Practice is over," Dad announces.

Jaysx throws her arms around me. "You're the best sister in the world."

I steady myself against her, hugging her back. Did I heal her? Awe surges through me. "You did good, little sister," I tell her.

We both laugh since Jaysx isn't so little anymore. We jog double-time toward the exit.

Jaysx isn't limping or even holding her side. I'm not sure how I healed her, but she's better. Pride surges up in me like I haven't felt since I was a kid. Healing! What a wonderful feeling. I would love to be a healer. I wish I could heal the whole world.

A small voice inside of me scoffs. A healer? What a joke. Bitterness curls in my belly like an edge of burning paper. Mom and Dad would never allow it. I'm too good at killing.

When I was about eleven, I wanted to be an airplane pilot. Mom and Dad actually laughed when I told them, like it was amusing. *We're soldiers,* they said. *That's what we are.* Like, even the dream of being something else was silly.

I wish I could escape. I know it's selfish because we're all fighting to restore peace and heal the earth. Each person is supposed to do their part. People who desert the military are shot, after all. Treason is a capital offense. If I dream of escape, I can't tell anyone.

US DEPARTMENT OF DEFENSE
SPECIAL OPERATIONS
WASHINGTON, D.C. 20223

CLASSIFIED

ULTRA
TOP SECRET

NO DISSEMINATION OR DECLASSIFICATION

DEPARTMENT OF DEFENSE
Office of the Under Secretary (R&E)
VIA COURIER
EYES ONLY   ULTRA TOP SECRET

FROM: Dr. Joseph Duroc, MD, PhD, US Under Secretary
TO: General Conrad Barnes, USSOC
      General BB Grasbach, MD, PhD, JSOC
      Senator George Mitchell, Chair, Armed
      Services Cmte
      Dr Richard Montrose-Beck, DARPA
      Major James Hamilton, Director of Operations
      Lt. Colonel Monica Nowak, Project Director
RE: PROJECT SAMSON: PLANNED OBSOLESCENCE/CLONING
DATE: 6 April 2088

As you know, Project Samson's long-term goal to increase US military efficacy has already far exceeded expectations. Each Project Samson operative's skill and reach is much greater than we had anticipated.

On the other hand, such power represents an unacceptable threat. Only now has it become evident how much we risk, what the entire world risks, should even one more operative go rogue. What might they do to human culture if, as a group, they joined against us? We must not allow these young chimeras to reach maturity.

Our eldest operative is about to turn 16, and we should replace it. Since it has not been able to reproduce naturally, we must consider cloning and termination at the earliest possible date.

We will discuss at our next SCIF meeting in
Washington.

Do not file.
Project Samson forbids use of text or instamail.
Deliquesce this memorandum after reading.

CHAPTER 7

In the sunroom, I sit with my feet dangling in the pool, totally miserable. Mom told us this morning that SamJay has a surprise mission, and he won't be back for a week—not until my birthday. At least he won't miss that. At the other end of the pool, a new guard, PaulTee, stands alert, watching, like somebody might actually drown.

I have a headache again. It feels like a tight band around my forehead and an ache in my neck. Nana gave me what she called an "analgesic." I think it helped a little. Nana, as usual, is sitting under the shadow of her umbrella chair. The special sun lamps in the ceiling keep us healthy, but Nana doesn't like them.

"Eten, come on," says Gefor.

"It's your turn," says Gethre.

"I got up to 237 seconds," Gefor says excitedly.

We're practicing holding our breath underwater. Of course, it's a competition; the boys are so excited, I pretend like I care. The girls are not participating. Jaysx swims laps and Teetu floats.

"Okay, watch out," I say. "I'm going to beat my record this time." I jump in, take a bunch of big breaths, swim down, and grab the bottom rung of the embedded ladder. I float, holding my breath. My record is 276 seconds. My feet start to rise and I slowly bring them toward my hands, anchoring my toes under the ladder. The stretch relieves the ache in my back.

I wish I could stay here forever, water filling my ears with muted, wavy sounds. Jaysx's breaststroke. Teetu's occasional splash. I close my eyes, willing myself to Sense nothing, feel nothing. I am weightless, free, tethered only by fingers and toes.

Dimly, I hear voices. Then Gethre calling my name. I Sense urgency. Then panic from Jaysx. I let go of the rung and shoot to the surface.

"Blood," shouts Gethre, pointing at the pool.

They're all shouting. Nana speaks into a ristcom. Jaysx and Teetu are climbing out of the pool.

"Eten, you're bleeding," says Jaysx, coming to the edge of the cement, wringing her hands. Teetu hops from foot to foot beside her. I'm the only one still in the water.

"What?" In the water, I turn in a circle, looking around myself.

"Eten, get out of the pool," says Nana

All around me swirls bright, red blood, spiraling and fanning out, staining the water pink at the edges of the cloud.

Frantically, I feel all over my body. Where is the wound? I can't find the wound.

"Eten, get out of the pool," Nana says again. She strides to the intercom and punches a button.

Panic rising, I almost Jump myself out of the water, but at the last moment, I remember to climb the ladder. Blood trails me.

"What is it?" I stamp my bloody feet on the cement apron surrounding the pool. Blood runs down the insides of my wet thighs to the floor.

"Her legs are bleeding," shout the twins. They run to me and Gethre shouts at Nana to call Mom. Which I think she already did. Jaysx grabs Teetu's hand, and all four of them press up around and against me.

"What is it?" whispers Jaysx.

"I don't know," I say. Nothing exactly seems wrong, and everything seems wrong. I ache. My belly aches. "My body hurts."

A quiet moan sweeps through us.

"It's all right." Nana comes over to us, not exactly touching us, her hands hovering. "Don't worry, I think she'll be okay."

After a few minutes, Mom throws the door, and suddenly it seems a lot of drama over nothing. "All right, all right," she says briskly. "Come on now, Eten is fine, just back off." She's holding a large, multicolored towel and a dusty, gray bag slung over her shoulder. "Come on, children," she says, dropping the bag down at our feet. I see dust poof out of it as she pulls on Jaysx's shoulder, muscling us apart. "Get back, now."

"Eten's bleeding," says Gethre, stepping back. "Look."

There's a puddle of blood and water around my feet.

"I know," Mom says calmly, wrapping the big towel around me and picking up her bag. "And don't you worry about it. It's perfectly natural."

We all gape at her.

With her arm around my shoulders, Mom guides me toward the large bathroom that adjoins the sunroom. "Eten's going to be fine. She's just a healthy young woman."

I look back and see the others' wondering faces. I'm leaving a trail of blood across the white cement.

"Nana," Mom says over her shoulder, "take the others back to the bedroom. And Sergeant Trevino, hose off the floor, please."

The bathroom is large, with shelves of supplies, several private toilet stalls, two showers, a bunch of chairs, and a low table. Mom drops the bag onto one of the chairs, pulls out a dark blue towel from the shelf, and puts it on another chair. "Sit down, Eten," she says.

I wave my hand under my butt. "But I'm…"

"It's okay. Don't worry about it. I can wash the towel." Then she smiles. A real smile this time, not one of her distracted, military grimaces, but something like warm, genuine affection.

My heart lurches as I sit down. Is this Mom? I remember that sometimes, when I was little, Mom looked like this. Once I'd been very ill with simian flu, and I had to be in complete isolation. Nobody could see me for two weeks, except Mom. She was there, right by my side, every day, every night. It's hard to remember—the fever makes it blurry. But I remember her bending over me with that smile, telling me I was going to be okay, patting my face with a cool washcloth.

"I'm sorry, Eten, I think I made a mistake," she says. I just stare in astonishment. "I know you love babies so much. You know, your brothers and sisters—even when you were just a little thing, you always loved them and took care of them so well, but I didn't think…"

My mouth has fallen open. I shut it. I don't know what she's talking about.

She sighs. "I mean, we just didn't know if you would be able to…I mean, with your—uh—skills—we didn't know if it would even happen. Then after you were thirteen and nothing, I was sure it wouldn't, but…"

Now she's not looking at me and she genuinely seems at a loss for words.

"Mom," I say. "Has this got anything to do with why I'm bleeding?"

She takes a breath, holds it, and nods. "You've got your period." She blows out the breath, her cheeks puffing up. "It's menstruation; you're menstruating."

"Okay," I say carefully. I don't know what these words mean. "And that is…?"

She waves her hand around in circles. "Reproduction."

My eyebrows shoot up. "What?" My heart begins to pound. Am I having a baby? Is that why she's talking about babies? A thrill shoots through my entire being.

All these years, Mom and Dad have refused to explain reproduction to us. Dad says, "Ask your mother," and Mom says we don't need to know yet. But we do know this much: Females get pregnant with babies and somehow give birth to them. That's why we celebrate birthdays. We know this because Ma on *Little House on the Prairie* got pregnant and had a baby. But we could never figure out how.

"Mom, am I pregnant?" I breathe.

Mom frowns and startles forward on her chair, holding out a hand. "No, no, nothing like that." Reassuring me. As if that would be a terrible thing.

Disappointment rolls over me.

Then Mom explains the uterus, the ovaries, microscopic eggs, the lining of the uterus, and the shedding of the lining—menstruation.

I'm so pissed off nobody ever told me all this, I want to jump up and down and punch something, but I'm afraid to bleed on the floor. I squeeze the arms of the chair and it begins to rattle.

"Why didn't you tell me this before?" I demand, my chair shaking even harder. I should calm down. I'll whip up a tantrum and there will be trouble.

Mom jumps up, her face going white and grim. "Control yourself!" She looks up and around, as if for a vidcam, then mutters, "No cams in here, of course."

I take a deep breath, relax my shoulders. She's right—it's dangerous if I get too angry.

"Eten, you have to control yourself. Don't you want to hear the rest?"

"Yes, I do." I try to clear my mind, and I repeat the lines of my mantra. After a few moments, I open my eyes. "Okay. I'm okay now."

"Look," says Mom, relaxing again. "I understand why you're angry. But it can be…" She shakes her head and looks away. "Devastating news to learn you can't have children. I thought maybe you couldn't. Most girls menstruate by the time they're twelve or thirteen. Some women don't want kids, but for me, it was…" She shakes her head again.

My turn to frown. What is she talking about, for her? She *has* kids. Us. "Somebody said you couldn't have kids?"

Her head snaps back and I can tell she has made a mistake. Her mental walls shoot into place. The fake smile crinkles her mouth. "When I was young, yes. But then—Voila!" She flourishes a hand at me. "They were wrong. You and your brothers and sisters came along."

She's lying. I don't know exactly what the lie is, but she's lying again.

"And *how* did we come along, Mom?"

She holds up a finger. "That's the rest of the story." She then tells me about sperm; testicles; penises—not like I never saw the twins' privates when they were little, so I know what she's talking about. Egg fertilization and the growth of the child in the uterus—these I can understand. But the sexual intercourse thing? It's hard to imagine.

Then she's talking about how she and Dad fell in love and created us children. Mom in love with Dad? I don't think so. She goes on and on, and I tune out until she says something awful.

"And someday, when you and your brothers and sisters are a little older, you will all have babies. Together. You and Gethre. Jaysx and Gefor."

I shrink back. "What? Together? No way." Gethre stick his penis inside of me? The thought is so gross, I can't even picture it.

"Well, if you don't care to have sexual intercourse," said Mom, "your brother can be the sperm donor. Or we can do what's called 'in vitro fertilization.' A doctor gets sperm from a male and an egg from a female and creates a baby in a test tube. Isn't that amazing?"

In her mind, there's an image of a man dressed in white holding a huge syringe, standing between the legs of a half-naked woman who's lying on her back on a table. I maintain a stunned silence. It sounds like torture.

"You children are very special," she continues, "and we believe that your offspring will be even more powerful than you are. That's very important for the war effort."

I shiver.

"Anyway," says Mom, standing, "you need to get in the shower. I left clothes and a pad for you. Stick the pad to your underwear. Nana will give you more. Don't think about any of this now. You'll feel differently when you're older. You're still too young. I've got to get going."

She starts for the door. She and Dad leave most evenings by dinnertime. They go on nighttime missions. Tonight, they'll leave for the weekend.

I don't stand. "Where's SamJay, Mom? It's Friday."

She looks back. "He's on a mission, I told you.

"He doesn't go on missions anymore. He's too old."

Her face goes hard and her mind clicks tight. "Don't talk back to me, Eten. There are missions about which you are totally uninformed."

I lift my chin, feeling reckless. "So inform me."

She stands stock still for a moment, blue eyes blazing. Then she shakes a finger at me. "Be careful. I mean it. You have to trust me, Eten. There are powers at work here that you can't even imagine. Powers that can destroy us all."

And then she leaves.

And I'm left wondering how I'm going to explain things to my brothers and sisters. Forget about "powers that can destroy us all." They're going to want to know why I'm bleeding. I cringe as I think of that new guard cleaning my blood off the floor. It's embarrassing. As much as I miss SamJay, I'm glad it isn't him cleaning up after me.

I slide into the shower, grateful for the hot water drumming down on my body. I decide I'll tell the others everything—except the part about us having babies together. That is really just too gross to mention.

CHAPTER 8

The night before the mission, something weird happens. Something weirder than getting my period and learning I can have babies; weirder than being told by a prisoner that I'm "fighting for the wrong side."

Nana hasn't yet locked the door, but my brothers and sisters have already drifted off. I lie in my bunk in the dark, brooding, so glad to have my sixteenth birthday over with. Birthdays are grueling. Testing all day, physical and mental challenges, IQ tests, blood tests, DDR scans, skills testing, stress tests. The only good thing about a birthday is the party at the end.

Today, even the party sucked. I didn't like the cake, I didn't like the gift—a new rifle—and Dad kept making stupid soldier jokes. The really bad thing was that SamJay didn't show. Even though it's Friday and Mom said he'd be back. This is the first time he's ever missed my birthday party. Now, he won't even get to say goodbye before my mission.

But just when Nana is about to lock the bedroom door, I hear him coming. SamJay's walk is distinct because of his limp. He's hurrying; I can Sense his agitation.

"Wait, Nana," SamJay calls out. "Wait for me."

My brothers and sisters immediately jolt awake. Of course they do. As SamJay slides past the heavy door into the room, they all chorus hello.

I'm so annoyed. It's my birthday. Why can't I have SamJay to myself for just a few minutes?

"I'm sorry I couldn't get to the birthday party, babygirl," SamJay says, feeling his way along in the dark.

"Don't you want the light, Sergeant Jones?" says Nana.

"No, no, thanks. It'll wake them up too much," says SamJay.

Nana mutters indistinctly and leaves.

SamJay's nervous. I Sense he's hiding something. He feels his way along by touching the top, empty bunks. He can't see in the dark like we do.

"It's okay about the party, SamJay," I tell him. I don't want him to feel bad. "I'm getting too old for parties anyway." I'm too old to be called "babygirl," too, but still. It reminds me of the old days. I prop myself on an elbow and watch him approach.

"I'll just tuck you in," he says.

That's weird. He hasn't tucked me in since I was about eight years old. My heart goes pitter-patter. What's he hiding?

"It was a great party," says Gefor, as usual not bothering to Sense anybody else's feelings. "We had chocolate cake with chocolate icing and chocolate ice cream. Eten blew out the candles and got a new Colt MK20."

A new rifle is the last thing I want for my birthday. But we don't get to choose the gift, only the cake. I would've chosen carrot cake, my favorite, but lately Jaysx seems to be allergic to nuts and nuts are in carrot cake and the boys love chocolate, so I asked for chocolate everything.

"I hope we get new rifles for our birthday," says Gethre. Their birthday isn't for another two months.

"Yeah, by the time you're thirteen, you'll want something else," says Jaysx, always the practical one. "Anyway, you'll probably get pajamas."

"Nooo," the boys groan simultaneously because Jaysx is probably right.

Teetu signs something from her bottom bunk under Jaysx.

"Teetu says if you guys didn't fart so much…Teetu, that's rude." I laugh and everybody else giggles. But not SamJay.

"Do you have to leave early for your mission tomorrow?" he asks.

"Oh-four-hundred," I say, trying to stay calm. I think I've come to terms with it. I'm feeling pretty confident I'll be okay.

I lay myself flat so he can tuck me in. But he doesn't. He kneels, pulls the covers up and, as he does so, slides something under my pillow.

"Don't show that to anyone," he whispers.

My heart really starts thumping as I nod. Then I realize he can't see me nod and I whisper, "Okay."

"Something's going on," he whispers. "You might be in danger. Just be careful tomorrow, okay? Try to figure things out."

I thought my heart was racing, but now it's pounding out of my chest. SamJay has *never* said anything like this before. "What's happening?"

"I don't understand myself. I saw part of a memo I wasn't supposed to see. But I…"

"What's a memo?" I whisper.

He doesn't explain. "Something's going on. There've been staff changes, secret meetings. I got sent away for a week, but there was nothing for me to do. Learn everything you can. Keep your eyes open." He pokes the pillow to indicate whatever he's left under it. "I don't know if this will help you. But you're sixteen now. You deserve to know what I know."

"What is it?"

Taps begins to play over the intercom. "Come on, Sergeant Jones," Nana calls from the open door. "Bedtime."

SamJay whispers, "Don't let *anybody* see that." He steps back. "Happy birthday, babygirl," he says too loudly. He's not good at lying. "I'll see you when you get back, okay?"

"Okay. Thanks, SamJay. I'll see you soon." I sound polite, but I'm boiling with frustration and anxiety. What's a "memo"? I feel like I'm sliding down a slippery surface, like my feet have gone out from under me and I can't get myself upright. Everything's moving too fast. I wish SamJay had told me more.

Nana heaves the metal door shut with both hands and sets the electronic lock.

I lay there, wide awake, counting to 100 while the boys fall back to sleep until they're sharing a dream, something about exploring the surface in hazmat suits. Jaysx sleeps dreamless as a hunk of concrete, and in the bunk below her, Teetu is flying through a world of color, dreaming about rescuing some strange creature in the times before.

From under my pillow, I pull out SamJay's gift, and my scalp prickles. It's a book. We don't have paper books in the pod, only the digital books we read in class and for fun. It's not very thick and it's held together with plastic along one edge. There's writing on the front, but it's too dark for me to read.

I probe Gefor's bed with my Senses, find the calculator under his arm, Jump it into my hand, and turn on the flashlight.

The book is only 22 pages long, with a cover made of heavy, gray paper. I begin to read:

Project Samson
Employee Handbook
TOP SECRET

CLEARANCE LEVEL 4 OR HIGHER ONLY
You are cautioned at this time to discontinue reading
if you do not have a Department of Defense Security
Clearing Level 4 or higher.

How exciting, I think. Or alarming. Both, I decide. I grin as I turn the page. More warnings on the second page. A lot about what charges will be brought against me if I read on when I'm not supposed to. A little shiver sneaks up my neck. I flip a few pages, looking for clues as to what Project Samson is.

A page heading reads:

HOW TO LEAVE YOUR JOB AT WORK.

It's natural when you go home from work to speak to friends and family about your job and for others to ask questions about your job. You may not put others off by telling them that your work is classified. Such answers provoke more questions. You must be prepared with a work scenario that is rote and mundane, with answers that will

not encourage more questions. Training class #17 will help you develop your narrative for what you do at work.

So, whatever Project Samson is, it seems to require a lot of lying.

I flip through more and find sections of the Handbook about Employee Benefits, Health Insurance, and Military Compensation.

Big yawn. I shake my head to keep myself awake. There's got to be a reason SamJay gave me this book—he wouldn't have risked it otherwise.

Then, a section called "Duties" catches my eye:

Your primary duty is to guard the Project Samson subjects, numbering _5_ at this time, and to keep the underground pod functioning smoothly.

The "underground pod?" So Project Samson is housed in an underground pod like ours. And there are five subjects. The number "5" has been filled in by hand, as if the number of "subjects" keeps changing and has to be updated. An uneasy feeling ruffles the back of my neck. I sit up in bed, all sleepiness gone.

The children may wish to interact with you, but you are to keep a physical and emotional distance.

A stone drops to the bottom of my empty stomach and I catch my lip in my teeth. I don't like this. There's "Project Samson" and there are children—five of them. And they live in an underground pod. My eyes quickly scan the rest of the page.

You are to maintain in-person and electronic surveillance of the children at all times. Check surveillance equipment every six hours. In particular, inspect auditory listening devices for damage. Your job is to protect Project

Samson children from harm and to ensure they do not escape. Unauthorized visitors must be escorted from the pod immediately and detained at 10B for questioning. Although you will carry a service weapon, the use of force is not authorized. If the children do not obey your instructions, contact Major James Hamilton or Lt. Col. Monica Nowak immediately. Under no circumstances should you try to enforce orders by physical confrontation.

As soon as I read "Major James Hamilton" and "Lt. Col. Nowak"—Dad and Mom—I know for sure. It's about us. Me, my brothers and sisters, Mom, Dad, and Nana. We're Project Samson.

Queasy, I lean back against my pillows. I thought we were Delta Force. Dad said we were Delta Force. I don't understand this. Plus, there's something else weird, something I skipped over that's even more disturbing. I scan the page again and find it. *Your job is to protect Samson Project children from harm and to ensure they do not escape.*

Escape?

With a zing of adrenaline, my head jerks involuntarily toward the heavy, locked bedroom door. My mind slams through all of the other locked doors in my life: the offices, the lab, the corridors, the elevators, the travel pods. Mom's mind.

I think of the prisoner from live target practice, the American who said he was a climatologist. He must be locked up somewhere.

Even as I try to assure myself that "escape" must refer to our impulsive curiosity about the outside, our desire to ride up the elevator and see the desolate landscape for ourselves, I know it doesn't. "Escape" means to run away, to flee a prison, to liberate oneself.

Just what my older brother Beeta did. Just what I want to do.

Does SamJay want me to consider escape? *Something bad is going on,* he said.

But everything above is uninhabitable. Destroyed. There's nowhere to go. Except another pod, maybe SamJay's pod, Bulee Creek.

It's impossible because I could never abandon my brothers and sisters. I'd miss Dad and Nana, sure; maybe even Mom. She's tough but she keeps things predictable. But I couldn't live without my brothers and sisters.

I've got only until 400 hours; I read the handbook again and Jump it inside my mattress. If I fall asleep without hiding it, and the others find it, there will be a full-scale crisis.

I drift off, thinking of how SamJay said to be careful. He meant more than just taking care of myself on my first mission outside. He meant take note, look around carefully, figure things out.

I dream I'm in a stone tower. I reach my arm through a window of iron bars towards a mysterious space outside. Cool air swirls around my hand. My body, pushing against the restraints, becomes so flexible, so malleable, I'm able to squeeze myself through the bars. Then I'm falling, but it feels like flying. I can see nothing but light. The sky is so beautiful, it makes my heart ache, until I realize with a terrible, sinking sensation that I have been exposed to radiation and I'm about to die.

CHAPTER 9

On the autoplane to South Kongolia, I sleep for 13 hours straight. Mom always says sleep is my Achilles heel, my weakness. It's hard to wake me when I'm tired. By the time I wake up, the plane is on the ground. I get dressed, eat and wait for Dad, pacing the small space, unable to concentrate on anything. Finally, he unlocks my travel pod door, enters, and shuts the door behind him. "You ready?"

"Yes, sir." My heartbeat ratchets up to double-time. I grab the back of my travel chair. "I'm ready." I'm burning to ask him about Project Samson, and I press my lips together so questions don't tumble out.

Dad's dressed in loose beige pants and a flowing white shirt. A patterned disk, which probably conceals a vidcam, hangs from a leather neck thong. A bit of blue scarf dangles from beneath his dingy shirt cuff, signifying revolution in this district of South Kongolia. His light brown hair is dyed black, his eyes covered by sunglasses, and his skin has been darkened with stain. It looks weird to me but hopefully will look real to strangers.

I wear a white dress with long sleeves, loose and shapeless, and a wide, blue scarf on my head. Canvas shoes. I don't need stain to darken my skin to a warm gold. But I wear soft contacts to hide the purple swirl of my irises.

"Your first time outside." Dad looks serious.

I squeeze the chair, trying to hide my trembling fingers.

"Just follow me, okay? Just follow orders, like I said. Nobody pays any attention to girls around here. You'll be fine." Even though he's acting casual, I Sense he's worried and my belly goes weak. *Straighten up*, I tell myself and I take a calming breath, swallow, recite the first line of my mantra.

"Yes, sir." My voice sounds embarrassingly faint, but Dad doesn't react. He turns and exits the pod, leaving the door open.

For the first time ever, I step out of my travel pod into the belly of the autoplane.

Dad leads the way. The inner metal walls of the plane glimmer. I look back. The featureless cube of my travel pod seems strangely small inside the plane.

"Come on," says Dad. A door at the far end of the plane frames gray light. The light of *outside*. Dad ducks through the door and disappears.

I run toward the light and halt atop a flight of metal steps, awestruck.

A few steps down, Dad stops and looks up at me, frowning.

No lecture, no vid could have prepared me for this. A long, flat vista. Behind it, dark mountains. Behind the mountains, a sky so blue, it strikes me like a gong.

A mysterious, rich aroma fills my nose and chest, tingles down my throat into my legs and toes. Fathoms of air, a sea of air, seething with life, drenching every part of me.

Up higher, the sky deepens to black, and way overhead—stars. Shimmering chips of light, crushed into the darkness. Too many to count. A dusty sweep of spangled sky.

I have to tell Gethre about the stars.

Moving air ripples my dress and I turn, suddenly feel it on my cheeks. Wind!

"Come on," says Dad. "There's going to be lots of new sensations. We have a job to do. You have to ignore it for now."

But how does one ignore the universe? Dad didn't tell me it would be beautiful.

Keeping a firm grip on the railing, I take a step down, then stop again. "Dad!"

Something's happening to the mountains straight ahead of us. They might be on fire, except there's no smoke. "Dad." I point.

He looks, glances at his wrist, then seems to realize he's not wearing his ristcom.

Something devastating crushes the horizon. A red-orange crater appears between two mountains. Above it, a strip of clouds glows pink and purple. I think maybe it's a nuclear bomb.

I clutch the railing.

"Okay, Eten. The sun is rising, that's all, okay? We've got to get going."

Sunrise? There's the orange shimmer edging up, with the long wisps of pink-purple, orange-rose, different and unnamable blues behind that. It's as if I'd never known color before.

The airport below me is tiny. There's the long strip we've landed on, and a tall building with a tall, metal pole poking out the top. A couple of small planes are parked behind the building, plus the big transport plane Dad and the other soldiers flew in on. The light from the rising sun burnishes it red-gold. I'm filled with a peculiar longing, but for what, I don't know. Maybe music. I can feel "The Rite of Spring" from Dad's music class echoing through my body.

"Eten!" says Dad.

Below us, on the road, a motor vehicle that looks like something from times before blows smoke out a tailpipe. An internal-combustion engine? I thought they didn't exist anymore.

The truck's back door opens and light spills out. Several soldiers skid by, so quickly they're mere flickers. They disappear into the vehicle.

"Let's get in the truck, come on!" Dad climbs back up the steps, grabs my arm, and hurries me down to the heavy vehicle. As he helps me clamber into the back, he says, "Don't speak inside the truck. That's an order."

I stand up in the back of the truck and freeze.

Four soldiers, three men and one woman dressed tunics similar to ours, sit at attention on metal benches. All four wear white blindfolds.

Alarms blare in my head. I crouch and try to back off the truck, but Dad murmurs, "Don't worry, it's okay," and pushes me down at the end of one bench. He sits across from me, pulls his ristcom out of his pocket and calls, "Move out."

The truck lurches into motion.

I stare at the others, but they doze or lean on their knees as if being blindfolded were the most natural thing in the world. The blindfolds are like scarves but with elastic bands around the back of the heads.

And then, we drive on for several hours. There are no windows. Nobody speaks.

I use a tiny, private toilet stall once. I don't really have to go; I just can't sit still. The others shift and lean but never rise, not even when the truck finally veers to our left and stops. Dad gets up and motions to me. We exit the back door.

"Dad, why ..."

He cuts me off. "Don't speak English," he says in Mongolian. He slides sunglasses on again, twin mirrors across his face, hiding his blue eyes.

Why were those soldiers blindfolded? The one time I'm not in my minipod and can see the others in our Unit, they can't see me.

Because they are Delta Force, and I'm Project Samson?

I look up at Dad, but he's already shutting the rickety, wooden gates behind our truck. I'm afraid to ask, afraid to speak. People flood the streets. White and brown buildings crowd the street, some made of what looks like hard, brown earth, some concrete blocks. They look similar to the ruins in the gym, except some of the houses are round instead of square. I spin toward Dad again, the truck now hidden in an alley beside one of the earthen houses.

Behind me, the people are chattering, wearing clothes like Dad's and mine. I can see further down the dirt road, there are guards. It's easy to identify the guards. They're the ones with the guns.

Dread churns in my stomach.

I don't have time to think. With a hand on my back, Dad turns and propels me forward. We join the flow of people, walking fast. Images from those around me flash through my mind: a pot on a stove, a woman running ahead, a child giggling, a man grinning and waving, an old woman coughing. Not one person shields their mind! It's too much. I withdraw my Senses, shield my consciousness as Dad pushes me along.

Just ahead of us, a guard shoves a man roughly. An elderly woman, holding the man's arm, staggers sideways. We almost run into them. I gasp as Dad jerks to a stop.

"Hey, watch out," the man shouts at the guard.

I clutch Dad, my heart pounding, but he just guides me to the side.

"Put your hands up," the guard shouts at the man, brandishing his rifle. I Sense fear, excitement, riot.

"We're just here to see President Hann," says the man, "like everybody else."

Dad's already pulling me away. "Dad, *President* Hann? What?" I'm speaking quietly in Mongolian, but Dad shushes me.

"He's just a terrorist," Dad mutters into my ear. "Keep your head down."

I stare at the dirt, my hand wrapped around Dad's arm. Dad's words echo in my head. *Just a terrorist.* So why did that man call him "President Hann"? A president is not "just a terrorist." SamJay told me to take note and figure things out. But it's more like figuring out what doesn't make sense than understanding anything.

We walk quickly, dust rising all around. The heat is monumental. Sweat runs down my back and sides. Or maybe it's the crush of people. I never imagined so many people. My head feels on fire. The canvas shoes rub my heels and the little toe on my left foot until I think I'm going to scream, but I say nothing. Soldiers don't complain.

I hear Sayan Hann before I see him. Calling out to the people. *Can American oil make clean water for your children?* The crowd roars, *No!*

Using his elbows and broad shoulders, Dad squeezes us into a huge plaza and guides me to the very back, where there's more space. At the front, the man I'm supposed to terminate stands on a narrow stage, ranting.

Everything is so different from when I Sense the target through Dad's mind. The surging and the pulling, the heat, the emotions of the crowd. They love this man. They hate Americans. I don't get it.

"You see the target?" Dad asks. "The man talking?"

I nod.

"Sure?"

I nod again.

Hann's face glows with passion. He sways on his narrow platform, exhorting people with slim, flickering fingers and booming voice. The crowd is rapt. He looks *illuminated*.

I don't want to kill him. I want to understand him.

"Go ahead," says Dad. "We're ready."

The feelings of people surge with excitement and hope, with their love for Hann. Their minds threaten to overwhelm me, and again, I have to withdraw.

Next to me, Dad mutters, "Hurry up, child."

"I'm not a child," I retort in the same patois.

In front of us, two men jostle and push, trying to get closer. They hesitate as Hann sweeps his hand upward like the conductor of an orchestra.

Have Americans brought you rain?

No, roars the crowd.

Have Americans saved your crops?

No, no, sings the crowd.

The two men ahead of us curse America, using a word I don't know. A woman next to them spits on the ground. I cringe.

Their hatred stings like a slap. Don't they know we're trying to help them? Of course Americans can't bring rain. Do they expect us to be magicians?

Dad edges me further back toward a filthy wattle wall, which gives way to an alley. An escape route.

"Hurry up, Eten," he murmurs. His anxiety hums like a wire on a fretboard. He's worried about our disguises. "We can't stay here. We have to get back to the truck."

In front of us, a boy stumbles backward as the two men push ahead. He leaps wildly as everyone cheers, fists pummeling the air.

My whole being goes still. I've never seen a boy my age before. I move closer. I can smell him, an acrid odor like burned coffee, not at all like my brothers. I can Sense his *pneuma,* his inner spirit, his life-force, swirling through his lungs like blue flame.

He burns with resentment. In the boy's mind, I Sense pictures of his mother holding his wasted and dying father and himself rushing in the door, dressed as a doctor, waving medicine. "I can save you, Baba," he cries.

But that didn't happen; it will never happen because his father is dead. It's just his fantasy, which merges with hatred and desire, with the frantic cheering of the crowd and the boy's wish to shatter windows at a certain clinic.

Grief uncoils inside me, and I, too, am steeped in loss. I want to step forward, to fold the boy's thin body into mine, to heal his anguish. *We are here to help you*, I want to tell him. His essence is so…is so…

Dad grabs my arm and shakes me. "Wrap it up," he growls in English, too loud. The boy whips around, staring with incredulity. His face is beautiful, the fine bones of his cheeks and chin etched with fervor, his black-fringed eyes glittering.

"American?" says the boy, in English.

Dad shoots him.

"No," I scream as the crowd cheers again. I reach out to the boy, and Dad grabs my already bruised arm. I hardly notice. A fire rages in the boy's mind.

My insides fracture. A column of glass holding me upright shatters. I merge with him: I am the boy; the boy is me.

Agony blazes. Our belly! *What happened?*

The world recedes as our minds merge. We tremble on the edge of consciousness. Have we been shot?

"Eten!" says Dad, shaking my arm. "Withdraw."

The scene waffles; *me, him, us, him, us*…We see Dad from a distance holding a girl by the arm, her eyes wide and blank, long black hair, blue scarf sliding off, silver hairs lifting like static.

Then we see nothing but dust, a white glare. Our belly boils; our heart races and kicks; warm piss trickles down our leg. *Where is Mama?* Sadness leaks from our body. Tiny sparks glint in the air. *Mama?*

Dad shakes my arm again, growling. "Withdraw!"

I can hear Dad. But it's hard to separate from the boy.

Dad squeezes my arm so tightly, I cry out. My eyes fly open. I swallow hard and withdraw my Senses, but I'm reeling.

Only a moment has passed. Dad's other hand still rests on the fracgun in his pocket, a pinprick dark hole in the cloth of his pale, dust-colored pants.

The crowd roars again. Before us, the boy sinks gently to the earth. A sob wrenches my gut and tears flood my eyes. One of my contacts swims loose as I jerk away from Dad and rush to the limp figure on the ground.

CHAPTER 10

He's not dead; he's lying very still, holding his side. I crouch down and put my hand on his arm. As soon as I touch bare flesh, I Sense his entire being as clearly as a vid. He's bleeding inside. I can Sense where the wound is; I can almost touch it.

"Help," the boy pants weakly. His eyes turn up toward mine, then go wide with terror. He recognizes me.

"Do not fear. You will be good," I say awkwardly, horror jangling my nerves. I pull my scarf from my neck, my hair cascading as I push the scarf against his wound. I Sense the burning metal pellet in the boy's side and Jump it into my hand. It singes my flesh, and I drop it.

Blood pools under him, so much blood. My Senses shudder through the boy's veins, his torn flesh, searching for something to heal, but arms grab me around my middle and jerk me backward. Dad lifts me from behind and we stagger away from the boy. People jostle against us, not even looking, then cheer again for Hann.

"Dad, let me help …"

"Hurry," whispers Dad. He puts me down and shakes me in time with his own pounding heartbeats. "Hurry. You *have* to complete the mission."

From somewhere, a voice rises sharply, high and quavering, barely cutting through the cacophony. "Americans!" It's the boy.

Terror like I've never known twists through me, freezing my mind. My head expands like a basketball.

A woman struggles past us, pointing toward the boy. "Help," she shouts. "He's shot."

Someone else shouts, "Americans!"

A few more people take up the cry, then suddenly people around us are turning, searching, shouting "Americans." I'm trembling. Is "American" scrawled across my face? But Dad holds me from behind, crying out "Americans," just like everyone else, until he leans into my ear and whispers, "Now."

Without thought, I hurl my Senses into Hann. I take hold of the man's flesh and bones; I push and, at the same time, pull his body, pinching space/time.

Hann explodes. Like a pumpkin.

Horror rushes me. Exploding is easy; witnessing it is hard. I scream and can't stop screaming as I watch.

By the stage, the gore that was Hann spatters across panicked people. Everyone is screaming. I can see Hann's ruined flesh spin through the air. White and red globs. A gob smacks into a screeching woman's head and she vanishes. I can smell blood. Madness dissolves my mind. I am terror. Dread from the struggling crowd floods me.

Running bodies collide. A wave of panic ripples like shadow across the people.

Dad's no longer behind me. I turn to one side and vomit. My body goes burning hot, then cold.

Guards leap to Hann's platform, their guns up, rooting in the sky for a sniper, firing at nothing. Shrieking women push each other, jammed up; a little boy scrambles like a rat over the shoulders and head of man. Next to me, an old woman with white hair stumbles and falls; an old man hauls her to her feet before she's trampled.

"Dad," my voice quavers.

Suddenly, he's there and grabs my sore arm. "What did you do?" he hisses, jerking me backward. I lean over and retch up my insides again. "You were supposed to stop his heart."

"I'm sorry." I'm shaking. "I made a mistake."

"Move, Eten." He's trying to push me. I can't feel my feet. "Oh my God!" he says, finally lifting and dragging me down the narrow alley. "Now they're hunting us. Why didn't you follow orders?"

Guilt and dread mingle with rage, burning up my insides. I see the boy's eyes again, the blood pooling under him. "I did! I tried, I was ..." I say, but he's not listening. He looks up and down the narrow alley, drags me to the shadows on the other side, and pulls his ristcom from his pocket. He mutters into it. I hear something about the truck.

It's way too hot. I'm dizzy and my mouth is salivating, like I'm going to throw up again. The alleyway stinks of urine. I gag.

"Come on," says Dad, still speaking Mongolian. He breaks into a jog. We shouldn't run; it makes us look guilty. But everyone's running now.

Running releases my tongue, and I blurt, "Why did you shoot that boy?"

"You know I had to eliminate him," Dad says. "I'm sorry, but he heard us speak—" Dad stops. He doesn't want to say it aloud.

Nobody can know Americans are undercover in this rebel-held district. I don't understand it. We're trying to help everyone recover from the ravages of war. I thought people would be grateful to be a part of New America. Instead, everyone hates us.

We turn a corner of the street, everything a withering beige, and see the truck creeping down the block. I Sense relief wash over Dad. He turns toward me, and opens his mouth, but his eyes register shock as he looks over my shoulder. I whirl around.

Two soldiers run toward us, boots slapping the broken walkway. They carry a couple of ancient AK-15s. One is young, the other not so much old as withered. Their clean-shaven faces look gaunt, their eyes hungry. "Stop!" they both shout.

We hold up our hands. "Terminate," says Dad, without moving.

"I can Jump the weapons," I protest. I've never disobeyed a direct order. But why do we have to kill when we can just disarm them?

"Terminate," he says again.

The two men dart looks at the truck as they approach, their dull gray uniforms coated with fine sand, crusty where they've sweated through the fabric. They both stare at me, and suddenly, I remember my mismatched eyes, one brown, one purple. The younger one has blood leaking from his nose and keeps sniffing. His elder snaps, "Who are you? What's that truck?"

He's speaking English. Bad sign.

Dad responds in the local patois. "Officers, what's the problem?"

The younger soldier yelps as I Jump both rifles into the truck. As far as they're concerned, their AK15s simply vanished. The two men shake their hands and stare at their feet as if, perhaps, they had dropped the guns.

The younger soldier's chin stiffens and retracts, like he's been punched, his mouth turning upside down. He stares at me—my eyes without the one contact must look bizarre. I was hoping the men would just run away when they lost their guns, but the older man lifts his ristcom toward his mouth. He's going to call for backup.

"Eten," murmurs Dad, barely moving his lips.

I have no choice. My Senses slide into their bodies with practiced ease, the panic I'd felt earlier replaced with resignation. Mind, flesh, bone, blood.

I crush their hearts.

The men grab their breasts and fall to the ground in a slow, unwinding suspiration. Heavy knees hit the dirt. The younger one twists, lands on his back, head snapping forward, then back. I squeeze my eyes shut, hope they don't have families.

Then I Sense their final images. *A woman smiling; her long, wavy hair shines. A little boy, laughing.* Of course they have families.

"Move," says Dad.

I follow him into the truck, blinking back more tears, dark thoughts battering my mind: *I'm not a coward. I'm not a traitor. I'm a good soldier. Obedient. Loyal. But he killed that boy. Why did Dad have to kill the boy?* I imagine the boy alive. I imagine somebody stopped the bleeding, and he's getting better.

Not likely, sneers the bitter voice in my head.

The entire ride back is a repeat of the trip to the town, only worse. Blindfolds. Silence. Bumping along as if trapped in the center of nothingness. My brain on fire. There are no windows in the truck, just cool, filtered air. The whole world contracts and contracts until it's nothing but a seething core wrapped tight inside my belly. Tears keep leaking from my eyes. I breathe deep. I must exercise self-control.

And then before me, the boy appears, his beautiful face, his vivid eyes. "American?" he says. Dad shoots him. Again, I die with him. Above me, the shadow of Hann hovers. His slim hands dance; his voice swells; the crowd cheers until it screams. Hann explodes. I can smell the blood.

Termination shudders through my body.

"You're fighting for the wrong side," said the American.

I am not a part of all things. I do not rise with the light. I am not embraced by the stillness.

Chapter 11

Then, I'm standing outside the truck on the ground. I don't recall having exited the vehicle. Behind me, it's empty.

"Hurry up," says Dad. He's 20 meters away, mounting the metal steps of my autoplane. "You've already had enough radiation exposure."

I walk to the bottom of the steps, trembling. I will be trapped again. In the travel pod. In our home pod. Not a window, not a crack, not a word to the world outside. I take a step back. "Dad," I say, loud, almost shouting, fear lashing me into something rash. "What is Project Samson?"

He has his back to me. He stops. Straightens. Terrified, I look away as he turns. But he says nothing till I look back. His twisted, darkened features look seared. His index finger hammers repeatedly towards the autoplane's top step, as if his nail could drill a hole through the metal. His voice is a growl. "Get! Up! Here! Right now. That's an order."

What if I disobeyed his order? I could blow him right off the steps, hurl him into the desert, blow up the entire autoplane. The thought terrifies me.

I run up the steps. "Sir, I'd like to fly with you and the other soldiers in the Unit," I gasp, my words running all together. "Requesting permission, Sir. I'd like to fly in the plane with the others. Not in my travel pod." The sun pierces my eyes, dazzling off the side of the plane. For a moment, Dad appears to be a dark shape, alien and inscrutable.

"Permission denied." Dad snaps back into human form. I stare at his flushed, angry face, his broad shoulders and flowing shirt, flapping a little around his hips, his loose cotton pants marred with a brown fracgun hole too tiny to discern. My hands ball into fists.

"Why, Dad?"

Dad leans forward and grabs the recording medallion on his chest, covering and muffling it. "Don't you ever, *ever* mention that project name again. You hear me? Not if you value your life."

Inside my head, a huge, metal gear is turning, screeching, and attached to it are all the strings of my heart and my gut and everything's getting wound tighter and tighter. I lean in toward Dad. My breath is volcanic, molten. "Do *you* value my life, Dad?" I whisper.

Dad wheels around and strides into the autoplane's dark interior. I race in after him. "Tell me what's going on," I scream. Rage, that hard, hot rock in my belly, begins to expand. I tremble like a mountain about to explode.

"Keep your voice down," Dad says over his shoulder. He disappears through the travel pod hatch, leaving it open.

I leap through the hatch and slam it behind me. "Why did you kill that boy?"

"I had to," Dad shouts. "I told you. Americans—"

I can feel the actual moment my self-control departs. Like a cool ribbon spooling through my burning fingers, thinner and thinner till it's smoke. Some part of me gropes after it, knowing no good can come of this, and yet, if no good can come of rage, then let me have the bad. I would rather burn down the kingdom than be its slave for one more moment.

"I want to know what's going on," I scream, backing up until I hit my chair. "We're supposed to be healing the earth. Why does everybody hate Americans? Why are we killing all these people? Why can't I talk to people in other pods at home? I want to meet other kids. I want to go outside at home. I want to see for myself."

"You can't," shouts Dad. "Home is a wasteland, a desert. You're going to have to trust me on this. I'm doing this for your sake, Eten. I'm doing what is best for you."

What's best for *me?* That's the last straw. Every last vestige of what holds me back is gone, and I erupt. My mouth drops open and a long, raucous scream spews out of my throat like lava. My entire body shudders.

Once the scream is loosed, I can't push it back. My hair whips straight upward, tornado-like, as if I were being pulled off the floor. My arms rise like a benediction. Turning slowly, I see Dad, the wall, Dad, the wall, faster and faster until I'm spinning in a blur.

My screams howl through the travel pod. The table and chair shake, unbolt, tumble back. Dad smashes up against the wall. I'm not breathing, I'm breath itself. I'm wind. Heat. Blood. Rage. I am conflagration. Obliteration. Termination.

And then, piercing agony rips up my spine. It starts at my tailbone, like a blow with a hot metal rod, and tears up my backbone toward my skull.

I fall to the hard plastic floor. Unrelenting pain ratchets my body backward and I scream again, cough, gag, wretch, nothing in my stomach left to come up.

Dad is using the wand. My implants light up each vertebra like incendiary bombs.

The room begins to fade away. I struggle to drag in a ragged gasp.

"Are you done?" Dad bellows. He's panting.

"Ya…" I croak, waving my fingertips.

The pain subsides like a blanket of mercy. I groan and close my eyes.

"What is the matter with you?" Dad cries out. "Are you crazy?" He coughs. "Oh my God, what have you done?"

"Sssor—" I say, still trying to recover. "Sor—"

There's silence, and after a time, I look across the travel pod. The table is cracked and the chair is upside down, the bed mattress and covers draped over it. Dad sits slumped against the wall. There's blood all over his face.

"Dad," I gasp.

He moves a little, licks his lips. "I'm all right." The blood is coming from a cut on his forehead.

I shut my eyes. Guilt and remorse well up, and I'm so angry at myself. I promised myself I'd never do something like this again. Lose my self-control. I hear a bitter laugh in my head. How twisted is this? I'm angry I have to be a soldier and assassinate people, so I hurt Dad? Smart!

I hate violence. I hate the violence in myself even more than war. "Dad," I tell him, tears stinging my eyes. "I'm sorry."

"I know." He struggles to his feet, staggers a couple of steps sideways, puts a hand to the side of his head. It comes away bloody. "Oh, God." He glances up at one of the vidcams. "It's in the vid. It's already in the vidstream."

"No, I…" I try to sit up, dizzy. "I didn't mean it. Dad. I didn't mean it." I groan and draw in my knees, sheltering my head with my arms. Mom will see what I did. That means another punishment.

From under my arm, I can see the wand in Dad's hand, the thin, black rectangle with its fierce buttons of pain. It's shameful—being wanded like a child. Somehow, I always manage to forget how bad it is. Why the implants don't burn right through my spine is a mystery.

"Don't show the vid to Mom. Please."

"Mom?" Dad says, disconsolately. He gives a humorless laugh. "You have no clue."

I want to say that if I have no clue, it's their fault, his and Mom's. But I do have a clue. In Dad's mind, I Sense a clear image of that man again: pale skin; stiff white hair; heavy black eyebrows; wire-rimmed glasses. His crooked front tooth. A general?

"Dad?" I begin hesitantly. "Who is that?"

Dad jerks his head down and makes a funny noise, not exactly a "*shush*"—more like the hiss of an animal.

I shut my mouth. The vidcams and soundbugs are still recording us. It's not something we can talk about.

Dad turns stiffly; he doesn't look at me. "I'm all right. Just clean up the mess. We have to get going."

I watch him limp toward the door. He looks defeated. He looks—weak. All this energy, I realize, all my rage and frustration with Mom and Dad. What if it's misdirected?

A cold determination sweeps over me. Not rage; rage will see me through a battle, but it won't get me any answers. Whoever is in charge of this war, whatever "Project Samson" is, I'm going to find out.

CHAPTER 12

It's one hundred hours the next morning when we get home. I don't see Dad. Nana makes a fuss over me, asking if I want food. I tell her I just want to go to sleep. She locks the bedroom door behind me. My sisters and brothers don't wake, don't even stir. I stand in darkness, calculating. Risk versus result.

It doesn't matter. I've already decided. I'm not going to sleep. I slept on the plane. Rested and planned. And now, adrenaline sings through my body. I have eight hours. From now until 9 a.m., the time Mom and Dad return to the pod each weekday morning.

I'm going to break into Mom's office.

She must be hiding secrets in there. There will be no surveillance, either. Only Mom is allowed in her office. Why would she surveil herself?

I Jump the boys' calculator into my hand—always helpful to have a flashlight—crouch in the middle of the room and press my other hand to the floor. I lick my lips and swallow- my throat has gone dry—before I raise the *thisness* of Mom's office. I focus on the spot where I sat at age five while Mom repacked my backpack because she didn't like how Nana did it. My first mission. I pull the office space into myself, folding it into the *thisness* of here and now.

And then I'm there, crouching inside her locked door, one hand on the floor, the other clutching the calculator.

Excitement pulses at my wrists, in my throat, each heartbeat tripping over the next. Holding my breath, I scan the space, moving only my head. Everything stands out in black and white. The carpet feels hard, tight, almost crunchy under my fingers; the room smells like Mom.

I can't Sense any sound bugs or vidcams. I don't see any red dots. There are some in the corridor, but not in the office. I'm relieved but not surprised. Of course, nobody would *dare* invade her space.

I risk standing up.

The room is neat and disappointingly empty. To my right stands a huge desk with a chair pulled up to it and a vidscreen on top, an empty glass next to the screen. Against the wall to my left, empty shelves. But all along the back wall stands a row of metal cabinets, each one with five drawers.

Moving like a shadow, I gently pull on a drawer, but it's locked. I look at the door. The window blind is up and some light from the corridor comes in. *Relax*, I tell myself.

Drawing in a deep breath, I press the palm of my hand against the drawer and move the little pieces inside the lock. It clicks open.

The drawer slides out easily and keeps sliding. It's a really long drawer. I catch my lower lip in my teeth. My head swims. This is it!

The drawer is stuffed with massive quantities of paper, thick and bulging files separated alphabetically. I shine the calculator light across them. This is a "D" drawer, with sequential D files, D–1, D–2, and so on. I pull out a big D–5 folder, sit at Mom's desk, and lay it down. The mound of paper spills sideways from the folder. Each page has writing on it, some printed, some with uneven handwriting.

I'm so excited, my fingers tremble. I focus the light with two hands.

"DARPA: SUBJECT SERIES D HUMAN DNA REPLACEMENT: INCREASED TO 1%." Under that: "Subject Series D, Number 5." Then, there are columns of abbreviations and numbers, which mean nothing to me.

I don't know what "DARPA" or "DNA" are, but I can see that there's a "subject," and it's something to do with humans. The papers kind of look like a medical file. Maybe it's records of the tests they do on me and my brothers and sisters. I don't see our names, though.

The next pages are more promising: images. Large, shiny, color pictures with names at the bottom. Shana V. Gordon, donor. John H. Williamson, donor. "Donor?" I'm wondering. Where did I hear about a "donor" before? The edge of comprehension teeters in my mind.

Shana is very pretty, with high cheekbones and wavy, thick, chestnut hair and very white teeth. John has a square face with a dimple in his chin. He looks a little like Dad. There's another one, too, labeled: Maria A. Garcia, host. I've never seen images on paper before. I touch the two-dimensional things with wonder. So different from a picture on a vidscreen.

Other papers look like test results and measurements. Most of it related to "D-5." It looks like "D-5" is the subject of an experiment.

```
D-5 viable: 1 week.
D-5 malformation of ulna: 5 weeks.
D-5 malformation temporal bones: 11 weeks.
D-5 12 weeks: evidence of displacement theory.
```

A flicker of excitement. If there is a "theory," then this is an experiment. You test your theories with experiments. And they'd found "evidence." This whole file is about an experiment, for sure.

Next to "evidence of displacement theory," there's a handwritten note in faded red: *24-hr surveillance.*

"Surveillance!" I know all about surveillance. Then I hit another roadblock: "D-5 12 weeks, 5 days: evidence of widespread displacement theory." What the hell does that mean?

The back of my neck burns, like somebody's watching me. I spin to look at the door again. Nothing. I feel spooked. Scared and excited and frustrated…and so nervous. As if Mom were about to march around the corner and unlock her door.

I turn back to the papers. The next note is handwritten. I can decipher only a few of the scrawled words: "*floor*" and "*Lab*" and "*blood.*"

Then another handwritten note: Dr. Ted Larsen, deceased.

So there was blood. And Dr. Ted Larsen, whoever he was, died.

On the last page in that folder, there are large red letters that I can read and understand: TERMINATED.

So much for the experiment D-5, I think. Whatever it was, that experiment had been terminated.

I flip through the pages inside two other folders and see similar reports, Series D with different numbers. They look much the same, with "terminated" in red at the end, or "not viable." "Not viable" means the experiment didn't work. There are lots of test reports with numbers and letters, all experiments. But experiments of what?

As I put the papers back, I Sense the night guard, JoeyEss, approaching from another corridor. *Shit!* My heart starts banging again as I push the drawer shut and turn my calculator light off.

I don't know JoeyEss very well because he works only at night, but I can Sense him clearly. He is doing a routine walk through the whole pod. He's shining his flashlight into different rooms, checking that all is well. He heads toward me.

I crouch. I can Jump myself back into the bedroom, but if I wake my brothers or sisters, I can't come back here. They'll insist on knowing what I'm doing and then they'll follow me. On the other hand, I can't let JoeyEss discover me.

As he turns the corner, I scuttle toward the back wall. In the corner, I discover a narrow space between the wall and cabinets. I slip in and stand still.

Pausing at the office door, JoeyEss shines his flashlight into the room. It's a powerful beam, a hundred times brighter than my puny little calculator light. For a moment, it brightens the back wall where I'm hiding. Panicky, I look both ways.

A small, dark door, briefly illuminated, hides behind the cabinets! Too small to see from the room. It's a secret door. Excitement pounds through me.

Jackpot.

CHAPTER 13

JoeyEss takes his time looking into Mom's office. I can Sense he's curious about Mom's private space. But there isn't much to see.

Finally, the guard moves on. He didn't Sense me at all. I blow out a long breath, unsurprised. Most of the guards can't Sense worth beans.

As soon as he leaves, I sidestep to my right, press my ear to the cold, windowless metal door. I hear nothing, Sense nobody. It must be a closet.

Laying my palm above the door handle, I unlock the door. Slowly, I turn the chilly knob and push it open, just a crack.

Total darkness. Even so, I can Sense this room is no closet; it's big, cavernous. My breath thins into nothingness. It's cold. It smells of stillness and something bad, some shut-in thing.

I push the door open wider with my foot. A squeak shatters the silent void, and I freeze. But nobody's here.

After a moment, I step into the room and allow the door to close gently behind me and feel gooseflesh prickle my arms. The pod is always the same, mild temperature. In here, it's cold.

I swing the calculator light to the right and the left. Metal shelves glint. As far as the light extends, there are metal shelves with things on them. The floor looks like cement.

This is a storeroom. A really big storeroom. It's bewildering—awesome. A huge storeroom hidden down here in our pod that nobody knows about but Mom. With stuff on the shelves. The back of my neck prickles, and my armpits get suddenly damp.

I look up, wheeling around, staring into darkness, Sensing upward and outward. No warm, red dots. No vidcams in this room. No soundbugs.

I risk a grin into the darkness. Why no surveillance? Because it belongs to Mom, and it's secret. Reaching back, I fumble for the light switches, hold my breath, and flip them. The room blazes to life. No alarm blares. Nothing moves.

Huge glass jars sit on the shelves. Marching rows of them.

To my left, the letter **A** sticks out on a tab from the first shelf. About five shelves along, a **B** sticks out on a tab from another shelf. There are more tabs, more letters on more shelves lined up alphabetically down the huge room.

I cross left to the first shelf and pace along the row of jars. Each one is filled with liquid. A bumpy lump of meat floats in the liquid. Some have strings floating out of them.

It's gross, and there's a faint, funky, bad smell. Formaldehyde, I think. I recognize it from Mom's lab.

I trot quickly up and down the rows. The jars are labeled sequentially. **A-75 A-76 A-77 A-78**…In the third row, I get to a jar that has a blob with more shape and stop. It looks like a giant bean with lots of strings floating from it. But the weird thing is that this thing has a big black dot toward the top. The dot looks like an eye.

Cold prickles again. I frown. An eye? What is this stuff, animals? Rats?

So many dead rats. It's creepy, cold, and disgusting. Definitely experiments. I know Mom and Dad sometimes experiment with rats.

Crossing my arms over my chest, I jog back out into the main aisle to see the other rows.

B shelves come after many rows of **A** shelves. **C, D,** and the rest of the alphabet stretching way back into the room.

I pass a few **B** rows and turn the corner into a **C** row, where the jars aren't set up right by the aisle. My fingers are getting cold, and I rub my hands briskly on my arms and walk faster.

I stop before the first jar, labeled **C-1**. The creature in this massive jar is much bigger than the rest, not just a lump. If it's a rat, it's the biggest rat I've ever seen.

I stare at a curved, bumpy process under smooth skin. A ridge? A spine? The skin of this animal is hairless, golden brown. It seems to have a head, curved away from me, and I sidestep to get a better look.

There's a face. Legs. Arms. Fingers.

It's a baby. A dead and preserved baby.

I scream. I can't help it. My eyes squeeze shut and my hands fly to my mouth, stuffing back more screams.

The stench in the room, so faint at first, sickens me and my stomach heaves. I lean over and try not to throw up. Sweat pops out on my forehead and saliva floods my mouth. I heave once more, but nothing comes up.

I will not look. I will not look.

I look.

The back of the baby's head is cracked open, like a split melon. Long, silver, ropy tentacles float from its scalp. Its arms and legs are ropy, too, like they have no bones.

I reach out and touch the jar. I try to turn it, but it's too heavy, and I manage only to jostle it. The baby rotates slowly. I see two milky eyes, a button nose, a hole for a mouth. Strings come out of an opening in its chest. Not strings; veins. With a blob attached, an inner organ, floating, attached by the strings to its insides.

Next to the jar, another jar. **C-2.** Another misshapen human baby.

I proceed down the aisle. Then I'm running. The jars—they all hold dead babies. They're experimenting on babies.

CHAPTER 14

Back at the door, I yank the cold knob before remembering it's blocked. I have to get out of here. I hit the light switch. Darkness falls like a blow and I sink to the floor with a moan. I want oblivion, to Jump back into my bed. I want to sleep and forget I ever saw this. I need to unknow it.

I press my face into my knees, try to slow my breathing. Suddenly, my mantra rises within me, unbidden: *I am embraced by the stillness, and the stillness fills me with power.*

I breathe in stillness. Feel the power within. *I am a part of all things, and all things lift me toward the center.*

I can do this. There is some atrocity here, as bad as the Nazis in World War II. I need to know what they're doing.

Go back, I order myself. *You have to go back.* I take deep breaths. I tell myself to have courage.

With a shiver, I stand and turn the lights back on, turn around, stiffen my resolve. To my right, the little tags stick out from the tops of the shelves into the aisle. Clenching my fists, I stalk to the very last row of shelves with jars, the **T** row. Beyond that row, the shelves are empty. There's a **U** row and a **V** row…the rows keep going as if they expected more, but more never arrived.

In the **T** row, there's only one jar, toward the center of the row. I bow my head, refusing to look until I get right in front of it.

I look up.

It's baby Teetu. Dead. Floating in a jar.

A throat-splitting, belly-ripping shriek barrels out of me and crackles through the silence.

The next thing I know, I'm back in my bedroom, panting. I'm crouched between the bunk beds in darkness. I Jumped myself back without even thinking. The only sound is my brothers and sisters breathing, the only smell is their living, warm bodies.

I fall to my knees next to Teetu's bed. I can Sense her. Though I see her outline, I still need to touch her shoulder, her cheek, her hair, just to be sure.

Relief shudders through me. Whatever floats in that jar, it's not Teetu. Of course it isn't. A baby floats in the jar. My sister is five years old.

But that baby looks just like Teetu. The hairs on the back of my neck stir like hackles rising.

Teetu tosses in her sleep. I force myself to radiate calm, reassurance. She falls back into deeper slumber. My sister is fine, but I'm not. My mind feels like a room full of cold steam, seething and foggy. Only one thought keeps echoing through that blur: *What is going on?*

I want to crawl into bed with my sister. I don't want to go back to that awful room. I press my chilly knuckles against my teeth, biting down, then turn and sit on the floor, my back against the bed.

The horrible image of the dead baby-Teetu keeps appearing in front of me. What happened to that baby? Why does it look so much like Teetu? Is it her twin? Panic edges my thoughts. Something is wrong. The whole world is wrong.

In her sleep, Teetu stirs and reaches a hand toward me. She touches my shoulder and sighs. Little by little, the terror ebbs away. After a while, I rise and go into the bathroom, stare at myself in the mirror. I blow hot breath on the mirror, then wipe away just enough fog to see my eyes.

"Be brave, Eten," I whisper to the girl in the mirror. Whatever is going on, I have to know the truth. Gritting my teeth, I Jump myself back into the storage room.

The lights are still on. I march from the door straight back to row **T** and again confront the thing that looks like my sister.

It does look like Teetu when she was a baby, with dark golden skin and a button nose and big, violet eyes. But not a twin. Now I can see obvious differences. The ears are little more than flaps. This baby has the same curly black hair, but the silver strands are much thicker, like rope. Plus, the place where there are scars on Teetu's neck, there are great big gashes in the sides of this baby's neck, and the skin seems fluted. Like gills.

And there's a bullet hole right in the middle of its forehead.

Again, I reel with shock. I feel tears slide down my cheeks.

Terminated.

The light glints on the bottle's surface, glazing reality with a sharp and brittle skin. It seems if I move, I might shatter.

The baby. The experiment. **TERMINATED.**

"Teetu is safe. Teetu is safe," I mutter, wiping my cheeks with my shirt. I drop my eyes, see a label on the shelf under the jar. **T-1.**

Carefully, slowly, as if unscrewing an overfull bottle, I turn my head to the left.

Next to the first label, there is another. It reads: **T-2.**

Above it, there is no bottle. There is a thick piece of paper that is folded over so it stands up on the shelf, and something is written on it. One word: **VIABLE.**

I catch my breath. That means something worked. Something lived. **T-2.** Teetu. Teetu had lived.

I press my knuckles against my teeth and bite down, but a moan comes out anyway, and then my heart is pounding impossibly fast.

I spin and sprint back to the main aisle, down the aisle to the **E** row.

I halt, knowing what I'll find, terrified to look. Head down, I force myself to march into the **E** row.

The shelf lies just above my head, holding jar after jar. Peripherally, I can see the labels. **E-7, E-8, E-9, E-10.**

The last label. **E-10.** I look up. There is the white card: **VIABLE.**

A weird noise rises from my throat. Like a machine that's whining and straining to work.

Unwillingly, my eyes dart toward **E-9.** I breathe in a jerky gasp and cover my face with my hands, another cry slipping through my fingers.

Don't look. Don't look.

I look.

I peer through my fingers as if my hands might protect me from this raw new truth. The floating baby has warm golden skin and purple eyes, like mine, and a full head of straight black hair. Heavy silver tentacles grow from the head; long flaps hang where ears might have been; gashes line the sides of the throat. It looks like a monster.

My hands smooth back my own long hair, feeling the silver strands move gently.

My fingers hit the jar behind my head and I jump, literally, my feet leaving the ground. Row **D**, behind me. Pale, golden babies float in jars.

Spinning, I run around to the **D** rows. The babies in these jars are more misshapen than in the **E** row: **D-2, D-3, D-4**.

I find **D-5**. The one I'd read about in Mom files.

D-5 looks like a regular baby boy, with pale golden skin Except for two things.

One, he's bald but has those ropy, heavy silver tentacles growing out of his scalp.

And two, he has a bullet hole right in the middle of his forehead.

His purple eyes stare sightlessly out underneath the hole as the body drifts gently.

The papers in the metal drawer said *terminated*. They shot D-5, just like they shot T-1. *Evidence of displacement theory*, the papers said. And *blood*. And *Dr. Ted Larsen, deceased*.

Oh my God. "Displacement" theory? I bet D-5 was Jumping things. And he hurt Dr. Larsen. I remember my brothers and sisters as babies, how important it was that I help to control them, to teach them to control themselves. But they weren't very powerful, not as babies. Was D-5 *too* powerful? What if he got scared and killed Dr. Larsen, and the guards shot him?

Just like they tried to shoot my big brother, Beeta, when he *escaped.*

Heart pounding, I run back to the **B** row. **B-1, B-2, B-3**…I keep my eyes focused on the floor until I come to the last one in that row, **B-10.**

There is no jar. Instead, there's a heavy piece of folded white paper, gray with dust, on which is written: **VIABLE.**

B-10. It has to be Beeta. I touch the card, fingers trembling. I couldn't say Beeten, so I said Beeta.

Every time I ask about him, Mom stands there and cocks her head, her yellow hair pulled back into its tight bun, her pale blue eyes crinkling sympathetically as she says, "Beeta isn't real. He's just a dream you had."

But Mom lies. The card reads **VIABLE,** and that means my brother lived. I wasn't dreaming; I remember him.

Wheeling, I run past the **G** row. It is all the same. **G-1** and **G-2** have the white, folded papers reading **VIABLE.** There are more misshapen babies with pale golden skin, one with no eyes, its whitish yellow hair streaked with heavy, ropy, silver tentacles.

J row. **J-1** and **J-2** look barely human, but the jars after that hold babies. Two tiny and misshapen babies. The next one looks a little more like Jaysx, with her square chin and big feet. But it has no nose, just the same big eyes, a thin mouth, gashes in its throat, and the fat, silver tentacles growing out of its head. It makes my stomach lurch. More monsters.

Next to that, where the shelf label says **J-6,** there's the white paper that reads **VIABLE.** Jaysx. There are three more misshapen babies after that.

I sink to the floor, my face in my hands. Me, Beeta, my brothers and sisters. We're not a normal evolution of human life, as we'd been told. We're experiments. Monstrous experiments.

CHAPTER 15

I have to move. My face feels swollen; the tears trickle slower now. I want my big brother back. I want SamJay to hug me and call me "babygirl." I wish somebody could make all this go away.

But I have to move. I can't be caught here in this storage room. Rising stiffly, I turn the lights off and ease through the door back into Mom's office.

For a moment, I sit in her chair. As soon as I do, I feel something crinkle underneath my butt. Another paper. I jerk it out angrily, ball it up, and stuff it into my PJ pocket.

I need to regain control before I go back to the bedroom. There's no way I'm telling my brothers and sisters about all this. It's beyond comprehension. I wipe my face with my T-shirt, clear my throat and swallow hard, take deep, even breaths.

Again, my eyes fall on the tall metal cabinets. How could Mom do this to us?

A sudden surge of hatred electrifies me.

Striding to the E drawer of the tall cabinets, I jerk it open. The drawer screeches and wobbles. The entire back half of it is labeled E-10, with folder after folder of papers. I grab one and throw it on the floor, pulling the small calculator light from my pocket.

Pictures of me. Pages and pages of notes. Test results. Medical measurements. I pick up the whole pile of papers and hurl them to the floor again, then jump on them, stamping with both feet. If I could set a fire, I would burn them.

How dare they experiment on me? On my brothers and sisters? Like we're *rats*? How dare they experiment on babies? *Shoot babies?*

Maybe I don't know the outside world, but I know the difference between right and wrong. You only kill terrorists, who are evil. Mom and Dad killed innocent *babies*. They're the ones who are evil.

The face of the American in the gym rises before me. *You're fighting for the wrong side,* he said. He was right.

Inside my chest, the rage churns. It tightens my throat. My hands clench as I scan the room for something, anything, to destroy. My fingers fly out. The empty water glass on the desk springs into my hand, and I hurl it against the office door as hard as I can. It shatters with a satisfying crash and falls to the floor.

Throwing my arms out, my whole body rigid, I Sense with hatred every single thing Mom has ever touched.

The cabinets tremble. The desk begins to lift. A howling blows from floor to ceiling and whips back down again. My entire body twists, and I lift the living darkness, blackness swirling close like a winding sheet. My body rises and I fling my head back, the juddering, irrepressible scream rising.

I will smash it all. Mom's office—the whole pod. Everyone will die. I will take my brothers and sisters and we'll go far away. We'll find our own pod.

My head snaps left. JoeyEss is coming. I Sense his fear, and I'm glad. Let him come. Let him fear me. He edges down the hallway toward the creaking, groaning, murderous wind.

I'll blow up his head. And when they all come back in the morning, I'll kill everyone else.

Except SamJay.

SamJay, who is a guard.

Just like JoeyEss.

As quickly as it began, the rage vanishes. My feet hit the floor and I steady myself. The air, the furniture, the cabinets settle back into stillness.

How could I think this way? Shame burns up my neck into my ears. Kill everyone? Me, kill everyone? I'm thinking like a terrorist. Like Mom and Dad. I'm thinking about murder.

A horrible image rises: SamJay, looking at shattered dead people I killed, the blood and the bones; SamJay looking up at me with hatred and disgust.

I could have done that. I could have been that person.

JoeyEss approaches the door.

Suddenly weak and wrung out, I Jump myself back behind the cabinets.

He shines his flashlight into the office through the window. I Sense his heart pounding. He's picturing his wife and new baby girl.

He's afraid he will never see them again. He hates this job. He sweeps the office with the beam of his flashlight through the window.

Crouched behind the cabinets, I taste his fear. Why is he so scared? Images tumble chaotically in his mind—the smiling woman with brown hair, pulled back into a ponytail, the baby with black curls and brown eyes, laughing, reaching for him. Four children dressed in bullet-proof gear holding semi-automatic rifles, sliding into the gym. Us.

He's afraid of us. And he's right to fear us. Because we're monsters. Experiments. My eyes fill with tears.

JoeyEss sees papers scattered on the floor.

Dammit! The papers from the cabinet. I forgot them, and now white pages glimmer all over the office. JoeyEss hunts through his ring of keys, tries one that doesn't work, tries another that doesn't work.

I edge around the cabinets so I can see the papers. JoeyEss isn't looking; he's searching for his keys. I Jump all of the papers behind the cabinets. Debris by the door glints in the light—glass! Chunks and slivers of it, sticking out of the carpet, the remains of the water glass I smashed against the door. The broken shards are right in front of the door, and JoeyEss has just found the right key. He's slipping it into the lock. I Jump the glass shards into my hands and duck back behind the cabinets.

But JoeyEss doesn't enter. "What the…" he mutters in the corridor. "Damn it." The key doesn't work after all. Of course not. Mom would never give her office key to a security guard. Not with all of these secrets in here. He shines his flashlight into the window again, sweeps the floor and ceiling above me. Nothing there. "Oh, screw it," he mutters and hurries away.

My relief is so profound, my knees go weak.

Pain in my hands surprises me. I am clenching the broken glass, and now I drop everything to the floor with a gasp. My palms ooze blood. What have I done?

I try to Sense my veins, the tiny capillaries, the sliced pieces of skin. I reach into my hands to merge and knit and heal. The bleeding slows, but I can't stop it. I can't calm myself enough. As I try to sink into my own body, exhaustion crashes over me.

I lean against the wall and slide down to sit. I could pass out right here behind these cabinets and sleep till Mom woke me. And then what terrible things would happen?

Dragging myself out from behind the cabinets, I Jump the broken and bloodied glass into the secret storeroom under the "T" shelf. Then I Jump all of the papers from behind the cabinets onto the floor. I press my hands into my PJs, just light sweatpants, to stop the bleeding. Finally, I neaten the papers up into a stack and stuff them back into the cabinet drawer under "E."

After sleeping for hours on the autoplane, I shouldn't be tired yet, but I feel broken. Like all the stuffing has been pulled out of me, and I'm nothing but a floppy skin. I just want to go lie down and sleep. Sleep, my Achilles heel. Or maybe my saving grace.

I take a last look around the office. Mom can't know I was here. Everything looks like it did when I arrived. Did I put all those papers scattered around the office back into the right place? I think so. I look at my hands. No longer bleeding. I hope I didn't get blood on the papers. But Mom would never look through those old papers. It doesn't matter.

The only thing wrong with the office is the paper that was on Mom's chair. I slide my hand into my pocket and touch it, a crumpled ball. Can't put it back now. My eyes close. A helpless darkness steals across my brain.

I call up the soft center of my blankets and pillows, Jump myself straight into my bed.

I want to read the paper in my pocket, but my mind sinks like stone. I lie motionless, too heavy to climb under the blanket.

Only one image looms before sleep takes me: SamJay. I have to talk to SamJay.

EYES ONLY   EYES ONLY

US DEPARTMENT OF DEFENSE
SPECIAL OPERATIONS
WASHINGTON, D.C. 20223

CLASSIFIED

ULTRA
TOP SECRET

NO DISSEMINATION OR DECLASSIFICATION

THIS DOCUMENT CONTAINS INFORMATION AFFECTING THE NATIONAL DEFENSE AND SECURITY OF THE UNITED STATES OF AMERICA. TRANSMISSION OR REVELATION OF ITS CONTENTS TO UNAUTHORIZED PERSONS IS PROHIBITED BY LAW. REPRODUCTION OF ITS CONTENTS IN ANY FORM IS STRICTLY FORBIDDEN BY LAW.

DEPARTMENT OF DEFENSE
Office of the Under Secretary (R&E)
VIA COURIER
EYES ONLY   ULTRA TOP SECRET

FROM: Dr. Joseph Duroc, MD, PhD, US Under Secretary
TO: General Conrad Barnes, USSOC
      General BB Grasbach, MD, PhD, JSOC
      Senator George Mitchell, Chair, Armed
      Services Cmte
      Dr Richard Montrose-Beck, DARPA
      Major James Hamilton, Director of Operations
      Lt. Colonel Monica Nowak, Project Director
RE: **PROJECT SAMSON: KILL ORDER**
DATE: 19 April 2088

Emergence of disturbing adolescent behavior [Ref. vid#4238, South Kongolia, 18 April: 16:27:22] unfortunately confirms our predictions. Subject E-10 was insubordinate, argumentative, and violent, delayed vital action, and expressed frustration with orders. This is only the beginning of a predicted adolescent rebellion. No doubt it will be worse in the male subjects once they mature. <u>A kill order is recommended.</u>

As you know, Project Samson's Random rDNA Hosting Program [RRHP] was suspended four years ago due to rising costs, increased liability, and the high rate of failure.

At that time, we determined the best course of action would be to breed our existing operatives, if possible.

However, the recent success of XVERT, in combination with CRISPR, now makes cloning a safer, more cost-effective and reliable way to move Project Samson forward. [See INCEPTION: CLONING AND IMPLANTATION OF FIVE RHESUS EMBROYS, Georges T.B., Rosen M.J., Haversham, J., et al. N Engl J Med; v.453(2):385-397.]

This new protocol will eliminate rogue behavior and the risk of escape. After the escape of B-10 with the help of an employee, we cannot risk the escape of a second operative, who might join the first if it has survived.
With a ready supply of subjects, employment at age five and termination at age thirteen will be viable, which gives us a promising eight-year window of complete control.

The schedule of a Cloning and Termination Program [CTP] will be discussed at the next SCIF meeting. Be advised that although we can't expect replacement clones to be ready for at least five years, <u>termination of subject E-10, age sixteen, is herewith recommended</u>.

Do not file.
Project Samson forbids use of text or instamail.
Deliquesce this memorandum after reading.

CHAPTER 16

I wake abruptly. The room is empty, the lights are on, the door ajar. I sit up. It's past 1300 hours. Lunch must be over already. Why did they let me sleep so late? Did Mom discover my raid of her office last night? My heart starts thrumming as I look around the room. I Sense my brothers and sisters in the gym. Something's wrong.

The half-opened door swings wider; I Sense SamJay before I see him. "Good afternoon, sleepyhead."

Relief explodes through my body as SamJay enters the room. Leaping from bed, I run and throw my arms around him. He's my rock, my touchstone. Silver tendrils of my hair creep over his arms. Tears leak from my eyes—so annoying.

"Hey, hey," he says. He pushes me back to look in my face, takes my hands, and I yelp, pulling them back. He grabs my hands again, sees the still-healing crisscross wounds on my palms. I jerk them away.

"What happened to your hands?" he murmurs, glancing back at

the surveillance vidcam. Which he really shouldn't do; it's so obvious.

"Nothing, I fell," I mutter. "On the mission." I clear my throat and shake my hair out, blink away the tears. I even try to smile while I Jump the soundbug into the toilet. It's probably still dead from Thursday, but just in case. Then I Jump Teetu's toy rabbit over the vidcam. I've never blocked the cam during the day before, when the room light is on, but it's a risk I've got to take. "I saw something terrible," I whisper.

"On your mission?"

"No. Yes, on the mission, Dad shot a boy. An innocent boy. Just because he realized we were Americans. It was horrible. But that's not all. I saw *dead babies*. In Mom's office."

"What?" he says, incredulous. "What are you talking about?"

"There's a secret storeroom behind her office, it's huge, with dead babies preserved in big jars. They're experimenting on babies."

SamJay covers his face with a hand. "Oh, my Lord, Eten, why did you go into your mom's office? Do you know how dangerous this is?"

My voice is shaking. I Sense SamJay's nerves stretched tight; his pulse races and I'm flustered as I try to explain. "There's babies they *shot*. Preserved in jars. And there's drawers and drawers of papers, all about the dead babies because they're experiments, SamJay, all the babies are experiments, and...." My voice cracks upward as my heart shatters all over again. I can hardly say it out loud. "We're in there too, me and my sisters and brothers. We're experiments, too."

"What? No, what are you talking about?"

"SamJay, we're experiments."

"No, Eten. You're not ..." SamJay is staring at me, stricken. He knows it's true.

"Yes, we are. We're not normal." I cover my face and rock forward. The darkness inside of me swirls around a singularity of hatred. Hatred of Mom and Dad, hatred of myself. "We're rats! Nothing but lab rats."

"Stop it, Eten. No." SamJay grabs my hands, forcing them away from my face. "You are a special, wonderful, beautiful girl."

I wish it were true. I squeeze my eyes shut, falling into a black hole, a collapsing, infinitely dense nothingness, sucking in all light. "That boy in South Kongolia," I whisper. "A boy who lost his dad because they had no medicine. And I wanted to help him, but Dad shot him." I stare into SamJay's eyes as if daring him to deny it. "Dad shot him because he heard us speak English and knew we were Americans, so Dad *killed* him. And *I felt him die,* SamJay."

"Oh, my God," SamJay says. He drops my hands and steps back, closing his eyes, shaking his head. "I'm so sorry. Sometimes, in war, there's collateral damage…"

"Sorry? What are we even doing there? Those people hate Americans. I think I killed the President of South Kongolia." My voice cracks. "Dad said he was a terrorist, but somebody called him President Hann. And one of our prisoners the other day, when we had target practice? He said I was fighting for the wrong side. Was he right, SamJay? Are we fighting for the wrong side?"

SamJay looks up. For the first time, he seems lost. Confused. "I don't know," he whispers. "We have to defend ourselves."

"But if we're fighting for world peace, why are people attacking us? Why do they hate us?"

"It's complicated." He shakes his head. A cold mist rolls through his mind, and he seems deflated. His mind wanders to images of a road and an explosion, a man next to him screaming, falling out of a vehicle. Two tears leak from the corners of his eyes.

Fear twists my gut. My pillar, my rock! I've broken him. I've never Sensed such unhappiness in SamJay. It's my fault. "It's not you, it's me," I say. I'm not *evolved*. I'm not even human. I'm an *experiment*."

SamJay gently takes hold of my hands, his voice is low and calm. "Stop it, Eten. That is nonsense." His gentle strength rushes back, his sure grit, even stronger than ever before.

"Experiments?" he says. "Who among us is not an experiment? We're all experiments, Eten, experiments of God, or Nature, or Gaia, or Allah, whatever people call it. You learned about evolution. Nature tries this and that. We evolve, we change, we are all different, and nature keeps whatever works. Who isn't an experiment? Some of us are black, some are white, some are pale golden, like you. Some have black and silver hair, some have no hair at all, like me."

He laughs, and against my will, my lips twitch.

"Come on, Eten." He drops my hands and pokes my shoulder.

"It's not the same," I protest. "Mom and Dad and the military aren't God or nature, are they? They just think they're God." Even though I'm arguing, I feel better. He's got a point; maybe calling myself and my siblings "monsters" is going too far. Teetu certainly isn't a monster; she's the cutest, sweetest little girl in the world. I stuff my hands into the pockets of my pj's, and my fingers touch the crumpled-up piece of paper. I pull it out. "Oh, I forgot this."

"What is that?"

"It was on Mom's chair. In her office."

"Oh, my God," he says, anxiety flaring. "We have to hide it." But instead of hiding it, SamJay smooths it out on my bed and picks it up to read.

A sinking sensation grabs my stomach as I glance over and see words in big, black letters: PROJECT SAMSON: KILL ORDER

"Oh, no," I groan, turning away. I'm sure it's another mission for me. Too soon. I don't want to know.

"It's only the first page," mutters SamJay.

Behind us, Mom stalks into the room. "What's going on here?"

I spin, Jumping the stuffed toy off the surveillance vidcam back to Teetu's bed. "Nothing," I say. "Ma'am. We were just talking."

Beside me, SamJay turns, hands behind his back. He salutes.

Mom looks behind her, up above the door, and SamJay stuffs the paper into his pocket. "The vidcam stream stopped."

She turns back and eyes me suspiciously. I shrug, shake my head.

Mom huffs and her mouth puckers like she just ate a lemon. "Eten, get dressed and join the others in the gym. Sergeant, I'll see you in the living room."

"Yes, ma'am," says SamJay. He turns to give me a look before he leaves. With Mom staring at us, it's not like he can say anything. His eyes are intense and wide, his brows raised, and he nods once, without smiling. He knows I can Sense his feelings. And SamJay is filled with determination. Whatever's wrong, whatever that new "kill order" is, he'll find out.

I watch him exit the bedroom.

"Eten," says Mom. She's angry. Does she know I blocked the vidcam all the time? Probably. But it's more than that. She seems—scared. "Hurry up. Get dressed and join the others in the gym. Let's go."

I must be mistaken. Mom doesn't get scared. Her mental shield clangs down as I meet her eyes. But already, I saw an incomprehensible image in her mind. I can tell it's not a memory—it's something she imagined. It's like a picture from a vid that froze. A soldier in shadows is shooting a woman who's running away from him—a woman in a white shirt and khaki pants, her blonde hair pulled into a bun, her black boots faltering as the red stain spreads out across her back.

And she's shielding someone else, pushing her out of harm's way: a tall, skinny girl, her long black hair lit with silver. Me.

DEPARTMENT OF DEFENSE

Special Forces

VIA COURIER

EYES ONLY   ULTRA TOP SECRET

FROM: Lt. Colonel Monica Nowak, MD, Project Director
      Major James Hamilton, Director of Operations
TO: General Conrad Barnes, USSOC
      General BB Grasbach, MD, PhD, JSOC
      Senator George Mitchell, Chair, Armed
      Services Committee
      Dr Richard Montrose-Beck, DARPA
      Major James Hamilton, Director of Operations
      Lt. Colonel Monica Nowak, Project Director
RE: PROJECT SAMSON: DELAY KILL ORDER
DATE: 21 April 2088

We feel termination of Project Samson operative E-10 is premature at this time. E-10 has been instrumental in subduing revolt in almost all of Norasia and significant parts of Afrikanz, and it is an integral part of our upcoming campaign in the Levant. The G-series operatives do not have E-10's accuracy at a distance; operative J-6 is still unable to work reliably in the field; and operative T-2 is not yet operational.

While a cloning program may produce the best possible outcomes for the future of Project Samson, even if we begin immediately, new operatives won't be ready to deploy for another five to six years.

<u>Recommendation:</u> At this time, we recommend to

reinforce the loyalty of operative E-10, and
evaluate its behavior after the next deployment.

Do not file.
Project Samson forbids use of text or instamail.
Deliquesce this memorandum after reading.

CHAPTER 17

Two days have passed, and SamJay is missing. The last time I saw him was the morning I told him about the storeroom with babies and Mom told him to go to the living room—as if he were a disobedient child.

After lunch, we have languages lab. We're all sitting with headphones, but I can't concentrate. When a finger taps my shoulder, I leap around, pushing the headphones off.

Not a finger, the wand. My belly tightens. It's Mom. The others push their headsets back, too, watching warily. "Where's SamJay, Mom?" I hate how pathetic and whiny I sound. I want to shake Mom by the shoulders and demand she tell us. But one look at her face, and I'm all jelly inside.

Not that she's angry. She's calm—too calm. She steps back, her mind a smooth, white, featureless wall. "SamJay's here."

"Where?" I ask. We all stand, ready to go.

She pauses. The wand dangles conspicuously from her fingers. Tightening her grip, she uses it to point to the others in a broad sweep. "We're meeting in the living room. Right now. Let's go."

Gethre and I exchange a look. Why are we meeting in the living room? Wait—*who* is meeting in the living room? A muscle twitches and flutters in my neck, and I press my fingers to it as we follow Mom. Somewhere, a pit yawns open, waiting for me to fall in.

The living room door is closed. Just outside of it, Mom stops us. "Our guard and friend, SamJay, is leaving us," she announces.

Deafness bludgeons me. I see Mom's mouth moving, but roaring blocks all sound. My hair lifts; my face flushes hot. I rock backward, then forward. I think I might pass out. I hear the word "separation." I hear the word "goodbye."

Gethre grabs my arm on one side and Jaysx grabs the other. Mom has stopped talking.

"I don't understand," I whisper, my throat dry. "I don't…"

My brother and sister pull me into the living room.

"We have to say goodbye to SamJay," says Gethre. Anger swirls around him like a dense cloud.

"He's leaving," says Jaysx. Tears are running down her cheeks.

"No," I say automatically. My heart pounds; my breath comes fast.

In the living room, SamJay sits stiffly on the couch, wearing civilian clothes—dark pants, a soft, blue pullover shirt, shoes instead of boots. He wears a stiff, civilian smile. I balk as soon as I see him. "What?"

"Come on," says Gethre.

"Mom's got the wand," says Jaysx.

SamJay meets my eyes. He smiles a real smile at me and nods just a little, holding out a hand. I don't realize I'm walking until I find myself standing before him. He touches the hard sofa, and I sit down next to him. "Okay, Eten. It's going to be okay." He's whispering.

Why is he even saying that?

Because his mind is a riot of anger and confusion, images of me and my brothers and sisters are all mixed up with battlefield images, memories of men and women being shot. His mind is so upsetting, I withdraw and whisper, "What…?" My lips stick to my teeth; my throat is scratchy. I lick my lips. "What's going on?"

"SamJay is resigning from the military," says Mom. I look up. "He's going to be leaving us today, and I gave him permission to say goodbye to all of you before he goes."

I shake my head. "Resigning?"

"I'm going to work in a new job, Eten." His smile is all fake again. "A civilian job."

I look at Mom. Right now, I hate her more than anything or anyone in the whole world. She did this.

Mom smiles her hard little smile and taps her foot, playing with the wand, twirling it.

"Lieutenant Colonel?" asks SamJay.

Mom nods. As if a reminder to us all, she looks up at the living room vidcam with its bright red dot. It's streaming everything, recording everything. Mom can watch us from a screen if she wants to. She looks back at SamJay. "You have fifteen minutes," she says, then leaves the room.

As soon as Mom leaves, my brothers and sisters crowd around SamJay with hugs and tears and questions. SamJay is going to work as a civilian guard. No, his home pod is not far away. He hopes the Lieutenant Colonel will allow him to come back and visit.

I sit voiceless. Mom will never allow SamJay to visit. It's Mom who's sending him away.

Darkness flickers at the edges of my vision. I hear, but voices sound dead, without volume. The world flattens and seems far away. My heart beats too fast. I taste fear like sour fruit in my mouth.

SamJay leans back and says, "Who wants presents, huh? I have a present for each of you."

The others crowd close again, and he pulls his big duffle bag out from the edge of the sofa and unzips the whole thing.

The boys get light-up yo-yos; Teetu gets a soft doll. He gives Jaysx a rainbow-colored, light-up jump rope, so she can practice being "light-footed."

I sit numbly on the couch. The world seems unreal, a color picture floating atop a black mirror.

"Now, let me say goodbye to Eten alone, okay?" says SamJay. My brothers and sisters hug him and say goodbye and leave the room.

"Eten," he says, turning toward me and taking my hands.

I look into his warm eyes, and suddenly I'm present in my body again. "What's happening?" I whisper.

SamJay smiles and jerks his head back, ever so slightly, his eyes looking up. I look up. The vidcam is behind him, recording.

"I have a very special gift for you," he says. He speaks slowly, opens his eyes wide, and winks.

I'd have to be an idiot not to know what SamJay's wink means. He's going to break the rules. He always winks before he whispers things about the time before. He's going to find a way for us to get together. Hope spikes in my chest, painful, almost like terror.

He bends over his duffle and opens it wide. There's practically nothing in it, just some clean, army brown and white T-shirts. I'm leaning over, too, thinking it's weird that the bag is almost empty when he laughs and pulls up the sides, shaking it a few times. "I guess this duffle bag I bought is too big," he laughs, then murmurs, "It's practically big as you, isn't it?"

Surprise and fear make me pull back. Does he mean what I think he means?

"Yeah, it's big," I whisper. I Sense images in SamJay's mind: me hiding inside his duffle bag. He *wants* me to hide inside his duffle bag. To escape. My mind reels.

"Only one present left." From a side pocket of the duffel, SamJay pulls a toy, a stuffed animal. It's my old teddy bear from years ago.

I'm amazed to see my old friend, my beloved childhood toy. Holding it calms my frantic brain. Could this be my original bear? It was so precious to me, and one day, it just disappeared. Sort of like what's happening to SamJay right now.

"Oh," I say, stroking its head. The teddy bear is small and made of a soft, brown, woolly material. The nap is worn from his ears and face; one of his button eyes has been replaced with a different button; his little bit of a tail is sewn on tight. "How did you find Teddy?"

"I rescued him when your Mom threw him away. It was years ago," he says, grinning. "I gave him a good wash and sewed him all up, and he's almost good as new. I've been saving him for a special occasion."

"Thank you, SamJay." I try to keep my eyes from glancing at the duffle bag. "Thank you for everything."

The living room door opens wide. "The colonel says it's time," says a new guard I've never seen before. Already, I hate her. "Here's your cart," she adds.

Behind her, just outside the living room door, Nana's kitchen cart stands piled with SamJay's stuff on the top shelf: a vidscreen, plants, a toothbrush, a bottle of pills. The bottom shelf is empty.

SamJay zips the duffle bag, and I follow him to the door. He goes down the two steps, places the duffle bag on the bottom shelf, and carefully straightens it out. The bag spreads the length of the shelf, about four feet.

SamJay turns and gives me a hug and a kiss on the forehead. "I hope I'll see you soon, babygirl," he says.

I duck my head and run.

CHAPTER 18

Nobody's in the bedroom; the others are in the gym. The light is off and I pull the door shut, so it's dark. Then I run to my bed and throw myself onto it like I'm going to suffer and sulk in darkness all day. At the same time, I Jump the hollow rabbit over the vidcam.

I place my old, beloved Teddy under the covers and stuff my extra pillow under there sideways so it looks somebody's still lying there. I leave Teddy's head just peeping out.

It's easy to Sense SamJay, still rolling the cart in the hallway toward the elevator.

I know exactly where I want to go. Inside the bag, the zipper above me, the T-shirts under me. I smell the fresh linen, pinch the *here* of the bedroom together with the *thisness* of the duffle, the *inside* of the duffle, and like folding myself inside out, like tumbling, I Jump.

And I'm inside the duffle bag. Scrunched. I can't breathe. The metal lip of the cart digs into my ribs; my body's hanging off the edge.

I curl up smaller, pulling myself and the bag back onto the shelf. I stick my finger into a small hole at the top of the zipper and open it a little so I can breathe. Through the gap in the duffle bag zipper, I can see the underside of the steel shelf above me.

The cart stops.

"Thank you for your service, Sergeant Jones," says Mom.

I freeze. What will Mom do if she catches me?

"Good luck," she continues in a low voice. "I'm sorry it's come to this, but you understand. She's in danger now. We have to move very carefully. I can't control her when she always turns to you."

Inside the bag, I freeze. They're talking about me. Mom needs to control me because I'm in danger? Is that what she told SamJay? That she's *protecting* me?

"Ma'am, if only you'd let me help," SamJay begins. He sounds calm, but inside, he's seething. "I think if we explained things to her ..."

The elevator dings. The doors rumble open.

"Sergeant Jones, we discussed this already. I have to do what I think best."

There's a beat of silence. Then I feel the cart move onto the elevator. Bump, bump. I squeeze my eyes shut and my fingers into fists.

"Thank you for your service," says Mom. She's not in the elevator. "I mean it."

"Yes, ma'am," says SamJay.

The doors close.

We're getting away with it! I feel the elevator rise.

I try to breathe quietly, but it's hard to be still. I want to jump out of the duffle bag and hug SamJay. He's saved me. Again.

Slowly, the elevator comes to a halt. The doors open with a ding.

The cart bumps as it emerges, rolls forward, then stands still. I hear footsteps. A young voice, a little girl, cries out sharply, "Uncle Sammy!"

And SamJay shouts, "Babygirl!"

The word pierces my heart like a spike of ice.

I push the zipper down with my fingers, turn over in the duffle bag on my hands and knees so I can see out.

A little girl in a pink dress about Teetu's age runs into SamJay's arms. He scoops her up and holds her tight, kissing her head. The little girl squeals.

"What are you guys doing here?"

My insides squeeze up to the size of a dried pea. Desolation sweeps me. Two children crowd in toward him, a boy and a girl. SamJay told me he didn't have family.

I push upward a little so I can see better. The room is big, though not as big as the gym. The floors are shiny stone with men and women walking quickly, shoes clicking and echoing. At the far right, there's a long counter with two people in uniform working behind vidscreens.

A woman in a pretty red dress catches up with the children. "Julia?" SamJay says. They all crowd around SamJay, and they stand out in vivid color against the rest of the room. SamJay switches the little girl to one arm and hugs the woman briefly. "What are you guys doing here? Where's Darius?"

"Darius told me what happened. This is worse than anything they did to you guys when you were on active duty," says Julia, lowering her voice. "He couldn't come. He's got an emergency meeting. I told him I'd come instead."

"Thanks so much, Julia. I don't know what I'd do without friends like you. I didn't even have time to get my car."

So, not his family. His friends from the war.

The little girl in SamJay's arms looks over his shoulder straight at me, and suddenly, I realize I'm no longer inside the duffle bag. The zipper has come all the way open, and I'm kneeling on top of SamJay's clothes.

"Sammy, who's that?" the child asks, pointing. "Who's that girl?"

"What?" SamJay turns.

His eyes meet mine.

"Oh, no. Don't point, Letitia." Eyes wide, SamJay grabs the little girl's hand and shakes his head at me, mouthing, "Down."

I drop flat. Panic roars. I squirm back into the heavy canvas sack, try to reach the zipper, but a man in a uniform who's passing by stops and bends over. "Hello," he says. His lips are smiling, but he's coiled as hard as a scorpion. "What are you doing in there?"

Shocked, I stop trying to re-zip the bag and stare at the man.

He stands straight again and waves. "Williams. Over here."

"Run," I hear SamJay say.

I scramble off the cart but then realize he's talking to Julia. He's pushing her and the children through a circular glass door divided into rotating wedges.

"Go, go home," says SamJay, pushing a glass partition to make the door revolve faster. Julia looks fearfully over her shoulder as she herds her children before her.

"Stop," somebody calls from a distance.

The spinning door is framed on either side by large glass windows that let in big squares of light. The entire wall is made of glass windows.

And just outside the glass windows…

Green. Lush. Trees.

Grass, a hedge, leaves. Like in times before the nuclear holocaust. Blue sky, sunshine, people walking, strolling.

Where's the radiation? Where is the devastation, the mud, the slag, the desert?

Outside, through enormous glass windows, I see SamJay's friends hurry away.

Many people are walking out there. Several men in uniform. Two women in dark suits. A man and a woman in jeans are working on something in front of a large, enclosed car. No hazmat suits. No protection from the sun or radiation. Not even the children. Nobody wears protection.

Because they don't need protection.

It only takes me an instant. One instant, and I understand. I understood it before, but I didn't want to know it. The yawning pit opens under me again.

Two squirrels, "extinct" rodents, chase each other up onto the branch of a tree.

Colorful flowers line the walkway.

Cars drive in a parking lot outside.

People walk briskly, without fear.

It's all perfectly clear.

Everything Mom and Dad told us about the world is a lie. To keep us prisoners.

My brothers and sisters and I, we've been living a lie.

The world outside our pod is beautiful, vibrant, alive. There's no nuclear radiation. No bombed-out devastation. No nuclear holocaust. My brothers and sisters and I, we've been tricked. Nobody lives in underground pods.

Nobody but us.

CHAPTER 19

My world cracks in half. And in the middle, I pulse like a strip of flesh that's lost its shell. I don't even look at SamJay. "You lied to me." I sound more amazed than accusing.

SamJay presses my shoulder. "Get back in the duffle. You have to hide."

I hardly notice. Beyond the grass and the flowers and the walkway, there are cars, "obsolete" vehicles, internal combustion engine cars of all colors that supposedly were "incinerated" in a nuclear war decades before I was born.

"Eten, what are you doing? We'll be caught. Get down."

I hear SamJay, but it seems irrelevant. These cars are referenced in the *Project Samson Employee Handbook*. And the "parking lot." Outside, right here, is the parking lot. It's all in the handbook. How to work for Project Samson.

Doors slam open down a long hallway of questions, and all the answers spill out. I am a prisoner, and so are my brothers and sisters. We're weapons, experiments, made powerful to fight for the military. No wonder the war is never over.

"Go, go, go!" SamJay's pushing me now, toward the doorway. I stumble, my legs paralyzed with wonder and horror.

"Hold it," someone shouts from the other side of the room. Dully, I look over and see a man from the big desk waving an arm.

"We have to get out of here," hisses SamJay. "Jump yourself."

I can hear his words, his anxiety, but it doesn't touch me. The world recedes. I am a trace of smoke, a puff of dust.

An alarm blares. SamJay throws his arm around my shoulders and propels me toward the door. "Come on. Jump yourself."

My feet are numb; they don't work. I stumble and SamJay's hands slide under my arms. He drags me the last few steps into the revolving door and hurls his weight against the glass.

It doesn't move.

Rapid shoes slap the floor behind us. I glance over my shoulder. Black uniforms. Guards approaching.

Again, SamJay heaves against the glass. The door won't budge. "Oh my God, it's locked." He reels around, pulling me with him into the far corner of the glass wedge. Across the huge room, with its mirror-like floor and its potted plants and sun-dappled ceiling, four guards advance slowly, cautious now.

"You've got to get out of here," says SamJay.

I stare at the guards, and I don't care. My whole life is based on a lie. The lie is so big, so awesome, reality tilts on its axis and spins.

Everyone—including SamJay—conspired to keep us underground.

All these people! Do they know what it's like to live underground? Do they know what it's like to live in a pod 24-7? To never see the sky or feel the sun? To never meet other people? I don't think so.

SamJay leans back in the wedge of space between glass doors. As I look at him, he seems to collapse in on himself. Who is this man? My hero? My savior? He *lied* to me.

"So there's no radiation," I say, bitterness twisting my mouth. "Was there even a nuclear war?"

"Jesus, Eten. No."

My face is hard and tight. Tears leak from the corners of my eyes, and I brush them away angrily. I don't feel sad. I feel…dumbfounded. "How could you lie to me?"

"I had orders. How could I tell you the truth? I tried to tell you things. I tried to tell you it was classified." His face is pleading, urging me to understand.

I don't. "To keep us locked underground forever! Why?"

SamJay rubs his head with one hand and looks down. "Come on, Eten," he mutters. "You're a smart girl. Why do you think they lie about the surface?"

I do know. "To control us. Because we're nothing but weapons to them."

"Not to me, babygirl."

"Don't call me babygirl," I say, turning away. I clutch my arms around the pain in my chest.

Two men and two women in black guard uniforms stand meters away. The taller woman cocks her head; she's listening to something though an earpiece.

The alarm stops. Everyone is still. A viscous silence rolls across the huge room. I think of something I saw in Dad's office: an insect from long ago, caught in amber. I am an insect, caught in amber.

"Back to the elevator," says the lead soldier, pointing. "Please." She doesn't even have a gun—not that a gun could stop me. SamJay grips my shoulder. He wants me to run, to Jump myself out of the building. But without him, where would I go? How can I leave my brothers and sisters?

I look up at SamJay. Can I even trust SamJay? Desolation crushes everything I am with breathless weight. I wonder what Mom will say, now that I know the truth—how will she control me now? She can't.

That bad vortex of rage begins to spin in the pit of my belly. But I control myself. Because nobody else will ever, *ever* control me again.

I walk away from SamJay, pushing his hand off my shoulder. He follows. The few people left in the lobby stare curiously. I don't care about any of them.

The elevator rocks back and forth as it falls meter by meter. I scrutinize the guards. They're not afraid. They're just doing a job. *I could squeeze their hearts to death,* I think. *In one moment, I could kill everyone in this entire building. They have no clue.*

The elevator doors open onto Mom. Her face is grim, with those extra white lines she gets around the edges of her eyebrows when she's especially mad. But I'm not afraid of her anymore.

The soldiers take SamJay in one direction, and Mom takes me into the living room. She sits in the big, stiff armchair, and I throw myself onto the uncomfortable settee.

"Sit up!" says Mom.

"Don't order me around," I say. Her eyes go wide. "You lied to us. You lied about everything.'

Mom's blue ice eyes are stone cold. She does that thing with her mind where I can't tell what she's thinking or feeling. There are no images. She perches on the edge of the chair, her mouth a tight, hard line.

"You stupid child. You don't even know what you've done."

"I know everything now. There was no nuclear war."

"Oh, grow up. What does that matter?" Mom leans back. She stares at the ceiling. "Eten, I can't protect you if you won't obey me."

I laugh and it comes out hard, incredulous. "Protect me?"

Mom leaps up, stalks over to the couch and leans close to my face so that I shrink back. Her breath is hot, venomous. "Do you think I give the orders?"

"You…" My throat feels raw, and I cough. "Yes."

"Do you think there are no generals, no higher-ups? The entire military of the United States? The politicians, Eten. I *take* orders!" Her face tightens in a passionate frown, a grimace of irony twisting her lips as she turns away.

My insides shrivel. I picture the man with the crooked teeth, the man even Mom and Dad fear. I don't want to believe her, but I know he's in charge. Not Mom. Maybe I don't know the whole story. Of course it's true. Mom is a lieutenant colonel. A general outranks her. Even a colonel outranks her.

Mom speaks into her ristcom. "Let me see the security tapes," she says, then shouts, "Yes, from the lobby, you nitwit." She whirls back and I cringe.

"Mom."

"Sergeant Jones should not have done this."

For the first time, my thoughts shift from myself to SamJay. SamJay is in trouble.

CHAPTER 20

I can see Mom turning her wrath from me toward SamJay. "Mom," I say. "SamJay had no clue. He didn't know I was in his duffle. It's not his fault. He didn't know."

She waves a hand. "Of course he knew," she snaps.

"I swear he didn't know, Mom."

She ignores me. "I've got to do damage control," she says. "There are vids everywhere. Oh my God. Just ... stay here, okay?" She presses her hand to her forehead as if it were aching. "Can you just stay here, please? Don't move from this room, okay?"

"Okay, okay," I say, holding up my hands. She leaves the living room, slamming the door behind her. I Sense my brothers and sisters crowded together in the gym. They know something bad is happening. Especially Teetu. She Senses everything so vividly. She's crying.

I will not allow her to grow up in this underground pod. I will not allow her to become a killer. We'll escape. I can't wait to tell my brothers and sisters everything—the lies about outside and the nuclear holocaust. The experiments on babies, on *us*.

I pace the room, reviewing everything I'm going to tell them, planning our escape. An hour passes, then another. The quiet echoes all around me, and my eyelids grow heavy. I stretch out on the sofa. Eventually, Nana comes into the room. She takes me to the bathroom in the hallway, then back to the living room. She brings me a tray with food: an egg salad sandwich, milk, an apple. She sets it on the coffee table in front of the couch; the smell of egg salad turns my stomach.

"What's happening?" I murmur to her. "Where's SamJay and Mom?"

"I don't know." She's scared. I Sense an image in her mind: guards running to the elevator. "Eten," she says, leaning over. I raise my head, and she puts her rough, old hand on my cheek. "Be careful," she says and turns away quickly.

A funny feeling curls in my belly as Nana leaves the room. Like, does she know I'm planning to run away? I try to eat but can't, and I get up and pace the room again until I'm exhausted. By the time the door flies open, I'm sitting on the floor, half-asleep, my head against my knees.

The door crashes back against the wall. I leap up. "Mom...."

Just behind Mom, a squat, powerfully muscled guard swaggers in. I've never seen him before. He wears a sergeant's insignia on his black sleeve and a sneer on his rough, reddened face.

As soon as he enters, I Sense malevolence. A large folded plastic sheet is tucked under his arm. The sergeant pulls furniture back and spreads the plastic. It covers a four-by-four-meter space.

My throat tightens. I know what that is. Once before, I stood in the middle of a big sheet of plastic in preparation for a very bad punishment. The wand can make me vomit repeatedly, bleed from the nose, break a bone. Mom doesn't want the rug ruined. But I won't allow it. I won't be wanded, not ever again.

Suddenly, I have to pee. A short time ago, I felt numb, but not anymore. Dread and rage shake me. What is she up to?

"Mom, can I use the bathroom?"

"This won't take long." She's not looking at me.

"You can't wand me," I blurt out, not meaning to. I won't let her do it. I'll throw her across the room if she tries it.

"I'm not going to," says Mom. Behind her, the malevolent sergeant and three soldiers march into the room, two blank-faced men and a woman. They could've been uniformed robots. They're half-carrying, half-dragging something.

I scream, horror fizzing down my body.

The something is SamJay.

Blood covers his face and shirt. His eye is swollen shut, and his right cheek looks swollen. His lips and nose are bleeding. One boot sticks out sideways—his bad leg—and he's trying to keep his balance with his good leg as two of the soldiers drag him toward the square of plastic. His wrists are bound behind him.

"SamJay," I shriek, lurching forward. Mom holds my arm in a vice-like grip. "How could you do this to him?" I shout at her.

"He's in trouble. Because of you, Eten." Mom's eyes blaze.

As SamJay is lowered to the floor, he tries to look at me. "Ak-k," he mumbles through swollen lips. "Brae, na." *Okay. Brave, now.*

I am not brave. I am not strong. I am nothing but a stupid child.

I sob, wrench my arm from Mom's grip and slide to my knees beside him. "It's not his fault. What did you do to him?"

"You can't keep disobeying orders, Eten," says Mom. "You put everyone else at risk. Every time you disobey me, Eten, others will suffer."

"You beat SamJay because of me?" My voice rises to a squeak. My skin burns all over; nausea lurches in my stomach. I touch SamJay's arm gently, probing with my Senses like I did with Jaysx. He's one big ache all over but no bones are broken.

"SamJay didn't even know I was there," I say to Mom, still probing inside SamJay. "How could you do this to him?" But maybe she knows I'm lying. SamJay did help me. I lean over, my Senses flowing into his bad leg. *Not broken, twisted.* "I'm so sorry," I murmur. "Please forgive me." I should have Jumped us both away when the guards caught us. I should have run with him.

SamJay breaths something so quietly, I just barely hear him. It sounds like *dn-ger.* His eyes lock onto mine. His lips don't move but I can hear his last word, riding a warm breath. "Run away."

"Come on. That's it." Mom yanks me backward.

A kaleidoscope of images explodes in my brain. Mom, her face contorted; a little girl in a pink dress, twirling; men holding SamJay by his arms while another man punches him; me, running under blue sky and burning sun. These are images from SamJay's mind. I can't leave him like this. My mind is chaos, swirling.

I have to escape. I can do it. I'll find SamJay in Bulee Creek, where he lives.

"All right, Sergeant," says Mom.

I think Mom's talking to SamJay, but I hear feet shuffle behind me. I writhe in Mom's grip, then finally *throw* her off me. There's a thud and a grunt as she smacks against the floor. To the side, I glimpse the sergeant—her sergeant—a mass of flesh as heavy as a truck. I didn't Sense him. The beefy man draws a pistol, hurries to the living room door, and looks out into the corridor.

"Who's coming?" I gasp. Apprehension trembles in my belly. My shield flies up around me. Is he going to shoot someone?

"Mom," I cry out, glancing back at her. She's getting up from the floor, from where I threw her, hair undone, her face curiously blank. "You have to understand," she says. "You can't run away. You will put others in danger. When you run, others suffer. Think of your brothers and sisters. Who will you hurt next? Think of the people you love."

As she speaks, the sergeant pivots. I glimpse him to my left, and everything runs in slow motion as I see him lift his arm, a gesture so casual he might've been tossing a used tissue. He shoots.

He shoots SamJay.

I scream, jump the gun away, but it's too late. Pain slams through my back, up my vertebra to my head. I'm arching backward. It's the wand. I didn't know she had it. The pain pierces my gut, coils around my waist, crushes my breastbone. I can't breathe. I can't see. A fiery serpent drags my heart through my mouth. The scream goes on and on, soundless, inside my brain. My head hits the carpet, my arms and legs jerking. My consciousness shreds, black ribbons before my eyes, fluttering until darkness closes in.

CHAPTER 21

I'm lying on my side in my bed, the pillow damp and crusty with tears. Teetu snuggles within the circle of my body. My arm drapes over her shoulder.

Vaguely, I remember being carried into the bedroom, my brothers and sisters crowding around me.

SamJay is dead. Tears leak from my eyes again. A fearful agony prowls through my body, waiting for me to wake up. I want oblivion.

Teetu pokes me in the leg with her heel.

"What?" I murmur. "I'm sleeping."

She pokes me again, then turns over and starts signing.

"I can't see you." What could possibly matter now? "Let me sleep."

Teetu pushes my arm more insistently and signs again. It's no use. She's going to make me wake up. I sit up. In the faint light of the bathroom, I can see her words.

"I said SamJay's not dead."

What? My hands grab hers. My thick, slow mind shudders between hope and despair. She pulls her hands away from me, nodding, eyes big. "SamJay's not dead. They tricked you."

I jump the stuffed rabbit over the vidcam and the soundbug back into the toilet, then speak, my heart thudding in my throat. "What do you mean they tricked me?"

"They used a fake gun," she signs. "We all Sensed it. We could tell he wasn't dead, but you were unconscious."

There's a storm inside of me. It's true that Mom hit me with the wand at the same moment SamJay was shot. Maybe…? I stare at Teetu in the dark and hold perfectly still as if a single movement might shatter this possibility. "But SamJay," I whisper. "He was all beaten up and hurt. I know he was; I Sensed it."

Teetu nods. "They beat him. But they didn't kill him."

I grab her hands again. "Are you sure, Teetu? Really sure?"

She pulls her hands back and says, "Yes, I'm really sure."

A rush of relief undoes me, and I throw my arms around Teetu, sobbing. The more she nods and pats my back, the harder I cry. SamJay is alive.

How could Mom fake "kill" him right in front of me? To trick me like that! I push my sister away and wrap my arms around my knees, my whole body shaking with sobs. Will they never stop lying to me? Lying to control me, lying no matter how much it hurts? I can't stand it. My cries rise to a shout. A scream. "How could they do this to me?"

"Hey." Gefor scrambles down from his bunk. "What's going on?"

Gethre rolls from his bed and turns on the bathroom light, leaving the door open to illuminate the bedroom. Jaysx creeps in next to me on the bed, putting her arm around my shoulders. "Eten?" she says anxiously. "It's okay."

Gethre grabs my shoulder. "SamJay isn't dead. It was all a trick. We Sensed it."

"I know, but it's not okay." I cover my face with my hands, rocking back. "How could they do this to me?"

"Tell us what happened," says Gefor. "Why did they beat SamJay like that? Why'd they pretend to kill him?"

It's moments before I can get my voice under control. I rock back and forth, look up, try some deep breaths. "I tried to escape," I say finally. "SamJay helped me."

"That's crazy," says Gethre as the others murmur exclamations of surprise.

"What do you mean, *escape*?" demands Gefor.

"SamJay said I was in danger, okay? He saw a kill order. He *wanted* me to escape." I describe to them how I Jumped myself into his bag and went up in the elevator with him.

"Holy cow," says Gethre.

"Mom couldn't tell?" asks Jaysx.

"She didn't Sense you?" asks Teetu.

"No, I'm telling you, I don't think she can Sense things."

"But why did SamJay say you're in danger?"

I frown because I'm really not sure. "There was a paper in Mom's office. It was a kill order, and I grabbed it, but only SamJay read it."

"So," says Gethre, "it was another mission. Probably a mission to go outside again. And you'd be in even more danger than before."

"Wait a minute," says Jaysx. "What if it was a kill order to terminate *me*?"

"Oh my God," mutters Gefor.

"What? No way," I say.

"That's just stupid," says Gethre.

"It's not stupid," Jaysx says angrily. "Mom hates me. I'm bad at everything."

"It's not a kill order for you," I say as a dawning suspicion wakes a whole new level of dread. "But it might be for me."

Gefor startles me as his voice rises to a shout. "Come on, are you guys kidding me? You're nuts."

Gethre shakes his head. "He's right. This is crazy."

"Hurt us? *Kill* us? Are you crazy? Who would do something like that?" says Gefor. "Mom and Dad? Are you kidding?"

"That is so wrong," says Gethre.

"Okay, you got a new mission that's dangerous," rants Gefor. "That's our job. Missions are always dangerous. We're soldiers. We protect America. I'll do the mission if you and SamJay are too scared."

"That's not ..." I begin to protest, but Gefor cuts me off.

"What you did was wrong, Eten. It was *wrong*. You should never have run away like that. SamJay was wrong. He should never have helped you. Mom and Dad need us here. Our country needs us here. To fight."

My voice rises as I try to break into his one-track mind. "What if we're fighting for the wrong side, Gefor? What if we shouldn't be fighting at all?"

"How can you say that?" He's gone all red in the face. "Everything we do is for the good of the world. We're fighting for world peace."

I lose it completely. "I can't believe my own brother is so stupid. You don't go around killing people for world peace."

"You do if they're bad people." His chin lifts, and he clenches his fists. His violet eyes blaze. At his side, Gethre is frowning, turning back and forth between us. He nods when his brother says this. Teetu has retreated to her lower bunk, her hands over her ears. Jaysx huddles next to her.

This argument is crazy. The boys believe everything Mom and Dad tell them. I guess I did, too, once upon a time. I have to break through to them.

"Well, you're so smart. Do you know Mom and Dad lied to us about the outside? There was no nuclear war. There is no radiation. It's all a big lie." I wave my hand up at the ceiling. "Everything's just hunky-dory up there. They just want to keep us prisoners."

"Bullshit," burst out Gefor, but it's even worse when Gethre laughs.

"Oh, come on," he says.

"It's true. I saw it for myself."

Gethre makes a *phishing* sound of complete disbelief.

"What did you see, Eten?" Jaysx asks in a small voice, leaning forward on the bed.

I turn to her. "I saw out the window. When I got off the elevator with SamJay. I saw outside, through the windows, and I saw grass and bushes and flowers."

"Flowers?" echoes Jaysx, awestruck.

"And I saw people walking around out there, *children,* too, I saw children outside, and nobody was wearing a hazmat suit." I swing back to my brothers. "Can't you Sense what I saw?" I know the images are clear within me. I can picture it all so clearly.

"Yeah, vids," says Gefor. "Vids of the times before."

"Yeah, they probably project vids outside the windows," adds Gethre. "Like Nana's painting of the window in the kitchen."

"They wouldn't even have real windows," says Gefor. "This is such bullshit."

"There are real windows and it wasn't vids," I shout angrily. "Can't you Sense what I saw?"

"I believe you," Jaysx says.

This seems to make Gefor even angrier. "You should never have tried to run away. You're a *traitor*. You and SamJay. No wonder he got beaten up. You're both *traitors*."

I pull myself up, the sting of those words coming from my little brother's lips bringing heat to my face. "How dare you!"

Gethre puts his hand on his twin's shoulder, but Gefor shrugs him off. "It's true."

My belly tightens, and my hands curl into fists. "You're a stupid little boy. You don't know what you're talking about."

"I hate you," says Gefor. "Don't ever talk to me again." He Jumps himself up into his bunk and turns away from all of us, pulling the pillow over his head.

His brother stands there and looks at me with dismay. "I...I don't..."

"So you think I'm a traitor, too?" To my immense annoyance, tears leak from my eyes. I don't bother to brush them away.

Gefor shakes his head. "No. But..."

"But what?"

His mouth twists up like *he's* trying not to cry. "You shouldn't run away."

"Oh, my God," I say. They don't understand anything. "Okay, I'm sorry, okay? But Gethre, they did lie. About outside." I'm about to go on, but Gethre shakes his head and holds up his hand.

"I don't want to hear it. It doesn't matter. We have to do what's right. We have to follow orders." He rolls back into his bunk and turns to the wall.

I breathe out a long, slow breath of liquid fire. I'm so burnt. How could somebody refuse to know the truth?

I was the same way. I used to be so proud of my skills. Proud of the way Dad depended on me. Yeah, depended on me to kill people. Suddenly, it fills me with shame. I felt like an important part of something bigger, something better: Fighting for world peace. What a joke. I couldn't see the lies until today, when I saw them for myself.

Teetu crawls to the edge of the bed and tugs on my PJ sleeve. I turn. "I believe you," she signs.

I drop to her bed. Jaysx and Teetu put their arms around me. They don't truly understand what I'm saying because they're not reeling from this new information. They're not aghast to discover the nuclear holocaust is a lie, a hoax perpetrated on us to keep us docile prisoners, fighting military battles.

Instead, Jaysx says, "We'll protect you."

Teetu echoes her sister's words with her hands. It's sweet and pathetic at the same time. Do they think they can protect me from the whole U.S. military? Even if they could, the danger is so much more insidious. Who protects you from lies? From tricks and betrayal? Who protects you from the people you love?

"Don't go outside for missions anymore," says Jaysx. "It's too dangerous."

"You can't," says Teetu.

"Okay," I smile at them, nodding. Weariness hits me like a truck. "We better go back to sleep now." I leave Teetu in her bed, and Jaysx climbs back to the upper bunk. As I slide between my sheets, an unfamiliar loneliness fills me.

Finding the truth and saving us all—even if my brothers don't want to be saved—that's my job. I'm so much older than them, and not just by years. I love my country, and I'm loyal to my mission, no matter what Gefor thinks.

But something is wrong with my country. Something rotten is going on. And my mission has changed. From now on, my mission is to stop the killing. My mission is real world peace.

CHAPTER 22

By the next day, I've collected everything I need. A backpack. Water bottles. A change of clothes. That part was easy, but it took me all afternoon to find a map of the U.S.A. It's from an old lesson on World War II. I can see North Carolina, but I can't see any place marked "Freedom" or "Bulee Creek." Somehow, once I'm outside, I'll have to find my way to SamJay.

My brothers aren't speaking to me, and my sisters keep giving me mournful looks. Nana asked twice what was wrong with us. We're too quiet. For sure, she'll mention it to Mom if she hasn't already. There's a time bomb ticking in my belly, cold and heavy. I've got to go quickly.

An hour after lights out, when the others are asleep, I cover the vidcam and pull the backpack and my clothes from under my mattress. I dress quickly and take a small note from the front pocket of the pack. It says, "Don't worry. I'm safe. I will come back for you. Destroy this note." I Jump the note into Jaysx's bed, under her arm. She mutters something and I freeze, but she doesn't wake.

I am going to find SamJay in Bulee Creek. And he will help me find a place that is safe for all of us. The United States is huge. There's got to be a place where we can be safe, where Teetu can grow up without knowing what it is to kill another human being, where Jaysx can be free of constant fear, and the boys can learn another way of life that doesn't involve blind loyalty to lying parents. I want us to learn the art of healing, not war.

I crouch low, one hand on the floor, my pack balanced on my back, and hesitate. My heart races as adrenaline pours through me. Suddenly, I have doubts. Maybe this is all very stupid. How can I possibly find SamJay? How can I ever escape Mom and Dad or the U.S. military? Maybe I should just do my job and forget all this. Why should I fear danger in my own pod? What I'm about to do is more dangerous than anything else I can imagine.

I scrunch my eyes shut and shake my head. I believe, I *know*, SamJay wouldn't steer me wrong. But it's more than that. The image of the boy in South Kongolia rises up in my mind again. The way he burned with passion. The way Dad shot him. The way I blew up President Sayan Hann and killed those soldiers on the roadside.

I can't do this anymore.

I have to go. I call up my vision of outside. I can Sense it as it appeared through the windows—the flowers by the path, the concrete walkway, the parking lot. I pull the edges of *here* and *there* together, feeling the *thisness* of where I want to be. I Jump.

But I'm not outside. I'm crouched just beyond the elevator, the shiny floors all around me. The revolving glass door glimmers ahead. The huge, dark windows reflect the light. I stand up, disoriented. I'm back in the big entry room, where I was with SamJay when I saw outside.

To my right, the long desk with two guards.

Who look right at me.

Shit.

I run for the door. I can't Jump myself outside; I can't even see outside. Everything is reflection. Everything glimmers. The grass I'd glimpsed earlier, the bushes and trees, all swallowed by night.

Both of the guards shout. A shattering alarm blares and honks. As I reach the door, I glance sideways. A guard is speaking into a ristcom. New surveillance cams glint from the ceiling. They were ready for me.

I push the glass. It doesn't budge. Locked.

But just outside, the concrete walkway is illuminated. I can Sense it. I Jump.

My sneakers land on cement and I race forward. There's a line of tall bushes to my right, the trees beyond, the cars parked in pools of light all around. The alarm from the building goes suddenly silent.

I look back. Nobody coming. I run straight for the wall of densely packed bushes, using my shield to push my way through.

Then, an aroma hits me. I stumble out of the hedge and pull up short, my feet on living grass, trees before me. This smell I'd never imagined, never experienced in South Kongolia, never understood from vids of the time before.

A green smell. Smell of living things: plants, leaves, hedges, grass. As if the freshest water were suddenly falling around me. As if an incredibly beautiful song coated my skin with light. I breathe in through my nose as deeply as I can, breathe out, breathe in again. I run forward and turn, arms out, embracing the night.

I know I have to move, to Jump again, but I take a moment, just one moment. Outside, it's quiet. Nobody's following me. And if they do, I'll just Jump away.

Escape into the outside isn't terrifying; it's easy. Easy and wonderful.

To my left, where the thick hedge has fallen away, a car moves quietly up a black road, its red lights vivid. The air churns all around me. A "breeze." I almost laugh out loud and turn my face toward it.

This is so beyond, so far beyond what I expected. I'd thought it would be like South Kongolia. But this is ....

I look up.

This is infinite. I see stars. Sparkling in their infinite numbers. Other suns, other worlds we cannot see. I reel and fall onto my back with a thump on the grass behind the hedge. My hands sweep across the silky blades of lush growth on the ground. I can smell the earth. The smell of freedom. I feel more alive than ever before.

"Eten!"

A powerful light shines from the building.

I leap up to a crouch, my heart pounding again.

"Eten, get back here this very instant. That is an order."

It's Mom. Why is she here? I thought she'd already left the building for the night. Nana! She must've warned Mom. I've made a terrible mistake.

And then there is pain.

My body jerks and goes rigid as my whole spine lights up. The universe morphs into pain. A scream rips past my lips and then another.

I can't think. I can't see. I can only scream.

The pain stops. Mom and Dad stand over me. They pull me to my feet.

"What are you thinking?" shouts Mom. She grabs my shoulders and shakes me, spittle flying as she shouts. "I warned you, I…"

"I hate you," I scream, tearing myself away. "Get away from me."

"I told you this would happen," says Dad.

"Shut up, Jim," Mom snarls.

He cranes his neck, looking for somebody, his SIG Sauer in hand. Horrible images swirl in his mind: Me, laid out on the grass, a bullet hole in my forehead. But not just me. Mom, too, and himself, all shot. He pictures guards shooting all of us. I don't get it. Why would guards shoot Mom and Dad? I Sense a flickering image of Dad whirling, crouched, shooting the guards.

His heart thunders. *He is scared!* Is Dad planning to defend me? Against the guards?

The moment slows. I see the individual bubbles of spit gather at the corners of Mom's mouth. Her white teeth, the glinting incisors, her stretched lips dark in the artificial light. The single tone of her furious voice. Next to her, Dad's white-knuckled grip on his handgun.

At the same time, close by in the parking lot, a car's lights blink on. A man holds his car door open. I Sense him slide inside the car, slam the door shut, and start the engine. I see the empty seats behind him.

Suddenly, Mom straightens up and looks toward the parking lot. "Don't you dare!" she spits.

I Jump.

CHAPTER 23

In a high, clear voice, the young man in the front seat sings a song with a catchy rhythm. Something about love and disaster.

He accelerates out of the parking lot. He's a soldier not much older than I am, dressed in a uniform, his hat pressed on his ears so they stick out. He's already half a kilometer down the dark road leading away from the parking lot before he glances toward the flicker in his mirror that is me.

"What the *fuck*?" he shouts. The car swerves to the right as he slams on the brakes. He throws open his door and struggles to get out without unfastening his seat belt. He turns, looking at me over his shoulder. "Where did you come from?"

I smile. "I'm really sorry. I need a ride." Already, I Sense his fear subside. To him, I look harmless. "I'm really sorry. I snuck into your car. Can we keep going?"

He sits back, looking at me again in his mirror. "You can't just get into somebody's car! Are you running away from home?"

"No, of course not." I smile. "Please, can we keep going?"

A very loud, amplified voice announces: STOP YOUR VEHICLE. STEP OUT OF THE CAR.

I twist around. Back by the parking lot, a car with flashing blue lights pulls out onto the road. They must have a handmic. Another vehicle is even closer, approaching from behind.

The soldier, his anxiety spiking again, unbuckles his seat belt and scrambles out of the car.

A truck screeches to a stop behind the soldier's car.

But I've already Jumped myself to the side of the road, where it's dark. I can't just run. I have to get a ride out of here, far enough away to evade Mom and Dad.

"Hey, bud," calls the truck driver, leaning out the window, glancing at the dazed young soldier, then back at the approaching vehicle with the flashing lights. The second driver isn't a soldier, and he's older, more like Dad's age. "What's going on?"

HALT, announces that ear-splitting voice again. STEP OUT OF YOUR VEHICLE.

I shrink back further into darkness, but I want to hear what these two are saying.

"I don't know," says the young soldier, pointing to his car. "She was…" He leans forward, taking his hat off, peering into the back seat of his car. "She was just here. And then those guys, on the handmic, they said halt and get out." He turns around and looks. "This girl. She wanted a ride."

"Huh?" says the truck driver. I grin to myself. The truck driver has no clue what the soldier is talking about.

"There was this girl, she's gone, this girl with long black hair, she was really pretty…"

A weird sensation tickles my insides. *Really pretty?* Really?

"…she was glowy, weird, you know?" the driver babbles on. "I mean, she just appeared! On my back seat."

Okay. I'm pretty but weird.

The car with the flashing lights pulls up, and I Jump myself further back, flattening my body to the ground.

Mom and Dad burst from the car, guns drawn. Two guards from the building are running up the road to join them. Mom and Dad speak to the young soldier, too quietly for me to hear.

"Eten," shouts Mom, holding up her hand. She isn't holding a gun after all. What does she need a gun for? She's holding the wand. "Come back here. I know you can hear me."

Panic leaps into my throat.

"We're not going to punish you, Eten. You just can't run away, it's too dangerous, please believe me. Dad and I are trying to help you."

Mom says it's dangerous to run; SamJay says it's dangerous to stay. I believe SamJay.

"Come back here," she shouts, waving the wand, "or I will wand you."

Reflexively, I stretch my fingers to the hateful thing. And suddenly, I'm gripping the wand with my own hand.

Mom screeches. "The wand! She's here. She's here. She took the wand right out of my hand."

Rolling onto my back, I stare at the wand. Unbelievable! That was so easy, and I'd done it without thinking. Jump the wand away from Mom. *Duh.*

They shine their flashlights across the grass, and I Jump myself further back. I have to fight not to laugh out loud. Maybe I'm in shock. Why didn't I ever Jump the wand away before? Why didn't I destroy it?

For years, I just stood there and let them punish me. Because I thought I deserved it. Because they were in charge—Mom and Dad. I knew nothing else. It's not like I could run away. The "nuclear holocaust," the radiation and slag remains of American soil, made that impossible. No wonder Mom and Dad made up stories. Of course they lied to us. It worked.

I always tried to be a good soldier. I always tried to please them. Not anymore.

They really can't force me to do anything. The thought is so amazing, so liberating, I am in shock. All I can do is stare at the people on the road.

The young soldier wearing the over-large hat slides back into his car, slams the door, and drives off as fast as he can.

"Stop him," shouts Dad.

One of the guards hops into the car with the flashing lights and makes the soldier stop. The guard searches the car and the trunk.

How idiotic! Even if I had Jumped myself in there, I just would have Jumped out while he searched and then Jumped back in. But it's a good idea to hide in somebody's trunk. If I can see inside somebody's trunk, if I can Sense it, I can Jump myself into it.

The older man who was driving the truck, dressed in blue jeans and a heavy red shirt, has gotten out to join the search. He's excited by all the commotion.

"Come back, Richardson," shouts Mom to the guard. She says to Dad and the other guard, "She's here. She's watching us. Just fan out."

It's amazing how often Mom is right. I still suspect she can Sense people; maybe she's just hiding her skills from us.

"We should get more soldiers over here to search," says Dad.

"No," Mom says sharply. "I don't want Duroc to know."

That image again. I can see him in Dad's mind. That man with the parched face and crooked teeth. Duroc.

The truck driver goes back to his truck, pulls out his flashlight, and joins the others in the search for me.

"Come on, Eten," says Dad in a loud voice, sweeping the ground beside the road with his light. "Enough shenanigans. Get back here now and you won't be punished."

But I won't be punished ever again. And I'm not going back. Not to them.

The two guards from the building—they're the ones afraid of being punished. They don't know what's going on or who I am, only that they somehow made a mistake. Their minds swirl with images of me running past them inside the building, triggering the alarm, and Mom's angry face. They hold big, heavy flashlights, as big as clubs, with their handguns alongside the lights, as if they could actually shoot me.

"Put the guns away, for God's sake," shouts Mom. As if Sensing my thoughts.

But if she can Sense, she's bad at it. My brothers and sisters would have found me in an instant.

And none of them can see in the dark like we can. I smile again, delighted at how much better I can hide than they can find.

Glancing at the brush behind me—to fix a place to Jump if I need to—I Jump myself closer so I can hear them talking.

My hand still clutches the pitiful, hated plastic wand. I crush downward until the wand implodes, sucking into itself and crumbling to tiny pieces that fall through my fingers.

As the wand breaks, one of the guards stops and shines his light where I just was. But I'm now standing behind him.

"Who are you looking for?" the truck driver says to the guard, shining his flashlight in the same direction. The truck driver pictures something he once saw in a vid: A hulking, beautiful, warrior queen with black hair, a machine gun, and very large breasts. I stifle a giggle.

Mom shouts from further down the road. "Come back, Eten. You are a soldier, Private! That's an order."

"We're looking for a girl, a young girl," murmurs the guard, then coughs as if his throat were dry. "You better move on, mister. You shouldn't be here."

"A young girl?" The driver laughs, derisive.

"She's very dangerous," the guard says defensively. "You better get in your truck and keep driving."

I'm very dangerous. I grin in the dark. I like being dangerous.

Dad's light sweeps toward me, and I Jump myself further up the road to the soldier's truck. Its front door hangs open, and a light from the inside spills onto the road. The back of the truck is an open rectangular space for carrying things, and there's something big in there covered by a sheet of dark plastic.

I consider getting into the back when I see Mom hurrying up the road toward the truck, shining the flashlight back and forth into the dark.

I Jump back to the grass with alarm.

"Check the truck," shouts Mom.

I Jumped further back.

The guards search the truck—even *under* it, by the wheels—and lift the big, dark sheet of plastic back up off an upside-down table. After they check under the plastic—no me—they lay it back down over the table. Perfect! Thank you for showing me exactly where I can hide.

Dad turns and points his flashlight at the driver, who's still standing next to the guard. Dad's still got his SIG Sauer in his right hand. "You," he says. "Get back in your pickup and be on your way."

"Yes, sir." The driver trots to his truck.

Do they think they can catch me like this? It's silly. Do they think I'm still five years old, the little girl they taught to kill?

Dad circles his light and shines it on the road. "Move on."

Don't they realize what they've created? I could kill all of them at once, right here, right now, in the blink of an eye. The thought makes me dizzy. I've always focused on destroying the enemy, on taking orders, like Gefor said. Sure, I've gotten mad and lost control, but I always felt so guilty about it.

It's like chains that have bound me all these years turned out to be mere brittle paper, and as soon as I flex my muscles, they tear and vanish.

The truck slowly rolls forward as Dad hurries off to the other side of the road. I let the truck get 10 meters away, 20 meters away. When it's almost too dark to see, I Jump myself into the back, landing in a crouch next to the covered table.

Air whips my hair. The night feels suddenly chilly. I've rarely been cold before, except in the swimming pool. I pull a narrow edge of plastic loose and crawl under it, onto a wide disk of wood.

Mom's calling voice quickly slips away, but my Sense of her and Dad grows thinner more slowly until I can no longer Sense them at all.

The truck slows, turns, then gathers speed.

I bump very slightly, up and down, up and down, lying on the wood, my head pillowed on my arm. It doesn't matter where this truck goes, as long as it's away. I'll find SamJay. I'll rescue my brothers and sisters. No one can stop me now.

CHAPTER 24

The seeping coldness saturates my T-shirt and the side of my sweatpants. I'm shivering. Each bump of the truck shoots a little pain into my shoulder. I've never been this cold before.

With stiff fingers, I pull my extra T-shirt and pants out of my pack and struggle to put them on over what I'm already wearing. It's April. Shouldn't it be warm in North Carolina?

Tucking my body into a tight ball, I resist my unspooling confidence. I press my lips together and pull the neck of my second T-shirt over my nose. *I am dangerous. I am powerful.* I repeat it again and again, like a new mantra.

But what I feel is exhausted. I try to stay awake as the upside-down table vibrates steadily but I end up falling asleep anyway.

I wake with a jerk as the truck slows and makes a series of turns. Then stops. Vibration and sound stop, too.

There's a rocking motion; the truck door slams.

My heart does a rat-a-tat. Adrenalin shoots into my veins. Time to take the next step.

It's very quiet and there's not even a breeze. The plastic covering the upside-down table is dark, but no longer completely black. Light shines on the other side of it. I lift an edge, stiffly crawl out, and raise my eyes above the side of the truck.

Emptiness and black road all around. A white grid painted on the road, a few empty cars here and there, parked within white lines.

Another parking lot.

Terror seizes me. Did this man just drive in a circle and we're back at Fort Freedom?

But no. The parking lot is similar, a huge square with big lights illuminating the emptiness. At one end of the parking area stands a massive building fronted with glass, all lit up inside. But it's not the building I escaped from. I breathe a sigh of relief.

A woman comes out of the building through glass doors, pushing a big cart filled with paper bags. I shrink back, still peeking over. The woman goes to one of the cars and, with a *beep*, opens a huge trunk in the back. She lifts bags out of the cart and puts them into her car.

She does not have a gun. She's not in uniform. She's wearing jeans with a shirt and a jacket.

For one shivering moment, I consider Jumping her jacket into my hands. Stupid idea.

Another person exits the building also pushing a cart filled with bags. He goes to another car and opens its door, putting bags inside the car.

He, too, does not have a gun. They're just regular civilians, and they're not looking for me.

The big, bright building is some kind of storage facility where civilians can go to get supplies. They seem to need a lot of supplies. I need only one thing: a map. A shiver shakes me. Or maybe I need two things: a map and a jacket.

Another car drives up close to the truck and a woman in a red coat gets out, closes her door, and starts toward the illuminated building. I Jump myself to the ground behind the woman's car. When I'm sure she's not looking, I follow her to the building.

As if by magic, the glass doors open as the woman approaches. I halt. Did the woman Jump the doors away? But then they slide shut behind her. I rush forward to catch them, but they open again as soon as I approach. Holding one hand out in front and one to the side, I blunder into the brightly lit space.

A hot pulse ticks in my throat. I try to squash down my fear.

Inside the door, metal wire carts line up, stashed one inside another. Another woman with pale skin and yellow hair like Mom's stands next to a cart.

She smiles, handing me a folded paper. "Welcome to Scupernog Road Big Green. Would you like a basket?" A white pin on her red vest reads, SALLY.

"Thank you, Sally." I clutch the cart with one hand and the paper in the other, trying to make sense of it all. Fruits and vegetables lie on a shelf to my right. Ahead and to my left hangs clothing, and between them sit glass counters. Beyond that, boxes crowd more shelves. The place is enormous.

"Can I help you?" asks Sally.

"I need a map. And a jacket."

"Oh, well, jackets are right over there." She points, but I can't tell what's she's pointing at. "I'm not sure about maps, most people use GPS, you know."

I look at her in dumb shock. Is she talking about the Global Positioning System developed by the Department of Defense in 1973? The top of my head throbs. This is when it dawns on me: I have no clue what I'm doing. Modern life in America? Forget it. I know history, and everything else I've been told is a pack of lies. I don't know how to do one basic thing. I try to hide my confusion.

"Oh, I think we might have maps and compasses for the Scouts," Sally continues, pointing. "Way over there in the back? By automotive?"

"Okay," I say, pushing the basket toward where the jackets should be. I turn again. "Um, thank you."

But Sally is already greeting a man in fatigues who's just entered. I go tense briefly, but the man doesn't glance my way. I see a few more people shopping who wear uniforms, maybe military, but I've never seen those uniforms before. Anyway, they're focused on their own shopping, not me.

Surreptitiously, I watched someone else with a basket. She's a very large, older woman who limps and leans heavily on her cart handle. She's got some hairs growing out of her chin. I've never seen anybody who looks like her. With one hand, the woman picks up a pink shirt from a table, shakes it, examines it, and throws it in her cart. Then she moves on.

Nobody reproaches her. Nobody even notices when she takes what she wants. Wow.

Suddenly, I see the truck driver—my truck driver, the one who helped Mom and Dad search for me. He's smaller than I thought he was, and older, but it's the same man, with short brown hair and a red shirt. He's got a basket with milk and cans in it, and he's coming right for me. The blood rushes into my face as I duck my head and walk off to my left.

But he doesn't sound the alarm. He doesn't even notice me. I look back and see him moving his basket back up toward the entrance. He's leaving. Why should he notice me? He didn't see me and he didn't know I was in his truck.

My basket bumps against something and I turn. It's a rack of jackets. They're large, black, and fluffy, with hoods, and they all look alike. Perfect. I push my cart aside, step in close and take one off its hanger. I hold it up, shake it, look at it closely, and toss it into my cart.

Turning, I scan the room. Nobody has noticed. I snatch the jacket from the cart and put it on. The soft, roomy jacket hangs down below my hips. I tuck a dangling plastic tag up into the cuff, zip it up, and hug myself, already feeling warmer.

The big, older woman who got the pink shirt has moved from clothing into the food section. I turn my cart and follow her slowly. My stomach growls as I watch. Many of the shelves are empty, but there's still a lot of food. The woman pinches something dark green— it's bumpy, oval, and mysterious—and then puts it into her basket. I creep closer. The woman picks up some speckled bananas and puts them into her basket.

Is this how food and clothing have gotten to our pod all these years? Mom and Dad said there were hydroponic and sun-lamp farm pods where all the food grew. More lies, of course. Maybe all of our food and clothes came from a storehouse like this.

I pick up an apple and put it in my basket, then glance around. Nothing. Nobody looking. I grab the apple from my basket and bite into the sweet, firm flesh. It's delicious.

Pushing on, I come to a long counter with shelves under it. The shelves are mostly empty, but there are a few sandwiches and plastic boxes of what looks like salads. The room behind the counter is dark, but the shelves are lit. I grab a sandwich and put it in my basket. I look around but again see no one. The old, large woman is heading out. After finishing the apple, I eat half the sandwich and put the rest in my backpack. It's turkey, kind of dry but another important resource for my journey. I'm beginning to feel like I might succeed; maybe I'll be able to navigate this strange, new world.

As I push on toward the map section, I get kind of lost. No more friendly people with name tags. I'm wandering through aisles of wrenches and cables and bottles of blue stuff when from behind me, a voice says, "Can I help you find something, dear?"

I turn, surprised someone could've come up from behind without my Sensing them. It's strange—the man's mind is a blank. But he looks very kind. He's smiling, with his head cocked to the side, inquisitive. He looks like a slightly younger version of Dad but dressed in civvies—a plaid shirt and dark slacks, a nice jacket with brown suede patches at the elbows. His light brown hair, combed back neatly, is a little gray at the sides, and he has a friendly face. He's holding a plastic bag with BIG GREEN printed on it. His pale blue eyes are lit up, and his smile is so warm, I feel the anxiety drain right out of me.

"Oh," I say, returning his smile. "Thank you. I'm looking for a map."

The man nods. "They're right over there. Come on, I'll show you."

He walks quickly and seems so familiar with the place, I'm pretty sure he must work here, though he doesn't have a name tag. I follow him to a section against the wall, near a display of motor vehicle tires. There's a tall rack with a picture of an eagle on top and folded papers—maps I hope—sticking into the slots. The man stands next to me and looks up at them. "Where are you going?

"Bulee Creek," I tell him. "It's in North Carolina." I realize the maps are organized alphabetically by state. Some are missing but I find the one for North Carolina and unfold it.

The man snaps his fingers and turns to me with a broad grin. "What a coincidence. I'm driving to Pennsylvania and I'll be passing right through Bulee Creek."

"Wow, really?" I am more relieved than I care to admit. Maybe I can ask this man for a ride. Before I even ask, he offers.

"I'd be glad to give you a ride if you need one," he says. "Or are you with your parents?" He scans the back section of Big Green, but there's nobody else around.

I'm trying to think fast so this man doesn't get suspicious and wonder if I'm running away from home. "No, my parents are on a mission, and I have to get to my, uh, uncle in Bulee Creek."

The man raises his eyebrows and frowns at the same time. I've said something wrong. "On a mission?" he asks. "Are they in the church?"

"Yeah, well, uh," I fumble, feeling my face get hot. I stare at the map. "No. They're in the military." I didn't want to say that. What if he figures out where I come from?

But he doesn't seem suspicious or disturbed. He says, "Oh, sure, okay. Lots of folks around here work for the government. I guess that's why we've got such a big store, here, eh?"

"Can you show me Bulee Creek?" I ask, waving to the map.

He takes it from me, reads something on the back, then leans over it and shows me a tiny dot. "Right there."

"Where are we now?"

"Oh, we're in Georgia now. It's not on this map."

I can feel the blood draining out of my face. Georgia! When I hid in the back of the truck, the driver must've gone much further than I realized—in the wrong direction.

"How far is Bulee Creek from here?"

"Maybe five or six hours. You want to get going?"

I'm surprised and delighted. "Can you leave now?" I look around and again notice how empty the place is. It must be late. "I thought you worked here."

The man lifts his chin and laughs. I notice how his Adam's apple sticks out of his thin neck. "Oh, no," he says. "I'm a customer, just like you." He lifts the BIG GREEN bag that's in his hand and sticks out his other hand. "My name is Tom Smith, by the way." We shake hands—I've never done that in real life before. I've seen it only on vids. It makes me feel oddly grown up. His hand is warm and dry and a little crackly. "What's your name?" he asks.

"Sally," I say.

"Well, Sally, want to get going?"

"Yes, thank you." The relief I feel is enormous. I wonder how I could have gotten to Bulee Creek otherwise. I didn't even know I was in Georgia.

"Okay, come on," says Tom, smiling warmly, He holds out a polite hand to guide me onward. "My truck is right outside."

CHAPTER 25

We approach the automatic sliding glass doors, which I now realize must be controlled by a vidcam. I'm feeling foolish about being so amazed by the doors at first, when Tom says, "Sally, do you have money to pay for that jacket?"

I stop dead in my tracks and look down at myself. The warm, black, fuzzy jacket falls to mid-thigh over my sweats. I look up again. "No, ah, I forgot." But I wonder: How did Tom even know I picked up the jacket here? Did he see me earlier?

"Hm," he says, pointing to a large, black plastic device attached to the bottom of the soft fleece. I sling my backpack off, quickly pull the jacket off, and hold it out to him. What an idiot I am. Of course, you have to pay for things. It's like Oleson's Mercantile, the general store in *Little House on the Prairie*. This place isn't a warehouse. It's a really big general store, and you have to pay. I'm so embarrassed. This man Tom might think I'm a thief and refuse to give me a ride after all. "I'm sorry, I was so cold when I came into the store, I put it on and I forgot."

But Tom is nice about it. He smiles and shakes his head and waves a hand. "Oh, that's all right. It does get chilly at night sometimes, doesn't it?" He takes the jacket back to a counter where a bored woman stands, looking sleepy. Again, I try to Sense his mind, just to be sure he's not angry, but his control is even stronger than Mom's. I can't Sense anything. I watch as he pays for the jacket and the map, using dollars and change. I've never seen money before. Not in real life. I've never been in a store before, never seen automated sliding glass doors before, never seen a map of North Carolina before. What I don't know is mind-boggling. Thank God I've found somebody who can take me all the way to Bulee Creek.

The woman at the counter takes the plastic tag off the jacket and hands it to me. I thank Tom profusely as we get into his car. The leather seat actually warms up beneath me as the car starts. Tom pushes a couple of buttons and a woman's voice says, "Destination?"

"Bulee Creek, North Carolina," says Tom. The car rolls out of the parking lot. Tom turns and pulls something from the back seat. "You thirsty, Sally? I've got the world's yummiest drink back here." He turns forward in his seat again holding a large brown cylinder with an upside-down cup screwed on top. Some kind of bottle or container.

I am very thirsty, I realize, having eaten that dry sandwich. I'm getting hungry again too. "Do you have any water?" I ask.

Tom frowns apologetically and shakes his head. "I'm so sorry, but I think you'll like this. Everybody does. It's thirst-quenching and tastes good, too." He unscrews the cup and another plug, then pours something creamy into the cup.

"Oh," I say, "chocolate milk?" He's right, chocolate milk is a delicious alternative to water.

"It's a lot like chocolate milk," says Tom. He gets another cup, pours some for himself, and gives me the first one. "It's called White Chocolate Russian, my own invention. Try it." He clicks his cup to mine and takes a big sip, then motions for me to try it, too.

I smell it first. It does smell chocolatey and it looks like chocolate milk. I try a sip. It's sweet and delicious and has a funny burning sensation as it slips down into my belly. "Mmm," I say, taking another sip.

Tom grins. "Good, huh?"

I agree and drink the rest down. It doesn't exactly slake my thirst, especially because it's so sweet, but Tom says again that he has no water. He opens a small compartment in front of me that he calls the "glove" compartment and I start giggling because it has some plastic spoons and forks, a big spool of wire, another spool of heavy twine, scissors, tissues, and a package of cookies, but no gloves. "There's no gloves," I say.

"Here are the gloves," says Tom, also laughing. He opens another cubby between the two front seats and pulls out a pair of thin white plastic gloves. He lays them on what he calls the dashboard, then opens the glove compartment again and grabs the package of cookies, which we eat. They're buttery and crumbly and we get crumbs everywhere as we eat them, but Tom doesn't mind. The cookies make us thirsty all over again, so Tom pours us two more big cups of White Chocolate Russian. I drink mine more slowly this time because I'm getting sleepy, and I have to keep closing my eyes and leaning my head back between sips. The seat is so warm and my stomach feels warm, too.

"Tom," I say, "I think I'm falling asleep."

"Don't worry about it," he says, removing the cup from my hand. "Just take a nap. We've got hours before we get to Bulee Creek."

I don't know if he says anything after that, because consciousness folds in on itself as I drop into a well of sleep.

ooooo

I wake, shivering. Something hard is poking me in the back. The air smells damp. Above, black swirly lines spin in a circle, making me dizzy and nauseous. I shut my eyes hard, open them again, and stare at the lines until they stop moving. They look like tree branches.

A bright moon pierces the black sky. The moon, how amazing. I'm seeing the moon. I must be outside. The sides of the tree branches glint with moonlight. Wasn't I just in a truck? My mind feels limp and fuzzy. I was sitting next to that nice man, Tom. Going to Bulee Creek. In a warm seat.

I'm not warm now; I'm cold. My legs and belly are cold. And something's sticking into my back. I reach my hand under my jacket and feel dirt. A rock. I try to grab it but it's mostly buried. I press my hand flat against it, Sense its edges dimly, and manage to Jump it into my hand. A heavy, fat rock. I push it to the side.

To my left, there's a low grunt. I turn my head, immediately assaulted by spinning again. Something is wrong with me. Did Tom stop the car because I was sick? I open my eyes and, in the bright moonlight, see him on his knees spreading out a blanket on the earth. We seem to be in a small clearing under the trees. I can see nothing but darkness beyond.

"Tom?" I croak. He stops what he's doing, but doesn't turn. "What's…?" I clear my throat.

In one smooth motion, Tom rises, turns, and kneels next to me. He is not smiling. I still can Sense absolutely nothing in his mind—no emotions, no images. It's like he has no interior life at all. Weird.

"I'm going to put you on the blanket," he says, sliding his arms under my shoulders and knees. He lifts me in another smooth motion, turns, and lays me on the blanket. "You'll be more comfortable."

I try to sit up and again my head spins. "Tom, I'm cold. Why did we stop here? Did I get sick in the car? I'm so dizzy."

As if on cue, I vomit. I manage to lean over the edge of the blanket, but that's it. I puke up my guts, and it tastes disgustingly reminiscent of tangy chocolate and cream.

"Oh, my God," Tom says from behind me. "That's lovely. Lay back down again."

Not that I mean to, but I collapse back onto the blanket. That's when I realize my sweatpants are gone. No wonder I feel so cold. "Did I puke on my pants?" I ask.

He doesn't answer but drags the blanket—with me on it—about ten meters away from the puke. I can hardly move. "Tom," I say, "that drink you gave me was bad. It's making me sick."

His response is weird. He imitates my voice, but not really. It's more like he's squeaking in a fake cartoon voice. "Oh, Tom," he says, "that drink was so bad!"

A cold shock courses up my spine. For the first time, I actually look at him. His jacket is gone, his shirt sleeves rolled neatly halfway up his arms. He has sharply defined, heavy muscles. His face is smooth, impassive, his flat eyes steady and unblinking. Gone is the warm smile, the cocked head, the reassuring manner. Another shock passes over my entire being. I go even colder. On his hands are the white plastic gloves from his car.

"Tom, what's going on?" I ask, trying to sit up again, fighting the nausea, my heart hammering upward into my throat. I twist, trying to see further into the woods. It's utter darkness just past the clearing. "Where are we?"

As I turn, brushing my legs together, I feel flesh meet flesh. I think my underpants are gone, too. Another thrill of horror zings through my belly. This is so wrong. Why am I half-undressed? My voice curves up into a frightened shout, "Tom, where are my pants?"

"Just relax," he says. He walks around close to my head as I struggle to sit up. He kneels beside me and, with remarkable ease, pushes my shoulders down so I'm pinned to the blanket. "I said, relax."

CHAPTER 26

His voice is calm and firm, as if he were simply giving instructions. He pulls a spool of wire out of his pocket—the wire that had been in the glove compartment. Before I realize what he's doing, he's got his knee pressing my shoulder to the ground and he's wrapping the wire around my wrists.

"Hey," I shout, and it's as if I just woke up all over again. A surge of adrenaline shoots through me as I bend my knees, roll upside down, twist my free shoulder sideways and clunk Tom in the kidney with my kneecaps. I don't hit him very hard, but he goes *oof* and loses his balance, and I Jump myself away. Not far. Just the other side of the clearing. I pull the jacket down over my nakedness.

I don't know where I am or what's close by. I'm disoriented and still nauseous. My fingers tremble and my heart's banging in my chest. Three tight loops of wire around one wrist cut into my flesh. But the pain of it begins to clear my head. I can feel myself getting angry instead of terrified. I pull the wire off and drop it to the ground. "What the hell do you think you're doing?" I demand.

Tom comes to his knees, his face unrecognizable. His mouth pulls back into a wide, leering grin, almost a snarl, and his eyes strain open. He wrinkles his nose and laughs, shaking his head back and forth. Then he snuffs the air like an animal on the prowl.

Is this the same man I got into the truck with? It seems impossible. Has he gone mad? I'm still trembling, still sick from whatever drink he gave me. *This man tricked me,* I realize. Again, I've been tricked by lies and deception. The rage begins to rattle in my bones.

"Oh, ho, ho," he guffaws. "This girl likes to fight. You want to fight me, girlie?" Still on his knees, he holds up fists, weaving them in a circle. But he's jesting. With a sucking rush, his inner being flames to life. I can Sense his mind and see the images there: Him, on top of my trussed body, coupling with me as if I were a piece of meat. Another image: My body, twisted, broken, stripped of clothing. And another: My head bashed in and bloody.

Finally, I realize, standing straighter as my trembling subsides, *I have met a real enemy.*

A high-pitched whine or growl emerges from the man's mouth. He leaps to his feet and rushes me, crashing through the brush, his arms and legs pumping.

Molecules of air shift into alignment and swirl blade-like around me as I form a shield. I lift a hand and hurl the man backward, the air itself my hammer. He hits a tree, bounces off, and lands below it.

He's not dead, but he may be unconscious. I take a few minutes, feeling my body all over to make sure I haven't been assaulted. Which

I haven't. I'm lucky on that score. What if I hadn't woken up? I create a new rule: Never, ever eat or drink stuff from somebody you don't know.

I see a glimmer of something under a bush. My pants and underwear snagged on stiff brambles just meters away. I grab them, pull them on, and look around the clearing. I've got to figure out where I am, how to get out of here. I can Jump myself only to places I can see or I already know. I'm not even sure how far I can Jump myself. Going from my bedroom to the surface of the pod is as far as I've ever Jumped.

I throw my Senses wide, trying to touch everything around me, to find anything familiar. And the weirdest thing happens: I can Sense the trees. Like seeing a color that is a sound, humming, dreaming. They are joined together underground, like a living chord of barely different shades of green.

Then, a disharmonious note. Tom, rising to consciousness.

Images flicker through his mind: an empty room in a house. A dog, whining. An old woman with vague eyes. Then another image strikes me so hard, I catch a breath and clench my fists. A naked girl with long, red hair crawls away from him, sobbing, screaming as he gets closer. They're someplace in the woods that looks very much like this.

Oh, God. This is worse. He's done this before.

I wrap my arms around myself, shaking my head, my stomach still queasy. The rage is rising within me again. The whirling. Leaves around my body lift and tremble. I don't like it; I want self-control. *I am not a killer.* Then I see the girl again, crawling on the dirt away from him. I think: This man is a killer.

"Tom," I call into the darkness, my voice rising. "What did you do, Tom?" I can feel my hair begin to lift; a cold breeze springs up around me. "Did you hurt some other girl right here in these woods?" I shout. "Did you kill somebody?"

Out of the darkness, he comes hurtling, his feet pounding, eyes wide, his teeth clenched, his mind a dark, seething blur. His jacket has vanished. His shirt is ripped at the shoulder, stained with blood from his nose, and caked with dirt. Leaves fall from his hair. He's gripping a knife in his right hand, held low, ready to rip upward. He leaps so close, I can smell his foul breath as I rise to meet him. I shove him backward with a whip of wind. He spins before he lands on the ground with a thud.

And the knife is in my hand. I heft it, switch my grip so the blade points down. I trot over to Tom's supine figure, where he's struggling to catch his breath. I Jump. He grunts as my body materializes on top of him, my knees digging into his soft gut. I shove my forearm under his chin. His larynx juts out, and the tender skin pulsing over the carotid artery begs to be cut to the bone. But no. I plunge the knife down, once in each eye. All the way to the hilt, but quick. One, two, done. I Jump away. He'll never see me or any other girl again.

He grabs his face, screaming. His cries are obliterated by the roar of a truck passing not far to my right. I turn and see headlights through the trees. We're not far from the road. The sky is getting lighter, the trees becoming more distinct.

Now Tom is screaming words, a string of curse words, some I've never heard before. His hands fall away from his bloody face as he tries to peer through his ruined eyes. He covers them again.

I crouch to the ground ten meters away, back where I began. I wipe the knife on the blanket and look at it. It's a good knife, heavy enough for combat but slim enough to fold and keep in a pocket. I don't want to keep it, though. It will only remind me of this night. I hurl into the woods and hear more than see Tom leap and land with a crash, blundering and staggering toward where I threw the knife. "I'll kill you, you bitch," he's screaming. "I'll kill you with my bare hands."

He slows and swings his arms back and forth. It's awful, to see him like that. I recall the man, Tom, who seemed to be a good person. This man is barely human, gouged by a rot deeper than the wounds in his eyes.

Another truck passes, juddering the air. I turn and jog toward it. We're not far from the road. I can even smell the oily fumes.

Behind me, Tom is still screaming curses. They are more coherent now; he's screaming about how he's going to smash my head in. I glance back. He's blundering after me; he can hear the trucks. Another one passes by.

"You little bitch," he keeps screaming. "You can't get away from me. Nobody knows you're here." He stretches his arms out, waving wildly, both eyes squeezed shut, and trips over something.

I could kill him right now. Crush his heart and he'd stay down. Dad would tell me to do it. But just the thought of Dad makes me angry all over again. Who are all these men who kill people and order soldiers to kill people? What gives them the right?

Stubbornly, I keep jogging toward the road. I can hear Tom crashing through the brush behind me.

I start uphill and the trees end abruptly. As I top the rise, there's a grass verge and then the road. I believe dawn is beginning. Only a few meters away to my left, Tom's truck sits parked on the side of the road, its blacktop gleaming. Far beyond it, headlights approach. Another huge truck.

I Jump myself across the two-lane road and turn. Tom emerges from the woods, swinging his hands back and forth, limping heavily. As he steps on the grass, he squats down and touches it. He straightens and runs straight forward onto the road, waving his arms wildly. I'm ready to Jump myself further up the road, but again, he stops, stamps his foot on the road, then leans over and touches the hard surface.

"Help," he screams, first one way and then the other.

The huge truck is still coming and the sound of it begins to vibrate through the air. It gleams brightly, a hot spot of approaching light. I look up the other way. The sun is just edging over the road, making the black surface watery with light, the sky all purple and pink above it. The approaching truck goes silver in the glow.

Tom turns one way and then the other. He waves his hands around again, shouting, "Help."

The truck doesn't slow.

Abruptly, Tom whirls, then bends down and touches the road, his hand sliding back and forth. He must feel the truck's vibration. He slides his feet sideways, a sliding hop, and I realize he's searching with his shoes for the dirt on the side of the road. But he's sliding sideways on the road, not across it, but toward the truck instead.

It's pretty close now, still charging forward at top speed. It's a monstrous vehicle, a huge, metal rectangle on wheels, the windshield in front glaring with light.

Suddenly, a horn blares with a long, insistent blast.

Tom flings up his hands as if he could stop it. Brakes screech. Then Tom whirls and races back down the road in the other direction, ahead of the truck, his arms pumping.

The truck closes the meters between them, its horn braying nonstop; the air shatters with screeching and squealing. I think I hear Tom scream as he finally tries to dodge sideways, but it's too late.

I imagine the screams of the girls he has hurt. I Sense the desperate driver as he stands on the big truck's brakes, struggling to stop.

The driver's scream begins just as Tom's is cut short.

CHAPTER 27

The front end of the truck strikes and Tom's body sails into the air, tumbling up and over, arms and legs wide and flopping. Below him, the whole huge mass of metal screeches, burning, and skids sideways across both lanes. I Jump myself further up the road. The truck finally comes to a rocking halt not far from me.

Tom's body lands with a wet thud on top of the truck.

I probe for his mind gingerly. Nobody there. He's dead. I'm glad, and I'm glad I didn't kill him. He'll never hurt another girl again. More than anyone I've ever fought, this man deserved to pay the ultimate price. Yet, as I stand there in the sudden stillness, I feel desolate. Not about Tom being dead. I feel bad that Tom turned out to be so bad. I've seen vids of war; I learned about Hitler and Stalin and other vicious leaders. But I never knew ordinary people could be vicious, too.

Still screaming, the truck driver leaps out to the road and runs around the back of his truck, looking for the body.

"Oh, my God, oh, my God," the driver cries. He rounds the truck's front end searching the side of the road. I want to tell him he shouldn't be upset. It's for the best.

Then he sees me standing here, and he's running for me, speaking into a ristcom as he approaches. He's very round and short, wearing sweats and brown, fuzzy slippers. He gasps, "Are you all right?" He's in a panic.

He babbles, almost incoherent. "I didn't see—he was *right there*, all of a sudden, I don't know—the glare! Oh, what the fuck, oh my God—Was he your—Oh my God, I can't find him, did you see? Who was that man?"

He spins around wildly, runs a short distance away, and spins back. "Maybe I didn't hit him? Did I even hit him? I can't find him. Where is he?" He rushes back to me.

I feel sorry for this man, someone who cares so much about the death of a stranger. So unlike a soldier. I stretch out a hand. "It's okay," I say. "He was a bad man."

But the driver's not listening. Another vehicle, a small, blue passenger car, pulls up behind his truck and he whirls again. The road is impassible. The new driver, a tall man in a suit, seems to unfold himself from his small door. The truck driver runs for him, shouting, "I called emergency." They confer briefly and the tall driver speaks into his ristcom, also. The short man runs back to me.

"Are you all right?" he asks again, as if he hadn't already asked.

"I'm fine."

"Did you see? Did you see me hit that man?"

He's slightly more focused now, no longer panting.

"Yes," I say.

"Was he, I mean…" The driver looks back toward the road and his voice drops. "Was that your Dad?"

"Oh, no." I want to reassure this man, but I'm not exactly sure what to say. "He was chasing me."

The driver turns back to me. I can Sense his anxiety melting into a sick concern. "*Chasing* you?"

I nod. "He was a bad man. You shouldn't be upset. It's better he's dead."

The driver's eyes go wide and I can tell immediately I've said something wrong.

"Oh my God," he says. "How old are you?" He swallows, then says, looking at me very directly. "Did that man hurt you? Did he touch you?"

"He tried. But I ran away."

"Good for you."

"Don't be upset. He was a bad man."

"Are you all right?" the driver asks me a third time.

"I'm fine."

He turns to look at his truck. "Where…Did he run away? Is he dead? Where's his body?"

"On top of the truck."

The driver sucks in a breath, stares back at the truck. From where we stand, you can't see the top of the truck.

"I'm pretty sure he's dead," I add.

He lifts his eyebrows and stares at me with a peculiar look on his face. I Sense I've said something wrong again, and I change the subject, pointing up the long hill to my left, the direction we were traveling in. "Is Bulee Creek that way? Is it close?"

The driver's eyes slide to the side, then back to me. He nods. He's stuck somewhere between horror and surprise.

I'm so relieved I'm close to Bulee Creek. Of all the places Tom could have driven me while I slept in his truck, he drove here, just as he said he would. Maybe he struggled with himself before he gave in to his evil impulses. Maybe that good man I glimpsed back in Big Green before I got into his truck really did exist as part of Tom.

Another car pulls up behind the blue one. A woman gets out, and talks to the tall man standing there. The truck driver abruptly jogs toward them, waving a hand. "He's on top of the truck."

The woman, shaking her head, gets back into her car and turns it around while the truck driver confers with the tall man.

The sun is rising behind the woods and down the road. The orange and pink wisps of cloud fade into white. Sunrise, the first thing I ever saw outside. My heart still aches with the beauty of it. How could Mom and Dad force us to stay underground all these years, to know nothing, to understand nothing, while everyone else in the world saw the sun rise every day?

The tall man is climbing a metal ladder attached to the side of the truck. He peeks over the top, hesitates, then comes back down double-time.

A siren wails.

To my left, a black car with flashing lights tops the ridge and starts down the long hill toward the truck. Another flashing car crests the hill and starts down, and then a third, this one a red car, with no lights.

A thrill of fear shoots up my backbone. The black cars look just like the military vehicles at Fort Freedom. If they catch me, they'll return me to Mom. I spin around, looking for someplace to hide.

Halfway up the hill, the red car stops, rolls forward, then turns around in the road and starts back the way it came. Toward Bulee Creek.

I focus on a spot ahead of the car, crouch and Jump myself, so fast it's like hurling myself off a cliff.

But it works. I'm crouching beside the road, up the hill. I whirl, rising. The red car approaches slowly. The sirens, still wailing, make my heart pound. I put on my best smile and wave.

A woman in the driver's seat stops the car so fast that I can see her body jerk forward. Her eyes are wide and her mouth makes a little "o." I Sense she's rattled, but not scared. She's excited. I jog to the side of her car, the passenger side. The glass reflects trees and the rising sun. Then it lowers halfway down.

"You need help?" she calls out.

She's a big woman in a bright red jacket, with puffy black hair and a broad face, now pinched into a frown. Fast-moving images jumble through her mind: Me, the truck, the flashing lights, the inside of a store, a child crying, a large piece of meat, hands cutting potatoes, then me again.

"I didn't see you. Were you sitting down?"

I nod eagerly. "Yes, I need help. Can you give me a ride to town?" I point up the hill. "I've got to get to Bulee Creek."

I don't want to distract her, but I can't help a glance back down at the truck. Two people in white uniforms are climbing up the side of it. I can see Tom's body, splayed out face-down.

The woman twists backward to stare at the flashing lights and the truck and the body. She's lit up with curiosity. "Oh, golly! What *happened* down there?"

"I don't know, ma'am," I say, trying to get her attention again. "I'm trying to find my uncle in Bulee Creek?"

She looks back at me and I try to smile again. "It looks like somebody got *killed*!" she breathes.

"Oh, I don't think so," I tell her. One of the military vehicles turns around, pointing uphill. If the driver of that car looks, he could see me. Adrenaline spikes in my chest. I press my body to the car, trying to be invisible. "Can you take me, please, just to Bulee Creek?"

"Well, sure, honey, get in," she says, and I slide into the seat before she stops speaking, relief bathing my every nerve. She's still twisted around, staring at the scene below us.

"Is Bulee Creek far?" I ask, trying to recapture her attention. I need her to move. "Somebody told me it wasn't far. Will it take us long to get there? I need to get there as soon as possible."

She's completely ignoring me. "It looks to me like somebody got hit and killed down there. Is that a man on top of that truck?"

Two cars zoom by us on the other side of the road, going downhill. Not military, no flashing lights. They slow when they see the road is blocked. A voice booms through a handmic.

TURN YOUR CAR AROUND. THIS ROAD IS CLOSED. PLEASE TURN AROUND AND GO BACK. THIS ROAD IS CLOSED.

The two cars that passed us turn around and slowly drive up behind us.

"Oh, well," says the woman. She starts her car again and we roll forward. "I'll find out what happened soon enough. I'm Mrs. Ellison. My husband is Richard Ellison, the County Executive? Were you hitchhiking? Hitchhiking is illegal, you know, it's not safe. You shouldn't take rides from strangers, dear. It could be dangerous. Oscar, music."

The car seat is soft and warm, heated. Reminding me uncomfortably of Tom's truck. Soft piano music begins to play. I know piano music; Dad used to play audios for us in music class. Chopin. Liszt.

"That truck was practically turned over on its side. What happened?"

"I don't know. I heard a screeching noise and the truck slid sideways. I don't think it hit anything." How easy it is to lie!

"Well, it looks to me like somebody got hurt. And now the whole road's blocked, that's the main road out of town. I've got to call my husband. And you—uh—what's your name?"

"Sally," I say. "My name is Sally."

"Sally what?"

"What?" A trickle of panic zings me. I have no idea what she's talking about. I'm filled with a floundering feeling.

"Well, it's all right." Mrs. Ellison sniffs. "You don't have to tell me your last name if you don't want to."

I fumble with the idea for a moment. I understand two names. SamJay has a second name: Jones. Mom calls him Sergeant Jones.

"Jones," I say quickly. "Jones is my second name."

"Well, okay! How do you do, Sally Jones? Oscar, 40 miles per hour."

A deep voice from nowhere says, "Thank you, Mrs. Ellison.

Continuing on State Route 137 North, 40 miles per hour. Mrs. Ellison, what is your destination?"

I lurch against the seat belt and try to see into the back seat. "Who's that?" I immediately realize my mistake, but Mrs. Ellison seems to enjoy it. She laughs in a high, tinkly giggle, covering her mouth. "Oh, my goodness, Sally. Oscar is the car. His voice only came out two weeks ago. Isn't he dreamy?"

"Oh, yeah," I turn my face away. I can feel a hot flush rising up my neck. I'm constantly making mistakes; I'm better off saying nothing. "I didn't recognize the voice."

"Well, you're right. It's a custom voice. Where does your uncle live?"

"Bulee Creek," I say. Behind us, the two other cars are turn off onto another large road that cuts through the woods. There's nobody else behind us as far as I can see.

"That's the town, not the address, dear." Mrs. Ellison pats my shoulder. I nod and say nothing. "What street does he live on?"

"I don't know." I look at Mrs. Ellison with dread. Everything is so complicated. Will she realize something is wrong with me because I don't know my "uncle's" address like I didn't expect the car to talk to her?

"No problem," she says. And before I can even feel relieved, she adds, "What's your uncle's name?"

Panic flutters in my belly. "SamJay," I blurt out. Immediately, I know I've said something wrong. Again. That's not SamJay's official name, I'm sure of it.

"Well, I can't just find an address for 'Uncle SamJay'." She speaks slowly, now, deliberately, as if I might be very dense, or maybe someone who doesn't understand English. But I Sense she's amused, not suspicious. "What's his first name and his last name? Like your first name is Sally and your last name is Jones. Is your uncle's last name Jones?"

"Yes, yes." I grab her words like a drowning person grabs a lifeboat. "His last name is Jones. Sergeant Jones." Hazarding a glance at Mrs. Ellison, I see her nod and smile.

"So, Sergeant Samuel Jones. Oscar, find address. Sergeant Samuel Jones, Bulee Creek, North Carolina."

In about three seconds, Oscar's disembodied voice says, "I have three names in Bulee Creek, North Carolina. S. Jones, 375 DePew Street; Sam Jones, 26 Harrison Road; and Sergeant Samuel Jones, 222 Dogwood Lane. Which one would you like to see?"

I'm so surprised, my mouth drops open. Mrs. Ellison grins delightedly and shakes a finger at me. "See how easy that is? Now you have your uncle's address. 222 Dogwood Lane, Bulee Creek."

A thrill shoots through me. SamJay is close.

CHAPTER 28

As Mrs. Ellison says the address out loud, a blue light flashes upward from her ristcom. There's a map inside of it. "Oh, darn it. Off, Dragon. Dragon, off!" Before I can see the map, the light goes out and she grins at me. "I named my ristcom 'Dragon' and my husband named his 'Rider.'" She giggles again.

"Oh," I say, smiling, squeezing my fingers between my knees. I don't like this woman who giggles like a little boy. We pass a big sign on the side of the road: WELCOME TO BULEE CREEK POP 12,437. Still, nothing but trees on either side of us.

"Oscar: Directions. Sergeant Samuel Jones, Bulee Creek, North Carolina," Mrs. Ellison says in a firm, clear voice.

Oscar says, "Yes, Mrs. Ellison. Go straight on State Route 137 for two-point-zero-three miles and turn left onto Plains Road." A map flashes up on a vidscreen embedded into the car's dashboard. I'm so close. I can see SamJay's home, a red dot on the screen, marked in tiny, white letters, 222 Dogwood Lane.

Oscar speaks again. "There is a militia car behind us, Mrs. Ellison."

Anxiety twists back into my gut and I turn. "Oh, no," I whisper. A black car with flashing lights approaches fast from about half a kilometer behind us. I push my chin into the back of the seat. "Um, Mrs. Ellison? What's 'militia?' Is that military?"

Mrs. Ellison waves a hand. "Oh, no, don't worry. They're not the military. They all work for my husband."

I watch the flashing lights get closer. Buildings line the street on both sides of the road. No more forest. To our right, all different colors of cars sit parked in a row, long cords running from them to white posts.

The black car pulls up close behind us, the flashing lights blinking inside Mrs. Ellison's whole car. "Oh, my goodness, Oscar, pull over." The car stops immediately.

"Please keep going," I say.

"We can't do that!" Mrs. Ellison shakes her head and glares at me with disapproval. I've said something wrong again. "That's against the law."

"Oh, right," I say, scooting as low as I can in my seat. The lights stop flashing.

"Uh-oh. My husband is going to be sooo angry if I get another ticket! But I'm sure I wasn't speeding." Mrs. Ellison leans across me and opens the glove compartment, fumbling for something, her ristcom visible. Behind us, a car door opens and slams.

Mrs. Ellison grabs a plastic card from the glove compartment and clicks it shut. As she turns to her window and begins to lower it, I Jump her ristcom into my hand and Jump myself out of the car.

Then I'm crouched behind one of the colorful cars. A militia woman dressed in a blue uniform approaches Mrs. Ellison, who holds her card up for the woman to look at. The woman touches her hat and smiles, taking a step back.

I can catch only stray words. I know I hear, "Sally." Mrs. Ellison looks at my empty seat and calls for me, then throws her hands up, still talking.

They *are* looking for me. That's all I need to know.

Over my shoulder, I see a vacant lot, then another building. I Jump. There's open land behind the next building, and I Jump again. More open space behind buildings, and I Jump again. I've never Jumped myself in rapid succession like this before. It feels a little dizzying, like I'm falling, but it works. I run around to the far side of the building, where I finally stop in a small alley.

On one side is a brick wall, the other, a tall brown wooden wall. Big green cans line both sides of the alley. The smell of garbage hangs in the air. I lean my back against the brick wall and open my left hand.

Mrs. Ellison's ristcom.

I immediately remember Tom paying for my jacket. I cringe. Stealing again.

"Dragon," I say. "Directions. 222 Dogwood Lane, Bulee Creek, South Carolina."

An image pops up immediately, hovering right over the ristcom. My relief is almost incapacitating; my knees feel weak. I'm almost at SamJay's. The ristcom image displays a red dot with "222 Dogwood Lane" next to it. There's also a static, dark green dot and a green arrow.

I think the green dot is me. And the green arrow points where I need to go. But it's right back toward Mrs. Ellison and the militia cars.

"Turn left," says a musical female voice.

Hastily, I stuff the ristcom into my pocket and jog around the back of the building through weeds and shards of broken green glass. Soon I see more houses on my right, and a wall angles in, cutting off the space behind the buildings. I turn into the last alleyway and slowly peek out onto the street.

"Turn left," says the musical voice from my pocket. Dragon's voice.

Mrs. Ellison's red car is gone, and so is the militia car. But I doubt "left" is a safe direction—not yet, anyway. I'll have to circle around. I cross the street as fast as I can walk without running.

At least half a kilometer later, I pull the ristcom back out of my pocket again. The directions flash up immediately. The voice says, "Turn left and proceed for point zero three miles."

I turn left. This street looks different, with plenty of buildings and a wide walkway. It's still early, but some people are on the street. A car rolls toward me, but it's silver, not black. All of the buildings on either side of the street have big windows, though some have boards over them. More stores, much smaller than Big Green. I pass one window with weird statues of faceless people draped in dresses and scarves, then another with colorful balloons, toys, and huge stuffed animals behind the glass. Teetu would love one of those furry elephants.

"At the corner, go right," urges Dragon's gentle voice.

In the next street, small homes crowd close together, with low fences and flowers growing in boxes. Cars line both sides of the street. I'm awed. It's a perfect image of the time before.

My shoulders finally unbunch. I'm pretty sure I've lost the militia car, and now the excitement of finding SamJay builds. It's not so far from here. The ristcom says 1.7 miles.

A woman, dressed in a dark suit, comes out of one of the houses and descends the porch steps, then freezes and looks up. Not at me, but beyond.

There's a *whoop* from behind me. My scalp burns hot. Militia car. I don't even need to look. I keep walking fast, my mind in a panic, trying to think of someplace to Jump.

A voice booms down the street. A handmic. THIS IS THE BULEE TOWN MILITIA. STOP WHERE YOU ARE. WE NEED TO SPEAK TO YOU.

My skin crawls as I Sense someone sighting me through a scope. My shield spins impervious air around me as I panic. My shield won't keep someone from grabbing me. I have to Jump away. But where? *Think*, I scream at myself. I stop short, keeping my back to the approaching car. Bowing my head, I cross my arms over my chest and squeeze my eyes shut.

I am a part of all things, and all things lift me toward the center. I blow out a deep breath and level my shoulders, willing my muscles to relax. I can do this. *I rest in light. My spirit flows forth unencumbered.*

The place flashes up in my mind, the big window with the sweet little toys and balloons behind it. I call up its *thisness*. I Jump.

A young woman is busy unlocking the front door of the building from the inside as I appear. She startles as she opens the door, but then smiles and waves at me.

"Good morning. Come on in." She has long black hair like mine, warm smiling eyes with dark lashes. "Sorry you had to wait."

I force myself to smile back, my heart still racing; my cheeks crack like they're made of hardened glue. "Thank you."

The *whoop* of another militia car bounces off the walls and I hurry after the woman into the shop. The door closes just before the car cruises by.

"Are you looking for anything special?" As she speaks, the woman straightens small, plastic figures on the counter, her fingers long and delicate.

"Um, for my little sister," I say, glancing back to the street. Empty.

The woman smiles again, cocking her head, her delicate, oval face full of fun. "Oh, so many great toys for little girls. How old?" She pushes her long hair back, and again, I feel struck by our similarity. My thoughts turn bitter: *She might've been my older sister, if I'd been normal. I might've worked with her in this beautiful toy place, safe and peaceful.* What am I, instead? Somebody's military experiment.

I have to force my thoughts into the moment. Stop feeling sorry for myself. "She's five. Maybe something like the elephant? In the window?"

The shopkeeper chats pleasantly about toys and children as she walks to a section of the store packed with soft, fuzzy, colorful animals.

I look out the window again. The militia car is back! It stops right outside. Two officers get out and head straight for the toy store.

Heart thudding, I duck behind the pile of toys, pretending to examine one on a low shelf. A bell jingles.

I hear, "Can I help you?"

"We're looking for a girl," says one of the officers. He mumbles something more.

Outside, a tall, light gray car creeps past the militia car. I can see and Sense the driver, an old man with thin, white hair who peers curiously into the toy shop. I can see him well enough to…

"Oh yes, she's right here," says the shopkeeper.

…to Jump. The old man cries out when I appear from nowhere in his front seat. He throws himself against his door, hands raised. The car shoots forward and an Oscar voice calls out, "Emergency. Engage autodrive. Emergency. Engage autodrive."

The car crosses the street at an angle ahead of the militia car and hits another vehicle. Horns clamor and an alarm begins to blare.

As I'm thrown forward, I Jump. Just down the block, as far as I can see. Behind me, people are shouting. The militia car *whoops* again.

Again and again, I Jump myself as far as I can see, fear driving me to the next corner, to the next street, and beyond. I run and Jump, I'm not sure how many times before I stop.

Sweat drips down my back and I'm panting. I stand on the side of a wide street, with a long strip of grass in the middle of it. A few cars drive sedately. No more militia.

There are fewer homes here. Behind me, stretches of grass give way to bushes and trees. Only one house in the distance. Another car drives by. Nobody looks at me. Maybe I've gotten away. For now, at least. Fingers trembling, I pull the ristcom out of my pants pocket.

The small round device is completely quiet now, no map, no voice. The screen is black. I look around again. If it doesn't work, I have no clue which way to go. I clear my throat and say, "Dragon. Directions. 222 Dogwood Lane, Bulee Creek, North Carolina."

To my relief, the ristcom wakes and flashes up a map, just as before. "222 Dogwood Lane, Bulee Creek, North Carolina. Go straight 1000 feet and turn right onto Peachtree Drive."

There's no one around and I break into a slow jog as I continue to follow the directions for about ten minutes. Still no militia vehicles. Now smaller houses appear on the side of the road, and some small parked cars. The further I go, the faster I run. I need to find SamJay and get off the streets.

"Go straight point-zero-two miles," said Dragon. "Then, turn right onto Dogwood Lane."

A thrill shivers through me. I'm almost there, less than a kilometer. I pick up my speed and race flat out for Dogwood Lane, flying as I take the corner.

Dogwood Lane. The house on my right has a number outside on a box on a wooden post: 527. All the homes here are evenly spaced, with neat grass and flowers and trees in front of each. More boxes mounted on posts display numbers. As I jog on, the numbers decrease.

I can see it. House number 222. It's white with dark green trim and a front porch with a swing on it. Then I'm running up the steps to SamJay's porch. I bang on the door with my fist.

Immediately, SamJay throws it open. His lip and eye are still swollen from the beating he got in the pod. But he's alive. "Eten," he says. I throw my arms around his neck, my eyes squeezed shut. I've never been happier. I've never felt safer. Finally, I'm here. SamJay will know what to do.

He hugs me back, pushing the door shut behind me. Relief crashes over me. It's like I've come to the end of a long swim. I'm completely exhausted. I'm about to ask him if I can just sleep for a while when he mutters, "Eten, I'm so sorry."

I jerk my head up and stare at SamJay, my eyes bleary with tears. "It's okay." I think he's talking about how Mom fake-killed him right in front of me. He pretended to be dead. "It's all right. I know Mom pretended to kill you."

"Yes, she did." He steps aside. The joy filling my body vanishes, replaced by horror at what I see standing there.

Mom.

CHAPTER 29

Mom holds up her hands. "Don't Jump."

I twist away from SamJay. He looks anxious and I can Sense his guilt. "What did you do?" My voice is filled with tears. The bottom vanishes from my world.

"I didn't—" he begins.

At the same time, Mom says, "I'm not—"

"How could you?" I shout at SamJay.

Viscous, black rage suffuses my being, every molecule of my body tensile and electric. SamJay, my last hope—my only hope—here with my worst enemy. After what she did to him! After what she and Dad did to me. I can't even trust SamJay.

A wind rushes up inside the broad, white room and down a side corridor, rattling pictures and doors. Nothing, absolutely nothing I have ever believed in is real.

"No, Eten," cries SamJay. "You don't understand."

"How could you do this to me?" I scream.

The wind curls back on itself with a roar. A lamp smashes off a table, and all the knick-knacks, papers, pens, yarn, books, magazines, and everything in the living room swirls upward, crashing into the walls.

Two sharp metal rods trailing yarn shoot by like arrows, pierce the wall and stick there, quivering. Something heavy and metallic in the adjacent room begins to rattle.

The whole room is alive with violence, and I'm rising through the center of it, a lightless vortex.

"Eten," SamJay shouts again, "stop! Let me talk to you."

The time for talking is done. What does it matter? I've been tricked and betrayed all my life. I'm nothing but a weapon. Not a person like other people. Not a girl like other girls.

Every light in the room sparks and explodes. The furniture trembles and creaks. The wind rushes around me faster, booming and shrieking.

"All you do is lie," I scream. "Everyone lies."

"Calm down and listen," shouts SamJay, crouching against the whirling blast of air. Mom's on the floor, holding an arm over her face.

"It's not what you think!" shouts Mom. Her voice catches and echoes through the maelstrom as she tries to say my name. "*Eeeeeee…*"

I could destroy them all; I *will* destroy them all. Who can match my power? "I hate you!" I bellow.

An armchair blows upward and crashes into the ceiling. Debris shatters off the ceiling and shoots sideways into the whirlwind.

"Eten, let me explain," shouts Mom, trying to edge away. "I'm not—"

Another blast of wind flings Mom back up against the wall, pinning her there. "You!" I tilt closer to Mom. "What did you do to me?"

Mom's eyes squeeze shut, her cheeks and mouth rippling under the force of the pummeling air, arms and legs splayed out, the wind pushing her deep into the blank white wall with bruising force.

Mom tries to drag in a breath.

"Eten, stop it," SamJay shouts from behind.

I don't care about SamJay anymore. I'm going to break Mom, beat her like she beat SamJay. Then I'll leave SamJay forever. I'll get my brothers and sisters and together, we'll blast all the new guards to a bloody pulp and just leave.

A door behind me slams open and a high-pitched voice screams, "Uncle Sammy!"

I whirl.

A little girl stands at the end of the long hallway. Her dress and hair blow backward in the fierce wind. She tries to move, her small fists punching out at the air.

"Letitia, get back inside," SamJay roars, struggling against the wind. Something big and black strikes him in the shoulder and he falls.

"Uncle Sammy," she screams again, "I'm coming."

She looks so much like Teetu.

A man I've never seen before struggles out of the room. "Letitia, no," he calls, stretching out an arm. The wind catches and slams him sideways as he reaches for the child.

It's the little girl from Fort Freedom, coming to save her friend, her "Uncle Sammy." She is so strong and so innocent. Children believe whatever you tell them. She could've been me, once upon a time.

Everything is quiet. I realize the wind has dropped. A cone of silence surrounds me, a silo of hesitation.

The man crouches next to his little girl, gathers her into him, whispering.

"Eten," says SamJay, panting. "I didn't call your mom. They were tracking you."

It's SamJay's friend, Darius, and his little girl. They were hiding from me in the back room. The child stares back at me unafraid, her small face twisted into a mighty frown, her little hands still curled into fists.

Out of everyone in the house, she's the only one who's not afraid.

"What's your name?" I ask her.

"Ticha."

"Ticha, did you ever get so mad, so really angry, you broke something you love?"

The child nods her head up and down. "I broke Lolly."

"That was her doll," says her father, smoothing back Letitia's hair. His fingers are trembling. In the open door, I see the woman from Fort Freedom, the one who'd come to pick up SamJay. Julia. She peeks out, the two other children crowding behind her. They were hiding from me.

"I'm sorry," I say, the rage draining from my body. From the crown of my head through the soles of my feet, it drains right down through the floor, leaving me hollow. SamJay's friends are afraid of me, and I feel miserable. "I'm so sorry."

CHAPTER 30

SamJay escorts his friends out the front door, then comes back to me. "Your mom just showed up. Not long before you. My friends were visiting, and…"

Mom breaks in, making me clench my teeth. "We tracked the ristcom you stole."

My heart sinks. Of course they did. How stupid can I be? I know nothing.

"Besides, I knew you'd head for Sergeant Jones," she continues. "Where else could you go? Then I heard about the truck accident near here. There were police reports of a girl."

As angry as I was before, I feel just as crushed now. Why did I think I could outwit Mom? Escape? I must've been crazy.

"Come on," says SamJay. I drag my feet as he leads us back into the living room. It's wrecked and I cringe as I survey the damage. When will I learn to control myself?

"Oh, my God," I say. "I'm sorry."

"Come on," SamJay repeats. He turns the armchair right-side up, brushes glass off the sofa. "It can be fixed, Eten." He urges Mom and I to sit, though I don't know if I can sit in the same room with her. I stand in front of the window stare at the floor.

"Listen," says Mom, "we have to move quickly. Before Duroc knows you escaped. We have a plan, and the generals want to help…"

A plan? I'm through with Mom and her plans. "How could you do this to me?" I turn and glare at her, tasting bitterness. I'm not sure which, of all the things she's done, I'm most angry about. "Fake shoot SamJay? How could you do that?"

"I'm sorry." She shakes her head, her pale face red from impact on one side, blood oozing from her nose. "I was trying to make sure you wouldn't…" She looks around. "Do this." Brusquely, she wipes her nose with her cuff.

She's dressed in civilian clothes, dark pants with a black turtleneck. Maybe it won't show the blood. Her hair has fallen around her face, making her look younger. "Okay, I've been harsh," she continues. "I know it. But Eten—you had to obey me. Obey without question, without hesitation. They're always watching us on the vidcams."

"They who? You're always watching us."

Mom shakes her head. "The generals. Dr. Duroc. They're always watching me, Eten. Me and Dad."

That lands on me with a boom. "You and Dad? The generals?"

"And Duroc. He's the United States Undersecretary of Defense." I see in her mind that same image of the man with the crooked teeth. "He's more powerful than the president. He *created* Project Samson.

You children have to obey me one hundred percent," she says.

"Or what?" I break in, feeling belligerent again. "We get the wand?"

Mom shakes her head. "Or be terminated," she says exasperated. "Don't you see that's why I had to be so harsh? I tried so hard to control you. Because there was always that risk, from the very start."

I sit, the wind and fury all blown out of me. I think of the dead babies. Of course they'd terminate us. They'd done it before.

"Can you show her the memo, Sam?" says Mom.

SamJay sits next to me on the couch and pulls a crunched-up ball of paper from his pocket, smooths it out on his knees, and holds it up. "This is the memo you took from your mom's desk. You remember?"

My eyes widen and shift to Mom. She nods. She knows I rifled her office. It's that paper with KILL ORDER at the top. *Emergence of disturbing adolescent behavior*, it begins.

"Here," says Mom. She crosses the debris-littered floor carefully and slides another page on top of the first. "This is the second page."

My eye skips automatically to the bottom where the words are dark black: <u>termination of subject E-10, age sixteen, is herewith recommended</u>.

It's like a punch in the gut, and I gasp. "What?" I whisper with a dry throat.

Mom hands something to SamJay which he takes and unfolds. "This is the original, complete memo," he says. "Let me read some of it to you." He clears his throat as if preparing for a speech. "Subject E-10 was insubordinate, argumentative and violent," he reads from the memo, "delayed vital action and expressed frustration with orders. This is only the beginning of a predicted, adolescent rebellion. No doubt it will be worse in the male subjects, once they mature. A kill order is recommended."

The words shock me so deeply, I reel back. I'm floating somewhere behind my body, my bones as heavy as concrete. *Insubordinate. Adolescent rebellion.* They'd kill me for insubordination?

"The threat was always hanging over us," says Mom. "I think Duroc's always been scared of you. From the beginning. He started Project Samson when he was just a young researcher at DARPA. And he told me, at first, some babies killed scientists. Infants!"

"Scared of me?" I shudder, involuntarily picturing the baby so like Teetu with the bullet hole in her head. "They should've just stopped the experiments."

"Well, that was before my time," Mom says. "Duroc instructed me that if you got out of control, he'd terminate you. I hadn't even seen you yet. I didn't realize you were just a baby!"

In the memo, Duroc calls me "it." Not she, not they. "He doesn't even think I'm human."

Mom lifts her chin, points a finger at me, then drops her hand to her knee. "Listen. I know I'm crap as a mom. All I ever thought about was trying to keep you five under control. But I'm going to tell you one thing. I am a good soldier and a good commanding officer. And the U.S. military does not assassinate its own." Her eyes flash. "I will not be part of it." She stands up, strides to the window and back, and stops in front of me. "We're better than this. Our country is better than this. I'm not going to do it anymore. I'm not participating in this shit." She flicks a hand at the memo.

I shake my head and look to SamJay. I don't know what this means. "Can I just stay here?"

"You're not safe here," says Mom. "SamJay wouldn't be safe either. And there's something else. Your brothers and sisters aren't safe, either."

My heart thunders as I stand up. "What do you mean?"

SamJay puts a hand on my shoulder and simply begins to read from the memo again. "With a ready supply of subjects, employment at age five and termination at age thirteen will be a viable paradigm. It gives us a promising eight-year window of complete control."

Now my whole body begins to tremble and, abruptly, I drop to the sofa. I lean toward Mom and whisper, "What does that mean? Termination at thirteen? Mom. *The boys.*"

Mom holds up a hand, flat. "Stop. Not yet. Duroc won't do anything yet, and we're going to take control. The generals and I have a plan." She takes the memo from SamJay, then shows me another paragraph. "See here, about cloning? He's got to wait at least five years. As long as the boys don't do anything stupid, they're safe."

Yeah, stupid like me. How likely is that? I don't even understand what she's pointing to. "What's cloning?"

Mom tries to explain it to me, turning this way and that, spinning her hands and fingers around, which is totally unhelpful: DNA. Double helix. How each person has an individual genetic code; how the placement of one person's DNA in a human egg can create a copy. How Duroc is going to put my DNA in somebody else's egg and create another me.

"He wants to copy me?" I laugh sharply. "That's insane." I'm furious that someone could do this to me. I'll have my own babies when I'm ready, not when some man decides to *copy* me! "I won't let them have my genetic code."

Mom rolls her eyes and sits back down on the big blue chair. "Eten, they already have it. It's in your blood, your skin, in every part of your body. And as Duroc's clone babies grow up, they'll replace you—not just you—your brothers and sisters, too. As you grow older and you discover the truth and rebel against him, he can just terminate you and still have his special little army."

SamJay had begun to pace, and now he turns, wiping his mouth and chin as if rubbing off grease. "He's a monster."

"How could you work for him?" I demand from Mom. "How could you help him?"

"This was never the plan. Eten, please believe me. I would never agree to this. Listen, if you come back with me now—"

"Go back?" I squeak. I stand up and, for a moment, consider Jumping myself away. Away, anywhere but here.

At the same time, SamJay steps forward. "No," he says as he puts a hand on my shoulder. The weight of it makes me feel grounded. I'm solid. She can't make me.

"Just listen," says Mom. "We can get rid of Duroc for good. But I need your help."

I eye Mom dubiously. No doubt her plan will be dangerous—for me. But to be rid of that monster forever? It might be worth the risk. "What?" I ask.

Mom's expression becomes animated. Her pale cheeks flush and her hands wave excitedly. Her mind is open like never before. "There's a mission Duroc has to get done. At the Hague World Court, there's a very important prosecutor who's going to charge the United States with war crimes. Duroc wants to terminate her. We're going to tell

Duroc only you can do it. But instead, when you get there, you're going to deliver evidence to the prosecutor that will finish Duroc."

"What evidence?" asks SamJay.

"Proof of Duroc's guilt. All of those memos, those files and folders, those horrible, preserved fetuses," says Mom. "Why do you think I kept all that? It's my insurance. My proof. I knew someday I'd need it." Her face lights up in a peculiar way I've never seen before. She looks triumphant.

"What am I supposed to do?" I ask, suddenly more eager. The image of what I saw in Mom's storeroom stokes me into simmering anger.

"It's too dangerous," SamJay breaks in.

"Wait. Maybe I can do it," I say.

"I can hide her," he says.

Mom stands up, her voice rising. "Really, Sam? You're going to hide her from the whole U.S. military? Besides, you think she's going to leave her brothers and sisters behind?"

SamJay tightens his mouth and looks away, wordless.

"Tell me the plan," I say.

CHAPTER 31

Dr. Duroc reminds me of the desert in South Kongolia. He's tall and cadaverous. His desiccated white skin contrasts with an oily smile. Tendons stand out from his neck when he turns his head. His short white hair stands straight up. I decide he looks like a vulture.

"Come in," says Dr. Duroc with the wave of a hand, standing at the door of our living room as if he owns the whole pod. *Maybe he does,* I think.

I can Sense my brothers and sisters, gathered in the bedroom. They sit, tense, Sensing us. Mom and Dad explained the plan to them because it involves all of us. For the first time, we stand together as a real family against the madness of this tyrant, Duroc.

All weekend, we talked about the plan. Gefor finally got over being mad at me and insisted I should just terminate Duroc. Then we got into another fight when I explained to him how stupid that idea was, how it would solve very little and just be another murder. Gethre and the girls wanted me to forget the plan, for us all to escape together and keep running. But they have no clue how complicated the world is—we'd never make it. Mom's plan is the best option. We have to turn the tables on Duroc and be able to control our own lives.

One really good thing—something between Mom and me has changed. She listens to me. She thinks about what I say. Dad seems different, too, bolder and more in charge.

In the living room, he sits at a table with some unfamiliar men, but he's not smiling nervously or joking. His mind is still. By their insignia, I recognize two of the strangers as generals. There's also a square, fleshy, civilian male with thick, white hair.

"E-10," says Duroc. He frames my whole being with those words. "Care to join us?"

I've been hesitating in the doorway. Mom presses me forward. I sit next to Dad and Mom sits next to me. Dad stands and introduces me to everyone—the big civilian is a senator—then he sits back down, sipping a bottle of water, eyes fixed on me.

The next few minutes will decide our fate. Dr. Duroc doesn't trust me. And he shouldn't. I hate him. His mind slithers like a bunch of snakes. The generals are trying to convince him to send me out on one more mission. The mission in which I'm going to destroy him.

"I've been told," says Duroc, "that you are a very good soldier." His face is a mask of benevolence.

I force the corners of my lips to turn up. "Thank you, sir. I hope so."

This whole meeting is all about making Duroc trust me again.

"Do you like being a soldier?"

"Yes, sir. I sure do. I've been a soldier all my life." I have to convince him, but can I fool Duroc? They say he's brilliant, a genius. "I feel it's the thing I'm best at. More than anything in the world, I want to defend our country and make America great again, sir. It's what I was born to do."

Maybe I'm laying it on too thick. I don't dare glance at Mom or Dad. I look straight at Duroc's grey, flat eyes like they told me to.

But Duroc seems pleased. I Sense his mind slow and his mood soften. He blinks.

"What you were born to do, eh?" He leans forward with an eager smile. "Why do you say that?"

I swallow hard. I said it because it's true. I was created and raised to be a weapon. But I can't tell Duroc I know this.

"I just really love my country, sir, and…and…well, it's so easy for me to fight. I'm a natural-born fighter. I just Jump the guns. I can just crush a heart, just like that."

I snap my fingers above the table and Duroc's head jerks back. A thrill zings me. He *is* afraid of me.

"And I'm really angry at all those terrorists who destroyed America." The words come more easily now. "They killed all our people in the nuclear war, and now they keep trying to take over and hurt us even more, so I'm really glad to fight and make sure we win."

Duroc nods, glancing at Mom.

I risk a quick look.

Mom is nodding, too, a smile plastered to her face.

"All I need are your orders, sir," I say, hoping to draw attention away from Mom. "I'm just waiting for orders for my next mission and I know I'll ace it."

"Orders." Duroc makes a laugh that is not a laugh. "You didn't follow orders so well in South Kongolia, did you?"

I can't hide the sick feeling that comes over me. He saw the vid from South Kongonlia. I Sense the images in Duroc's mind: Dad flying back against the wall in the travel pod. The vortex that is me. Dad with blood on his face.

"She was just upset—" Dad begins, but Duroc holds up his hand, staring hard at me.

"Let's see what E-10 has to say. What about that argument with your *dad?*" Mockery colors his voice. Because Dad is not my "true" dad, my sperm dad. As if that matters to me.

I concentrate on being small, on being a child again. "I am so sorry." My voice comes out high and quiet. "I know what I did was wrong. I haven't lost control like that in a year, more than a year." I let my voice get choked up as I look up at Dad. "I'm so sorry, Dad. You know I love you and Mom, I'd never do anything—"

"Shhhh," says Dad, putting his hand on my shoulder. He's actually tearing up! What an actor. "I know, I know."

"I think we've heard enough," says one of the generals. "General Grasbach and I agree she's committed, and Lieutenant Colonel Nowak says she's the only one of them that can do this mission."

"That's right," says Mom.

Duroc's pale eyes drill into me once more. "Are you ready?"

"Sir, yes, sir," I say, saluting.

"Are you ready to follow orders?"

"Yes, sir."

"This will be dangerous."

"I can do it, sir."

Duroc explains to me that I have to fly to Netherdeutsch, to the city of Arnhem, where the international Hague Court was relocated after half the Netherlands drowned in rising seas. The Hague is about to put the United States of America on trial.

I know all of this from Mom and Dad, but I pretend it's the first time I've heard it.

"Some rogue groups," says Duroc, "have dared to accuse America of poisoning thousands of people with an unregistered nuclear waste dump near Zinder, Niger."

With everything I'm finding out lately, I'm guessing that might be true.

"You'll meet a contact who will get you into the world court. As soon as you're there, terminate a prosecutor named Yara Bakker." He passes me two large pictures. The contact is a thin man in a business suit with black hair and big ears. Yara Bakker is short and heavy, with short brown hair and a sagging face. She looks tired.

"She's anti-American and she'll bury us if she can," says Duroc. "If you see any Nigeran witnesses, terminate them too."

"Yes, sir," I say, resisting the urge to look at Mom.

Our plan to destroy Duroc depends on me disabling Duroc's contact. Mom's contact, a young woman, will take me directly to Yara Bakker so I can give the prosecutor documents and vids to prove Duroc is trying to assassinate her.

The news will go 'viral,' meaning everyone will see it, and create an international incident. President McCarthy will have to suspend Duroc from his position pending investigation. And the generals will take over Project Samson.

As I listen to this arrogant, cruel man who wants to terminate me, I think about exploding his head. It would be so much easier. I'm not tempted—I don't want to hurt anybody. But I have to force myself to remember my argument with Gefor, in which I insisted it was a stupid idea. It doesn't seem so stupid right now.

"Are you ready for this?" he asks me again, for the millionth time.

"Yes, sir."

Another presence reverberates so violently inside my head, I stifle a gasp. Teetu. I can Sense her in the other room. Anxiety shoots through me again. I can't tell what's happening.

A shout splits the air behind us, a guard's voice. Teetu bursts in through the living room door, followed by the boys and Jaysx. Duroc's guards trail behind.

One of the guards grabs Jaysx's shoulder; the next second he's lying stretched out on the floor.

Everyone jumps to their feet.

Teetu signs fiercely at Mom and Dad, her eyes big, her mouth open. She spits stuttering, inarticulate noises. The boys and Jaysx crowd up behind her. It's hard to catch her words, she's signing so frantically. "Tricking. He's tricking you. Dangerous, bad, he's planning something…"

"Dad," shouts Gefor, "Eten can't go. Teetu says that man…"

Duroc roars, "What's the meaning of this?"

The generals start yelling. The senator flattens himself against the far wall.

Teetu blares in my consciousness with images of my own destroyed body, blood, my dead eyes staring out of my face. I grunt like I've been punched. Her power with Sensing is getting stronger than anything the rest of us can do.

From the hallway, a bodyguard leaps over the other, prostrate guard and points his gun at Gefor, who's still shouting warnings to Dad. General Grasbach, legs wide, points a service revolver two-fisted at Teetu. The senator crushes his water bottle and tries to hide beside the glass China cabinet.

Already, I'm next to Teetu, my shield all around us. Gethre disarms the general and the guards, Jumping their pistols into our bedroom.

Don't these men know we can't be shot? They're supposed to be in charge of us.

"Shhhh," I whisper to Teetu. "Shhhh, it's all right."

"What's this about," Duroc growls at Mom.

"Calm down, Teetu, you're making it worse," I whisper.

"He's going to trick you," she signs.

Mom looks grim; suspicion swirls inside of her. "I'm not sure what this is about, Dr. Duroc. Are you planning something the rest of us don't know about?" Though I'm afraid the whole plan is about to fall apart, I'm kind of thrilled with Mom. Calling out Duroc? That's brave.

"Don't you have any control here?" demands one of the generals, looking at Dad.

Mom turns her head towards us. "Sit down," she says, and all of us sit on the floor.

Duroc takes a step toward Teetu. "So you think I'm planning something? You *Sensed* something?" He doesn't sound angry; he's curious. "Or did you *hear* something?"

I tighten my arms around my sister, wondering a little myself. How much can she actually Sense? "Leave her alone." I glare up at Duroc. "She's just a child." I mutter to Teetu in a low voice, "You have to stop. I have to go on this mission."

All eyes snap to Duroc. His face is as blank as a stretch of barren sand. Behind his eyes, there is a decision, but I can't Sense what, exactly. I can Sense curiosity. And arrogance. Supreme confidence.

If he tries to leave without agreeing to this mission, I'll kill him. He will not terminate me or anybody else; I won't allow it.

But he doesn't leave.

He smiles.

It's a oily grimace, his lips thinning to nothing. He points at the boys, using a military voice. "You two. Attention!"

The twins jump up. They're used to obeying commands. They salute. Duroc grins more. "Tell me again why these two can't do the mission in Arnhem? Is E-10 so much stronger?"

"She's not stronger than me, sir," says Gefor. Gethre sticks him in the side with his elbow.

Duroc laughs. "Oh, no?"

Dad moves closer to the twins. "The boys are very strong, sir. But E-10 has more control at a distance."

It's chilling to hear Dad pronounce my name like that.

"We can't get close enough for the boys to do the job," he continues.

"I can do it, Dad," says Gefor.

"He can't," I say. "Not yet. He's only twelve."

Teetu and Jaysx glare at him.

Gefor turns and glares at us. Still such a baby. He understands nothing.

Everyone waits for Duroc.

"Okay," he says, nodding. "E-10 goes on the mission. And I take T-2 back to Washington with me."

"No!" I leap up.

Duroc raises his dark eyebrows. "No?" His mouth pulls back into another grizzly smile. "Why not?"

"She's too young."

"She's our sister," bursts out Jaysx.

"T-2 can return when E-10 gets back." Duroc turns to Teetu. "I think I'd like to get to know T-2 better."

I say nothing. He's going to hold her hostage. He'll probably try to turn her to his side. Good luck with that! But he could hurt her, take her by surprise, or while she's sleeping. My scalp prickles. I glance sideways at Mom. How can I complete the mission if Teetu's a hostage?

Mom nods at me, just barely, her smile as grim as Duroc's. Mom is picturing grabbing Teetu as the news about Duroc spreads worldwide. She's picturing Duroc being marched from his offices by guards; the generals standing by. She's picturing holding Teetu's hand. She looks at me as if to ask: Can you Sense it?

I nod.

"Pretend to be a helpless child," I whisper in Teetu's ear.

She nods. The merest whisper of a smile crosses her face.

I'm tied up in knots, but this scheme is all we've got. It has to work. It's our only way out.

I stand up. "When do I start the mission?"

CHAPTER 32

Rows of seats line each side of the autoplane. Seats *and* windows. No travel pod. Today, I fly as an adult. There's blue carpet on the floor; the ceiling is white, and the seats look the same as the seat in my travel pod: wooly blue, with seatbelts. There are two chairs on each side of the narrow aisle. I am the only soul on board.

My gut twists as I walk down the aisle. I couldn't eat breakfast. Nausea roils my belly. Everything depends on my getting this mission accomplished.

The windows in the autoplane are round and much smaller than I thought they'd be. I trail a hand down the soft seat-backs, peeking out. Bright green grass covers a big field on both sides of the plane. Beautiful. I try to focus on the pretty yellow flowers dotting the field.

Yesterday, Mom, Dad, and I spent hours going over the details, the papers I'm carrying in my overnight bag, the vidstick with audio and vid files. They show me two more photographs of the airport contacts,

Mom's and Duroc's, the agents who will meet me when the autoplane lands in Arnhem. Duroc's agent doesn't know about Mom's agent.

Mom's trying to get Duroc's contact neutralized, but if that doesn't work, I'll have to neutralize him. That is, kill him and hide the body, so it doesn't create an international incident. But I'm not going to do that. I'll evade him. Piece a cake, as SamJay likes to say.

I get to the twentieth row and slide into the seat on the left by the window. The seat Mom told me to use. Carefully, I place my bag with the false bottom, containing the incriminating evidence, under the seat in front of me. Then I push my fingers down between the seat cushions and work my hand under the cushion next to me.

I touch the edge of something slick and cool. A vidscreen.

Overhead, there are surveillance cameras. Every five seats. There's one four seats ahead of me and one just behind me. If I keep the vidscreen in my lap, it will be hidden from surveillance. Duroc is probably watching me right now.

As the engines rumble to life, I turn on the vidscreen. There's a vid of someone talking, but I can't hear it. The engine's too loud. On the other hand, the surveillance cam can't hear it, either.

After a few minutes, the plane rolls out smoothly and turns, and then I see earbuds swing from a pocket on the seatback. It doesn't matter if Duroc sees earbuds. I use them all the time when I listen to music. I grab the buds, stuff them in my ears, and plug into the vidscreen.

Now I can hear the woman talking. It's a news show. Mom said I should keep listening to the news throughout the whole trip, so if there are any "significant developments," I'll hear about them.

What might significant developments be? She said I'll know it if I hear it.

The woman is talking about the new flooding in Washington, D.C. About flooding in the parts that have not already been abandoned due to climate change.

Tremors move through my belly as I buckle my seatbelt and the plane starts down the runway. I'm not afraid of flying; I'm afraid of failing the mission. What happens if I can't convince the prosecutor, Yara Bakker? What happens if somehow I lose the evidence? Or it's not *enough* evidence? I pull the earbuds out, breathe in slowly. I can't concentrate. I have to center myself. *I am a part of all things, and all things lift me toward the center.*

Suddenly, I see a big, white car through the window, racing right next to the autoplane.

What the hell? Maybe cars normally accompany autoplanes as they take off? But already, I know this can't be true. The car is half on and half off the runway. It's driving dangerously.

I unbuckle my seatbelt and plaster my face to the small window, trying to see better. Someone is waving from the back seat, leaning precariously out the open window of the car. I draw a sharp breath. It's Mom. She pushes up, half out of the window, both of her arms waving at the plane, her hair loose and flying sideways.

I'm paralyzed. I have never seen anything more bizarre: Mom, hanging out of a crazily swerving car, hair blown wild. My throat closes up and I try to swallow. Should I Jump myself out of the plane? I don't know what she wants.

She shouts something as she signs, but I can't get what she's trying to say. Her hands jerk randomly. She stretches her mouth wide open, bringing her lips together, making an "o" shape. But it's not "no." Then she signs again. I slap my hands on both sides of the window, shaking my head. She's jerking around too much.

The car's driver swerves dangerously close to the plane and then spins away. As if in slow motion, the car hits something and flies into the air.

"No!" I scream.

In the air, the car turns sideways. I don't see Mom. She must've fallen back in. Then the car crashes down, rolling over in the green field.

The ground tilts sharply and drops away. I fall back into my seat. A *ding* sounds and an autovoice says pleasantly, "Please fasten your seatbelt. Please fasten your seatbelt."

I press my hands to my head. I should Jump myself back to the ground. But…. I look outside again and see nothing but white clouds below me. The plane rises steeply. I don't think I can.

I try to think as the autovoice continuously urges me to fasten my seat belt. Finally, I buckle it.

Sweat bursts out on my forehead and I feel sick. I made a mistake. I'm making a mistake right now. *Jump.* But I'm afraid. Too far to the ground, going higher each second. I can't do it.

What did she say? First Mom's mouth was open wide, then her lips came together, and—

Two musical notes announce themselves quietly. Not the seatbelt announcement. I jerk my head, looking. I don't see anything. Again, the two notes. They're coming from the floor. From the vidscreen, which landed upside down on the floor when the plane took off.

I unbuckle myself again so I can reach down and slide the vidscreen into my lap. The plane levels out. On the black screen, a word blinks, surrounded by a red square: *Notification. Notification.* I tap it.

A three-dimensional image forms and hovers over the screen, just like the map hovered over Mrs. Ellison's ristcom. The image is a large, square building, turning slowly. Tiny figures run out of the building.

My scalp prickles. I'm trying to see the figures more clearly, but it's hard to see from the top. The earbuds lie on the seat next to me; I stuff them back into my ears.

"A bold attack at The Hague International Court of Justice today in Arnhem, Netherdeutsch, has left two people dead and five more wounded," says a dramatic, low voice. "Officials seek three unknown assailants, one of whom was a recently hired security guard."

The Hague? The International Court? My heart slams in my chest. Something's seriously wrong. The images of the vidscreen flicker and blur. I bend sideways, trying to see more clearly.

The picture changes, showing a woman dressed in a suit sitting at a desk, holding a sheaf of papers. Under the rotating image, there's a name I can't make out. The voice in the earbuds goes on. "Using illegal automatic munitions, gunmen wounded five World Court employees and took the lives of Nigeran translator Abiodun Hassan and World Court prosecutor, Yara Bakker of Arnhem, who was about to launch a case against the United States…"

I cry out, leaping up, and yanking the earbuds from my ears. Adrenaline shoots through my veins, and my shield swirls around my body. I pace up and down the narrow aisle. Yara Bakker killed at The

Hague! Assassination of the very person I'm supposed to assassinate?

Did Duroc do it? I look up, straight into the vidcam. He must have. What is going on?

And the word Mom shouted at me before the plane took off. Mouth open, lips together like "o." Suddenly, I know. "Abort."

Abort the mission.

Oh, my God.

Get off the plane.

Duroc has betrayed me and the generals and Mom and Dad. He must have known about our plan. He's already assassinated my target. What's next?

My knees are half crouched, my arms outstretched. I can hear myself panting. Closing my mouth, I try to calm down. Deep breaths. In through the nose, out through the mouth. Again, I begin my mantra.

But frantic thoughts break in and I can't calm down. Why didn't I Jump myself when I had the chance? I don't know what to do. What will Duroc do? He thinks I'm in the dark. He doesn't know I have a vidscreen, that I know he already assassinated Yara Bakker. So he expects me to naively approach his "contact" when I get off the plane. That means his contact will be an assassin, meant to kill me. Yes, for sure. The contact will just step in quick and close to me, cut my throat before I can say hello or push them back.

Should I wait and run when I land in Netherdeutsch? Or should I try to Jump myself back home to the pod right now? What will happen to me if I can't Jump that far? I will fall to the earth.

The autoplane hits rough air, bounces up and down, the angles upward. "Fasten your seat belt, please," says the pleasant autovoice. I grab hold of a seat back, my heart hammering against my ribs like rapid gunfire. Should I try to Jump? Or ride it out?

"Make a decision," I scream out loud.

It's too risky, maybe impossible to Jump myself from this plane to the pod.

The plane levels out again. I sit down and make a decision: I'll Jump myself as soon as I arrive. Straight from the plane to the ground. Mom and Dad said commercial airports are crowded. I'll lose myself in the crowd.

The plane is quiet now, and deciding my next move calms me. I practice breathing. Repeat my mantra, feel the silence stealing over me. It's so quiet. Like the engines have stopped.

Wait. *Have* the engines stopped? Is it too quiet? It sounds like headphones clamped over my ears. Too much altitude?

The calm I was beginning to feel cracks. I jump up from my seat and back up into the tail end of the plane, my shield full strength. I crouch there. Something is wrong.

A roar splits the quiet length of the autoplane, slams me back against the wall, and the world shatters into a million pieces. I feel myself catapulted backward.

There's pain in my head and back. Everything goes black, then red, then black again. Suddenly, I'm tossed upward, upward like a rag, head over heels, and there is freezing, fierce wind battering me.

Another boom as big as the whole sky shudders through my ears, with black and white fire. Then I hear nothing, Wind blows past me, around me, but I don't hear it. Then there's fire all around me, spinning, screaming whiteness. My shield holds tight. Another shuddering *bam,*

bam, bam. I feel it instead of hearing it. And smell it. Smoke, bitter smoke. Am I on fire?

There was an explosion.

My plane exploded.

My heart pounds a million times a second. Gongs echo inside my ears. Red droplets circle my head as I turn upside down, or right-side up. More blood spurts from my nose, flattens against my shield. Droplets turn round and round like fat dots of red rain spattering my cheeks. Falling around me. Falling upward.

Everything, falling upward. My head pounds. I wipe blood from my eyes.

I try to climb upward, flailing my arms and legs, try to crawl up the buffeting wall of air. I scream. I can't hear myself scream. I flutter on the edge of fainting. I'm going to die.

Get it together, Eten!

Water glistens below. There's land beyond the water; I'm falling toward the water. A huge splash breaks the surface, something black, like a giant whale.

Pull yourself together! Think.

The splash is part of the plane. Falling into water.

There was an explosion.

Awareness slams back into my body. The plane exploded. Duroc is trying to kill me. He set a bomb and my plane exploded. That's why Teetu told me not to go. Why Mom tried to get me off the plane. I am falling, slowly it seems, through clouds. Below is the black and silver of water.

I focus, stretch my arms and legs out, my shield as big and strong as I can make it. I pretend Teetu and Jaysx are on either side of me, stretch my shield as if to envelope them both. Maybe I can make my shield function like a parachute.

My descent slows a little. I tighten all the muscles of my body to keep myself flat, to flatten and widen my shield.

Slowly, I stop tumbling. I fly, skimming air.

But always down. Still falling.

The water is far away, and then, suddenly, very close. Waves crest on the surface. I've never seen waves before. White spray, triangles of light flash up silver, shards of silver on the black water.

Water at speed, hard as concrete. It will kill me. I keep my arms wide and tuck in my knees, rotate until my feet are downward.

Then. SNAP. I am knifeblade thin. Legs long, toes pointed, arms up overhead. Shield tight, powerful. *Breathe!* Oxygenate. Heaving mighty breaths. *Gefor, I can hold my breath so much longer –*

Did I hear a shout?

Force breath. *All the way OUT.* Force breath. *All the way IN.* HOLD. Point toes toward the—

PART II: PEACE

Though little recognized, the renunciation of violence as a means to any end except defense is as much a cornerstone of democratic institutions as its widely recognized counterpart, freedom of expression.

Toward a Theory of Peace
by Dr. Randall Forsberg

CHAPTER 33

I float.

A tug.

Cold.

Am I moving? I'm in water.

A tug.

Oh, pain. Bad pain. *Stop touching me.*

Water gurgling. Floating on water. What happened?

A moan.

"It's okay." There's a low, gentle voice. "I got you now."

That voice, like life itself.

The sluice of water.

I'm so cold. Then the pain. I scream, open my eyes. The light is blinding.

Oblivion.

∞∞∞∞

"JP!" Someone is shouting.

"I got her."

I'm rocking. There's hardness, bad lumps underneath my back.

Forward motion jerks to a stop. There's a long crunch.

The light is so bright. I can't open my eyes.

Motion, up, slowly, with a long, sliding, grating noise.

It hurts. Everywhere, I'm moaning.

A cool hand on my forehead. "I got you," says that gentle voice again. A man's voice. "You're gonna be okay."

"Wha…?" I don't remember what happened. Why am I here? I Sense gentleness, help, caring in the people around me, but can't open my eyes.

Someone else, panting. "She's alive?"

"Alive!"

"Let's get her home."

"Off the beach, hurry."

"The Militia?"

"Hurry up."

"Maybe Ma can—"

"Careful!"

"Lift the blanket."

"One, two, three, up."

Pain as I swing back and forth in a sling. Pain as bad as the wand. Like crushing hammers. My skull pounds, my legs burn, my back splinters. A shrill scream tortures my throat.

I am totally wet. Have I pissed myself?

Blackness shreds my consciousness.

ooooo

"What are you talking about, hospital? Ma can examine her."

I wake slowly, eyes closed, and listen to voices. Vaguely, I can remember being in the water, and these people. Kind people.

"She needs radiology, she could be bleeding internally." The gentle voice, the good voice.

"…hospital will report her. And us." The other, higher-pitched voice from before.

Silence.

I am lying on a bed, lying still. Still is good, so good. We must be inside. The pain is steady, not shrieking, not roaring. As long as I'm completely still. I barely dare to breathe.

"You're right. Too dangerous."

The two who saved me from the water are talking. I want to open my eyes, to thank them, but my lids are so heavy.

"All right, all right. Call Dr. Mac then."

"JP, do you have two hundred creds for Dr. Mac?"

They're about a doctor. For me? I'll tell them I can heal myself. I don't need a doctor. But my lips, my tongue don't move. I swallow.

"Dr. Mac is Mom's friend. He'll make an exception."

A dismissive laugh.

I try to diagnose myself. What hurts? My feet, legs, chest, belly, arms, hands, head, back.

There's another voice, someone who just arrived. A woman. "I can pay for it."

"Ma!"

"Dr. Mac owes me."

My tongue pushes at my lips. So dry. I'm trying to tell them.

"She may be waking up," says the woman. "Nate, go call Dr. Mac. Now."

A rough hand with soft touch on my forehead, my cheek. "Hello, my dear. Can you hear me?"

I'm so, so thirsty.

"Wa…Wa…" My lips are glued together.

"Get her some water, John-Paul."

"Can you open your eyes? You've been in an accident."

Ah. I've been in an accident. Of course.

Here where I lay, it is just so soft. Be still, I think. It hurts to breathe.

My eyes fly open. Pain flares as my fingers clutch a blanket.

I've been in an accident. Except it was no accident. *Assassination.* I breathe faster, trying to sit up.

"Steady, steady," says the woman sitting on the bed beside me. Both hands press gently on my shoulders and I relax again.

She is possibly the most beautiful person I've ever seen. Her flawless, dark skin glows as if she were a beacon. Fine eyebrows arch above intense, wide eyes. Her high forehead glints like a crown, and a gold scarf holds her hair back.

"That's better," she murmurs again, stroking my forehead.

The steadiness she's urging flows from her into me. I Sense it. Her very essence is peace; her face shimmers with it. When she smiles, she illuminates all the nooks and crannies inside of me. It's a smile that speaks of welcome, of safety, of having already been taken to heart.

Tears come to my eyes.

Water touches my lips. She holds my head up so I can sip. Her voice whispers, *drink*. I swallow three times, liquid coolness soothing my raw throat. I close my eyes again and sleep.

∞∞∞

"You said she fell? How far?"

"Pretty far."

"Hmm. Into the water?"

"Yes, sir. Into the water."

"Hmm."

I hear restless footsteps, open my eyes. The back of my head pounds. I'm in a dark bedroom, lying on a wide bed, a bureau with a mirror glinting across the room. A boy stands near the door, outlined in light. I feel a soft coverlet under my hands. It smells like lavender. Nana uses lavender hand cream.

My body lists toward the indentation caused by the small man sitting on the bed next to me, his head turned toward the boy.

"Do you think anything's broken, Dr. Mac? Mom says no," says the boy.

"Wish I had a CT scan," grumbles the man. "We have to monitor her pupils for bleed or brain swelling. I brought the portable X-ray."

"Is X-ray good enough, Dr. Mac? It's such old tech."

"Do I look like a hospital, JP?"

"John-Paul, that's enough." The beautiful woman from before comes up from behind the boy and puts a hand on each of his shoulders. "Let Dr. Mac do his work. Give them some privacy."

Chortling, the man says. "Thank you, Maria."

"Ah, there she is." The small man, who must be the doctor, has turned and is looking at me now. He smiles, showing very white, even teeth. "Hello, young lady. I'm Dr. Mac. You've had a bad accident, but I'm going to take care of you."

He radiates well-being. I hardly need to Sense, his feelings are so strong. His inner being is filled with curiosity, like a child's, bounding forward, like somebody just let loose into a field of grass and flowers. He's a wiry man with a round face and a short nose and gold-rimmed glasses he keeps pushing back up.

Memory slaps me with dizziness. Durac tried to kill me. I remember the explosion, falling. Trying to hold my breath. Then nothing. "What happened?" I rasp.

The boy steps forward but still, I can't quite see him. "Your plane exploded," he says. "My brother and I, we pulled you out of the water."

The enormity of it shakes me. The room spins. My sisters, my brothers. Mom and Dad and SamJay. Nana. They'll all think I'm dead.

I try to focus on the wall, stop the spinning. There's a picture on the wall. A picture of a family.

The doctor peels back the thin blanket covering me. I'm wearing somebody's pajamas, somebody bigger than me. They're soft and dry.

"How do you feel? Any pain? Here? Here?" Dr. Mac pushes up the leg of my pajamas, and gently touches my leg down to the ankle, slowly turning my foot back and forth. I cry out, try not to shriek. My leg is covered in black and purple bruises. My feet and ankles are black and swollen. Anxiety surges with the pain, gripping me—sudden terror I might lose my legs.

"Yes," I croak. "My legs. Are they…?"

The doctor smiles and puts my foot down. "Don't worry. It's just bruising. It looks worse than it is. You probably have sprained ankles. You are very lucky there are no breaks, young lady."

I fall back, exhausted and relieved. "My head," I rasp. The headache is nauseating.

"You probably have a concussion." He feels my head, even more gently than before. "I'm going to X-ray your head, okay? We'll make sure nothing's broken up there." He smiles again, his warm brown eyes magnified by thick glasses. "You have a lot of bruises, but no breaks in your legs or feet. Can you remember what happened?"

I look at him blankly, see the steely surface of the bay getting closer and closer.

"Can you tell me your name?"

I say nothing. What can I tell these people? I'm afraid to tell them anything. It will put both me and them in danger. And then…they're so kind, but can I trust them?

"Okay, okay. Later. Later you can tell us what happened." He presses on my ribs, and I yelp.

"Huh. Maybe cracked ribs." He smiles.

Why shouldn't I trust him? I'm suddenly so tired, I can't remember why.

Dr. Mac pushes his glasses back up on his nose. His skin stretches over his bones like there isn't quite enough of it to go around. His skull is bald and shiny. But there is a looseness to his grin as if he has plenty of space inside for a good laugh.

Pushing in next to the doctor, the boy bends over me. He's a male version of the woman, Maria. His mom. High cheekbones, big eyes. A beautiful boy, about my age.

"Cracked ribs?" he says, his gaze turning fiercely onto the doctor as if accusing him. "Can you fix it?"

It's the same voice, the one who rescued me from the water. His voice is deep, resonant like a grown man, full of strength. His concern washes over me in a warm flood. Images from his mind flash: an expanding brightness in the sky, light and dark objects falling. Water. Me in the water. He's swimming next to me. He's the one who saved me.

I want to touch him, to thank him, but I don't think I can move.

He wears a too-tight, faded T-shirt and similarly ill-fitting, worn-out shorts. The outline of his body stands out under his clothes, the hard muscles, a vein pulsing in his neck beneath smooth skin. This boy is all taut energy, barely contained. He smells like salt and sweat.

And his eyes. Intense, electric. Such colorful eyes, yellow brownish-green, his gaze unwavering. Then he smiles, and my whole body responds in a way I've never felt before. As if my insides are lit up by a thousand suns. I want him to never stop smiling at me, ever.

CHAPTER 34

I have no words for what is happening to me. I can't stop staring at this boy, so different from anyone I've known. My whole body feels drawn to him, as if, when I Sense him, I feel like I'm touching him. Even though he's standing three feet away from me and I'm banged up, I feel my body pressed against his. I imagine stroking his sleek skin. A flush suffuses my cheeks and I shut my eyes quickly. I'm so embarrassed, I will die if Dr. Mac notices. But the doctor is still talking.

"John-Paul, I don't need to fix her ribs, okay? Cracked ribs need only rest to heal. You think you could help with that? Let her rest?"

I allow my lids to ease open again, to peer under my lashes. His name is John-Paul. What a wonderful name. He's worried about me, about my cracked ribs. Mom and Dad pretty much ignore minor injuries like that. Soldiers don't complain about a cracked rib.

"Sure, Dr. Mac." He turns that wonderful smile back on me.

My eyes go wide and my belly flutters. I'm…I'm…

"That means get out of the room now," says Dr. Mac. "I've got to X-ray this young lady."

John-Paul skips backward but pauses in the doorway, the sun blazing behind his silhouette.

Dr. Mac lays a heavy blanket over me. "Lead shielding. This will take a few minutes. I have to fix the machine. I just want to make sure you don't have a skull fracture."

"Okay." My throat feels full of rust and the sudden exhaustion rushes back.

"Okay. Try to go back to sleep now."

That will be easy. He wheels up some kind of ancient portable X-ray machine and starts to fiddle with it. No big deal. I'm used to tests. I close my eyes as the doctor slides a hard, flat disk under my head. A riptide of sleep sweeps me back to darkness.

The next thing I know, awareness *pings*. Something's wrong. I need to wake up.

Swimming to the surface of myself, I feel a hand in my hair. Someone touching, separating the strands, feeling my scalp.

My hand snaps up and grabs the offending wrist in an iron grip.

Dr. Mac yelps.

Opening my eyes, I stare. "What-r-you doin'?" My voice sounds harsh, unfamiliar. But at least I can speak.

He looks at me strangely. Half afraid, half curious. "Your hair."

"Don' touch." I'm ready to throw him across the room if he tries it again.

"But the X-ray." Dr. Mac takes a step back, and I drop his wrist. He rubs it. "The good news is, you don't have any fractures."

"Good," I breathe. I want to go back to sleep.

"But your hair."

Fear stirs in my belly and my eyes widen. What will these people do if they know I'm not normal? Dr. Mac seems kind, but I also Sense a driving curiosity in him.

He tries to smile, still rubbing his thin wrist. "Well, just some strands of your hair. Maybe the silver ones? They seem a little thicker than the rest. Loose hair doesn't show up on an X-ray." He pauses for a beat. "Normally."

"Jus'…don' touch." It's hard to talk right now. Of course, my hair isn't "normal." Nothing about me is normal.

But I don't see revulsion in his eyes. Only warmth. And curiosity.

"Don' tell," I rasp. Then regret it. Stupid! It's acknowledging what he suspects.

Dr. Mac nods, presses his hands together, and bows over them. "I apologize. I won't, I promise. I won't touch your hair again, and I won't tell anyone."

I'm too surprised to respond. Finally, I nod.

The spirit looms so large inside of him, it burns practically right under his skin. I can Sense no guile in him, only the desire to help… and that intense curiosity.

"Who are you?" he asks.

"Eten." The word comes out like it's scraping the sides of my throat. I swallow hard and Dr. Mac gets me another few sips of water.

"Eten what? Where do you come from? Where are your parents?"

My parents. Dangerous questions. "Dead," I say. "Parents r dead."

"The boys said you fell, Eten. Where did you fall from?"

John-Paul rescues me again. "She fell from an airplane." He's hovering just inside the door. "An airplane exploded over the bay."

Dr. Mac scoffs. "That's not possible. Nobody could survive that."

I go rigid. Nobody normal could survive it, maybe.

"I saw it," says John-Paul. "I saw her fall."

"There was nothing on the net about an airplane exploding." The doctor frowns. "Nobody can survive such a fall. It would be a miracle."

I close my eyes and watch through my lashes.

"I saw her fall, over drowned Jacksonville. The part where Camp Lejeune used to be. Nobody else saw, just me and Nate."

Dr. Mac puts his hands on his hips, his eyes narrowed, and hisses, "What were you doing there? Does your mother…"

John-Paul holds up a hand. "Please, Dr. Mac, don't worry my mother. We have to go over there to fish. We've been fishing there for two years now. It's not polluted any more, we did all the tests. Where else can we go? The New Jackson Wharf? I don't think so."

So, the place where the plane exploded, where I fell into the sea, that's the boys' secret fishing spot. A forbidden place. How lucky for me they were there.

Dr. Mac sighs. "Just be careful, boys. Polluted or not, you could get shot over there. The State Militia patrols everywhere now. They don't have enough to do."

My eyes fly open with anxiety. Militia?

Another boy crowds close up behind John-Paul. "Those assholes couldn't shoot off their own…"

"Nate!" snaps Dr. Mac.

"What?" He pushes past John-Paul, arms out, hands open, eyes stretched wide with innocence. "I was gonna say 'feet!' 'Shoot off their own feet.' What?"

I recognize his voice: the other boy who rescued me. It's got to be the first boy's brother. He looks like a skinnier version of John-Paul, except for the way his ears stick out from long, ropy hair.

"Be serious, huh?" says John-Paul. He lowers his voice. "We saw a DC Militia guy over there yesterday."

Dr. Mac's voice drops. "National military? Around here?"

A chill goes through me and the anxiety grips me harder. Was it Duroc's spies, looking for my body?

"Did you see anybody from EVE?" asks the doctor.

"No but just yesterday. We saw…"

"Shhh."

The mother enters the room and crosses to my bedside. Smiling warmly, she leans over and lays a hand on my forehead. "How is she, Mac?"

"You were right. Contusions, no fractures. Bit of a concussion, I think. Maybe a cracked rib. Lucky she has you, Maria. She just needs to rest."

Dr. Mac turns to me with a needle. "I'm going to give you something for the pain, okay?"

I shake my head. "No," I croak. "I'm just going to sleep."

The doctor takes the needle away. "Okay. You sure?" His eyebrows are raised.

I nod, shutting my eyes. I can't sleep. I have to heal myself

"Mac, you better come to Sunday dinner tomorrow," I hear Maria say as they step away from me. "The boys got us a whole lot of flounder."

"If this is my payment, Maria," the doctor says with that big, loose grin in his voice, "there better be pie."

Maria laughs. "Well, I do believe the boys brought home a big bag of wild strawberries. So I guess there might be pie."

"Well, thank you very much, Maria, I do believe I will accept that kind invitation."

They whisper the next words. They must think I'm asleep, but I can hear them.

"I got the antibiotics," says Maria.

"Thank God, two new cases of typhoid yesterday."

"How's EVE's pharmacy in Mayville?"

"Still empty."

"I'm going to put in a new order at the hospital," says Maria.

I go still with concentration, all sleepiness gone. These two are conspiring about something. Excitement surges up in me.

"You sure, Maria? Don't push it."

Maria makes an impatient sound. "I'm the head nurse on the floor, Mac. If we had enough staff to see me swipe antibiotics, maybe we'd save more lives."

"Just be careful," says Dr. Mac.

"You should talk!" Maria gives a snort of laughter. "What's the latest from out west?"

"Still gathering recruits, as far as I know."

"Anything from Rebecca?"

"Not this week." The doctor pauses, then says, "You're a warrior, Maria."

"Never mind. Typhoid rampant in the United States! It's criminal."

I gaze up through my lashes. Maria's bright eyes flash with contempt, the corners of her mouth tight and downturned.

"What's criminal, Ma?" Nate stands in the doorway.

"Shhh." Maria glances back at me. "Just you never mind, young man." She crosses the room and pushes Nate back. "You've got homework to do."

"The Disenfranchisement, that's what's criminal," says Nate.

I know that word. "Disenfranchisement." History of the 20th century. Women weren't allowed to vote. They fought and won the right to vote, August 18, 1920, with the 19th Amendment to the Constitution.

"Homework, Nathanael. You too, JP."

"It's Friday," Nate complains, and Maria responds with something else I can't hear.

I flow my consciousness into my body as they leave the room, finding the broken veins, the cracked rib, the swollen, bruised flesh. Slowly, I begin to mend.

CHAPTER 35

"Hey," says a soft voice. A hand on my arm. My arm on a coverlet. "Hey there. You hungry?"

John-Paul. I open my eyes and smile.

He grins. "How you doing?" His face is so open and welcoming, it's like we've been friends forever. I think of that boy in South Kongolia, and I hope that nothing bad will ever happen to this boy. This boy is full of life and hope, his spirit deep as a pool of clear water.

But violence follows me, everywhere I go.

"Better," I say.

He puts a cup of water to my lips and I drink. My throat no longer hurts.

"You must be hungry, too," he says. "You've been sleeping for two days."

"Two days?" My fingers clutch the light blanket covering me. How long since the crash? My brothers and sisters! They'll be frantic. I sit up abruptly.

"Whoa," says John-Paul, spilling some water.

I'm sitting on a different bed. I'm in a whole new room. Someone must've moved me while I slept. "Where am I?" This bed is in a little recess, with doors on either side. Outside of the recess, a long wooden table and chairs extend into a big room. I begin to panic and rise to my knees. "What's going on?"

"Hey, it's okay," says John-Paul as Dr. Mac appears by his side. "You're just in the living room. We gave my mom her bedroom back."

A glance to my right shows me the doorway to the room in which I lay previously. I sit back, nodding, and find Dr. Mac staring at me with his bright, curious eyes. I can Sense his wonder, his desire to probe, to discover my secrets.

"You seem to be moving much better, miracle girl," he says. "How's the pain?"

"Oh, much better," I say tell him. It's been 48 hours. I've got to get in touch with Mom and Dad. Or SamJay. I've got to let them know I'm still alive. Then I realize something even worse. Duroc. Our plan to incriminate Duroc failed. Somebody else assassinated that Hague Court prosecutor. My heart sinks.

"Mind if I…?" says Dr. Mac as he comes closer, and without really waiting for me to say whether or not I mind, he uncovers my legs.

The bruises are entirely gone, my ankles and feet no longer swollen. With my inner arm, I surreptitiously push on my chest. No pain. The cracked rib is healed, too. Dr. Mac gives a low whistle, covers my legs with the blanket again, his eyebrows raised. I try another smile. "Better."

"I'll say," he answers but says nothing more. I blow out a breath. He already knows there's something peculiar about me, but—to my relief—I can Sense he's letting it slide. For now.

John-Paul holds out a hand. He's still wearing the same clothes as yesterday, or something like it—an overly tight T-shirt, and blue jeans instead of shorts. They ride low on his hips. I can see the muscles of his belly ripple. "Want me to help you to the –?" He jerks his head. "You know. Outhouse?"

I nod. I don't need help, but John-Paul doesn't have to know that. Maria helped me to the outhouse a few times. She explained about the neighborhood, how there was no plumbing, no running water anymore. What she said shocked me. All of the houses here were abandoned due to flooding and then reclaimed by people who work hard but were still too poor to afford regular homes.

I'm wondering, if there was no nuclear war, how did this happen? Okay, people aren't living in underground pods. But in abandoned homes? No plumbing or water? Maria told me it's the climate crisis. Even their electricity is jury-rigged from a distant pole.

But SamJay's house wasn't like this. Why do these people have so little? Because they're not in the military?

I move to the edge of the bed and, as John-Paul's hands press mine, that quickening zings through my body again. He helps to pull me up from the bed and slides his other arm around my waist. My bare toes curl into the floor and I lean my head against his shoulder. Suddenly, I'm weak, but not from my injuries. As I look up, he smiles down at me, and squeezes me a little tighter. "Are you okay?"

"Uh—I think so." In fact, my knees are going to buckle. At the same time, dismay surges through my belly. I can Sense John-Paul's protective nature reach out for me like I'm a little kid, a little Nate, or a younger sister. How young does he think I am, anyway? I straighten up a bit taller.

As soon as we walk from the living room into the big kitchen, I balk, almost back up. More new people. Along with Maria and Nate are several others—two old men, an old woman, and a young couple with children. I feel John-Paul's arm tighten around me as if I were falling. Maria tells them my name. The children hide behind the parents while the adults nod and smile. With a grin, one of the old men mutters something to Maria about "you and your orphans."

Too many minds crowd me, each with its feelings and images, spewing out excitement, caution, curiosity. Especially the children—so wild and unrestrained. I shut down my Senses altogether.

I wish there were not so many people. I need to keep my rescue a secret. Because Duroc can't know. My heart twists as I think of Teetu, taken by that dried-out old man. What's happening to her? I have to get out of here, find a safe hideaway for all of us.

What Maria whispered to Dr. Mac comes back to me. *Out west,* she'd said. Somebody named *Eve* in charge. Maybe Eve can help.

I'm still dressed in the overlarge pjs, barefoot, and Maria fusses in a closet, finding a worn pair of shoes for me to wear. Once we're outside, I push John-Paul away. "I'm okay," I say, clearing my throat.

"Okay," he says, turning back to the house. He thinks I'm embarrassed to use the outhouse with him nearby. "Just call if you need me."

I don't need him. I'm better off not touching him and getting all of those sensations. My head already feels clearer. When I get back inside and wash my hands in the kitchen water bowl, the others have already drifted into the living room with platters of food that trail a smell of crisp, salty fish, of butter and boiled corn and baked bread.

I step out of the huge shoes but still shuffle slowly—I don't want them to know I'm already healed—and sit by John-Paul in the only chair left. As we eat, my arm almost brushes his. I try to focus on getting used to the strangers instead of my heady closeness to this boy. *He doesn't feel the same way*, I tell myself sternly. *Ignore him.*

The food is delicious, with big helpings of cornbread, something I've never eaten before. But something at the table smells a little funky, and I think it's the two ancient-looking men, Henry and Bart. Their clothes sag and their shoes are wrapped in rags, but—and this is strange—they can't stop smiling. I can Sense their physical pain—the throbbing feet—but they're both chatting cheerfully.

The battered-looking old woman named Andrea eats with a delicate touch. She's very thin, with hanks of her red hair tied up in pieces of shiny cloth. She smiles broadly, repeating, "Wonderful! Wonderful!" Her mind swirls with confusion. I try not to gape when I see she has only a few teeth.

The younger adults are the children of Maria's sister, who died of typhoid fever. Because Maria has a good, regular job as a nurse and her boys fish, she has more food than many others. And Maria likes to share.

Henry, one of the old men, says, "Bart used to work right next to Andrea's shelter, down by Lyman Road. That place used to be a hotel when Bart was a producer at CNH News. Remember CNH, Maria? Oh, maybe a little before your time, before the Disenfranchisement."

"I remember CNH, and I remember the Disenfranchisement," says Maria. "I was eleven. My mother cried for a week."

"What's the Disenfranchisement?" I ask. The question gets me some peculiar looks, like, how could I not know? I try not to blush and mutter, "I didn't learn about it."

John-Paul shrugs and gives me a reassuring smile. "That's okay. Lots of kids don't get to go to school anymore."

I cringe. Now he's going to think I'm stupid as well as unattractive.

"Disenfranchisement means losing the vote," says Maria. "Nobody votes for our leaders anymore. Not until the state of emergency is lifted."

Nate makes a rude sound. "State of emergency! What bullcrap. It's always a state of emergency."

"Watch your language," says Maria.

"It was because of climate change and riots," John-Paul tells me. "At least, that's what started it."

"President Wagner started it," says Henry. He turns to me. "Lots of people loved him. They thought he was strong, but he was just a bully, a criminal. He said he was going to save us, but he was a liar and a cheat and he destroyed democracy."

Bart says, "But there was an emergency. Back in 2049 and 50? Storms got crazy bad. They wiped out Florida and the coastlines. And tornados. The midwest was like the 1930s Dust Bowl all over again. California burned and flooded. Everyone ran from the floods and the wildfires. It was all over the news. People had no homes. They died in the streets. The government declared martial law. And it was bad back then, riots, no food, no clean water..."

Awful images flare in his mind: people shooting each other, people being beaten and bloodied.

"And people wanted ranchers to stop raising cattle," Bart continues, waxing loud, relishing his memories as a newsman. "There was a big fight over it, and then a lot of the land out West turned into desert anyway. They say nobody lives there anymore."

"Except for EVE…" Nate begins, but his brother cuts him off with a *shhhht* sound, and Nate falls silent. Bart and Henry stare at him, but the others look away.

"Who is Eve?" I ask, the excitement stirring again.

Maria leans forward, looking at her boys. "We don't discuss EVE. It's an illegal organization that opposes the government called Everyone Votes Everywhere, and we don't even talk about it in this house. Right, boys?"

"Right," the boys mumble and everyone at the table agrees, looking at their plates.

My cheeks flush as I look down. I bet the boys won't keep that secret. I'll ask them about it as soon as I get them alone.

"There's no free press anymore," says Bart with a sigh. "Global warming keeps getting worse because of fossil fuels, but we can't report on it."

"The government protects the fossil fuel industry, you know, oil and coal and gas," says Henry. "Those guys are all rich now"

"The government is *in* the oil business," says Bart.

I frown and stop eating. "Oil?" I say faintly. Only John-Paul hears me.

"Burning oil is the worst environmental hazard left," John-Paul says. "If we could vote, we could make the government ban it."

Oil! My whole body goes cold. Oil is the problem. And I am the weapon that protects fossil fuel, oil fields, and refineries. My throat goes dry. I picture the desert in the mid-west. The floods that destroyed Florida and the coasts. Caused by climate change—not nuclear war. There was no nuclear war. My mind, once again, flashes on the American back in the gym. The climatologist. *You're fighting for the wrong side.*

"You used to be rich, right Mr. Henry?" pipes up the little girl, Olivia.

"Oh, yes, I was a money man," says Henry, grinning. "Not much use for that now. I was what you called an investment banker. Regular people could get rich back then."

"Well, we do our best with what we've got," says Maria.

"No, Ma, we have to fight for something better," says Nate, his eyes blazing. John-Paul kicks him under the table. I wonder if the boys even know their mother conspires with Dr. Mac to steal antibiotics. Maybe they're both secret members of EVE.

I'm so uncomfortable. I need to make sure they don't find out what I've been doing all these years. I need to know more about EVE.

"I think that's enough politics at the table for tonight," says Maria.

"So, Mr. Henry," Maria's niece says with artificial cheeriness. "You said there's activity down by your shelter on the quayside?" She's trying to change the subject. "Are more people fishing? I thought it was usually pretty quiet down there.

"Usually," says Henry, glancing at his friend.

"No fishing. Some kind of helicopter buzzing around this afternoon," says Bart. "I think they headed for that drowned Lejeune area."

John-Paul's face goes still, but I see him nudge his brother's leg under the table. They're picturing me in the water, and suddenly my stomach drops. Is a helicopter looking for me?

"I was following 'em with my binoculars," continues Bart. He grins.

"Bartholomew," Maria says reproachfully. "You didn't. You could get jail time for that!"

Henry clears his throat and Bart makes a dismissive sound. "Oh, goodness, don't worry about me."

"The news-hound instinct dies hard, Maria," says Henry.

"No, not news," says Bart. "I just gotta have a bit of entertainment, don't I? I won't write anything, don't worry. I'm old, but I'm not stupid."

A loud banging on the door brings Dr. Mac and Maria to their feet. Panic lashes me. Are they already looking for me?

I'm not the only one who's scared. Everyone at the table looks frightened.

More pounding. Dr. Mac throws his napkin on the table. Maria holds out an arm. "I'll go," she says. "My house. You stay here."

"Ma," says John-Paul, getting up also.

Maria lifts her hand. "All of you, please stay here. Keep quiet."

Dr. Mac grabs my wrist with one hand and his bag with the other. "Hide," he says, and he pulls me from my chair toward the bed. He throws the medical bag on the bed and urges me into the nook. As soon as I climb on the bed, he pulls the doors together, hiding me and his bag. But the doors are made of thin, horizontal slats of wood, easy to peek through.

I hear a door crash open in the kitchen. A high voice shouts, "Where's Dr. Mac? I need Dr. Mac!"

"Here, I'm here," calls Dr. Mac, starting for the kitchen.

A tall, thin girl races into the living room, her wild hair swinging around her head in a red corona. "My brother. Dr. Mac."

Maria hurries into the room after her.

I shove the doors aside. In the girl's mind, I Sense a young man with the same curly red hair lying on a wooden floor in a puddle of blood, moaning, holding his belly.

"I'm coming," says Dr. Mac. He hurries back to me for his bag. I hold it out and catch his arm as he takes it.

"Take me with you. I can help."

"What? Let go." Dr. Mac shakes me off.

I know I should keep a low profile. But maybe I can do just this one thing. Heal. I have so much death to reverse. "He's shot in the stomach," I say.

The girl is sobbing. "The Militia, the curfew, they just left him in the street. Oh, hurry Dr. Mac. They shot him in the stomach."

Dr. Mac's head whips back toward me, his eyes wide.

He turns and runs.

I run after him.

Chapter 36

My bare feet slap the pavement, stinging. The overlarge pajamas threaten to trip me and I pull them up as I run. My body is stiff, my leg muscles complaining, my shoulders sore.

But my training takes over. I run behind Dr. Mac—who is faster than he looks—in the middle of the deserted road. Quiet houses, mostly dark, line the street. I can hear the sister's breaths as she races ahead. Maria, who paused in the house long enough to grab her medical kit, hurries behind us.

The warm, damp night echoes with our footfalls. Here and there, a light shines from a window. Overhead, the moon casts a hazy glow through clouds. On another day, in another world, I'd stop and stare.

We run past one street corner, and then turn left at the next. "It's just ahead," says the girl, a panting shadow.

At the other end of the block, a truck revs its motor, shattering the silence.

"Down," Dr. Mac calls hoarsely.

"Get back," Maria cries out.

Their anxiety spikes off the charts. Terrified, I Jump myself from the street, backward to some bushes in front of a house.

Darkness cloaks me. Though I can Sense the others, I can't see them. Headlights turn onto the street.

A bunch of young men pack a large, boxy-looking car. Two hang out the windows and two hang out an opening in the back.

They're dressed in white shirts with a dark insignia patch on the arm, and they all carry rifles. Soldiers.

Noisy voices, jeers, and retorts echo through the street, although someone inside the car keeps telling them to "pipe down." They sound like boys, not men. One pretends to shoot at the houses they're passing. "*Pop, pop, pop,*" he says in a poor imitation of gunshots.

"Curfew," shouts another from the window. "Everybody s'posed to go home now." His words slur together.

"Shut up, Jingles," says someone else inside the car.

I stretch my Senses and touch the mind of the one pretending to shoot. There's an image of a frightened woman quaking on the street as urine pools under her.

As the car approaches, I see "N C Militia" painted in white on the front. A white star glows on the door.

"Curfew patrol," shouts the first man again. A huge light from the car plays unevenly over houses and walkways. It reveals only homes and growing things. No people.

Anger rakes my bones. These churlish, poor excuses for men! They shot that girl's brother. In what reality does punishment for breaking curfew equal death?

To my left, I glimpse movement in the darkness. The redheaded girl races from her hiding place toward her house.

The soldiers' light is about to catch her.

I explode it.

A soldier curses loudly as the hot glass shatters with a pop. Two more inside the truck shout.

I could eliminate these men. I think of Tom Smith; the hard *pop* when I threw him against the tree; the thud of his body landing on the truck. A shudder takes me. I'm done with death. There's got to be a better way.

The car stops almost directly in front of me. I hold my breath. Chaotic voices emerge from the dark interior.

"Somebody shot at us."

"No, you idiot."

"The light broke."

"The spotlight broke."

"Yeah, it got too hot."

"I heard a gunshot, I'm telling you."

"Let's get out and check."

The car door with the big white star flies open; a man slides out.

"Marty, get back in. Geeze."

"I saw somebody."

I hover with indecision, heart pounding. Maria reaches the girl, and they creep together toward the back door of the next house. Another shadow joins them: Dr. Mac. That must be where the wounded boy lives.

The militiamen sound angry. Excited and angry. A bad combination.

Maybe they'll just leave.

Another man slides out of the vehicle and stands next to the first. They both raise their guns and peer through the scopes. My breath catches in my throat. If the scopes are infrared, in a moment they will see me.

"Oh, my God," says someone from inside the car. "Can we finish this patrol, please? I'm hungry."

A car door slams. Another soldier has gotten out of the vehicle. The three split up, trotting toward the houses and my heart sinks. Are they going to search house to house? I've studied that tactic a hundred times. I need a diversion.

Way down the street, a light shines in front of a house. I Jump myself to the edge of the illuminated sphere. A dark car glimmers by the roadside. I've Jumped something that size before, and I can do it again. I focus.

And Jump the car to the middle of the street.

Not *on* the street, but above it. The car drops with an explosive bang of tires. Alarms and lights bounce and blare. Wow! Incredibly satisfying. The soldiers run back, leap into their vehicle and it roars to life, screeching up the street toward the blaring car.

I Jump myself to the back of the house. The others have already gone inside, but the door is still open. As soon as I enter, I Sense the boy's agony like a slap. I rush in and see him right away, lying on the kitchen floor, dying. A second ago, he'd been writhing in pain. Now, he's still.

Maria presses a bloody towel to his stomach. "What happened out there?" she breathes. Blood soaks the boy's shirt. It spreads out from his side and runs across the slanted kitchen floor.

"I created a diversion."

Dr. Mac is by the stove, checking a pot. A man in an undershirt with flaming red hair hovers close behind. He must be the boy's father. Crouched over the boy, the mother cups each side of his head with her hands. She's staring at his face, tears flooding her cheeks, muttering, "Come on, baby, come on, baby, don't you leave me." Her agony is so great, it's hard to shield my mind from it. The sister throws herself down beside the mother, as pale as a sheet, her raised hands curled and helpless by her mouth.

Dr. Mac pulls a chair up beside the mother and grabs something from his medical bag. The dad turns and paces back and forth. His cheeks are wet. He leans over a big pot on the stove. "Is it ready now?" he asks, his voice raw and shaking. "Dr. Mac! Has it been ten minutes?"

Steam rises from the pot of boiling water. Something metallic sticks out of the top.

"Almost," says Dr. Mac. He attaches a plastic bag filled with dark red blood to a bent hanger, which is slung onto the back of a chair next to the boy. A tube snakes from the bag. Dr. Mac pulls on a pair of thin, blue gloves, rips open a small paper packet, and pulls out a needle.

I'm frozen in place. I've seen blood before. Torn bodies, bloody guts, death. But always through Dad's eyes. Never quite real. Not until the boy in South Kongolia.

This is too real. This is personal and up close. The grief and horror of it tolls inside me like a bell. The unfairness and stupidity.

"God dammit, he's going into shock," mutters Dr. Mac, crouching.

My paralysis breaks. Maybe I can save him. I rush to the boy's side, drop to my knees, and press my hands to his bare arm. His spirit flutters, cool and weak. His skin is clammy, and his face and neck are covered with sweat.

"What are you doing?" explodes the father. "Who is that girl? Who are you?"

The mother and the sister jerk their heads up in alarm. Maria, still holding the towel to the boy's stomach, stiffens.

"It's okay, Reuben," says Dr. Mac. He glances at me. "She's my assistant."

His assistant! Suddenly, I relax and focus. Dr. Mac *knows* there is something different about me, and he isn't afraid. He's hopeful.

"I'm sorry." The father sobs once, turning away.

The boy is utterly still as Dr. Mac slips the needle into his arm. His breathing is shallow; his eyes are closed. The doctor tapes the needle in place, hooking it to the tube.

Blood from the bag flows into the boy.

"Let's get those needle-nose pliers." Holding his hands up in the air, so the clean gloves won't touch anything, Dr. Mac herds the father toward the pot of boiling water.

Whatever implements the father is boiling on the stove, there won't be time to use them. Breathing deep and slow, I let my Senses drop into the boy and find the bullet immediately. The foreign metal is lodged in the wall of his stomach. Luckily, it is a small bullet, not very powerful. The militiamen had been carrying light rifles, probably .22 caliber.

I Jump the bullet into my hand and open my fist. The crumpled metallic lump is warm and slick with the boy's blood. It's revolting and a relief at the same time. I let it slide to the floor, unnoticed, and surrender my Senses to the boy's wound.

Somewhere a vein, nicked and pulsing, is filling the boy's stomach with blood.

The room and everyone in it recedes. I trace the bullet's trajectory, feeling the soft tissues leaking fluid, trying to find the bleeding vein.

Dimly, I'm aware as Dr. Mac kneels next to Maria. "Okay," Dr. Mac says. "I'm going to try to find the bullet. Let me see it."

I'm trying to Sense the boy's wounds and remain aware of the room, but it's hard to balance.

Maria pulls the towel back from the wound and I look. It's so small, just a hole in his stomach. Dark red blood pulses from the wound. It rises rhythmically, one spurt after the next like a tiny, red animal rising to the surface and subsiding again. His heartbeat. I sense the connection from the laboring pump in his chest to the blood that leaks from his vein to the head of that tiny, red pulse that's killing him.

"Damn it," mutters Dr. Mac, glancing around. "I can't operate here!" A black despair rolls over the doctor. In his mind, he knows what he can't say aloud. It's hopeless. The bleeding is too severe.

"I can heal him," I whisper, eyes closed, my palms pressing against his forearm.

"Mac," Maria whispers. "Look at her hair."

I let go of the outside world and allow my Sense to rise and create a whole world of images: the boy's powerful heart, the hot blood thrumming out of it, coursing down a supple pipe, branching off, branching off, and *there*. The leak.

Gently, I hold the ruptured edges of flesh in my consciousness. I stroke the shuddering tissues, urge, move the edges together, *desire* the tear to mend and visualize the blood continuing its journey through the vein. The cells reach, as if with longing, toward each other, toward harmony, integrity, wholeness. They want to mend.

"The bleeding is slowing," whispers Maria.

"Oh, my God."

Long moments pass like a held breath.

Everything has almost come together when there is a heave, a violent disruption, tumultuous, explosive. I fall backward as if physically struck, and a cry of anguish fills the room. His mother.

The boy is on his side, vomiting blood, globes of red, viscous muck with blackish granules. It looks like he is vomiting his insides out. Maria holds his shoulders and head to the side, so he won't choke, her hand covering and protecting the IV needle.

The mother starts screaming.

"Reuben, help her," Dr. Mac shouts, again pressing the bloody towel to the boy's wound.

The father goes to his wife and holds her in his arms, smothering her cries against his shoulder. One anguished sob escapes him.

As the boy rolls back, Dr. Mac dully holds the towel to the wound, not even looking at it. He's giving up. There's nothing more he can do.

But I'm not done. Pressing both my palms to his arm, I obliterate the outer world again and give myself over to Sensing. It's easier this time. I trace the route from the boy's heart through the veins. At the same time, I Sense the entry wound, extending from the small, round opening to just inside, where the bullet bounced off a rib, slowing the trajectory. Then a curve into the boy's belly to where the bullet lodged against the interior stomach wall.

The vein no longer gushes blood. It's now only a slow leak. In my mind, as I Sense the boy's stomach—the vessels and muscle, the skin holding him together—I see it as a tear. *There*, the flesh is torn. Again, I pull the edges together, like Jumping something, but slower, as if Jumping through viscous, liquid amber. As the edges close, I can Sense the very cells of his body long for wholeness, for completion. The separate edges of the vein merge. They cling, mending themselves to completion.

At the last, I focus on the rib, cracked by the bullet. Bone, so much easier, so resonant, and tenacious. Bone needs only a little urging to begin knitting into wholeness.

I open my eyes, still kneeling beside the boy. Only a moment has passed.

Mother, father, sister—sobbing. Dr. Mac, looking down, defeated. Maria, gazing into the distance, tears trickling down her face. They don't see as he begins to survive.

The boy has relaxed back and color is returning to his white face—a pink blush. And I know he is healed. Almost healed, close enough. He'll live.

Sudden tears sting my eyes. I saved him. Me. Where for so many years, I had been a killer, here, now, a healer knelt. No matter Mom's disdain for religion, I feel like an angel has brushed my heart.

I begin to speak, but my voice cracks and I have to clear my throat. "You guys. Look. I think he's going to be okay."

Quick gasps replace the sobbing. Dr. Mac and Maria snap to attention and stare at the boy, then at me.

"Oh, my God," says Dr. Mac, pulling his stethoscope from around his neck and hastily pressing it to the boy's chest.

He seems to be breathing normally again.

And then his eyes open.

"Donny!" his mother cries, dropping to her knees beside him.

"Ma," he whispers, raising a limp hand. His father grabs the hand in both of his. The boy tips his vivid blue eyes toward his father, then toward the rest of us.

"Don't move, Donny," says his dad, pushing the boy's hair back from his forehead. He turns to Dr. Mac. "Is he ...?"

Dr. Mac rocks back on his heels and straightens the blood pressure cuff around Donny's arm. He pumps and releases the pressure, counting, and looks up with a startled expression. "He's doing better."

"What happened?" asks Donny.

"You stayed out after curfew, lame brain," says his sister, her voice clogged from crying. "Those militia assholes shot you."

"I'm thirsty," says Donny.

Maria rises to get water. "Just one sip," says Dr. Mac. "See if he keeps it down."

Dr. Mac and the others lift Donny and get him onto a couch in the big room adjoining the kitchen, the sister holding the blood bag high. There's a dark red puddle spreading over the cracked wooden kitchen floor, not to mention the blood vomit. I can smell the metallic tang, the sour puke. Flies already buzz over it, which strikes me as particularly disgusting. I never saw insects in the pod; I believed flies were extinct. I get some dishtowels and a sponge from the kitchen to clean it up.

Maria comes to help me, but even as she crouches down, she grabs something and rises again. "Mac!"

It's the bullet. I let it fall to the floor after I Jumped it out of Donny. Dr. Mac hurries over and she shows him. The doctor whistles and my heart does a little flip-flop. But they don't even glance at me.

"Did he vomit this up?" says Maria. "I never saw that happen before." I think she probably has had a lot of experience with gunshot wounds in the hospital where she works.

"I don't know." The doctor frowns and touches the bullet with a forefinger. "I thought it nicked an arterial vein," he says and looks back at Donny. The parents and sister hover, their faces twisted with joy and anguish. The doctor lowers his voice. "It's a miracle he's not bleeding out. I don't get it."

Maria shakes her head. Then they both look at me. I duck my head and busy myself with cleaning up the floor as they go to show the others to the bullet. There's a lot of blood. I go back and forth to the sink, sopping up blood and vomit as I hold my breath so I don't have to smell it.

I'm washing my hands in the sink when I realize Dr. Mac is standing behind me.

"Remember when you said, 'I can heal him?'"

I shrug and blow out a breath, unable to meet his eyes. "I…I don't know. I thought maybe I could help."

"Why?" says Dr. Mac. "Why did you think you could help?"

Maria comes up behind Mac. I can see them reflected in the kitchen window. I stare past their images, into darkness.

"You had your hands on his arm," says the doctor. "And your hair…"

His voice trails off. I know that my hair moves when I use my skills. Dad once said it looked like a breeze ruffling me. "Did you do something?"

Maria murmurs, "Laying on of hands?"

I know what that is—a religious belief that some people can heal with their touch by channeling God. I look at my hands. In each palm, there's a small, white scar left by the cuts I suffered in Mom's office. My skill, which has killed so many and healed so few—probably not channeling God.

"No, Maria," I say, turning around. "I'm not religious. I just thought maybe I could help." The family is kneeling by their son, and the sight of it again shoots a thrill of joy through me. That boy is alive because of me. That family is whole because of me. Pride swells like I haven't felt since I healed Jaysx, the way I felt when I was five years old and I believed I was saving America. I can't help but smile.

"Hmm," says the doctor. Maria nods, smiling back. I Sense their utter disbelief. They know that somehow, I did something.

"Dr. Mac," calls the father, and the doctor and Maria go back to the recovering boy. They're going to let it go—for now. But what will come next? I have to get back to my brothers and sisters. I have to get them out of the pod, away from Duroc. And I don't know what to do after that. Where will we go? Maybe west—to EVE.

CHAPTER 37

A sound, or a smell, wakes me the next morning. I peer out from between the wooden slats of my bed-cubby doors. Dim window light outlines John-Paul and Nate as they sit on a bed across the room, eating and whispering. A delicious smell makes my stomach rumble.

I slide the doors back and scramble off the bed. "What are you eating?" I whisper.

"Breakfast," John-Paul announces loudly.

Nate giggles. He clicks on the lamp next to him.

"Isn't your mother sleeping?"

"No," says Nate. "She's not home from work yet."

"How do you feel?" asks John-Paul.

"I'm fine," I say, forgetting that "normal" healing would take longer. He's finishing off rewarmed fish and cornbread from the night before. "That smells good."

John-Paul digs an elbow into his brother's side. "Nate! Where's your manners? Go get Eten some breakfast."

Nate jumps up, looking surprised, and trots off into the kitchen. John-Paul swallows and grins. "Sometimes I just have to be his dad."

"You're not my dad," Nate calls from the kitchen. He brings me a plate and we finish eating quickly.

"We gotta go," says Nate, glancing at the window. A dim gray light seeps through the curtain behind the bed.

"Where are you going?"

"Fishing," says John-Paul.

My mood lifts. "So you're going back to that Lejeune area where my plane crashed?" I want to see the site, see if anything is left of the plane.

'Yeah—don't say anything to our mom about it."

"It's dangerous," adds Nate.

"I want to come." I stand up. For the first time, I wonder if Maria's home might be a safe place for us to hide, at least for a while. I want to find out everything I can about this place.

"It's against the law. It's not safe," says Nate.

"I want to see the crash site."

"We can't fish and take care of you, too," says Nate.

I level a glare at him. "I just fell from an exploding plane and survived. You think I can't take care of myself?"

Both boys stare at me. I stand up tall and defiant, willing them to see me as more than a helpless child.

"She does have a point," says John-Paul, and I grin at him.

"Come on, JP. We're…"

"What's the big deal? I'm going to give her some of Becca's clothes."

"Whatever," Nate says, taking my plate away. He surreptitiously spoons my leftovers into his mouth.

John-Paul leads me to Maria's barely furnished room. He opens a closet, reaches up, and pulls a big box off the shelf. "We have an older sister named Rebecca. My mother had her before she met our dad. Becca was about seventeen when she left. What are you, thirteen?"

"No. I'm *sixteen*," I say.

"Oh, sorry." He turns and looks at me with new interest. I lay a hand on the side of my neck, hoping to stop the blush.

"So where did Becca go?" I ask. He's got some complicated feelings going on, something he's angry about.

"She left about three years ago, to join EVE out west." He puts the box on the bed and opens it. It's packed with clothing. "I know Mom communicates with her, even though she pretends she doesn't. Mom is dead set against us joining EVE." The anger surges inside of him.

My lips pucker as I consider whether he knows his mother works for EVE. I don't think I should tell him. "Where is EVE? Can I get in touch with them?"

A look of blank surprise crosses John-Paul's face. "Why?"

I shrug. "I want to help, too."

His mouth twists. "I mean, it's great you want to help but ..." Again, he seriously underestimates me. "EVE is everywhere and nowhere. Usually, they get in touch with you."

"Guys, come on," Nate calls. "I left Mom a note that Eten's with us."

John-Paul gestures to the clothes as he leaves the room. "Hurry, okay? We've got to get going."

Hastily, I pull on the overlarge clothes, still wondering about Rebecca and exactly where she is. The pants are too big, and I'm glad there's a belt so I can cinch them tight.

The boys carry their fishing gear as we jog toward the pale dawn. The neighborhood's devastation becomes visible as we get closer to the water. Soon I see piles of rubble, rusting cars, twisted metal. Old homes with busted windows, broken and gaping windows.

Further on, only a narrow path down the street threads through piles of wreckage. Tall weeds, vines, and skinny trees grow up and around the debris, life springing from every crack, reclaiming formerly civilized property.

Soon, I hear a rhythmic, shushing sound. For a second, I think it's a vehicle approaching, maybe soldiers, but the boys don't hesitate. The sound gets louder as we continue to run through big bushes and tall grass, swerving away from an impenetrable thicket, then rounding a curve.

And then I stop, staring.

The sea crashes and sucks the land before me. Gray and white and massive, it surges and falls as if enormous underwater shoulders are trying to emerge. Close to shore, waves curl and smash into brown foam. Far away at the impossible horizon, where sea and sky shimmer with purple and pink streaks, the sun rises from its watery bed.

John-Paul grabs my wrist. "Come on, we have to hurry, there's no cover here."

I follow without words. I don't think the boys understand; they must be used to it. The sea to them, I think, is just another landscape in which to survive. I stop again to stare.

Here's something Dr. Duroc can't control—a wild, free, limitless power I've never before witnessed. The raw power of the earth itself.

John-Paul stops. "Come on, Eten. We have to hurry before the tide comes in."

I turn and run after them on the packed sand, then I pass them, pounding along the edge of the waves. A wild elation leaps in my chest.

"Eten! This way."

Nate is rounding a long, low wall of rock. John-Paul waves to me and runs back toward the trees.

Focus! I tell myself, racing after them.

Together, we scramble up a grassy ridge of land, hollowed out below, long weeds on top. I leap the last foot into the grass.

"I…" pants Nate, grinning at me. "Never saw…anybody … run so fast."

A rising whine drowns out his voice.

"Down," shouts John-Paul, pushing me and grabbing Nate. The three of us fall flat into the long grass. The noise grows louder, deafening. I follow the boys who crawl on their bellies under a flowering bush.

A shadow passes overhead and I Sense their fear surge.

"What?" I ask, terrified. "What is it?"

John-Paul flips over onto his back and peers up at the sky through the leaves. Nate lifts his head, looking north.

"Helicopter," says John-Paul.

I Sense the image in his mind. I've never seen a real helicopter before, though they're popular in battle. I remember a picture I saw in a book—soldiers with guns hanging out a helicopter's side door. After a moment, I can barely hear the noise.

Nate sits up. "That was not a North Carolina Militia 'copter."

"The NC militia doesn't even own a 'copter."

"Yeah, that's what I mean," Nate says, staring at his brother, raising his eyebrows.

"U.S. Military!"

"Remember, Henry and Bart said the military was poking around by old Lejeune?"

A dark fear starts up in me. It couldn't be Duroc, could it? How would they know where my plane exploded and crashed?

"Let's go see," says Nate, his eyes gleaming.

The same gleam lights John-Paul's eyes. He turns to me. "Maybe you should go back home."

"No way. I'm coming."

The boys shrug. "Okay, just keep up," says John-Paul. Nate grins at me as John-Paul scrambles out from under the bush and jogs to another thicket of bushes. "The boat is over here."

If Duroc is looking for me, this could be more dangerous than the boys realize. I clench my fists. I'll just have to protect them.

When the boys pull the concealing brush away, I realize the boat is small. Scary small.

The whole contraption looks like a patchwork quilt. The colorful interior of the boat—bottom, middle seat, and ends—is cobbled together, straddled by various kinds of wood and patched here and there with bits of metal. A big motor lies on its side on one of the end seats. My breath catches. Do they intend to go out on the waves in this flimsy thing?

They do. John-Paul pulls out life vests for each of us; Nate shows me how to clip it on. The boys drag the boat quickly off the land to a sheltered inlet, where the waves don't break. A breeze waffles around my hair and face with a pungent, salt smell. Which would be wonderful if I weren't horribly afraid. I bite my lip and feel my fingernails dig into my palms.

"In, in, in," says John-Paul, holding onto the back of the boat as the pointed front rises up and down on the water. "You know how to swim, right?"

My face flushes. "Of course, I know how to swim."

Nate leaps deftly into the boat, turns, and holds out a hand to me. "Come on. It's safe."

Blushing even harder, I take Nate's hand and step over the side. The boat rocks as Nate and I move forward. Abruptly, I lose my balance and sit hard on the middle seat as the whole thing lurches.

I look back. John-Paul is pushing us off the sand; he jumps and rolls into the back, his legs wet, his feet bare. The boat tips to one side. I gasp and grab the wooden seat, suddenly sure getting into this miserable craft was a terrible mistake.

CHAPTER 38

Nate thinks my fear is funny. He's laughing. "We rescued you in this boat, you know." John-Paul doesn't seem to even notice that I'm scared, thank goodness. I tell myself to toughen up. What's so bad about riding a patched-up skiff smaller than a sofa into the bottomless expanse of never-ending, surging sea?

"Up," says Nate, helping me to the narrow front seat. He turns to face John-Paul on the middle seat and grabs two, long oars. He may be thin, but he's strong and his strokes are powerful. The boat surges forward so hard, I slide on my seat.

John-Paul stands unsteadily in the back. When he crouches over the engine, Nate says to me, over his shoulder, "Hold on."

I grab the side of the boat as John-Paul quickly pulls a rope straight up. The machine roars and the boat surges forward hard, pushing wind through my hair.

Then it's like we're flying, and I forget about being afraid. It's the most exciting thing I've ever felt. The water moves with waves like small hills, and we surge up through them, then slap back down with foam spraying. The sea wind, with its heavy, weedy smell, blows through my hair as droplets of spray sting my face.

It seems like we're going straight out into the ocean, but the boat turns and we run parallel to the land. All too soon, flying through the sea slows to a putter. John-Paul steers the boat closer to the shore.

"Don't run the motor so close," says Nate. "If anybody's there, they'll hear us."

John-Paul turns the motor off and tilts it back into the boat. Without comment, Nate begins to pull on the oars again. Sweat streaks his neck above his life-vest.

I'm about to ask how far we still have to go when John-Paul puts a finger to his lips. I look all around but don't see anyone or anything to hide from. Ahead of us, a spit of land curves out into the ocean in a broad semi-circle. Ruins trail across the overgrown land, but I don't see any real houses or people.

There are hardly any waves at all now, just a mild up-and-down swell to the water. Strange, angular rocks dot the bay, sticking up out of the water which laps and slushes around them, sighing and gurgling.

As we approach land, the boat glides close by one of the big rocks. I lean over and see small fish near the surface of the muddy water nibbling at the edge of the rock. We round the side. A huge hole gapes in the rock where it rises from the water.

Something big splashes in the darkness. *Inside* the rock.

It isn't a rock at all. Splintered, weathered wood edges the hole.

It is a roof. The roof of a house. Shock rocks me back.

They are all houses. Horrified, I scan the bay. None of the rocks are rocks. They're all people's homes, swallowed by the sea. "These are houses," I say, leaning forward, my voice husky.

"It's low tide," Nate whispers over his shoulder.

John-Paul shushes us.

Knowing a concept and experiencing it are two different things. This is climate change. Floods. Drowned homes.

What happened to all of the people?

The boys say nothing. We glide quietly toward the far shore, navigating around the houses. The wild, open sea smell has given way to something more rank, as if more than homes are rotting.

Images of Harry and Bart and Andrea from last night's dinner flash across my mind, their ragged clothes and ill health. Maria's and Dr. Mac's struggles to get enough medicines, to help people too poor to afford a hospital. I see again the desperate people of South Kongolia, hungry, thirsty, living in the barren desert with mud and stick houses.

Something inside of me clicks, almost as if I were a jigsaw puzzle, and some missing piece of me has suddenly snapped into place. I see the big picture. Climate change, not nuclear war, is destroying the world. The American government and military—but not the people, who can't vote—worsen climate change because fossil fuels make them rich and powerful.

And my brothers and sisters and I have been fighting for the wrong side.

A cold sense of purpose fills me as, with one last, mighty heave, Nate drives the front of the boat up onto the grassy, muddy shore. A hill rises above us, covered in a wild tangle of trees and brush.

I will find EVE. From now on, my fight is not with ecoterrorists. It's with Dr. Duroc and the American military.

I jump out of the boat and the three of us drag the small craft uphill to firmer ground. A loud machine clanks in the distance as we sneak through the woods and make our way up the hill.

The machine sound stops, and John-Paul stops as well, holding his arm out. We stand motionless.

A man's voice comes from the other side of the trees. A woman responds. "Got it!"

We drop to the ground and crawl on our bellies toward the voices. Whatever these people are doing, they're doing it so loudly it's unlikely they'll hear us.

Tortured metal screeches. "Okay, bring it in," shouts another voice.

"Yes, sir," shouts the woman.

I smother a flash of fear. She sounds military.

John-Paul reaches the edge of the brush and stops. Nate and I crawl up next to him. Below, the land falls away—a steep hill with a narrow beach at the bottom. A big bay curves out to the sea,

Across the water, an enormous helicopter sits on a swath of burnt, flat land. Below, on the beach, a towering machine holds a metal arm stretched out over the water. A cable with a huge hook drops rapidly from the arm, and the machine screeches again.

Three boats float on the water. In the water, swimmers—dressed all in black with black backpacks—surround the boats. Their faces glitter in the sunlight.

"Oh," breathes Nate. "Divers."

"National militia," says John-Paul, barely making a sound.

Two men in one of the boats lean over the side, helping the people in the water. Another boat rocks as the huge hook that dangles from the machine drops into it. They start their motor and move in closer to the others.

"What are they doing?" I hiss. "Is it my plane?"

"I don't know," says Nate. "It can't be your plane. It crashed much further out."

"The tide could've brought it in," murmurs John-Paul.

My scalp prickles.

Suddenly, all of the boats pull way back. We wait, minute after minute. An impossibly tiny ant crawls up the side of my arm and I blow gently to make it crawl off. I can't believe how small it is.

"Look," whispers Nate.

An oily bulge ripples under the surface, surging toward the shore.

"Oh, no," I say. Foreboding creeps up my backbone, tightening around my throat. "Look, the hook is rising."

Both boys shush me.

But fear has already stopped my breath. The underwater object takes shape. The wing and engine of a plane. My plane.

I start panting, eyes wide. John-Paul puts a hand on mine. "It is my plane," I whisper. "They know I'm here." I feel like I can't catch my breath, like there's a stone on my chest.

"It's okay," says John-Paul. "Come on, we better get out of here."

We freeze as a voice, loud and clear, speaks just below us. "No sign of the girl yet."

Both boys swivel their heads and stare at me.

"Keep looking," says another voice. "Her body must be there. Find it."

"Yes, sir, Dr. Duroc."

I cover my mouth with both hands and stop breathing.

Duroc. Right here?

John-Paul tries to pull me back.

Eyes wide, I shake my head at him and put up a finger. I have to hear what they say. Edging closer, I peer carefully over the lip of crumbling dirt. Nate and John-Paul, completely silent, appear next to me. One man stands below on the beach, a man with long black hair pulled back into a ponytail, his camouflage T-shirt reveals darkly tanned skin. Not Duroc. A greenish image hovers over his ristcom.

"Report back later today," says Duroc's voice. But not Duroc. His voice is coming from the ristcom.

I'm so relieved, I push myself back from the edge of the cliff with a hard shove. From under my hand, I feel dirt crumble. I gasp and look over. Dirt falls straight down toward the soldier's head. I scramble back, pulling the others.

"Hey," shouts the soldier.

"He saw me," whispers Nate, crouching. "He looked me right in the eyes."

"Let's go," says John-Paul.

We run.

The soldier shouts orders, and in just a few minutes, the *thrump-thrump-thrump* of the helicopter pounds the air.

The boys run faster, exchange glances, and without stopping, catch the boat up by its sides, racing it down the steep slope toward the water, half running, half sliding. I follow them straight into the bay.

"Get in," gasps Nate, who had already pulled himself over the edge. He holds out both hands. I grasp one hand and the edge of the boat and throw my leg up over the side. The boat tilts crazily toward me but then rights itself as John-Paul scrambles over the opposite side. Nate leans back and drags me up.

I sit shivering as Nate digs the oars into the water and John-Paul lowers the motor and leans over it.

"Wait, there's grass," says Nate.

John-Paul either doesn't hear or ignores him and pulls the starter rope. The motor sputters. "Damn it," he mutters.

The beat of the helicopter grows closer.

The boat lurches forward again as Nate heaves on the oars.

John-Paul jerks the cord three times in a row, cursing as he does so. The motor makes a whirring sound but doesn't start. Then it gurgles.

"What's wrong?" I whisper. They don't hear me.

"You're flooding it," says Nate. His arms bulge as he heaves against the oars. We glide through drowned houses again.

This is my fault. I hunch down in the front of the boat. Wherever I go, I drag people into danger.

John-Paul scans the sky wildly, tipping everything sideways.

"JP!" snaps Nate.

"They're going the wrong way," says John-Paul, dropping to the motor again. He's right. The helicopter is flying west, low over the woods. He grabs the cord again, this time settling himself quietly, then tugs it hard and quick.

The motor clicks a few times and falls silent.

John-Paul and Nate stare at each other. The sound of the helicopter fades.

"Piece of crap," says Nate, dipping the oars in the water again.

"It'll start after a rest," says John-Paul. "You want me to row?"

Nate shakes his head. "I'm good for now."

John-Paul looks at me. "You okay?"

I nod, clutching my arms tightly around my life vest, though I'm not chilly. The air settles around us, breathless. We're getting close to the field of black rooftops sticking up out of the water.

Duroc is searching for my body. What will he do when he doesn't find it?

A voice shouts from shore. Another joins it.

Nate utters a curse and rows faster.

My heart pounds and I double over my knees. They saw Nate, but did they see me? I'm paralyzed. I can't let them catch me, but I can't Jump away. I have to protect the boys.

A voice becomes huge, shattering the air around us. They're using a handmic. "Stop where you are, or we will shoot. You are in a restricted area. We just want to talk. Stop where you are, or we will shoot."

CHAPTER 39

Nate tries to hunker down as he again heaves on the oars.

"Stop, Nate," says John-Paul.

A crack reverberates, and a bullet hits the water. We spin in our seats, gasping. There's a sniper on the shore.

"We give up. We give up," shouts John-Paul, his hands waving the air. "Nate, pull in the oars. Put your hands up."

Nate jerks the oars in quickly and we all put our hands up. "What the fuck is going on?" Nate's voice cracks. "Why are they shooting at us?"

"We surrender," shouts John-Paul.

My heart is hammering in my chest. Some men are getting into a small boat. I can't let them see me. I'll Jump myself. Once I know the boys are safe, I'll Jump before the soldiers can identify me. But how will I know the boys are safe? What if the soldiers just shoot them?

The helicopter roars back over the bay. Rapid fire strafes the water, not far from the boat.

"What are they doing?" screams Nate.

"Get down, get down," cries John-Paul, pulling Nate off the middle seat. "Eten, get down."

The blue sky stretches, elastic, and the moment expands. Calm descends on me. Arms extended, I launch myself across the middle bench and land on top of the two boys, wrapping them in my shield.

The boys scream as the guns rage.

"Let me up," yells John-Paul. He wants to shield me and Nate—a staggering, idiotic idea because, of course, he can't. He'd just get shot. I Sense his rage, his blunt refusal to allow his brother or me to be hurt. Even though it's idiotic, I'm awed by his courage. I hold on tightly to Nate's arms as he wriggles, sandwiched between us.

A powerful wind buffets the boat into circles as the helicopter sweeps overhead. John-Paul and Nate yell as rapid-fire bullets pummel us. Bullets slide off my shield, drained of all momentum. They clatter to the boat's floor. The helicopter sweeps onward and hovers above a rooftop, turning.

"Eten," John-Paul screams, his surge upward irresistible now. The three of us sprawl apart. His horror assaults my Senses. He's sure I am shot and he grabs me, pulls me in close.

"I'm okay," I shout. The helicopter hovers not far away.

John-Paul's strong hands twist me around so he can see the back of my life vest. He can't believe I'm not hurt—which makes a lot of sense, since he doesn't know I can shield.

"There's no holes."

"I'm okay!"

"Thank God!"

"Looks like they just want to sink us, not kill us," says Nate. He points at two holes in the bottom of the boat. The murky water is bubbling up through them.

"Oh, no!" says John-Paul. Nate grabs a bucket that was stowed under the seat at the back, along with their fishing gear, and bails out some water.

The three soldiers in the helicopter do want to kill us. Not because of me; they don't know anything about me. They just want to kill the people who saw their secret operation.

So this is the real America? Soldiers killing innocent civilians. Disgust fills me.

Gritting my teeth, I Jump the rifles out of the soldiers' hands, into the bay. The helicopter dips and comes straight toward us again as Nate tries to scoop the water out of the bottom of the boat. He scoops and tosses as John-Paul slides the oars out and pulls on them. The helicopter's roar pounds my head. I force myself to let go of my ears so I can cup my hands and scoop more water out of the boat. But I fall sideways as John-Paul digs the oars into the water again.

The helicopter is on top of us. I don't Sense any more weapons up there. Maybe they're trying to use the helicopter as a weapon, because they keep coming down, closer and closer. The soldiers are shouting. The helicopter's huge rotors blast wind and the boat rocks, almost turning over. We bang into a rooftop.

The helicopter rises and turns in the air.

We're back at the house with the hole in its side. "There's the hole," I shout. But it looks smaller. "Are the houses sinking?"

"No, the tide's coming in," Nate shouts.

The helicopter dives towards us again.

John-Paul grabs an oar, and lunges to the back of the boat. "Take cover in the house. Hurry!"

But the water is *rising*.

Nate manages to grab the splintered edge of the hole and pulls the boat to the interior. In another second, we are out of sight. In hot, dank darkness.

The helicopter roars overhead, as if about to land on the roof.

"Duck," shouts John-Paul as he pulls us toward the bottom of the boat. But there are no more bullets. Just deafening noise. I hear a long, low rumble and hiss from the darkness beyond us. The growl seems to be coming from inside the house.

"What's that sound?" I ask nervously.

"They must be out of ammo," says Nate.

I think there might be an animal in the black recesses of the house. And the tide is rising fast. "The house is flooding," I say. "We have to get out of here."

"The boat is sinking," says John-Paul. "We have to patch it first."

Dismayed, I looked down. Water swirls around my ankles, and my feet and shoes are entirely submerged. I hadn't even noticed. "Oh, no."

"Get the putty," says Nate.

"You get it. And the patches. I'll get the motor."

Nate lunges toward the back of the boat.

Something floats into my leg and I yelp, pulling it up with a slosh. It is just one of the fishing rods.

Next to me, John-Paul holds the motor in his arms, and he's *standing* in water, and not because of his life vest. "Eten, come on."

My mouth opens and no words come out.

Nate slides over the side of the boat into the water, stands up and grins. "It's the floor." He takes the motor from John-Paul. "We're in the attic of the house."

The pounding in my head dies away. Of course. We're in a house.

Something else hits my leg as I stand in the flooding, rocking boat. I yelp again, louder this time. The oar nods in the water by my shin. I do not like this place. I can Sense all kinds of life wriggling around in these waters.

"It's okay. Don't be scared. Just grab the rods and the oars and climb out," says John-Paul. "We have to fix the boat."

"I'm not scared!" I press my lips together, grab the rods and the oar, and slide over the edge of the boat into the dark water.

The floor is slippery and I slide back, the life vest making me bob in the water. It's an odd sensation; I've never I'm so glad my head didn't go under.

"No helicopter," says Nate.

The silence is almost spooky. I throw out my Senses as wide as I can and stiffen. I Sense people out there. How can there be people in the middle of the bay?

"Somebody's coming," I say.

"Hurry up. Let's just fix the holes," says John-Paul.

Without a word, both boys reach under the water. Dark, murky wavelets swirl around my life vest and tug at my clothes. Again, I hear a hissing noise from the far end of the house. It sounds like air flowing out of a pipe. My night vision can't penetrate the darkness back there, but I can Sense something back there.

The boys burst upward, flipping the boat over so the damaged bottom is exposed.

"Go around, Nate," pants John-Paul. "Give me some putty. I've got the patches."

I've got to look out of the house. I'm afraid that the boat I saw earlier may be approaching us. Still clutching the poles and the oars, I stretch out a foot and find I can walk. Laboriously, feet slipping, I push my way toward the light. The hole we entered through keeps getting smaller. That is, the water is still rising. Can we even get the boat out?

I push harder through the water. I Sense soldiers.

My foot goes down into nothingness, and my face plunges forward into the water. I come up sputtering, water in my nose. I hate this place!

 Quietly, I side-stroke to the edge of the hole and look out.

My throat goes tight and I swallow.

Glossy, black lumps glide toward the house. Soldiers in the water, shrouded in skin-tight, black suits. Guns hang across their backs. There must be ten of them.

My heart pounds as if about to burst. I Jump the guns off their backs into the water, where they sink. Most of the soldiers don't even notice; a few pause, turning. Then they keep coming.

I swim back into the house. "Soldiers," I whisper. The boys don't hear. I regain my footing and half swim, half run for John-Paul, then Jump myself right behind him. Nate's looking right at me as I appear.

"Hey!" he shouts.

"Shhhhh."

"Where did you…"

John-Paul jerks around.

"Soldiers!" I tell them. "Soldiers are coming."

The sudden hissing noise from the dark end of the house brings all three of us to a halt.

"What is that?" I ask.

A low growl echoes across the water.

I can Sense something. An animal.

A splash.

"Uh-oh," says Nate. "Crocodile."

That was a *big* splash. "A crocodile?" I ask. If I recall correctly, it's an animal that looks like it should've gone extinct with the dinosaurs. And it should only live way south in Florida.

John-Paul grabs the floating oars and holds it up. "Get in the boat. Nate, flip it over."

"Soldiers are out there." I point back. "In the water!"

"What?" John-Paul turns toward me, confused, his face contorted.

Nate lurches forward. "The motor," he says, plunging toward the side of the house where the motor lies half-propped against a shelf.

"No," shouts John-Paul. He tries to run after his brother, holding an oar above his head.

A growling bellow shocks the air, blasting the pitch-dark walls. Even the water trembles.

"Get back," screams John-Paul, rushing toward Nate.

The scariest sight I've ever seen in my life lunges out of the darkness. It's a huge log of thick, crisscrossed flesh with flailing claws and a lashing, battering tail. Its gaping mouth, full of jagged teeth, surges straight for the boys. I'm frozen. I can't even scream.

John-Paul whips the oar back with both hands and lets loose. It hits the monster across the eyes and bounces off. The animal sinks for a moment, giving John-Paul enough time to reach his brother. The two of them grab the motor, which looks like it could be a tidbit in the crocodile's maw.

Slashing its huge tail in the water, the crocodile shoots toward them, its teeth flashing again. Together, Nate and John-Paul throw the motor right into the animal's mouth. The teeth snap shut on the machine and the crocodile sinks as the boys fall backward.

John-Paul stands, pulling Nate to his feet. He lunges for the oar, which has floated close again. It's not going to help. The crocodile could snap the oar like a toothpick. They back up against the shelves, gasping.

Maybe the motor has hurt the beast. I can't Sense any pain, though. Only hunger. For a moment, there's silence.

"We have to get into the ..." begins John-Paul.

With a crash, the monster surfaces again in a rush of water, the motor in its mouth, actually *standing on its back legs*. It thrashes its head back and forth, then flings the machine toward the boat.

I Sense its resonating power, its massive bones and lust for blood, its blurred view of prey and its driving hunger, and suddenly I'm unfrozen and screaming.

The boys scramble sideways, splashing, falling, unable to get their footing. Growling again, the creature leaps at them with its mouth gaping, the teeth glinting like shining rows of broken knives.

I explode its head.

The boys, still yelling, scramble backward as the monster crashes to the water, gobs of flesh, blood, and bone spattering everywhere. John-Paul runs around the thrashing body toward the boat and Nate follows.

Next to me, they turn and stare at the massive, ruined animal shuddering in the water. Its huge claws judder and splash. The tail, as big as the boat, lashes sideways. Then the crocodile lays still and sinks.

"Did somebody shoot it?" asks John-Paul, turning to me. "Did you shoot it?"

I stare at him, not knowing what to say since it's kind of obvious I don't have a gun. I reach out a hand. "You have, uh, gunk on your face."

As if in shock, John-Paul touches his cheek, his forehead. His fingers come back bloody.

"Aww, yuck," says Nate, scooping up water and dashing it over his face. "Bro, it's in your *hair*." He dunks his head under. John-Paul shudders, then dunks himself, too.

Trembling as I go colder and colder, I point back to the opening in the house, now only about a few meters high. I'm not sure we can even get the boat through. "Soldiers. They're in the water. They're coming!"

"Oh, my God."

"Flip in the boat," says Nate, grabbing the edge of the craft, which is low in the water. John-Paul grabs the edge too, and they rock it.

"Where are we going to go?" I ask.

A voice booms from outside, mechanical and strident, from a handmic. "The house is surrounded. Come out quietly and you will not be harmed."

I shake my head and the boys stare at me. Their faces are still smudged with blackish blood. "Don't go. They're going to kill us," I tell them. "I can Sense it."

I'm so cold. I wrap my arms around myself and clench my teeth. Some of the soldiers still don't realize they've lost their guns. Others draw knives. I can Jump the knives, too, but the soldiers will still attack, fighting with bare hands. A shield doesn't do much in hand-to-hand.

Jumping is the only answer, but I've never Jumped three people before, and what if I can't do it? Despair makes me suddenly weak in the knees. These soldiers intend to kill us. I *have* to do it.

Taking a calming breath, I focus on quelling my fear. *I am a part of all things, and all things lift me toward the center.*

"We're coming in," booms the magnified voice.

CHAPTER 40

I can hear them swimming, almost at the opening. "You're under arrest," echoes the booming voice. "Keep your hands where we can see them."

I breathe deep and focus on Sensing: the boys, the boat in the water, the rods, the sunken motor. I take my time to be sure, to be thorough. I vaguely hear the boys talking anxiously, something about *racing, the motor, the line, and hooks.*

I visualize the place where we began: the beachhead where the boat lay hidden under brush. I smell the wind off the sea. I feel the hot sun on my head, the rough ground under my knees and elbows.

"We're armed," booms the voice. "Stay where you are, and you will not be hurt."

Eyes shut tight, I gather the boys and the boat, the sea, the sun, the scratchy bushes, and the land. I pull the edges together. I Jump.

Saltwater crashes over my head, knocking me sideways, and splashes away into the grass. The boat rocks back and forth, settling on its side, and the motor lays half embedded in the dirt, fishing poles and oars next to it. The sun beats down in hot waves.

Something smells terrible.

I lay on the ground, breathless and exhausted. Nate and John-Paul sprawl in a puddle next to the boat.

Never before have I Jumped so far, or with two other people. And a boat. And a motor, rods, oars, water. I can't believe it. I didn't know I could do this. I took a portion of my surroundings with me. Giggles burble hysterically inside of me. I did it, but I was so anxious about the boys' boat, I Jumped too much. Like, half the bay, including the dead crocodile.

My brothers and sisters would be in awe. I ache to see them again. Could I Jump myself back to them? I wonder how far I can Jump. I don't know the limits. Maybe there are no limits. Maybe I keep getting stronger. Though I do feel very weak at the moment.

The boys sit up groggily. They seem disoriented. I bite my lip, wondering if I have to tell them the truth. Maybe I can just say I don't know what happened.

"Oh, what's that smell?" says John-Paul, covering his face with his hands and rubbing his eyes.

"Wait...where are we?" Nate turns, viewing the brush, the grass, and the boat lying on its side. He scrambles up and grabs his brother's arm. "What happened?"

John-Paul gets to his feet and grabs Nate's shoulders. "Holy shit. Where are we?"

"I don't know!"

"Did we pass out?" John-Paul looks up and turns around.

"There were soldiers," says Nate. "Where are the soldiers?"

"We were in the water. Inside that sunken house."

They look at each other. "The croc!"

"Somebody shot it," says John-Paul.

"A soldier?"

Finally, they look at me, where I'm sitting on the ground, biting my lip. I want to tell them the truth, but I'm afraid. How will John-Paul see me, once he knows? What if he finds my special "skills" repulsive?

They're waiting for me to say something.

"The 'croc'? You mean the crocodile? It's right there." I point behind the boat. "I think that's what stinks."

They shout and skitter backward from the bloated, gruesome corpse.

Even without a head, it measures about six meters long. It lays belly-up, the bottom a pale, leathery yellow with rows of deep lines running sideways. A bit of spine pokes out of the neck hole, with pink and yellow tissue twined around it. Bloody water drips. Already, buzzing insects swarm the exposed flesh.

Its stubby legs hang sideways in the air, looking kind of pathetic. The front feet are almost like hands—well, vicious hands—each with five long, taloned fingers. Webbing joins the toes of the back feet.

"Don't worry, it's dead," I say.

"Yeah, I can see that," says Nate. "But what is it *doing* here?"

"What are *we* doing here?" asks John-Paul. "We're back at the boat launch! How did we get here? I feel like I…" He shakes his head and presses his hands to his brow. "I feel like I just lost a chunk of myself."

"Maybe it's one of those, you know, psychological thingies," says Nate, dropping to the ground. "What's it called? When you just black out for a while?"

"Yeah, a fugue state," says John-Paul. "But not *both of us* at once. That doesn't make sense." He turns to me. "What about you? Do you remember what happened?"

His half-angry bewilderment and fear leave me aching to just get it over with. There's no point in being secretive anymore. Duroc knows my plane is here. Secrecy and lies are just going to cause more trouble. I've already put this family in danger—and what's worse, they don't even know it.

Swallowing my anxiety, pushing back that longing for John-Paul to see me as a normal girl, to like me the way I like him, I say, "Yeah, I know what happened."

But once I explain, they don't believe me.

"You what?" laughs Nate.

"Is this a joke?" John-Paul asks coldly.

The sun has started to beat down on us as we stand behind the boat in the hot grass. On the far side of the boat, the crocodile carcass is starting to smell even worse. I'm sure it's getting late, and their skepticism is annoying me.

"Don't you know of anyone else who can Jump things?" I ask.

"Move things with their mind? No," says John-Paul.

Perhaps there isn't anyone else like me and my siblings. Another lie from Mom and Dad—saying other children have "evolved" like us. I think of the storeroom behind Mom's office. All the jars. All of the experiments. Something twists inside of me. Of course, we didn't "evolve." We're experiments. But I will not be ashamed of being different. I refuse. If my brothers and sisters and I are unique in the world, then—oh, God, then it will be tough.

They already know. I may as well demonstrate. "Okay, watch," I say, and I Jump the crocodile from where it's lying on the far side of the boat to our feet. The boys scream and leap back. Nate gags as the nasty odor puffs up.

"Oh, all right," shouts John-Paul, holding out his hands. He's a bit shaky. "I see it. Okay."

The stench is unholy. "Sorry," I mutter. "That was a bad thing to Jump." Hurriedly, I Jump the carcass to the water's edge, where the waves will carry it away. The boys keep staring at the empty spot where the croc just lay. "Okay, look at the boat," I tell them. When I'm sure they're looking at it, I Jump the boat to the nearby bushes where the boys keep it hidden.

"Whoa," says John-Paul, turning around and looking for it.

"Where is it?" says Nate.

"There," mutters his brother, taking Nate's arm. They move closer to each other, like closing ranks. I Sense their fear with a sinking sensation.

"Listen," I say. I can hear the pleading in my voice. "Don't be afraid of *me*. I'm on your side. We need to be afraid of the military."

"I'm not afraid," says Nate, just as his brother says, "The military!"

John-Paul's face looks grim. "They were looking for you."

Nate takes just a moment longer. He looks at me with new eyes, then at his brother, then at me again. "You're not an orphan, huh? Dr. Mac said you had no family."

I shake my head. "I've got four brothers and sisters at home."

"Brothers and sisters like you?" Nate murmurs. I Sense his fear drain away, give way to awe.

I nod.

"The military's after her," says John-Paul. He looks up at me. "Right?"

Again, I nod, shame burning into my cheeks. "I'm sorry. I put you in danger."

"Are you kidding?" He shakes his head. "You saved us. You saved our lives."

"But it's my fault those soldiers were there. I can't stay here. I'm a danger."

"Don't be afraid of them," scoffs Nate, as if we hadn't been cowering moments ago. "We've been running circles around them for years."

"You don't understand. There's this man named Duroc. Dr. Duroc. He ..."

John-Paul's head snaps back. "Wait. Duroc?" he asks. "He was the one on the soldier's ristcom, right?"

I nod.

"Uh-oh," says Nate.

"You know who he is?"

"Like, yeah," says Nate. "Everybody does. He's the puppet master behind our so-called leader, President McCarthy. Everybody knows Duroc has the real power."

A chill runs up my backbone.

"Why is the military after you?" asks Nate. Then he slaps himself in the head. "Duh. I guess they know what you can do?"

"I'm guessing she *escaped* from the military," says John-Paul. "Right?" He's got that look again: gentle, serious, concerned. As if I were the only person in the world who mattered right now. How does he do that?

I nod. "Yes. I escaped. I've got to get my brothers and sisters out, too." I stand here, pulsing, dumb as a post, staring at John-Paul,

He smiles his warm, wonderful grin, his eyes soft. Oh, my God! I think I might collapse right here. Holding out his hand, he says, "Let's go talk to my mom."

CHAPTER 41

There's a very good reason why I don't Jump the three of us back to the house. I don't want John-Paul to let go of my hand. We leave the life vests in the boat, push through the long grass and John-Paul helps me through the brush. The moment is as fragile as a soap bubble; I'm afraid to breathe. But as soon as we reach the path, he drops my hand and moves behind me. My heart sinks. He's only interested in being kind, I realize.

Nate doesn't notice. He's walking on the other side of me, in the street, dodging debris and whacking at rusted cars with a stick. He starts asking questions, and I tell them

about our pod, about Teetu and the others, the fake nuclear war, and how Mom and Dad told us America was uninhabitable. But I say nothing about assassination. I'm hoping they never find out about that.

Inside the house, all is quiet. Maria's handbag sits on the kitchen table and dishes from another meal lie in the sink.

"Mom's home." Nate shoves the fishing poles into the corner.

"Shhh," whispers John-Paul, taking off his wet shoes and shirt. "She might be asleep." I take my shoes off, too, and try to wring some of the water out of my clothes.

"Nah, she never sleeps before we get home," says Nate, peeling his socks off.

"Be quiet anyway. We're really late."

"I'm being quiet!" insists Nate. He is not being quiet.

"Is that you, boys?" Maria's voice comes from the living room.

Nate gives John-Paul a look of derision, turns, and runs into the next room. "Ma," he calls, "you're never going to believe what happened." We hurry after him.

"Good Lord." Maria stands up behind the big table, her hands still holding the book she'd been reading. "You're soaked. Did you capsize?" She points a finger. "Did you have life vests on?"

"Yes," I say.

"Ma, listen ..." starts John-Paul.

"Ma, Eten is telekinetic," Nate blurts out. "She can move things with her mind. It's incredible. And the military is after her."

Maria surveys us with a frown, her mouth half-open, then sits back down. "What?" She wrinkles her nose, staring at the three of us as if we're speaking gibberish.

"It's true," says John-Paul. "The military is looking for her. We have to get EVE to help her."

Maria's face loses its vague expression. She glares at John-Paul. "Nobody is getting involved with EVE, do you hear me? That's a dangerous organization."

"Ma," Nate begins, but John-Paul interrupts him.

"Just show her," he says to me.

I Jump the book from under Maria's hand into mine and hold it up. "Your book?" It's a thick, soft-cover book, well used, and I fan the yellow pages with my thumb and Jump it back down on the table again.

Maria glances down and back up to me. She's incredulous, but she doesn't leap up or gasp or get scared. She just whispers, "Oh, my Lord. I knew there was something."

John-Paul and Nate look disappointed. "Did you know?" asks Nate.

"I thought, when Donny Abrams lived, at the neighbor's house last night," says Maria. "Mac didn't save him. You did something, didn't you?"

I nod. "I Jumped the bullet out of him." I try to explain what I did. I know it sounds confusing and imprecise because I don't exactly understand what I did, but they don't seem to care.

"You saved him?" John-Paul whispers. "You saved his life?" That look is back on his face again, the intense glow that makes my insides melt.

"Child," says Maria, her voice soft, "what you could do for people."

"I want to," I tell her. "That's just what I want. I want to be a healer, not a ..." I break off before I say the word. Killer.

The boys don't notice. But Maria does.

"Did you say the military is looking for Eten?" she asks.

"Yeah," says Nate, "they were pulling up pieces of her airplane out of the water."

"And we heard them talking," says John-Paul. "Over a ristcom. This soldier was talking and we could hear his commander over the com, and Mom, it was Dr. Duroc."

Maria starts as she hears the name. "*The* Dr. Duroc?"

John-Paul nods. "He's looking for Eten. That's why we have to get in touch with EVE."

For the first time, Maria seems agitated as she turns to me again. "Is Dr. Duroc looking for you Eten?"

I cringe inside as I nod. I should have left these people already. I've put them all in danger. "I'm sorry."

John-Paul moves closer to me. "She escaped from the military. And she's got brothers and sisters still in prison there."

"They're not in prison," I say, but how do I explain it? Should I say out loud that my "parents" are just soldiers who trained me to kill? That I'm the product of a military experiment, an assassin, just a cloneable, expendable weapon? The words die in my throat. "My parents are in the military," I say to the floor, my mouth dry. I feel hot and feverish under my chilly, damp clothes. The words come out haltingly. "I think—um, Duroc—doesn't trust me anymore. He tried to kill me."

"Nate," Maria snaps. "Go run to Dr. Mac's house and wake him up. Tell him to come over here right away."

"Yes, ma'am," says Nate as he turns and sprints from the room.

CHAPTER 42

Maria makes coffee while John-Paul and I change into dry clothes. Before long, Nate and Dr. Mac arrive. The doctor rubs his eyes and gratefully takes a mug of coffee.

"I'm sorry to wake you, Mac," says Maria, "but I think we need your help on this. It's…" She pauses. "It's a little out of my league."

The doctor settles at the table opposite me.

"Joseph Duroc is looking for her," says Maria.

Dr. Mac almost spills his coffee. Suddenly, he isn't so sleepy anymore. "Joseph Duroc? As in Under Secretary of Defense?"

Maria nods.

He frowns and makes a deep, disturbed growl in his throat as he pulls on his small beard. "Why is that, Eten? Why is Duroc looking for you?"

I'm about to say something about the military but Nate pipes up.

"I told you, she's telekinetic," says Nate.

Dr. Mac shakes his head, his brow crinkled. "Can you show me?"

I bite my lip. A small bowl on the table holds three apples. "Okay, look at the apples in the bowl."

When I'm sure they are looking, I Jump the apples onto the table next to the bowl. They roll around a little and I Jump them back.

To my disappointment, Dr. Mac just frowns.

"She can do way more than that!" says Nate.

Dr. Mac shakes his head. "I'm sorry, but it kind of looks like a parlor trick."

That stings. I raise my eyebrows. "A trick?"

I Jump Dr. Mac to the boy's bed.

Maria leaps up. "Mac!" she shrieks.

Dr. Mac falls harmlessly backward on the bed. "Whoa," he bellows.

I smile.

"Mac?" Maria cries out again.

"I'm all right," says Dr. Mac as he sits up. He looks right and left, then at us, sitting at the table. "What happened?" With a hand to his throat, Dr. Mac pants a few shallow breaths, as if he's been running.

Nate starts to laugh. Maria shushes him angrily.

"Do you want me to Jump you back to the table again, Dr. Mac?" Caution has melted away beneath my pride. Let him call my skill a "trick" again! He'll see what I can really do.

He puts up a hand. "I believe you. I'm going to walk back to my chair, thank you."

"I told you!" says Nate, triumphant.

Maria sits down heavily, pushes her chair out, and leans her head between her knees.

"Ma," says John-Paul, scraping his chair back.

Gripping the arms of her chair, she lifts her head and takes a long breath. "I'm fine, just a little…surprised, is all."

"I'll get you some water." John-Paul hurries to the kitchen.

"I'm sorry," I say. Once again, I acted without thinking, out of pride and anger. "I guess that was a little bit overkill."

But Dr. Mac sits back in his chair and gives me that wry, loose grin. "Okay, I needed convincing. And that," he points back toward the bed, "was convincing!"

Even Maria chuckles a little. I sit back down as John-Paul brings in two glasses of water, one for his mother and one for Dr. Mac. They both sip in silence until Dr. Mac clears his throat. "Nate said you have brothers and sisters? Who can do what you do?"

I nod, wondering what else Nate told him. "I have to rescue them. Dr. Duroc wants to clone us and then he'll…" Somehow, I feel ashamed of what comes next. Why should I? Duroc is the monster, not me. But to be cast aside like a worn-out shoe, a manufactured weapon that's no longer useful, like garbage.

"He'll what, Eten?" asks Dr. Mac.

"Terminate us," I whisper, closing my eyes. "Once the clones grow up."

"Oh, my God," says Dr. Mac.

John-Paul sits next to me. "Is that why your plane blew up?"

"Yes," I say. "I think he already has my DNA."

"He tried to *kill* you?" Nate's voice goes ragged with disbelief. "Why? Why would he even want to do that?"

"Because," I say, feeling the bitterness rise, "I don't want to do his dirty work anymore."

There's a silence. "That's why we need EVE," John-Paul says.

This time, his mother doesn't object.

"EVE can hide them," says Nate. "Right Dr. Mac? In the Free Zone out west." Nate is vibrating with excitement. He's picturing a town in the middle of nowhere—mountains in the distance, sunny fields of grass and crops, a bright stream, children playing. Nate's fantasy of the Free Zone. I'm thinking probably a little too good to be true.

But Dr. Mac is nodding. "We better get your brothers and sisters away from Duroc as soon as possible." He rises from the table. "Just keep a low profile until they send somebody, Eten." He looks at the boys. "Don't tell anyone anything about Eten. Not any of the other kids at school. Nobody. And Eten, just stay put. No need to spread word around that there's a new girl in town. I'll get word to EVE."

I think Maria is going to object again, but when Dr. Mac leaves, she gets ready for bed and the boys get ready for school. Before they leave for the day, Maria sits next to me where I'm curled up with one of John-Paul's medical books on the soft, wide couch. She leans in and addresses me seriously. "Eten, you need to understand something. EVE is dangerous. They're violent." She shakes her head. "They do important work, too. They transport medications and try to help the homeless. But they're killers."

My entire being cringes. If only she knew.

"But Mom," says John-Paul, coming to sit on the other side of her. "Where would we be without EVE? If nobody fought for our rights?"

"Do they have to fight for our rights by blowing things up? Shooting people?"

"Ma," Nate says. "What kind of country are you leaving us? What are we going to have when we grow up? It's not right. Dad knew that. We have to fight."

Maria sighs. She speaks to Nate sideways, without looking at him. "I don't want another death in my family."

Both boys embrace her and she sighs again. "We'll be careful," says Nate.

"All right," she says. "All right."

EVERYONE VOTES EVERYWHERE

04 MAY 2088

Garfunkel,

A midlevel operator based in North Carolina (code name: MD25) has brought something extraordinary to the table and we have to act fast.

He claims to have a teenager who escaped from the National Military. They are using her and her four siblings as weapons. Yes, no typo, dude, "weapons". MD25 claims this kid has telekinetic powers, strong enough to kill somebody. Okay, it sounds nuts, but listen to this:

The kid started going on "missions" 10 or 11 years ago. Remember when Rider and Bill Aronson held the Fort Worth refinery hostage in 2080? They all got whacked in like, 15 minutes? And the one guy who escaped, everybody thought he was crazy, he said their guns just "disappeared" right before the military moved in?

Maybe not so crazy. I've heard rumors like that from other operations. And what about those foreign assassinations, the "secret weapon" people are talking about?

MD25 and his people want our help to hide and

protect the 5 kids. The one who already escaped
claims she can bring the other 4 to a meeting
place. I can see your face right now, shaking
your head and saying I'm a fool, but I'm going.
And I'm taking the new van.

If even one of these 5 has that kind of power,
we can NOT let the National Military keep them.
I will verify if it's real when I get there,
instamail: #1 if it's a yes, #2 if it's a fake.

                              Iggy Pop

CHAPTER 43

"Call me Joe," says the man from EVE.

It's late afternoon, more than a week after Dr. Mac informed EVE about me and asked for their help. It's been so hard to wait. I'm supposed to be hiding, but nobody is looking for me. John-Paul brought me books to read from his school, amazing books about biology and the structures of the body. I wish I could go with the boys to school. One evening, John-Paul walked me there. It's an old building that looks like all the rest of the buildings, four levels high, with worn, stone steps that go up to a wooden door and a big window decorated with cut-out pictures of animals and flowers. What I'd give to be a regular girl going to a regular school.

We all sit at the big living room table, with Dr. Mac, Maria, the boys, and me at one end and Joe at the other. If this man says EVE will help hide my brothers and sisters, I will leave tonight to get them. It all depends on Joe.

His name isn't Joe.

His face looks much younger than the heavy glow his spirit suggests. His wide, bright blue eyes and easy smile engage even Maria. He takes a sip of water. He has freckles across his nose, and ears that stick out sideways from his head under short brown hair, and it reminds me of something. An old TV vid? A vid about a goofy boy always getting into trouble? He's supposed to be charming.

"We want to help you," says Joe with another pleasant smile.

He's lying. He hasn't made up his mind yet.

I glance out the window, suddenly wishing I were anywhere else. Not that I've gone out much in the last week. We've avoided two militia patrols, and even more scary, a late-night, slow-driving car carrying a woman from the military police. She cruised by with headlights off. But didn't stop.

I wish I were on the shore of the sea, and nobody ever wanted to hurt anybody ever again.

"Dr. Mac told us that, uh, you have certain skills?" I haul my attention back. Finally, Joe is looking at me.

My skills. The price of EVE's help.

I've thought about this a lot. I'm not going to let them know everything I can do. Especially not the assassination part.

I stand up. "Okay. Let's get this over with."

The others stand up, too.

Nate picks up a bag from the floor and dumps every knife and fork from the kitchen onto our end of the table.

"What's this?" says Joe, frowning.

"Just watch," says Dr. Mac.

"Okay," I say, "imagine your enemy has all these knives or guns or weapons." I Jump the silverware to the other end of the table, right in front of Joe. "I can disarm them."

Joe is staring down at the pile of silverware. He looks up at us, shaking his head. "What did you do?"

"She's telekinetic," says Dr. Mac. "She just disarmed the enemy."

"So she can do a trick with silverware?" says Joe. He doesn't believe his eyes. Just like Dr. Mac. It's like you have to put on a show to make people believe their own eyes.

"Oh, good grief," says John-Paul.

I know I should've been more patient with Dr. Mac, but this guy Joe—he's totally annoying. I Jump him into the outhouse.

"Oh," says Maria, staring at the place where Joe was. She turns. "Uh-oh."

Dr. Mac twirls around, searching the room, then frowns at me. "Where is he?"

I raise my eyebrows. "He's perfectly safe."

A shout comes from outside.

Nate rushes to the kitchen door. "I think he's stuck in the outhouse," he calls back to us, then the kitchen door bangs.

John-Paul starts laughing.

"Eten!" Maria says disapprovingly.

Dr. Mac is angry, even though I think it's funny. "Eten, these people are trying to *help* us." He hurries to the kitchen and through the door, and we follow.

"Yeah, well, they're not helping us for free, Dr. Mac," I mutter, but he doesn't hear me.

Outside, already having escaped the outhouse, Joe excitedly approaches Maria's picnic table that sits under a huge tree. Nate trots after him.

"Wonderful!" Joe says. "What else can you do?"

I figured he'd be at least a little bit shaken up after finding himself in the outhouse. But no, the man from EVE looks like he wants to pin a medal on me. He's grinning from ear to ear, holding out a hand, headed straight for me.

I just get mad. I don't know why, I just do. I don't want to show off my skills. I don't want to prove I can fight, just so I can rescue my brothers and sisters. There is nothing "wonderful" about any of this.

I blow up the bowl of strawberries I just spent an hour collecting from an abandoned garden down the street. Not the bowl, which is still sitting on the table. Just the berries.

Strawberry mush spatters Joe's nice, white T-shirt. And his face. And his hair. I'm hoping it got in his big ears, too.

Nate leaps back. "Strawberry bomb!" he shrieks, laughing.

"*Eten*," thunders Dr. Mac.

"Oh, my goodness," says Joe, wiping his face and hair and looking down at the strawberry mush dripping from his shirt. I'm a little shocked to realize it looks like blood. Bright, pink blood.

But Joe doesn't see it that way. I bet he's never even experienced the blood of someone he's killed. The blood of someone killed next to him. Does he know about the horror? He's still smiling. Not upset at all. If anything, he's happier! "You can blow things up too?"

"No, oh no, I can't do that." Joe nods like he doesn't believe me. Stupid me. Joe shakes everybody's hand and leaves in a rush. He's supposed to come back tomorrow, because tonight, I'm going to Jump back to the pod to get my brothers and sisters.

A thrill shoots through me—to be reunited with them, finally. But it's also a thrill of fear. What if this very big Jump lands me in the center of crushing dirt eight hundred meters under the surface? Or worse, leaves me hanging in the middle of no-time and no-space, drifting nowhere forever? All sorts of disasters flash through my head.

I'm not able to eat dinner, and afterward, I pace back and forth in the living room as John-Paul reads aloud from a book called *Survival Medicine*. It is both very boring and at times completely chilling, especially when it describes how to survive a bear attack. I didn't even know bears still existed.

Then I hear Maria greeting Dr. Mac. It's time.

"All ready, Eten?" he asks.

No, I want to yell.

I climb off the bed and nod. "All ready."

The plan is simple but monumental. Jump myself back to my home pod and Jump my brothers and sisters back to Maria's—if I can.

It's late enough that Mom and Dad should be gone for the night and my brothers and sisters will be in bed. I'll Jump myself into the bedroom, blackout the vid and audio, then wake them up. And then I'll Jump each one individually back to Maria's house.

Tomorrow, EVE will come pick us up. Take us to hide, out west.

Piece of cake.

I kneel on the floor of Maria's living room, the others gathered around me. Steep my consciousness in the thisness of my bedroom, the beds on either side of me, and Jump.

CHAPTER 44

Terror flickers through me like lightning. I strain my eyes wide open but see nothing.

A moment ago, I Jumped from Maria's house to my home pod, but…I wave my arms around from where I kneel in darkness. Where am I? Across my brow, skin prickles, and sweat pops out on the back of my neck. The air smells musty, old. I can Sense no human presence. Where are my brothers and sisters?

Am I in some kind of stasis, a nothing place, a nowhere in-between space? I hear myself groan.

You can't hear yourself in nothingness, right?

"Hello?" I whisper out loud. No reply. I rock forward to my hands and knees and feel the smooth, narrow boards, the tiny seams between. A floor, a normal floor.

Quickly, I crawl forward and promptly smack my head on something hard. "Ouch!" I cry out. Then freeze. Again, no response.

Only silence rushing in my ears. Reaching my Senses outward again, I find no one.

I touch the thing I banged my head on, explore it with my fingers. Cold, metal, horizontal bar. A squishy mattress on top. Blanket.

I draw a sharp breath and stand, groping in front of me. Bed. Bunk bed.

I'm home.

Where are my brothers and sisters?

I can't Sense them. Where can they be? On missions?

The darkness confounds me, though. No red dot from the surveillance camera. No night light in the bathroom. The smell is wrong. Stale. The bedroom is never this dark, never this quiet. Some essential background noise no longer whirs. I feel the upper bed. It's neatly made, with sheets and a blanket tucked tight. Under the pillow, my fingers bump something hard and square. The calculator.

Eagerly, I turn on the light and shine it around the room. All of the beds are neatly made. I look into our dresser. One drawer is empty. The next is almost empty. I throw open the sliding door to the boys' closet. Most of the clothes are gone. The bedroom door stands open. Darkness invades every corner of the corridor beyond.

A chill sweeps me and I shiver. It's *cold* in here.

Everything, everywhere, is dark.

Not expecting it to work, I flip the light switch just inside the bedroom door. And choke back a yelp as light floods the room. In the light that spills out of the doorway, I hurry along the corridor to Nana's room.

The door handle turns, unlocked. I throw the door open and turn on the light.

The room is empty. The bed is stripped down to the white mattress. The white bedside table and the brown, anonymous dresser are bare as if they never were cluttered with Nana's little bottles of pills and tubes of cream. I jerk open the drawers, the closet. They're all empty.

With a papery taste in my mouth, I turn all the lights in the pod on, room by room. There's no food and no smell of food in the kitchen. The dampness in the sun and pool room smells musty. The pool has a greenish tint.

I press my chest, try to slow my heart, and think of what could have happened. My head is pounding and I feel the swell of a cry mounting inside. I shout their names out loud. The silence presses in on me like a mountain of earth. I've lost them. There is only the wheeze of my breath as I sob.

It must be Duroc. He has my brothers and sisters. He already took Teetu; he must've taken them all. Maybe that was what Mom was trying to tell me when my autoplane took off. I'll kill him. I'll find my brothers and sisters, and I'll kill that bastard Duroc.

I try the door to Mom's office but it's locked, as usual. As soon as I Jump myself inside, I freeze. Something's different. The long row of metal cabinets. They've been moved back. They're now flush up against the back wall, hiding the secret entrance to the storage room. I pull on a cabinet drawer. It's not locked, and it slides out easily.

Empty. Quickly, I pull out more drawers. All empty. All of the papers that documented the experiments, vanished.

Did Duroc destroy everything? And arrest Mom?

Nausea. My fingers tremble. Duroc must have raided the pod. Found the files, and taken my brothers and Jaysx. Right now, he might be holding them hostage. It seems so likely, I taste metal on my tongue, like blood.

The shelves are blocking the storeroom door, so I have to Jump myself just inside the hidden door and fumble for the light. As it flickers on, my breath explodes with relief.

The storeroom is full. Full of evidence!

Piles and piles of papers block the aisles, stacked carelessly, as if in haste, some spilling to the side. They're all from the metal cabinets. And I can see the glass jars, glinting from the shelves. Everything is still here.

Mom must have saved the papers back here. And obviously, the files were moved in a big hurry. Which means…what? She knew a raid was coming? Or she knew she was leaving the pod? Whatever it was, at least she had a little time to prepare.

I drop to my knees in the middle of the mounds of paper. All of the evidence of Duroc's sick experiments could destroy him. But then, once people see it all, everyone will know I'm one of Duroc's sick experiments. The thought makes me queasy, but…this is more important than just me. This evidence may be a way to stop Duroc. To find justice.

I don't need to kill him. Let the truth destroy Duroc.

Carefully tip-toeing around, I search through the folders. They're still in order, even in the tumbling piles, and I find a folder entitled D5. The one about the baby they shot. This, for sure, is gruesome enough to put Duroc away forever! I take the final few pages and photographs from D5, fold them up, and stuff them in my pocket. Then I see something else, on top of other papers. KILL ORDER. It's the page with the kill order for me. In fact, there's a whole stack of papers from Dr. Duroc. It's not the one I saw already, but the one where Dr. Duroc says I should be cloned and killed. I put that and some of the other orders into my pocket, too.

Someday, I promise myself, everyone will see this room of horrors. The world will know Duroc is the monster. Not me.

The only place I haven't checked yet is the gym, and with a thrill, I realize I haven't yet checked for the travel pods. Maybe my brothers and sisters are away on missions. I don't want to think about how unlikely this is. Why would our whole pod shut down if the others left on missions and were coming back?

I Jump myself to the gym, and before I even stand up, lights blaze, and air whooshes over my body in a massive gust. The big metal gym doors stand wide open in front of me, warm, fresh air blasting from the white grill opposite the doors. I crouch lower, shielding myself.

Lights flash on all the way down the corridor. I Sense the pod's entire system coming back online. Cameras activate.

Worried somebody might figure out I'm back in the pod, I quickly Jump myself to the huge elevator at the back of the gym, where the travel pods are lined up in a row against the wall. All three sit like squat, blocky sentinels. The three minipods are there, too.

My hopes sink. So they're not on a mission. Duroc's got them. Did he know about the plot to expose him at the World Court? He must have. Did he arrest Mom and Dad?

I'm staring and staring when I see something's *off* with the boys' pod. The door's open, hanging at an odd angle. And it seems dirty. I move in closer. The door's *broken*. And the dirt on the door seems peculiar, flaky. There's more on the bottom edge, on the sill you step over to go inside.

The gym lights, full on daylight, glare harsh and bright. The dirt looks like…

A stain. Shaped like a bird. Or a hand.

I move closer.

It's brown. Reddish-brown and black.

With hair stuck in it.

Blood. I can smell it. I stuff my knuckles into my mouth, managing to stifle a scream.

Stuck to the blood, stiff blonde hairs with a single, limp, silver tendril. My brothers' hair.

Are my brothers dead?

I launch myself into the travel pod, slapping my hand on the light switch.

And scream for real, long and loud. Terror shakes me. There are streaks of blood all over the white floor. Long hanks of curly, golden hair with deflated silver strands, all clotted with blood.

Clumps of hair, everywhere.

I gag, try to hold back the bile rising in my throat.

Blood pools under each thick, silver strand. My hand smooths back my own hair as I step back. I yelp as I step on something squishy: A filthy yellow bathroom towel, crusty with blood and hair.

Blackened blood smears the twin blue travel chairs. The table between the chairs is smashed forward. It rests upside down and some silvery implements I don't recognize lie on the floor. Except for the gleaming scissors, the blades smeared with blood. I recognize those.

I gasp as I see restraints. On the chairs' arms and legs and backrests, restraints made out of some white plastic. They're edged with blood and crisply cut apart in the middle.

Restraints couldn't hold my brothers. Not unless…

They were unconscious.

Something black and lumpy lies in the mess of blood and hair behind the chairs. I lift it gingerly, with two fingers. It's a kind of mask. Two big, round goggles for the eyes; a kind of plastic grill over the mouth, and two big, round cans screwed in on the sides. Straps and a mesh hold the mask to the head, and there's more blood on the mesh.

I know what it is, though I've never seen one in real life before. A gas mask.

Somebody gassed the boys into unconsciousness. Then cut off their hair.

Trying to destroy the boys' power.

Dropping the mask, I cover my face with my hands. I don't know what to do.

"E-10," echoes a loud voice, a voice I recognize, and I can't suppress another yelp.

It's Duroc.

CHAPTER 45

Whirling, I fling my Senses as wide as I can. Duroc is not here. He's speaking through electronics.

"I thought you might return. I'm so glad," says the hateful voice, shuddering off the walls and the huge dome of the gym. Duroc is using the gym's speaker system. No place is safe from this man.

I Jump back to the gym entrance. The red dot of a camera glows just to the side of the door. My breath catches as I try to reach my Senses *into the camera*, willing myself through the wires, the speakers, buzzing like electricity into Duroc. But I can't; it doesn't work. If only I could strangle that voice.

"What did you do to my brothers?" My voice cracks and I hate allowing Duroc to see my dismay.

"Nothing!" booms Duroc. "I didn't do anything to your brothers. And I don't know where the others are, either."

My heart lurches and grinds as I listen to him lie. But I'm ready to play his game. I force myself to calm down. I even smile. "I think you do know, Dr. Duroc."

"No, really. I don't. No clue."

Duroc has the advantage here. I can't Sense him. I can't tell if he's lying. I have to find him. Confront him in the flesh.

"I've been waiting for someone to show up," he goes on. "I've been hoping *you* would show up! We didn't know if you were alive or dead."

"I guess I disappointed you."

"*Tsk, tsk*," comes from Duroc. It's a wet, unpleasantly fleshy sound over the loudspeaker. "E-10, I assure you. You are my most important asset. I did not try to hurt you—that plane malfunctioned. I'm very grateful you survived."

"Grateful enough to tell me what happened to my brothers? Their blood and hair are all over the travel pod. They were…"

"Blood?" Duroc attempts to sound shocked. "Blood and hair?"

My composure cracks like an eggshell. "It looks like they were butchered!" I shout. "Isn't that your department?"

"Oh, no," says Duroc. "I thought that was *your* department, E-10."

Shock reels me back, takes my breath away. Images of people I killed flicker through my mind like lashes of a whip. The depths of this man's cruelty in unfathomable. My fingers ache from clenching, and I have to regroup. There's no way Duroc doesn't know what happened to my brothers, not with cameras all over the place. I change tactics. "You took Teetu. Where is she?"

"Now that's an odd thing, I will admit. Your mother came to visit, although I had not invited her, and brought J-6 with her. She wanted to see T-2, just when I was discovering some very interesting things about your younger sister. Did you know she can actually hear people's thoughts? So strange for someone who can't talk."

Sweat breaks out on my forehead. "No, she can't," I say, keeping a tremor from my voice. Did he *do* something to Teetu? I may have to kill him if he hurt Teetu.

Duroc continues as if he hadn't heard me. "And then, that blockhead of a girl J-6 had a tantrum and said she had to see her sister. She was making quite a scene, breaking furniture and such, so I did allow T-2 to come into the room, and wouldn't you know, as soon as they hugged T-2, all three of them vanished. How's that for gratitude? I don't know where they are."

I'm sure Duroc is lying. This is futile. I have to find him. If I can find him, I can pry out the truth.

As if he Senses my thoughts, he says, "E-10. Why don't you come see me? I mean it, you are my greatest asset, my most valued soldier. Come see me in Washington. I can help you find your brothers and sisters."

At first, I'm shocked. Why would he risk getting close to me? Isn't he afraid I might kill him? Then, I get it. He's trying to trick me. Again.

I have to catch him unprepared.

"Come to D.C., I can…."

I cut him off. "No, thanks. Not going to happen."

Something clangs from further back in the gym. A muffled, metallic *bump*. There's a low hum, coming from the elevator shaft. And then I Sense people. Soldiers from the surface lobby, the same ones who caught me when I was with SamJay. Four of them in the elevator. They're armed.

I turn back to the camera, suddenly scornful. "What are you doing? Sending your pathetic squad after me? Are you kidding? Are you aware of what I can do?"

Duroc makes a low sound. "E-10. Don't feel threatened." He makes that rumble in his throat again, as if he thinks it's reassuring, and it's so creepy. "They're not going to hurt you. Their job is to escort you to me here in Washington."

Somehow, I'm pretty sure that's not what he has in mind. "Yeah, they *can't* hurt me. I hope you know that."

I Sense the soldiers descending rapidly. Maybe thirty seconds until the elevator doors open. Duroc is talking again, but I'm not listening. Because I suddenly realize the soldiers have more than guns. *They are putting on gas masks!*

How could I be so dense? Gas! Just like they did to the boys. They'll gas me and kill me.

I crouch, pull up the *thisness* of SamJay's living room as I grab hold of the essence of here and now. I pull them all together and Jump.

Then I'm here, at SamJay's. It's quiet, dark, and full of scents in his living room: a smell like Nana's rose soap, lingering traces of warm bread, and another, indefinable air that smells like outdoors. From the street, a glimmer of lights outlines the window shades. I pull the edge of one and see homes and cars glimmering down the street, unbroken. So unlike Maria's neighborhood. It gives me a little shock. SamJay is my most trusted and beloved friend, and it's shocking to realize he lives in a privileged place. Probably because of his military service. I'm guessing the state Militia doesn't even patrol here.

Sleep drifts through the house, a cloud of stillness as the night crosses over into the next day. Almost one hundred hours.

As I look around, shame flames up in my cheeks. I remember the wreck I left here. SamJay's living room shows no trace of the chaos. A faint glow from the kitchen illuminates the pale living room carpet, the new armchair, a delicate vase holding flowers. He's repaired everything.

I have to control the rage. Rage makes me do things I don't want to do.

Suddenly very tired, I sit on the pale living room carpet, head pressed to my knees. A longing for my brothers and sisters reaches from my bones to the tips of my fingers and toes, to the backs of my eyes, through the ends of my hair. If SamJay can't help me, what will I do?

What I do is recite my mantra. Over and over again. *I am a part of all things, and all things lift me toward the center.* The stillness seems to enter my body and little by little, the fear and stress drain from me. My thoughts drift into limbo. Sleep carries me away.

CHAPTER 46

Only moments later, it seems, a door bangs shut and I wake, my heart pounding. I scramble to a crouch. Already, dawn leaks in around the window shades. I glance around in confusion, preparing to Jump. Then I remember where I am.

SamJay pads through the living room without seeing me, as if the gloom in the room were inside of him. I ease to the side as he shuffles by, rubbing his neck. He seems too quiet, thick and slow. He goes into the kitchen, opens the refrigerator and leans into it, staring. Then he shuts the door without taking anything out. He stands quietly.

Strange images revolve in his mind: an empty beach with the sun rising, sea birds crying from above, a wide tree brimming with red leaves. His body aches; his mind is like syrup. He seems miserable. What has happened to him?

"SamJay?"

His back goes rigid, hands gripped at his sides.

"SamJay," I say again, closer behind him now.

He spins about, sees me, then rubs his hands over his eyes. "Eten?" He looks at his hands, turning them back and forth, glances toward the clock on the kitchen wall, then at me again. "What…"

I close the gap between us. Of course! I realize he doesn't know. "I'm alive."

"Eten!" he cries quietly, holding out his arms. I step into them and the tears begin.

"Dear Lord, I thought you were dead." Face against the top of my head.

"I survived." Muffled against his shoulder.

His elation is dizzying. "Of course you did. Supergirl!"

He pushes me back, hands gripping my shoulders, not even noticing his own overbrimming eyes. "Let me look at you. Your mom thought you were dead. We all did. That bastard Duroc."

Hope thrills me. "You saw Mom? Did you see Teetu? The others? Do you know where they are?"

SamJay leads me back to the sofa and we sit. All of his slow melancholy vanishes. "Your mom came here with Teetu and Jaysx just a few days after—what happened to you …" He looks at me like he still can't believe I'm real. "She was scared for Teetu. She knew Duroc wasn't going to give her back. She took Jaysx and they went to Washington, D.C., supposedly to "visit" Teetu, but the three of them escaped. After that, Duroc tried to have your mom killed. He was trying to recapture Teetu and Jaysx."

I freeze. "Oh my God."

SamJay pats my shoulder. "It's okay, they're all right. She didn't tell me the whole story, but they got away and went into hiding. Your mom came here to see if I could get a message to your dad. We didn't dare use a ristcom."

"Do you know where the boys are? SamJay." I squeeze my eyes shut, trying to block out the images. "The boys were attacked."

"What?" he whispers. I turn to him. His face crinkles. "What happened?"

I describe the scene, the hanks of hair, the gas mask. "It was horrible. The blood…" My throat closes up. "I don't know what they did. If they killed the boys…Oh, God."

SamJay puts his arm around my shoulder. "No, I'm sure they're alive. I once overheard your mom and dad talking about something like this, years ago. Your mom said Dr. Duroc wanted to shave off the hair of one child to see what it would do. If it would eliminate their skills to Jump things. If the hair would grow back."

There's no way for me to know if cutting their hair really took away their skills. But the picture of my brothers, helpless, their skulls shorn, their skills gone…it makes me writhe inside.

"I think that's what Duroc did," says SamJay. "He wouldn't want to kill them. He wanted to make them—vulnerable. So he could take them and keep them."

"I have to find them." The thought of leaving them helpless in Duroc's hands makes me sick. "If I could find Mom and the girls, they could help me. Did she say where she and the girls were going to hide?"

SamJay shakes his head. "No, I don't know. I got a letter to your dad through a guard there, a friend of mine. I told him to watch out for Duroc, about what happened to your mom and the girls, but not where she was going to go."

My tears dry up as rage pulses through my throat and chest. My fists unfurl and I press my hands to my face and stand. "That bastard. He's got them. I'm sure he does. You know a really weird thing? He invited me to go see him. Duroc did. When he saw me in the gym, he said, 'Come see me in Washington.' Why would he do that? He says he didn't try to kill me, but I know he did. He planted a bomb on my plane. He should be *scared* to see me."

SamJay squeezes his knees with his big hands and leans toward me. "If he has your brothers hidden away, and if they can't escape, he may try to blackmail you into doing whatever he wants."

That stops me. "What's black mail?"

SamJay's head rocks back and forth as he tries to think of a clear explanation. "Blackmail. That's when somebody uses their power over you to force you to do something. So, Duroc can threaten to hurt the boys if you don't obey him. That's blackmail."

It's like a sharp slap in the face. My thoughts scatter. Here's one more way to control me. Blackmail. So many ways I can be hurt or manipulated that I never imagined. I shake my head. "What do I do?"

SamJay's heavy body rocks very slightly back and forth on the sofa. He's staring at the floor, frowning, imagining different scenarios. Finally, he looks up at me. "What do you *want* to do?"

"I have to go see him," I say. "Duroc." No matter what the pros and cons, I have to know, for sure. "It's the only way I can know. I can tell if he's lying. I have to see if he has the boys."

SamJay nods, thinking it over. "If he admits he has them hidden, I think you should Jump away before he can make any demands. Pretend you know where they are. Duroc won't know one way or the other if you can Sense where the boys are. He'll go check on them, or he'll have somebody check on them."

I'm nodding along with SamJay, the idea forming in my mind. It's risky but it might work. "I can Jump myself away from Duroc but someplace nearby, so maybe I can still Sense him or see him. So I'll know if he calls someone to check on the boys. Or if he goes to check on them, maybe I can follow him."

SamJay holds up a finger. "And you can say, before you Jump, you can say, 'I'm gonna to get them out of there,' or something like that, so he thinks you're Jumping yourself to wherever the boys are."

I twist my lower lip between my fingers, trying to picture it. This is not a plan; it's a Hail Mary. But it's better than nothing. I have to see Duroc face-to-face. Only then will I know for sure.

"I'll call in sick to work and drive you to Washington." SamJay looks grim. "I'll take the week off."

"Oh, SamJay, you have a new job." Of course he does. I'm so wrapped up in myself, in my own troubles, I didn't even think of that. "I'm sorry."

"It's okay, it's bank security." He shrugs. "I can get a substitute."

He meets my eyes and points at me. "You can do it, Supergirl." He's scared. I think he's trying to convince himself.

I nod, half-grinning, half-frowning. "No more *babygirl?*"

He shakes his head, heading toward his bedroom. "Nu-uh," he says over his shoulder. "You're my Supergirl now."

CHAPTER 47

My belly lurches. Why the heck did I eat breakfast? I should know better by now.

Ahead is Duroc's building, The Pentagon, the five-sided concrete heart of the U.S. military. It appears to be crouching in the shadows of a miles-long, man-made hill that holds back the Potomac River.

SamJay says nothing as he inches the car forward in a long line of traffic. To the right rises the steep, grassy hill. To our left, endless parking lots surround the Pentagon.

Yesterday, it was he who decided I needed rest before this confrontation. We arrived at the outskirts of Washington in the early afternoon and stayed for the night at a small motel. Much of the area was deserted, some buildings completely destroyed. The motel was surrounded with a high fence of barbed wire. It was a scary place, but SamJay was right. I needed rest. I slept for fifteen hours straight, and before we left, SamJay paid to keep the room another night. He said it's our "safe-house." If we get separated, we meet back here.

On the drive, I told him about surviving the plane explosion, about John-Paul and his family. What it was like where they lived, the poverty, the food and medicine shortages. He told me that many of the people who live in Bulee Creek work for the government or the military, America's biggest employer. That's why the houses were better.

Ahead, a dark blue car flashes its red back lights, and we stop suddenly. We're surrounded on all sides by cars and trucks. I've never imagined so many in one place. SamJay is brooding. When I ask him why the road is so crowded, he shrugs and says, "Rush hour." I'm not sure what that means, but I do know why SamJay isn't talking.

He's afraid to let me go into the Pentagon alone. But if Duroc sees him, SamJay's life will be at risk. His home won't be safe. There's no real reason he needs to come inside with me. We argued over it yesterday, and finally he agreed when I said his house needs to stay a "safe-house" for me. I will go alone.

Again, I open myself as wide and deep as I can, but I Sense no trace of my brothers. Somehow, somewhere, Duroc must have them. But maybe not here. I try to push the disappointment away. They might be here, somewhere. It's a huge city. I have to keep trying.

Finally, SamJay turns the car into a small road leading to a parking lot. We sit in another line of cars, shorter now. Ahead, a uniformed, military officer speaks to each driver before waving them through.

I scrunch down in my seat, suddenly alarmed. What if they don't let us in? Or even try to arrest us? "SamJay?"

"It's okay." He pulls a small, metal shield from the pocket of his jacket. It's a dark blue jacket with his Sergeant's insignia on the shoulder. Below that is another patch with MP in black letters. Military Police, he tells me.

It looks great. Except for the fact that SamJay resigned from the military as soon as Mom transferred him out of the pod.

The cold gaze of the guard in the little booth makes my toes curl. SamJay hands him the shield. The man stares at SamJay, and, with a line between his brows, leans over to stare at me. I hold my breath and do something with my mouth that hopefully looks like a smile.

The guard touches a hand to his cap. "Go ahead, Sir," he says.

The steel railing rises, the car rolls forward, and my breath whooshes out in one long sigh.

"Are you sure you want to go in alone?" SamJay asks for the fifth time this morning.

And for the fifth time, I fight the churning desire for SamJay to stay with me.

"Yes, I'm sure."

He drives around for a while to find an open spot, parks and turns off the car. He points, even though he doesn't need to. Crowds of people flow from the parking lots toward the front entrance.

"That's where you go."

"I know." My heart thuds. I unclasp my seat belt.

He doesn't look at me. "We can call it off if you want."

I rub my palms together, touch SamJay's arm. He turns. "I'll be fine," I tell him.

SamJay grins. "I know you will, Supergirl. I'll be waiting right here."

Just seeing him smile like that gives me courage. He believes in me. I will get through this, and I will find my brothers.

Outside the car, it's already hot under the glowering sun. The crowd streaming toward the doors sweeps me with them, until we reach more lines in front of huge, metal doors.

The vein in my neck throbs and leaps. I ignore my fear and walk slow and steady into the building, not looking at the guards, as SamJay instructed.

Nobody stops me.

Inside, a huge and gloomy room echoes. People murmur in low voices. Shoes squeak and click on floor tiles of glossy stone. The ceiling stretches up into darkness.

A second row of guards stands by white pillars that look weathered, like they were once outdoors. Bright lights illuminate the crowd. At the top of each line, machines scan each person and their belongings. Some people are scanned again with hand-held devices behind the machines, or physically patted down. They must be looking for weapons.

Fortunately, I carry nothing. I *am* a weapon.

I wear "appropriate" clothes SamJay purchased for me yesterday: Dark navy pants, a little too short. A plain white shirt, black socks and new, black sneakers. The pants are too big around my waist. SamJay gave me a safety pin which now I don't touch, resisting the urge as I go through the scanner.

Two female guards finish searching a woman ahead of me. They look at me curiously, turn, and whisper to each other. I try to ignore them and walk on. A drop of sweat runs down beside my ear.

"Excuse me, Miss," says the taller, middle-aged guard, stepping in front of me.

I lurch back. People turn to stare.

The guard smiles and holds up her hands. "I didn't mean to startle you, sorry. Can I ask you why you're here? Are you here for a tour?"

I shake my head and say what SamJay told me to say. "Appointment." My throat, dry as the scuffed floor, catches on the word, and I cough. "I have an appointment?"

"Do you have your ID?"

My heart bangs again. I don't know what she's talking about. My eyebrows must be raised with horror, because she says, "A driver's license? Or a school ID?"

I shake my head. "I have an appointment with Dr. Duroc."

The guard's eyes go wide. Then she recovers her bland expression and holds out a hand. "All right. Let's go over to this counter over here."

We walk up through one of several open doors into another big room, over to a small white counter. There, the guard leaves me. A young man with very short hair and a round face behind the counter is talking, but I can't hear him. He looks beyond me, and—as I stare at his mouth—I realize his lips are blurred.

Cold prickles go up the back of my neck. Is he skilled, like me? But he'd be a soldier if he were like me. Or is there some kind of new shielding technology here? My knees feel watery.

Suddenly, the man looks at me. His hands drop out of sight. "Can I help you?"

His mouth no longer blurs, and I can hear him normally. Maybe I imagined it.

"I have an appointment."

He smiles reassuringly. "With whom?"

I don't feel reassured. "Dr. Duroc."

His thin eyebrows shoot up, but he smiles again. "Of course. May I have your ID?"

My heart sinks twice over. "I don't have ID."

He nods, glancing down. Then he smiles a fake smile. "Your name?"

"E-10," I say, purposely saying my name the way Duroc does.

The eyebrows scrunch together. "Eten?"

"No. Like the number. E. 10."

His mouth opens but no words come out. He looks to the side of me, then to another person at the other end of the counter, then back to me.

"Yes, miss," he says with his fake smile. He snaps his left wrist upward then begins to talk. His ristcom glows, and again there's that weird blur on his face. I can't hear him.

He definitely isn't manipulating the air; I could Sense it if he were. They must have some kind of shield, some new technology. What else can it do, besides blur the air? The watery feeling comes back in my legs. If Duroc can shield himself, will I be safe?

The young man behind the counter turns his back on me and continues to talk. I Sense anxiety. The shield must've dropped, because his voice suddenly comes through loud and clear. "No, *E-10*, that's what I said. Yes! She doesn't have ID. Should I tell the guards to take her away?"

He pops up straight with a pang of fear, looking around. He says something else, but it's blurred and silent again.

Behind me, random footsteps click and echo through the lofty room.

Moments pass and my throat goes drier. The room begins to fall quiet. Some of the people have moved down on of the many corridors into the building. The young man clears his throat and says, "Uh. Miss?" I turn. His face looks stiff. He is not smiling. "Someone will be right down."

I'm relieved. Then I'm nervous. I step aside, though nobody is in line behind me, and turn to face the room. All the people who come and go are dressed neatly, but there are few in military uniforms. I wait and wait. The anxiety in my belly rises as I turn back to the counter man. Maybe he needs to call again. But the stiff expression vanishes from the man's face, and surprise stains his cheeks pink as his mouth falls open. He's staring over my right shoulder. "Oh," he says, and I turn back.

From the elevator emerges a group of heavily armored guards, all in black—black bullet-proof vests, anti-ballistic goggles, helmets and chin-shields, weapons in black holsters as well as rifles in their arms, antiballistic pants, steel-toed boots. I know the uniform well. We use it for target practice.

In their midst, protected from public view, Duroc approaches in a wheelchair. He pushes on a lever which propels the wheelchair forward. The people still in the room fall back and murmur. Why is he in a wheelchair? A short time ago, he walked just fine.

Furthermore, Duroc's dry, sharp face looks all wrong. Abruptly, I realize why.

He's smiling.

CHAPTER 48

"Eten!" he calls, for the first time pronouncing my name like I'm a real person. He holds both hands out in front of him and a guard pushes the wheelchair rapidly. Involuntarily, my hands rise to meet his and he grabs me, gazes into my eyes. His hands are dry, hard and very strong. I step closer, a little off balance, baffled by the wheelchair.

"I *hoped* you would come," he says. "I'm thrilled to see you. You are *vital* to our country, Eten." With each emphasis, he jiggles my hands.

I manage to jerk myself free. His excitement is more than disconcerting; it fills the air with uneasy tension. The whole room seems to hesitate and glower. There are maybe twenty people in the vast chamber, and I Sense their stillness, their awe, as if Duroc were some kind of king from medieval times.

I am so not safe here. I need to escape as soon as possible. "Where are my brothers, Dr. Duroc?" I ask, trying to make my voice sound firm.

The six guards move in closer around Duroc and me. As if I couldn't disarm and disable them all in a moment. Does Duroc even know what I can do?

He sweeps up a hand. "I'll tell you everything I know. Please, come to my office. We'll be much more comfortable there." With a jerk of the joystick, he turns the wheelchair sharply and he advances down one of the many corridors. Four guards surrounding him, and the other two crowd me forward; we march double-time to keep up.

As we move into the building, I throw my Senses as wide as I can, but I get no hint of the warm, familiar pulses of Gethre and Gefor.

We trot down a long, white corridor lined with doors. On the walls hang photographs of officers in uniforms or dark suits, mostly men. As we pass, others in the corridor stop talking and step back. They salute.

I do not Sense my brothers. Fear and anger tremble within me. A horrible image crosses my mind: my brothers lying bloody and dead on the gym floor. What if Doroc's already done the unthinkable? I take deep breaths, push these thoughts away. *Focus*, I tell myself. He must have them somewhere else. Probably shorn of their skills, unable to Jump or defend themselves.

We turn into another, shorter corridor and stop at an elevator. Duroc leans forward, presses his right hand against a screen, and the elevator doors open. The guards stand back and Duroc advances. Wondering if I'm making a mistake, I get on the elevator with him and we rise toward the top floor—number five.

He never stops talking. He tells me how special I am, how vital, how America owes me a great debt. He tells me how the American people are suffering, about all the wonderful things he hopes to do for

America and how I am so important to that effort.

My brain spins, suffocated by words. I can't think. "Dr. Duroc," I ask, "what happened? Why are you in a wheelchair?"

He tsks and waves a dismissive hand. "Just a little problem with my leg. It's temporary."

The elevator opens into a sprawling room, sunny and carpeted in spotless white, furnished with comfortable brown and white chairs, a white leather sofa and a big desk.

"Welcome to my office," says Duroc, advancing himself into the room. I follow, then halt when the elevator doors abruptly close behind me.

Duroc and I are alone.

"Where are my brothers?" I ask again. In this quiet room without distractions, I'm sure I'll be able to tell if he's lying.

He smiles and shrugs. "I don't know. Best guess? Your dad has them."

Hatred rakes through my body. I hate his smile and I hate his shrug and I hate his mind. I don't want to believe him, but he's telling the truth. I Sense a picture of the boys in the pod, when they barged in with Jaysx and Teetu to warn me against him. The last time he saw them.

But I Sense another image, one he's trying to hide. It flickers lightening-fast, just enough for me to see a vidscreen. He was watching a vidscreen. Did he see what happened to the them?

His mind is a maze of corridors, doors slamming in my face as I try to Sense his thoughts and memories. He's almost as skilled as Mom at keeping me out.

"You saw something. On a vidscreen," I say.

"I'm surprised you didn't ask about your little sister," he replies, and my heart lurches.

"I can Sense she's not here." I'm praying she's safe with Mom and Jaysx.

Duroc shrugs again. "Neither are your brothers." He wheels himself to an enormous wall of windows and pulls back filmy curtains, and I rack my brains about how I can force him tell me about the vid he saw—he knows something he's not telling me.

The view out his windows is panoramic. Not far away, the broad Potomac glitters, with high, protective dams on both sides. Beyond the river sprawls the huge city of Washington, D.C. According to SamJay, it used to be the most powerful city in the world—and I realize now, it still is—a place of vast riches, where wealthy men and women decide who will eat and who will go hungry, who will be healed and who will suffer, who will find justice and who will be broken.

Duroc turns his chair toward me with a smile, spreading his hands. "All this could be yours. Join with me, Eten. Please. Stop fighting me."

I'm so flustered, I close my eyes. How does he manage to twist things like this? He tried to *kill* me. Didn't he? I go closer to the window so I don't have to look at him. "I'm not fighting you," I say. Which sounds totally lame. "I just want my brothers and sisters." My voice verges on trembling, and I clear my throat. I can't allow him to see me as weak.

"We'll find your brothers and sisters," he says. "Together. It won't be hard. Just join with me to lead our country to greatness. Once we're in charge, we can create world peace. We can help those in need all over the globe. Don't you see how amazing it will be? With your special abilities and my leadership, we can do so much good. Your brothers and sisters can help—we can save so many people, Eten."

My mind is swirling. Could he be right? With the whole world united, there would be no more war, no more killing. Hospitals would have the medicines they needed; I could be a healer. Maria and all the people like her would have decent housing and…

But I remember, suddenly, the town militia. The people in charge, shooting people for breaking curfew. I turn sharply to face Duroc. "You'll make us kill people."

The smile on his face doesn't waver. "No, no, not at all," he says. "If you don't want to fight, you don't have to. You can help in so many other ways. You'll be rich beyond your wildest dreams. You'll have a big white house surrounded by green grass, all for yourselves, full of sunshine and happiness. You'll all have your own special bedrooms and there will be flower gardens and swimming pools, and toys for little Teetu…"

Disgust twists my mouth into a sneer. What am I thinking? This man won't be giving Teetu toys. He wants her to be a killer. Like me. Killers in his personal army. Maybe he'd give us a house, but we'll still be fighting.

"Dr. Duroc, you tried to kill me. I don't think you're interested in helping other people."

"That's. Not. True." He angrily shakes a finger at me as he enunciates each word. "That plane suffered an electrical fire and engine failure. Nobody tried to kill you. I'm *thrilled* you survived." He looks more pissed than thrilled.

I pull Duroc's two-page memo from my pocket, unfold it and throw it into Duroc's lap. "It's true, Dr. Duroc. Read your own memo.

Clone and terminate E-10."

Duroc face goes pale. Literally, as white as the pieces of paper. He snatches the memo from his legs. "Where did you get this?" he says thickly as he bends to read it. His face goes from white to red. He crumples the pages and shakes his hand at me, thundering again, "Where did you get this?"

On the other side of the room, a door opens. A uniformed soldier leans in. "Is everything all right, Dr. Duroc?"

"Get out," shouts Duroc, waving him back. The soldier hastily shuts the door.

I sit back on the luxurious, white leather sofa and watch him. The seductive veneer of kindness has burnt off this old man's face, leaving only his bone-hard eyes and thin lips. He shakes the paper again. "This is a forgery," he says, his voice is low and harsh. He rolls himself to his desk, wads the memo into a ball and throws it in the trash can.

"It's not a forgery," I tell him, enjoying my moment of triumph. "I have plenty of memos like that. Hundreds of them. And I've got more than papers. I've got dead babies. *Murdered* babies floating in jars, *Doctor* Duroc. Your experiments." I spit the word. "I've got a room full of evidence against you. Leave me and my brothers and sisters alone, or everyone will see it."

He throws his head back and laughs.

My hands bunch into fists. I can't believe he's laughing. "I'm telling the truth. I can bring you pictures of your experiments if you don't believe me."

"Take a picture of yourself!" he says, grinning at me. "*You're* one of my experiments, my dear. You wouldn't exist if not for my experiments.

Shall we tell the world what kind of experiment you are?"

A hot flush creeps up my face and I stand up. "You're a monster."

Duroc shrugs. "Maybe. But then, so are you." I back up a step, glaring at him, and he adds, "Ah, I can see the anguish in your eyes. Too true, too true. To be less than human."

I turn and head for the elevator. *Monster.* My heart is cracking up the middle. *Experiment.* I can't allow him to see my tears. I've gotten what I came for—he doesn't have my brothers, and I showed him the evidence against him. I'm leaving.

But searing pain rips up my back and I twist, a howl wrenched from my gut. White carpet rises to meet my face.

"I didn't give you permission to leave," says Duroc. Still behind his desk, he's holding a wand above it, pointing it at me, pressing a button.

I gasp and try to not cry out again. How did he get a wand? I squirm, helpless.

As if hearing my thoughts, he says, "I found a few of these in your pod, after your Dad so gallantly rescued your brothers."

My brothers! His words land like a splash of water in my face. Where did I get the idea I was helpless? Despite the pain, I Jump the wand out of Duroc's hand—just as easily as I Jumped a thousand rifles from a thousand soldiers in all the years growing up. I drop the wand to the floor, stand up and stomp on it. It doesn't crack much, so I Jump it out to SamJay's car.

"Hm," Duroc says, unphased. "I wondered if the monster-controller would work. I don't know how your Mom taught you any discipline."

I ignore his clumsy barb and take a few breaths. The pain is gone. "What do you mean, Dad rescued my brothers?"

Duroc waves a dismissive hand. "Well, it is true I ordered their hair to be cut. How else was I going to get them to obey me? With wands? Please. But at the last minute, your Dad swept in with a gas mask on and took out my agents. Well, they were busy cutting hair, which was difficult, so he had the advantage. I didn't see what happened after that. He disabled the vidcams, and then he vanished with the boys."

"How could you," I grind my teeth, trying to find the right words. "How could you *mutilate* my brothers like that?" My voice rises to a squeak.

"Oh, don't worry," says Duroc, flapping his hand like a town gossip. "It'll grow back. I'm pretty sure." He snaps his fingers, grinning again. "Hey, I've got an idea. Let's go see your real mother."

"What?" I sway back and drop to the couch again. My mother? My egg-donor? Is she like me? I don't know what to say. "My *mother?*" I echo numbly.

"Oh." Duroc puts his fingers to his mouth, feigning contrition. "I'm sorry. Did you think your 'Mom' was your real mother?"

Ironically, his nasty gesture helps to ground me. I stand, tighten my belly, press my toes to the floor and steel my backbone. "No, Dr. Duroc. I'm aware of how I was created." I think I understand it anyway—the donated sperm and egg, the host who incubates the baby.

He leers in a very unpleasant way. "Not exactly."

I don't move. He's not lying. There is something—though I can't Sense an image of it, I can tell it's some secret about me.

Duroc powers his wheelchair toward the elevator. "Come on," he says, not looking back. "She's in the basement."

CHAPTER 49

She's in the basement.

The elevator drops to the ground floor, and when it opens, Duroc's squad of guards is waiting for us. This time Duroc is driving himself; he never actually needed the guards to push him along. It was all a show. His wheelchair is fast, and two guards clear the way in the lobby as the others clip my heels from behind. There's more of a crowd now, and I Sense.... I turn frantically, even as I'm propelled forward by the guards. I Sense SamJay, though I can't see him. He shouldn't have come into the lobby—he's afraid for me. He should've stayed in the car.

Then we're in another corridor again, into another room, down another elevator, leaving the guards behind.

At the level of BB, the silver doors slide open with a *ding*. Cement pillars face the elevator and lights engage as Duroc propels his wheelchair out. Lights come on as we proceed in a long tunnel with a tiled floor. The air smells dead. Even though the white walls are perfectly clean, it's grim.

"Right this way," he says, glancing back. He's still smiling. He leads me though a warren of tunnels, punctuated by office doors. He plunges so quickly into the darkness, a shadowy helmet forms about him and I imagine he's a beast, until the automatic gleam from the overheads dispel the illusion. I have to jog to keep up.

On my left, solid wall gives way to double-paned glass. A shiver trembles through me. Through the glass, I see equipment on counters; bottles and vials on shelves and in cabinets. A secret lab down here? Something shoved in a corner stops me in my tracks.

A white wicker baby bassinet. There's a small mattress inside of it, made up with a white sheet and blue blanket. A chill creeps up into my skull. It's so much like Teetu's old bassinet, it could be the very same one.

Ahead of me, Duroc stops. "It's this way."

"What is this lab?" I put my hand on the cool window and, for a moment, I'm holding myself upright against it. Could this be the place where I was conceived?

"It's nothing," he says, continuing down the corridor. "An old lab. Decommissioned. We're going to a different room, up here."

I am so still, the motion-activated overhead light suddenly goes dark. I can see lights at the back of the lab. If it's decommissioned, why are lights burning? My neck prickles. I can Sense people back there. Are they working?

Are they working on clones?

Lights come on way back in the passageway. Someone else has

gotten off the elevator. But there are offices all along these halls. It seems deserted and mysterious down here, but other people must come in to use the offices.

Duroc says, "Here." I turn, and he motions toward another door. He presses a handkerchief to his nose and clears his throat. "Come on."

A momentary thrill flickers in my chest. What if it really is my true mother? Could she be imprisoned, living down here like my brothers and sisters and I lived in our pod? Are we going to another pod? Duroc is capable of anything. I hurry toward him as he pushes his hand against a big, square glass scanner. The door pops open.

The tiny, bright antechamber might be the entrance to a pod. An airlock. Overhead lights glare off a steel floor and steel walls. Vents perforate the ceiling. The room is entirely empty. My breath comes quicker.

The door swings shut behind us, as if on a spring or with electronic eyes, like the store doors. Already, Duroc is opening another door on the other side of the room, this time with a keypad and an eye-scanner.

I wrap my arms around myself, trying not to shiver.

The door, almost seamless in the steel wall, pops in just a crack. It looks as thick as our bedroom door in the pod.

My Senses flare as I reach out. Is someone there?

"Here we go," says Duroc. As soon as he pushes the door open and moves his wheelchair forward, I know I'm wrong. I Sense no one. It smells like the inside of a refrigerator. It's larger than the first room, but also clad in bright, silver steel with vents at the top. It's entirely empty. The room hums. The floor vibrates.

Duroc rises from the wheelchair and closes the door behind him.

It's flush to the wall, with only the hand-scanner beside it.

"Dr. Duroc, your leg," I say, disconcerted. He's not even limping.

He walks briskly to the side of the room, where there's a large bar sticking out of the wall, like a door handle. Beside it, vents perforate the steel from the floor to the ceiling. Warmer air from the vents flutters my hair.

Reaching for the steel bar, Duroc turns, his smile manic. "Not to worry," he says. "It feels much better now." Excitement thrums in him; he actually fumbles as he reaches for the bar and watches me at the same time, his mind surging with waves of triumph I don't understand. I withdraw my Senses and try to block him out.

"Only a few people have ever seen this," he says. "But I was there at the beginning. I saw the potential. I created Project Samson."

He grabs metal bar, pushes a button and pulls.

It's not a door. It's a drawer. An enormous, long, heavy drawer that pulls out half the wall—from just above the floor to shoulder-height. Rollers flip down and support its massive weight as the drawer emerges. It beeps as Duroc walks backward, until it's completely open.

Inside lies a huge glass dome filled with fluid and mist. Tubes emerge from the sides, and at the back, against the wall, electronics glow.

"Is this...?" I try to see through a white mist swirling inside the glass. "Is something alive in there?"

"No, no. Dead." Duroc's lips twitch "Nothing to fear."

"I'm not afraid!" Anger and disappointment flare in me. Of course, all this is another one of Duroc's games. I'm angry at myself for allowing him to draw me in. I actually thought I might meet my birth mother down here. What a joke.

He pushes another button on the side of the drawer and, with a low hum, the mist above the fluid begins to dissipate, vacuumed into the tubes. "The fluid is liquid nitrogen. This is a Dewars tank. For cryopreservation."

Duroc begins a story as I parse the thing in the Dewars tank, trying to figure out what I'm seeing.

"I was on a field trip with my boss, Dr. Mattea, near Fort McDermott in Arizona," he says. His voice sounds almost wistful.

An animal take shape as the mist disappears. It's huge and looks like an octopus. Except for the face, which looks like a human. Sort of. Except the mouth is round and has sharp teeth. Some kind of unusual sea monster? I don't get it. "What is this, Dr. Duroc? Why are you showing me this animal?"

Duroc goes on, as if I hadn't spoken. "We were doing a genetic study at the reservation. I was an assistant researcher at DARPA, the Defense Advanced Research Projects Agency—eventually I was the director there, but then, I was just starting out—and my boss got a call to report asap to some kind of classified disaster at the Groom Lake air force base in Nevada. I was just 20—it changed my life."

The animal's at least 200 kilos of pale golden, wrinkly, human-like flesh. It's almost three meters tall, more than a meter wide. Hard to tell for sure, because tentacles float out to the sides.

I think maybe it's a sea creature. Behind its head, there's some kind of ruff or sack, floating loose under the body. There's a short, thick neck before the body fills out, not exactly into shoulders but there are tentacles—two on either side, extending like arms, each ending in a bunch of wormy-looking fingers.

My body sways as I lock my knees and hold my breath. There is no stench of formaldehyde, and yet I seem to smell something bad. Fighting the urge to turn away, I stare at the monster's face, at its eyes, which are huge and purple with round, black pupils at the center. They're recessed, held by bony sockets, and fringed with wrinkly lids, even eyelashes. The nose lies almost flat but has flared nostrils, and that mouth! It's little more than a gaping hole, black edges pulled back, exposing sharp, brown teeth. Carnivorous teeth. Three slightly-open reddish-brown slits line each side of the stumpy neck. They look like gills.

Now I see the beast's lower limbs are legs, not tentacles; they seem to emerge from under a mantle of skin. Two heavy, jointed limbs end in splayed-out, webbed toes with claws. Except for the disconcertingly human-like skin, the feet look much like those of the crocodile I blew up—how long ago?

"We were lucky we had to drive so far, or we would've been dead," Duroc is saying. "Just as we got there, a tremendous explosion ripped a building apart. Had to stop short to avoid the debris."

Duroc motions toward the monster in the tank. "When the alien first arrived, when its ship crashed, they found it lying on the ground. The ship disintegrated, they said, within hours. Maybe it was organic. They thought the creature was dead. The four airmen who first approached it, they were carrying weapons, and suddenly, their rifles just vanished. *Pffft.*" Duroc flicks his fingers. "Just—disappeared. The airmen were looking all around for their guns, like dopey blockheads, and suddenly, the airmen vanish, too. *Pffft.*" Duroc flicks his fingers again.

I'm stuck on the word, *alien.* Does he mean, like, something from another planet? Like *War of the Worlds*? *Superman* and *Supergirl*? I'm staring at the creature as I realize that the most disturbing thing about it—the silvery hair on its head.

"Just when we drove in," says Duroc, "it blew up the whole building and everybody in there. Eleven people killed, ripped apart. Then it just walked out, steady as you please, totally unharmed. I saw. It was... magnificent. Intelligent."

It isn't hair, really, but very fine, silvery tentacles, glinting in the light, massed into a thick mat. Some strands lift and waver in the fluid. My hand flies to my head, stroking my own hair back.

"We just sat there in the car—we were scared to get out and scared to lose sight of it. We watched things appear in its hands. Its hair was lifting and snaking around like Medusa, holy Christ." He points, "And those tentacles there, the ones that end in fingers, its hands. Things appeared in its hands, then disappeared again. Appeared and disappeared. Chunks of the building. Equipment. Somebody's bloody *head*, good Lord. That was a shock. Like it was trying to figure out what we're made of. Then *the creature itself* disappeared. I remember the moment—my boss, Dr. Metea, shouted. After a minute, I spotted it, further away. That's when I grasped the meaning of it all; I realized what was happening. It was moving things around with its mind. *Jumping*. you call it. Jumping things. Jumping itself. True telekinesis. It Jumped those soldiers into the desert and disoriented them. And the others, the ones who just walked out of the airbase into the desert. Some kind of mind-control."

What I'm hearing doesn't make sense. My heart pounds. "Jumping?" I whisper. My mouth and throat are dry.

"Right then, the entire strategy came to me. I saw the full program, as if I'd already accomplished the whole thing. I even knew what I'd call it: Project Samson."

Suddenly, I'm sitting on the cold, steel floor, my head to my knees, eyes closed, arms wrapped around my legs. Duroc's words continue like hurled rocks, like bullets I can't shield against. A moan escapes me.

"Do you realize what a miracle you are? We experimented for years. Splicing the alien's DNA into human embryos. Years of failure, but we were getting closer. Then, the first miracle. B-10. A fully realized chimera, part human, part alien." His voice lowers to a growl. "That bastard, Goswami, he got too close to the child, helped him escape. Dr. Dev Goswami, the great genius, yeah right, not without my help he wasn't a genius. But by then, we had you, too. E-10. Another miracle. Less than one percent alien DNA; the surprise was we needed so little."

Bright images of Beeta swim before me, his yellow hair like the twins, the power of his small body as he lifts me from my crib. Then the strangest thing happens. Beeta talks to me. He says, "You better get up now." I try to struggle to my feet and find that I can't. My legs splay out before me; my hands tumble to my sides. My head, resting on the drawer, seems to weight a ton. I look up at Duroc. Beeta, a shimmering boy, stands right next to him.

"What did you do?" I rasp. "What did you do to me?"

"Do?" says Duroc. "I created you. You wouldn't even exist without me."

I don't want to exist. I'm contaminated, not human—a monster. But words don't form on my lips. I look up at Duroc, who's bending over me, and see something in his nostrils. Two flesh-colored plugs. He's breathing through them. And the vents in the steel walls. I can see a faint blur as the air ripples. Some kind of gas.

"He drugged you," says Beeta. SamJay is standing next to him.

"SamJay?" I groan. Out loud, I think. Duroc grabs my wrist and feels for my pulse.

"Jump away, Babygirl," says SamJay. "Jump yourself away."

Duroc laughs as he drops my hand. "Oh, is a friend with us?" He peers in SamJay's direction and shakes a finger. "Tell E-10 here she'd better rethink her choices." He turns away and pulls a gas mask out of the pocket that hangs on the back of the wheelchair, fastens it onto his head. It covers covering his eyes, nose and mouth. I can hear him breath hard he grabs me under my arms and drags me backward and up onto the wheelchair.

SamJay and Beeta look on with frightened expressions. I don't understand why they aren't helping me.

I can Sense Duroc, his gas mask, the wheelchair, but as I reach out to Jump the mask from his face, nothing happens. Icy fear fills my veins. I focus all my consciousness on Duroc and try to push him backward.

Nothing.

"Do you really think I would allow you to run away?" he says from behind me, pulling me higher up in the wheelchair. My body is entirely limp; I fall sideways. In his mind, I see images that were hidden before. My brothers inside their travel pod, limp like me, completely unconscious. Two guards with gas masks shearing the boy's hair off, wiping the blood off as they work. "Did you think I would let all my work come to nothing?"

Duroc comes around front, shaking his head, his eyes squinting behind the mask's goggles. His muffled voice drips with sympathetic derision. "And you kids are supposed to be so smart. Advanced calculus, ten languages." He tsks, shaking this head again.

Eleven with Mongolian, says Beeta, and I tell him to be quiet, although no sound emerges. I can't move my lips. I have to Jump away. I can pull up the *thisness* of SamJay's car, the warm, leather seat, the still air, pull it toward me, but nothing happens. Duroc buckles a strap around my chest to hold me upright, another one across my lap and Velcro across my ankles and wrists. He speaks into his ristcom. "You ready?" he says loudly.

"Yes, sir," responds a voice.

Oh my God. He's been planning this from the beginning. Of course there's nothing wrong with his leg. The wheelchair was meant for me all along.

Chapter 50

"When I tested this gas on your little sister, T-2," he says, closing the huge drawer with the alien in the Dewar's tank, "she was able to breathe on her own for seven minutes before we had to intubate her."

Teetu! Inside I'm screaming. For the first time, I burn to kill him. Crush his heart, blow up his head, nail him to the wall, any which way. But I can only stare at Duroc with hatred in my eyes.

"Oh, don't worry," he says as he rounds the wheelchair and grabs the handles from behind. Our wavering image is reflected from the bright steel of the wall. "She recovered fully. Though she did cry a lot."

"He's baiting you," says SamJay, who is standing half-in, half-out of a steel panel, his hands clasped before him. "Don't react."

"He hates you," says Beeta from the corner of the room, floating near the giant drawer. "He needs you, so he hates you." He looks very grave, much wiser than his six years would suggest.

Duroc slaps his hand against a glass panel on the side of the slender crack that indicates a door is there, and the door pops open. Someone pushes it from the other side. He wheels me just inside the next room, leaving the door open behind.

Six guards stand in the bright anteroom, the door to the corridor shut tight. Now, in addition to the body armor, they're wearing gas masks, their faces invisible. They seem to be outlined in a haze of rainbow. What kind of gas has me drugged? One is holding on to a metal pole—a blue plastic bag and tubing hang from it. An intravenous bag, I recognize, but viscous, blue stuff in it, not blood or saline.

Beeta floats above their heads and SamJay stands glimmering in the corner of the room. "That drug isn't good for you," SamJay says, shaking his head.

Help me, I scream at them, soundless. But they don't Sense me.

"Hurry up. Insert the IV," says Duroc, motioning. He leaves me and the wheelchair in the opening between the rooms as he steps toward it. "It will take hold in two minutes. Then we can clear these rooms of gas and open the door."

The guard with the IV pushes the pole ahead of himself. But is it a guard, or…?

The guard blunders and crashes to the ground on top of the pole.

"You clumsy idiot," shouts Duroc, rushing up. He leans over the fallen guard, reaching for the IV, and the guard leaps up with his elbows lifted, knocks Duroc backward. "Oh," the guard cries out as he blunders forward and falls again, on top of Duroc this time, "I can't breathe," he shouts, "Something's wrong with my mask."

Duroc's mask has been knocked off his face and he scrambles to push the guard away. "Get him off me," he shouts, much louder now without his mask. He shuts his mouth to a tight line and breaths in through his nose. He still has the nasal filters.

Two other guards rush to the fallen man, who's still on top of Duroc. But as they bend over, the fallen guard leaps up and backward, as if he were on a springboard. His helmet crashes into the face of one guard and, at the same moment, he kicks the other in the belly. The kicked man flies back with an *oof* and crashes into the fourth guard. They both go down, while the fifth guard shouts, "Hey," as the one who got hit in the face screams. He's ripping his mask off, blood dripping from his smashed nose. The sixth guard, instead of helping, is crouched in the corner, holding onto his gas mask with both hands. "I can't breathe," he shouts. "I can't breathe."

"Don't take your mask off," shouts Duroc. But the guard does. He pulls his mask up over his head, gasps, immediately sinks to the floor and sprawls. He lifts himself a little, then sprawls back on the floor again. Duroc grabs the IV pole, sets it upright, and comes at me with the needle end of the tube. I can't even shout. Glimmering SamJay and Beeta are both leaning over me, obscuring my view. "What's that blue stuff in the bag?" SamJay breathes and Beeta is shouting, "It's the gas." Or maybe somebody else is shouting that. I want to tell them to shut up and move, I can't see what's going on, then feel a horrible sting in my pinned right arm. Duroc has pierced a vein with the needle. I roll my eyes toward him and he grins, lifting his chin.

Which might've been a mistake because the guard, the one who started the turmoil, punches Duroc's chin so hard, blood sprays from his mouth and he goes down against the steel wall, hitting his head and leaving a stain of red behind him. Rainbow SamJay and Beeta hover over the fallen man, exclaiming. Two of the other guards are staggering now, clutching their masks. "I can't breathe," bellows one, "the mask is—" The other guard pushes at the door to the corridor. It swings open wide and the man rips his mask off, gasping as he rushes into the corridor. But he's not quick enough, or there's too much gas. He lurches forward and sprawls to the floor, his legs still visible through the door. His black shoes jerk. The other guard stops moaning, pulls his mask off and gasps; he sinks the floor where he stands, without sound or protest.

Fluid from the IV slips into my vein. Is it more of the paralytic, or did Duroc decide to just kill me? I strain my Senses, arm, my body, my fingers, but nothing moves. I've never felt so helpless. I'm not sure if it's my imagination but it seems like I'm breathing faster, as if I can't draw in a full breath.

Two masked guards are still fighting, the one who started it and the one whose mask seems to be working just fine. The one who started the fight, a bit shorter than the other, runs toward me, reaching for the IV tube, but the other man catches his shoulder and spins him around. The smaller guy ducks under the second's swinging blow, backs up and, without looking, circles a hand behind. He catches the IV tubing in his fingers and it jerks from my arm with a painful twist.

And then I know. Behind the mask, the body armor, the uniform. It's SamJay. If I could've moved, I would have sobbed. Tears leak from my eyes. I'm panting shallow breaths and a spike of adrenaline stabs upward. If I can't get out of this gas soon, I'll stop breathing.

The bigger man weaves in with an upper cut that knocks SamJay's head back. The glimmering images of Beeta and SamJay gasp. As the bigger man follows up, SamJay lurches to the side, as if off balance, letting the man in close, then springs up with his hands rigid, fingers hooked, and pulls the gas mask up and off the other man's head. It goes flying. The man reaches after it wildly, and SamJay punches him in the neck. The guard coughs, then gasps. Then sinks to his knees.

SamJay doesn't even wait to see him go down. He runs for me, grabs the handle of the wheelchair, jerking me one way and then the other as he pushes off from behind and sprints out of the room, through the open door, the wheels crunching over the shoes of the fallen guard.

Lights snap on above us, humming as he runs. I can hear his uneven step, but his bad leg doesn't seem to be slowing him down. "It's me. SamJay," he pants, leaning low, his voice muffled by the gasmask.

Inside I'm saying *I know*, and I make a noise. A grunt. SamJay doesn't seem to notice, but it's the most glorious sound I've ever heard. The gas is wearing off. I manage to take one deep breath, then another.

As we run, an alarm blares, filling the hallway with a crushing throb; red and white lights strobe in time with the alarm. "Shit," says SamJay, and he runs faster, a catch in his breath each time he lands on his bad leg. Two office doors open, anxious eyes peering out, then bang shut quickly as we pass. He skids to a stop in front of the elevator, frantically punches the button. Even I can see it's not working. The up and down arrows blink red simultaneously, in unison with the alarm. He runs to the heavy door marked Fire Exit and tries to open it. It won't budge, and SamJay fights with the handle, jerking it and muttering, "Shit, shit, shit." He runs back to the elevator again, under the blaring speakers and flashing lights, and pries apart the doors. They slide back stiffly, revealing the black, empty interior, and he props them open, his back against one, his hands and one foot against the other.

I can't imagine what he has planned for the elevator shaft, but suddenly, the flashing lights and alarm stop. In the blessed silence, there's a ding and the elevator doors slide all the way open. SamJay almost tumbles into the shaft, and he staggers backward as the doors close. In place of the alarm, a calm and professional female voice announces, "Please, shelter in place. This is a temporary disturbance. Please, shelter in place."

We can hear the elevator rising. It seems to stop, and then the down arrow lights up. I Sense soldiers upstairs. With gas masks and guns. They're coming for us. I try to call SamJay's name and manage to produce a horrible, death-rattle sound. But it's enough to make him turn and look at me. I move my head just a little, side side, staring at the elevator and making the gurgling noise like water struggling through pipes. He looks over his shoulder at the elevator. "Somebody coming?" he says.

My head tilts up ever so slightly and I continue my wheezy groan, looking over at the fire escape door.

"It's locked, Eten," he says, rushing to get behind me. He shoves the wheelchair forward, ready to run down different corridor, but I tilt my head again toward the fire door and try to cry out louder. SamJay hesitates. The elevator is coming down. Sweat springs out on my brow and neck as I strain to wiggle my fingers. My hand is on top of the wheelchair's arm, so SamJay can see it.

As if he can Sense the image in my mind, he pushes me forward to the fire exit, rips the Velcro off my wrist and with one hand, presses my hand against the door. He wraps his other hand around the door handle—how many times have I bragged to SamJay I can unlock any door? Our lives depend on it now. I Sense the lock, reach into it and shift the tumblers as pain rips across the top of my head. And then it's open.

CHAPTER 51

The elevator dings as SamJay wrenches the door to the stairwell open, pushes the wheelchair through, and pulls the door shut behind us. He crouches next to the wheelchair and we listen to the soldiers' muffled voices as they get off the elevator and run down the corridor, toward where we left Duroc.

Duroc. So. Not dead. He called security.

The stairwell is shadowed, with one emergency light shining from far above. SamJay fumbles as he pulls off the straps holding my body in place; I slump forward. He catches me, throws me over his shoulder, and starts up the concrete steps. My heart is banging and my head swims, aching as all the blood rushes into it. SamJay moves up the steps in an agony of slowness, one at a time, stepping up with his good leg and bringing the damaged one up next to it. The fight with Duroc's men, and then the running afterward, hurt his leg more than I realized. I Sense the pain radiating up through his body with each step.

We're almost to the next level, having turned at the landing and progressed up the second half of the steps, when we hear the door at the bottom open. It whines for just a moment, then closes quietly.

Soundlessly, SamJay pivots, lowers my body to the step, and props me up against the wall. He's still wearing the gas mask. The air in the hallway is fresh but if he's seen here, or if a vid catches his image, they'll identify him. I Sense the question in his eyes as he takes my hand in his, and I press two fingers into his palm as I look down the steps and back at him. I Sense two soldiers. The rest ran on to search other corridors.

SamJay nods and draws the nightstick from his weapons belt. He crouches behind the wall of the staircase, opposite me.

I sit in the light and wait.

After a moment, we hear a sound. The shush of a foot sliding across concrete. A faint whisper. My eyes half-closed, I see their shadows first. Then they dart around the corner together, one slightly ahead of the other, both focused on me. SamJay springs out and shoves the man in front backward, and the two soldiers tumble down the stairs together with SamJay in close pursuit. I Sense all three of them, SamJay's surging anxiety, his tight focus, and the other two in pain as they crash down the steps. I try to squeeze the two soldiers' hearts, but nothing happens. Then, through SamJay's eyes, I glimpse his nightstick rise and fall.

SamJay dashes up the stairs to me, panting, tucking the nightstick back into his belt, favoring his bad leg, and not even conscious of his pained grunts. "Came on, we gotta move before more come in here," he says, picking me up again like an over-large duffle bag and slinging me over his shoulder. He makes it to the next landing. "Only one more flight to go," he says. The throbbing in my head is terrible, and my stomach where it rests on SamJay's shoulder feels bruised. I don't understand how he expects to get me out of the building. Does he think we'll be such a spectacle in the vast lobby, Duroc will hesitate to arrest us? Will SamJay call for the police or a hospital?

I want to tell SamJay. If he calls the police now, before more of Duroc's soldiers or guards catch us, maybe we'll have a chance of getting out. But I still can't speak, can't control my flopping arms or dangling head. I can only suffer the pain in my belly and the growing sense of panic as SamJay slowly makes his way up toward the lobby.

And then it's too late.

Above us, the door opens. "They're down here," shouts a voice. SamJay does an immediate about-face and starts limping back down the stairs. But a moment later, the downstairs door opens. "Here's the wheelchair," says someone.

"Eten," calls Duroc, "tell your friend to bring you back and we won't hurt him."

The sound of his voice crushes all hope. I hear boots coming up the stairs. SamJay backs up, shifts me off his shoulder, and slides me to rest on a step. He's panting. "I'm sorry, babygirl," he says. He takes hold of me under my arms and hoists me up so I'm leaning against the wall. Then he draws his pistol and crouches in front of me.

A faint cry waits in my throat. I want to tell him no, there is no point to this, they will shoot him, but he already knows it. I see Duroc's face slide into view as he slowly maneuvers upstairs. His face is streaked with blood and looks particularly grim as he smiles. I reach out with all my strength, pour my Senses into his body, his throbbing veins, his throat, his blood, and squeeze. Duroc tumbles backward.

Voices clamor from down there. "Dr. Duroc!" calls one. "Medic," cries another. There's a lot of boot-shuffling and cries of, "Hold it," and "Lay him down flat." The guards tromping downstairs hear the shouts and halt as they catch sight of us. I can Sense their confusion as they train their rifles on SamJay and listen to the calls for a medic. They're clad in black, like the other guards, but they're wearing gas masks like SamJay. "Stand down, soldier," one of them shouts at SamJay. Four guns bristle at him from four different angles. SamJay carefully lays his pistol on the step before him.

"Medic," the cry comes from below again. "Dr. Duroc needs a medic."

"Coming," shouts one of the guards above us. She turns around and darts back up the stairs, goes out the door. Dizzy blackness fills my head as I feel my Senses slipping away from Duroc's body, my grasp on his vital organs loosening. I did something, but I'm not sure what. I close my eyes, hear my breath coming harshly. SamJay turns, whispering, "Eten?"

I whisper. "I…I…"

Below they're shouting again. "Loosen his belt," says the voice from before.

The door above opens again and a young man in a service uniform carrying a large black bag dashes downstairs through the armed guards, who ignore him and keep their guns trained on us. The one who left to get the medic rejoins them.

I hear more yammering from below, then sudden quiet, and in the middle of it, Duroc's hoarse whisper echoes. "Arrest them."

In front of us, the four guards come to attention. "Get up," says the one in front, motioning with his gun.

"Okay," says SamJay, lifting his open hands, "but she can't move, okay? She's completely paralyzed. I'm just going to lift her."

The guard doesn't respond, but motions again with his rifle. SamJay gets up slowly, turns to me, and takes me in his arms, holding me under my knees and shoulders this time. He whispers to me, "I'm ready," then turns back to face the guards, who rise and move to the sides to flank us, two on each side.

I'm not ready. I'm exhausted. Blackness edges in on my vision. Bright spots appear when I blink. If I try anything, it may backfire, and get us shot instead of saving our lives. What if I try to Jump all four rifles and Jump only one? What if I Jump their rifles and they use knives or nightsticks as I pass out?

SamJay makes his way slowly up the steps, one step up, bad leg next to the first, pause. One step up….

"Move it, soldier," says a guard, poking SamJay in the ribs with his rifle.

"Bad leg," says SamJay, panting. He's not faking. "I'm—"

The guard who is now at the top of the stairs says, "Vargas, take the girl and carry her up to Holding B. Take this guy's mask off, get his prints, and escort him to Holding C."

Alarms blare again, this time inside of me. I can't let them separate us, can't let them touch me. Not if I want to save SamJay. I have to try, and I have to try right now. I turn my face into SamJay's shoulder, concentrate, and reach out to Sense SamJay's house. But no, it's way too far, easier to reach for the car—the black leather seats, the shining chrome. I pull these in close to me, the *thisness* of SamJay's car pulled right here to these concrete steps, and I strain mightily to fuse them, to Jump us there. SamJay lurches forward and almost drops me. He shouts.

I yelp as he stumbles, but I can feel the change in the air, the light. Turning my head, I see cars…the parking lot. SamJay's dark blue car under a blazing sky. SamJay's gas mask lands on its hood as he rips it off. "We did it," I rasp, my voice and tongue heavy. Relief pounds in my head so hard, it's almost painful. I grin up at SamJay's sweat-streaked face. He's grinning and frowning at the same time, still anxious to get away.

There's so much I want to say. I'd be dead if not for SamJay. Again. How dumb I was, thinking I could do everything myself. My mouth feels wet and I wipe my hand across it, see blood on my hand. I make a sound like, "Uh," the sight making me woozy.

SamJay limps fast, almost hopping as he tries to run around to the other side of the car with me in his arms. He puffs and mutters, "Oh my God. Let's get out of here." For a moment, he balances me on the front of the car, the heat seeping through my slacks as he plunges a hand into his pocket for the keys. The car beeps once, twice, then he's pulling the passenger side door open. He slides me in. I'm able to hold myself upright as he buckles my seat belt and opens the glove compartment in front of me, which he paws through, knocking stuff to the floor like keys and a little red box, some plastic silverware. Everything gets blurry as my head tilts forward; SamJay grabs what he was looking for, a wad of loose paper napkins, and presses them to my nose, tilting my head back. He kisses my forehead. "You did it, Supergirl."

And then, everything goes black.

CHAPTER 52

Consciousness reemerges all at once. I find myself in a bed, propped up on pillows, and I see SamJay's feet. Socks actually, resting on the bottom of the bed. He's leaning back in a tattered armchair, a small vidscreen on his chest, head back, snoring. The room is dark except for a lamp on the long, low dresser behind him. A thin strip of daylight meanders through a crack in the curtains.

An icepack slides off my head, which I catch in my hand. It's warm. We're in the motel where we stayed on our way to Washington. Quickly, I run through my memory of events. Duroc—I didn't kill him. But I think I disabled him. I know I Jumped us back to the car, but that part is hazy. I was bleeding. My fingers fly to my nose, but there's no blood. My right arm shows a bruise where the IV was inserted at the inner crook of my elbow, then pulled out.

The first question: Am I damaged?

Lifting the blue gel-pack in my hand, I Jump it to the dresser across the room, under the lamp. No problem. Then I Jump it back and forth a few times. It skips from here to there and back just as it should. But a sharp pain lances my skull and my head begins to ache. I feel a trickle of warmth in my nose. I massage the top of my head, touch my finger to my nose. Blood. Just a little.

Anxiety flutters in me. *I'll be fine,* I think. I just need rest. I'm sure I'll be fine. I'm not going to mention this to SamJay; he'll just freak out, and we still have to deal with Duroc. Because the second question is: What should I do about Duroc?

On the table next to the bed, there's a big paper cup of water with a straw, and tissues. I blot my nose with a tissue and drink, then drink more. I'm horribly thirsty—the water doesn't seem to quench it. There's a loud, slurping noise as the straw sucks up the last drops of water and SamJay jerks, clears his throat and sits up.

"How do you feel, Eten?" he asks, grabbing his reading glasses as they fall into his lap. His vidscreen slides to the floor.

"I'm good. I feel better." I quickly crumple the tissue with new blood staining it and toss it under the bed while SamJay fumbles to recover his vidscreen.

"He gassed me—something that made me paralyzed. I couldn't Jump, I couldn't do anything." My throat feels thick with tears as I remember feeling so helpless, and I push them aside. "He wanted me to join him. To rule the world." I laugh at the absurdity of it.

"Of course he did." SamJay isn't laughing.

"When I said no, he tricked me. He…" But I don't want to tell SamJay about the monster in the basement. Maybe Duroc was lying about that. I refuse to even think about it.

SamJay turns and grabs something off the dresser, shows it to me. The wand. "I found this in the car." Then he smiles. "I took the batteries out. Double A."

"Oh my God." It's obscene. That hideous wand, powered by a couple of ordinary batteries. "I Jumped it away from him. Please, just…" I wave a hand. "Break it."

SamJay twists it in his hands. It cracks in half. He grins and says, "Ta-da," holding the pieces out.

"Okay, okay, I stomped on it first." I grin weakly, recalling SamJay's awesome fight with the guards. I'm so used to thinking of him as soft and gentle, with a bad leg. I had no clue how strong he is.

Then I think of Dad—Dad fighting the soldiers who gassed the boys and cut their hair and tried to kidnap them. It still amazes me. "At least I found out Dad has the boys. He ran away with them. Duroc's goons cut the boys' hair, that's why there was all that blood. But Dad got in there and rescued them. Can you believe it?"

SamJay whistles. "Good news, then."

"I can't believe Dad did that."

SamJay nods and says cryptically, "As you get older, your parents get better."

"They're not my parents," I say bitterly. But even I can tell I sound petulant and childish.

"Of course they are," says SamJay.

"You're more like my dad than Dad is."

SamJay shrugs with a smile. "You're fortunate to have two dads then."

"Hmf." Not that fortunate, I think.

"There was news about Duroc," he says, holding up the vidscreen.

"He was taken to a hospital near the Pentagon. They're speculating he maybe had a stroke, but nobody knows yet."

"How bad?" I ask.

"Don't know yet."

I sit up a little straighter. "Did they say which hospital?"

SamJay's eyes suddenly flick up to meet mine. He nods slowly. "Yes, they did."

"Maybe I need to finish the job," I say. I can feel my pulse throb in my hands, my lips.

"Are you sure you want to do that?" His eyes don't leave mine. "Do you remember? When we talked about it, what you said?"

I look away. Of course I remember. It wasn't that long ago, the night we all played basketball and I confessed to SamJay the fighting makes me sick. The *killing* makes me sick. I was afraid I was a coward. But that night seems like another lifetime. As I think of us all playing together, a sudden longing for my sisters and brothers crushes the breath in my chest, makes my throat tight.

"You don't have to do anything," says SamJay.

"Is it wrong to…terminate him?" I ask. I can't bring myself to use the word *kill*. "Is it self-defense?"

"You have to decide, Eten," says SamJay. "You have to live with your decisions, not me."

I nod. I want SamJay to give me an order, because I've always taken orders. I was an assassin, but I did not choose to be one. I did not choose whom to kill. I was not responsible. Because I was a child.

This time, it will be different.

We circle the tall, medical building slowly; there are few other cars on the road at this time of night. "There he is," I say, pointing to one of the windows. "He's up there on the fourth floor. Corner room." I can Sense Duroc, incapacitated, in a bed. I think he is conscious, but he's weak. A fierce joy leaps up in me. I'm glad I hurt him. I'm sure of my decision.

We park nearby, in a big building that spirals up and up, all filled with cars, and walk to the hospital wearing civilian clothes that SamJay purchased from a big, all-night store like Big Green. I'm in black sweats and a brown T-shirt with my black, oversized Big Green jacket, an empty cloth bag stuffed into a pocket—that's for later. SamJay's wearing jeans and a sweatshirt. We both wear medical facemasks, spread out as wide as possible. Lots of people in the hospital wear masks, so that's a plus. Sunglasses would be too obvious a disguise at night, so we both wear what SamJay calls, "clear safety glasses," and we both wear stretchy hats, my hair piled up inside of mine. I hope it will be enough. Especially for SamJay. Duroc doesn't know his face; if they recognize him, they will hunt him down. But when he said he was going to help me, I didn't object.

The lobby is much like the lobby in the pod building at Fort Freedom, only smaller, with shining tiled floors and potted plants. We hesitate inside the door. There are no guards, only one woman sitting behind the desk, and she's looking down at something. To her right is an elevator.

"Come on," mutters SamJay, and he heads for the elevator. The woman behind the desk glances up, and then, without a word, goes back to whatever she was doing.

Inside the elevator, SamJay presses the number five button. As soon as the doors close, he kicks off his shoes—some new, slip-on, white sneakers—pulls off his jeans and sweatshirt. Underneath, he wears a nurse's uniform—plain blue pants with a drawstring and a pullover shirt. *Scrubs,* they're called. He pulls off his hat and puts on another one that looks like a bandana with a blue and black pattern and puts the glasses and shoes back on. I pick up his clothes and stuff them into the cloth bag, then Jump the bag into SamJay's car. Immediately, I feel my nose begin to run and curse to myself. I tilt my head back and press my nose with my jacket cuff; I don't want SamJay to see the blood. It seems to stop quickly, anyway.

The elevator doors ding as they open on the fifth floor.

There are two long corridors, one straight ahead and one to the left. We walk straight ahead, briskly passing an alcove with a desk and a few nurses on our left and doors to patient rooms on our right, some open, some closed. Everyone, except the nurses, is sleeping. The nurses are dressed just like SamJay. Without the hat. "Visiting hours are over," calls one nurse.

SamJay lifts a hand. "It's okay," he says, smiling. "She's cleared to come in."

The other nurse grunts, disinterested, and goes back to her vidscreen. I Jump her badge, hung on a lanyard, into my hand in my pocket. She doesn't notice. My nose doesn't run.

We keep going, out of sight of the nurses, pass a stairwell with a heavy glass window in the door, and finally see what we're looking for—a closet. "Employees Only" and "Housekeeping" read the signs on the white door.

SamJay grabs the handle and turns. Locked. I press my hand to the door, unlock it, and we slide in. It's almost pitch dark; I can see buckets, a mop, bottles and supplies on the shelves. It's small. "Can you stay in here?" asks SamJay. "You want the light on?"

I shake my head, then realize he can't see me. "No, I'm all right." Although the smell is sharp with soap and cleaning fluids, I think I can stand it for a while. I press the lanyard and badge into his hands. "I took this from the nurse who spoke to us," I tell him as he puts it over his head. "And remember, SamJay, try not to think or feel. Just see." I'm used to Sensing a target through Dad's eyes, by Sensing Dad and then the target. Dad could focus on the target perfectly. This will be SamJay's first time. I hope he can do it.

"Yeah," whispers SamJay, and he opens the door a crack, looks out, then slips out the door. He's trying hard to keep his mind clear, but images of fighting keep jumping up instead of the vision of what he sees—the corridor. He hurries back to the stairwell and, as he descends, I see the cement steps interspersed with images of Duroc and the guards dressed in black—he's picturing us back in the Pentagon basement.

"Come on, SamJay," I mutter out loud, willing him to clear his mind, to perceive only what his eyes can see. The staircase reappears, then he slips from the stairwell through the door to the fourth floor.

Guards opposite the stairwell door come to attention and challenge SamJay. My heart sinks. I'd hoped there would only be a guard by Duroc's room. SamJay seems startled into stillness, and my vision of the two guards becomes sharp and unwavering: one a young person who looks like a teenager, the other a man with thinning, red hair, and a lined face. I can Sense SamJay is talking with them, then suddenly, I can't see them again. SamJay is visualizing punching the young guard in the face while he kicks the older one in the privates.

Then reality reappears—I see the younger guard's face as SamJay flashes the stolen hospital ID—then reality is gone, replaced by SamJay's vision of the young man windmilling backward after being punched.

This is not going to work. SamJay can't keep his mind focused—who knows what will happen when he confronts Duroc. I raise the *thisness* of the stairwell, Jump myself there and sprint down the last few steps—though it's hard to run down steps and see through SamJay's eyes at the same time. I withdraw from him and crack the fourth-floor corridor door.

The guards are escorting SamJay further down the hall past many closed doors—I guess the other nurse's ID passed muster. Two more guards with rifles stand outside a room at the end of the corridor. Duroc's room. He's almost there.

But one of the guards by the room moves toward them, his rifle in a loose grip, easy to point and fire. "Who is that?" he says.

"Nurse from downstairs," says a guard next to SamJay. "He has to take Dr. Duroc's vitals."

"No, he doesn't," says the first guard. "Nursing isn't scheduled till four a.m. The nurses are right down there." The guard points down another corridor to his right. "We have a schedule." He raises his rifle to his shoulder. The second guard steps back and pushes himself against the room door.

"Whoa, hold it," says SamJay, holding up his hands. "No guns, okay? There was a monitor spike, okay? Downstairs. There's something wrong with Dr. Duroc and the floor nurse can't see it."

I can Sense the man with the gun wavering. He looks to his right again and waves. "Hey, Nurse. Nurse. Can you come over here and check something out?"

SamJay pushes his way forward. "All right, I've got to check his heart monitor, he could be having a heart attack right…"

As SamJay moves in, the partner of the guard with the rifle darts forward and pushes SamJay's chest, hard enough to almost stop him. "Not without clearance you're not. Show me your badge."

I'm biting my knuckle, breathing fast.

"Let me do my job, you morons," bellows SamJay, still pushing toward Duroc's room. "My badge is right here." He's got his hand on it, shaking it. "You're endangering this patient. He's a VIP, for God's sake."

"Wait a minute," somebody else calls from further away. From the nurse's station. There's the sound of running feet. "Wait a minute." Another person shouts, "Call security."

Several doors along the corridor open. A few heads pop out, then duck back inside.

The first guard with the rifle steps backward and aims at SamJay. I Jump the rifle into the stairwell behind me. "Hey," shouts the guard, waving his hands and looking at the others, at his feet. "Where's my rifle?"

It's kind of just a reflex to Jump all the other rifles, too—a skill I learned when I was five years old. I'm not focused on the guns; I'm entirely focused on the nurse who has run up to the others. I could hurt her from right here where I stand. I could squeeze her throat so she couldn't talk, couldn't breathe. I *should* do it, to protect SamJay, but I might kill her by accident—it's hard to do that sort of thing without killing.

She grabs hold of SamJay's arm, shouts, "Wait a minute, who are you?" And then she grabs for SamJay's mask as he struggles to slide between a guard and the wall so he can reach the door. Just as he does this, another of the guards pulls a pistol—oh, my God, I didn't Sense for other weapons, epic fail—and he fires it before I know what's happening. I Jump the pistol away. The nurse screams, but nobody has been injured. I Sense no pain, just confusion.

But the commotion is blowing our plan—we wanted to make it look like Duroc had a natural heart attack. Maybe, somehow, we still can, because SamJay finally bursts through the door of Duroc's bedroom—but then there's pain. Terrible pain in the back of SamJay's head, and then blackness.

CHAPTER 53

I don't know if I scream. I do know I Jump myself down the hall as far as I can see and barrel into the still-shouting group of guards standing outside Duroc's room. I explode, the air whipping around me as I shove these people so hard, they sail down the long corridors, back toward the nurses' station, back toward the stairwell. I don't wait for them to land. I slam Duroc's door open, see SamJay on the floor. Blood on his head. Then I do scream, and a stream of curses floods from me as I look up and see Duroc. He appears more cadaverous than ever on the hospital bed with tubes and monitors attached to his body. A terrified man in uniform stands beside his bed, and they both hold their arms stiffly extended toward me.

Pain, agony, rips up my spine before I understand they are both holding wands. They don't totally get how to use a wand, because if they were using the highest setting, I'd already be unconscious. I hear pounding boots from the corridor, shouts of "Police" and "Drop your weapons."

It's easy to fall down on top of SamJay. I wrap my arms around his chest, and Jump.

∘∘∘∘∘

I Jump us back to the motel room, on top of the bed. The room is dark, and I roll to the side, run into the bathroom and get a washcloth wet with cold water. My head aches, pounding, and I wonder if I'm just Sensing SamJay's headache as I fill a glass and go back to him. My hands tremble. We're safe, but it feels like they're still after us.

SamJay groans, returning to consciousness. In the light coming from the bathroom, I lean over to examine the back of his head. It's a small gash, not bleeding anymore but already swelling like an egg. I fold the cold washcloth across the wound. SamJay lifts his hand, presses the washcloth down with a groan. He clears his throat and tries to speak into the bedspread. "What…what…?" It sounds like a croak. Wordlessly, I push the glass of water into his hand. He lifts himself a little and drinks.

"What happened?" he finally manages to get out.

"Somebody clocked you on the head, Duroc and another guy wanded me, and I Jumped us back to the motel. Let me check your eyes." It's simple field instructions: Always check for brain bleed or swelling after a head injury. Ensure pupils react normally to light. If the pupil is sluggish, or fixed and dilated, bad news.

I pull the lamp as far as I can off the counter, closer to SamJay's face, and suddenly switch it on.

"Agh," chokes SamJay throwing up a hand in front of his eyes.

"SamJay, I have to check your pupils, you have a head injury."

He groans. "Later."

He's being stupid. If he has a brain bleed, it could damage his brain, or even kill him. And no way am I going into Sense the fragile capillaries inside his brain—I could damage something in there. This is a simple test. I make an impatient sound, but he doesn't react. I think he's falling asleep. I shake his shoulder. "Mmm," he says.

"Come on. Let me look at your eyes, then you can sleep," I say.

He grudgingly agrees and rolls onto his side, his head close to the foot of the bed. Holding the lamp to the right, I click it on and watch his right eye. He blinks rapidly, but I can see his pupil, dilated in the dark, constrict to a point in the lamplight. I turn the light off for a few minutes. By then, SamJay is sitting up, being a little more cooperative. I hold the light to the left and turn it on. His left eye responds the same, to my great relief.

"Looks good, SamJay. I'll check again in a few hours."

He grins. "Thanks, doc. Your nose is bleeding."

"Shit," I mutter and duck into the bathroom to grab another washcloth.

"We're a couple of doozies," he says as I collapse into the chair opposite the bed and put my feet up. SamJay lies back with a pillow folded under his neck and the ice pack I used earlier on the top of his head. He looks up at the ceiling. "So we didn't get him?" he asks.

"No." My voice is low, but I know he hears me

"Okay, then. We done?"

"Yeah," I say. "We're done."

The exhaustion I feel is more than bone-deep. It's soul-deep. I can't do this anymore. We're silent for a while, but I know he's not asleep. Finally, I ask, "Do you think he'll come after me again?"

"Truth?" he asks.

"Truth," I say, with a quiver in my belly. I know the answer.

"I think he will. Once he recovers. He's going to look for you, and he's going to look for your brothers and sisters. How can he not? He's got too many years invested in you. And you're too powerful for him to stop looking. He'll be afraid you'll fight against him."

"I will if I can," I retort, angry all over again. Why can't I just find peace?

"Yeah, well. Case in point."

We say nothing for a while after that.

Finally, SamJay takes the icepack off his head and sits up on the side of the bed, rubbing his face. "You better come home with me. We'll figure something out."

I shake my head. "No, SamJay. You've done enough."

He makes a scoffing sound.

"You won't be safe and neither will I. I'm going back to Maria's. I can hide there. I can look for the others. There's this organization there. They're trying to get American rights back, to restore democracy. They're called EVE. They'll help me look for the others."

SamJay stands suddenly and turns. "EVE! No, Eten. Not EVE."

He's a seething mass of rage and I'm so startled, I don't know what to say. He utters a few curses, paces the room, and turns on the lights. "What's the matter?" I finally ask.

He slaps his leg. "EVE is the reason I limp today. EVE is the reason I lost my career. They killed…" His throat closes on what sounds like a sob. "Someone very close to me." There's the face of a man in his mind, someone with clear eyes and a warm smile. "An IED, a car bomb. He got killed, and I got my leg shattered. They're terrorists." He seems to come to himself and turns, shaking a finger at me. "Do not get involved with EVE."

My heart is racing. It's true, they just want to use me, to use my brothers and sisters. But...

They're my only hope.

"SamJay, they're fighting for the good guys. They're fighting against Duroc and trying to reverse climate change."

"It doesn't matter whose side they're on. They're killers." His face is twisted up with bad memories. It won't help to tell him I'm already involved with EVE.

"You say you want an end to war!" he says. "You don't want to be a soldier anymore." I'm nodding but he's not noticing. "Promise me you won't connect with EVE. Not even to find your brothers and sisters. They're not working for peace. They're just trying to take over."

"Okay, don't worry," I say in a low voice. "I won't talk to EVE." This may be the first time I've ever lied to SamJay. I have to get help from EVE. But I won't allow them to use me. I'll use them—just until I find my family.

He turns to me with a stern look and I Sense his resolution. "You're coming home with me. I'll help you find your brothers and sisters. I've still got connections. You can live with me until we find them."

Standing up from the chair, I put my hands in my pockets, take a deep breath, and say, "SamJay."

He drops to the edge of the second bed.

"Thank you, but you know that's not possible."

"Of course it's possible," he says stubbornly. "The neighbors don't have to see you."

For the very first time, SamJay seems fragile to me. Breakable. "We won't be safe," I say. "Not you. Not me. Hopefully, they didn't recognize you tonight. But you worked with us in the pod for years. They'll be coming to talk to you. They'll be hunting for the man who helped E-10. What if they figure it out?"

He shifts uncomfortably and nods. He knows I'm right. He'll have to disappear, just like me, like Mom and Dad. And Duroc will expect me to run far away.

"I can go back to Maria. She's waiting for me."

SamJay stands up and heaves a sigh, then looks over at me. "Can't believe I lived to see the day when you're giving me advice."

I grin, and he holds out his arms. When he hugs me, I feel its finality.

"You're something else, Supergirl."

"You, too, Mister Father-Knows-Best."

He laughs. "Let's get some sleep. Tomorrow, we can get the car and disappear."

CHAPTER 54

In Maria's silent kitchen, dust rises on a shaft of midday light. I'm kneeling on the floor. The room smells of fried fish and toast.

It feels like home.

I feel my nose and my face with relief. I must be recovering. No nosebleed. No headache. SamJay drove me as far as North Carolina, and then I Jumped, straight from his car. Quietly, I rise and walk into the living room. All is still.

I have a bag holding my new clothes, and I leave it on the bed. In my pocket is the ristcom SamJay gave me, tucked into a little red box. He said the government can't trace our calls to each other with this ristcom. Wherever he goes, I can call him. I tuck it under the mattress of my cubby bed and smile, thinking of how SamJay sternly ordered me to call him every week on Sundays at 1900 hours. *I'll be hunting you down if I don't hear from you*, he said.

On the far side of the room, Maria's door stands ajar. I peek in. She lies stretched out in bed, one arm over her head, her chest slowly rising and falling, sleeping after her night shift at the hospital.

Another ordinary Friday. The boys must be in school. Yet nothing is ordinary. Because in this moment, I'm free. I don't know if Duroc will search for me here, but I don't think so. Not after encountering me in Washington, D.C. His mind will place me where he would go—close to the seat of power. I hope he thinks I'll try to assassinate him again, so he lives in fear. He'll be mired in maintaining his own self-defense. He'll be hunting for me close to Washington. Or maybe out west, where EVE hides its operations.

The street is just as quiet as the house. No cars coming or going. I do hear a bird, though. I turn this way and that, trying to locate the source of the song. It trills again, and finally, I see the little red thing, a cardinal like in Nana's picture, fluffed up on a tree branch.

To go outside in the sunlight, to hear a bird sing, and walk to school. These are marvels. Things I never knew. Things I now will never surrender.

"Hello, Eten," says a voice from behind me. I whirl and crouch, spinning up my shield, my arms crossed above my head in a reflexive battle stance.

"Hey, kid, hold it."

It's Joe, fake "Joe" from EVE. He must've been watching the house. He looks scruffy with stubble on his cheeks and dirty hair, and he stands on the quiet, sunlit sidewalk like an awkward, homeless guest. "Sorry, I didn't mean to scare you."

I stand, feeling awkward myself "You didn't scare me."

"You remember, I'm Joe ..."

I cut him off. "I know who you are." I'm not smiling. EVE killed the love of SamJay's life; they ruined SamJay's leg. Yeah, Nate loves them, Dr. Mac joined them, Maria and John-Paul help them, but are they really such good guys after all?

Joe looks around me, at the front door of the house. "Are your…?" He looks back at me, and now his face is eager, his voice breathless. "Did you bring them? Your brothers and sisters?"

I shake my head. "They weren't there. I couldn't find them."

The man lets out a breath with a sound of disgust, rolls his eyes, and throws his head back, half-turning. "Shit!" he mutters, looking down at his ristcom, then at the ground, shaking his head.

"Sorry," I say coldly. "I think they're all right, though.

He swings back toward me, looking hopeful. "Do you know where they are?"

I have to decide. Warnings flicker through my mind. EVE wants to use me as a weapon, just like Duroc. But without EVE's network, how can I possibly locate my brothers and sisters? "I don't know where they are," I say, "but I'm hoping EVE can help me find them."

Joe stands there nodding slightly, his hand rubbing the stubble on his chin. In this light, I can see that despite his youthful look—his muscular body, his colorful T-shirt, shorts, and sandals—he's older than I thought. His forehead is lined with fretfulness. His neck sags below the chin.

"I'm sure, with you helping our cause, we could help find your brothers and sisters." He smiles.

So. Not free. Here it is, the bargain. I help EVE with their war for democracy, and they help me find my brothers and sisters. Of course, I'm not really free. Not until my brothers and sisters and I are reunited. Not till we're safe from Duroc.

"All right," I say slowly. "I'll help you. But I won't kill anyone."

Joe looks shocked, but he's faking it. So obvious. "Of course not. You're just a kid."

He looks up and down the deserted street. "We'll be in touch," he says.

Before I can respond, he heads down the broken sidewalk, cuts through the overgrown yard of another house, and disappears.

I push back on my uneasiness—I don't have to do anything I don't want. EVE isn't going to terminate me if I disobey orders, like the military. In fact, I'm sure I can probably prevent killing. I can help them by disarming and shielding, like I did for Dad at first, when I was very young.

Meanwhile, EVE will start looking for my brothers and sisters. That's the important thing. I have to find them.

I turn back in the direction of John-Paul's school, and soon I'm running, not Jumping, just for the hell of it.

When I reach the school building, I take the steps two at a time and creep to the open door of the classroom, stand there, and listen to the murmurs from within. The sound fills me with hope. Soon, I will join them. Go to school like a regular teenager. I peek in.

A tall woman with flowing, colorful clothing bends over, conferring with a young boy seated at a big table with other children. Nate is across the room at a different table, sharing a book with a girl his age, scribbling furiously on a piece of paper.

Then I see John-Paul. He's sitting on a cushion with his back against the wall, books spilling across the floor around him. He looks up from the heavy book on his legs, right at me, as if he could Sense my presence. He grins and puts a finger to his lips, rises, and hurries out to me.

"What happened?" he demands as soon we're outside. He paces anxiously down the walkway in front of the houses. "I got scared when you didn't come back right away. Are your brothers and sisters at the house?"

"No, they were gone when I got to the pod. Nobody was there at all. Everything was dark."

"Oh, no!" Before I can continue, John-Paul drops heavily to some steps cut into a hill. I Sense the images in John-Paul's mind: boys and girls being shot dead.

"No, no, they're okay. They escaped with Mom and Dad."

Overhead, a huge, broad tree creates an island of coolness. I sit down next to him and explain how the girls escaped from Duroc with Mom. How Dad rescued the boys.

"So maybe they weren't so bad after all, your mom and dad."

I frown. "Maybe." Now that I know Duroc, I understand Mom and Dad better. And at the end, on the plane—Mom tried to save me.

"What about Duroc? And the military? Will you have to hide in the Free Zone?"

"I don't think so. Duroc is injured. He'll look for me but I don't think he'll look here. So, I want to say here, if it's okay, with you. And your Mom. And Nate." I don't want to think about the fight with Duroc. And the monster in the basement…I'm not sure I'll ever tell John-Paul about it, especially not now when he's looking at me like that. There's a softness in his eyes, a glow in his face, and joy in the curve of his lips that I haven't seen before. I hardly breathe for fear of dispelling this sudden magic.

"I missed you," he says. "I was worried." He slides closer to me on the foot-worn step. Leaves rustle overhead, and a warm, scented breeze caresses my cheek. My hair blows over my eyes, and John-Paul reaches out, smoothing the strands away.

His touch is electric. My skin is on fire. His hand slides down and cups my cheek and I'm melting into him. I Sense his heat, his yearning, and see myself from his eyes as if in sun-lit water.

His other hand gently touches my ear, slides down my neck. My blood surges, heat flares through my body, and my heart pounds wildly. I don't understand what's happened. I thought he wasn't interested in me, didn't care about me, and now…

He leans in close, brushes his lips across mine, and hovers. "Is this okay?" he whispers.

Okay? How dense can this boy be? Does he actually have no idea what I've been feeling since I met him? "Yeah," I whisper. "Very okay."

The sensation is more than mere touch. I never knew lips could feel such pleasure. My breath becomes shallow and I can't tear my eyes away from his. The world vanishes. He is the world.

Then his lips press harder against mine, his hands fall away from my face and gather me up, pressing me to his chest. His heart pounds against me as my lips part and his tongue slides into my mouth, as if he longs to touch the very essence of me.

My body arches up to meet his, and everything that was closed within me flies open.

After moments, or forever, we drift apart and lean back.

"Whoa," he whispers.

"Whoa," I say. I can Sense this is an appropriate expression of awe.

He twines his fingers into mine and stands up. "Come on."

I stand. "Where are we going"

I can't stop grinning. Neither can he, apparently, because he tries to look serious for a moment, then starts to giggle. I start to giggle, then neither of us can stop laughing.

"No wait, stop," he says, holding up a hand, pulling his eyebrows into a frown. "This is serious." Then he starts to laugh again.

"What is it? What's serious?" I laugh.

"I don't know," he says, wiping his eyes. "We have to tell my mom you're safe. We have to tell her you can live with us."

"But she's sleeping."

"Oh, right. I know." He grabs my hand again. "Let's go swimming."

"What?"

"Can you Jump us to the beach?"

I shrug, then grin. "Sure." Holding his hand tight. I call up the spot where I first saw the sea.

And then we're there. The tall grass on either side, the packed sand before us, and the endless roll of waves surging onto shore. John-Paul whoops and leaps toward the water, tearing his shirt off as he runs.

Laughing, I pull my shoes and sweatpants off, then just stand there, the warm wind whipping my T-shirt and hair. My bare feet hit cool sand as I dig in my toes, and the sun is hot on my cheeks and brow. And the sound—the low rumble and pause, and the rumble again, it's like a kind of language the waves speak. I breathe in deep.

I am a part of all things, and all things lift me toward the center.

I rest in light. My spirit flows forth unencumbered.

I am embraced by the stillness, and the stillness fills me with power.

John-Paul leaps high over the white foam of a breaking wave, springs upward with another gray-green surge, and crashes down into the water. He jumps up again, waving, and shouts for me to come in.

I saunter forth more slowly, each foot in the sand an exploration, each breath of salty, ocean air a discovery. Small white and dark shells litter the beach where an edge has been formed by a pattern of wetness. I press a shell into the sand with my foot. The seafoam curls up around my ankles, and I allow it. The surging water sucks the sand out from under my feet and I am planted by it. I kneel in the spent waves, lift foam and water in my cupped hands, and bathe my face in it.

John-Paul jumps and swims down the crashing side of a wave, and it carries him toward shore. He splashes through the shallows, comes to me, kneels beside me.

"Your first swim in the ocean," he says.

"Yes," I smile. "My first time." Then I point out to sea. "You see that?"

He squints, shades his eyes with his hand. "What? I don't see anything."

Low in the bright blue sky, there's a glittering streak that seems to be neither water nor air, a space where they become indistinguishable. "Right there. Where the water meets the sky. That's where I want to live, like, forever."

"Um, well, you can't actually *go* there," he says gently. Then he tries to explain "horizon" to me. "I mean, it's like the earth…there's a curve, and we're here, and when you move up or forward, it goes on…" He looks like he's working up a sweat. "You know, it's an illusion."

I grin at his discomfort. "It's not illusion; it's perspective."

And I laugh, because if you looked at us from out there, we are the horizon. I, a prisoner who grew up to know only walls and doors and death, now am horizon, a blur of being where water meets air and land and goes on.

Grinning, John-Paul takes my hand and pulls me to my feet. "Come on," he says, and I allow him to lead me into the ocean, where a wave crashes against my shoulder, and the next one lifts me into the sky.

Acknowledgements

To Leanne Pankuch, many thanks for great coaching and editing and for getting me through to the finish when I started flagging. Also, to Eric Smith, thank you for stellar edits and ideas about how to improve the story flow. I'm grateful to Kat Brzozowski for incisive comments on early pages and to the incomparable Nova Ren Suma, whose feedback at the Highlights Foundation gave me more encouragement than she knows. The writers at SCBWI have been wonderful, reading many drafts and offering perceptive suggestions. Thanks to dear friends Lisa for her steadfast encouragement and faith in my work and Nancy for her reads and rereads, proofs and comments, always there when I needed her.

Look for

THE SAMSON PROJECT - II

BOY WITH THE SUN IN HIS HANDS

Coming to readers in 2026

Subscribe to Celia Seupel's newsletter at

www.celiawatsonseupel.com/newsletter